Liberty's INHERITANCE

BOOK ONE IN THE SERIES

A WOMAN OF ENTITLEMENT

BY **MARY ANN KERR**

THINK WELL BOOKS

thinkwellbooks.com

Second Edition: Published in part by Thinkwell Books, Portland, Oregon. The views or opinions of the author are not necessarily those of Thinkwell Books. Learn more at *thinkwellbooks.com*.

Design and Cover illustration by Andrew Morgan Kerr
Learn more at **andrewmorgankerr.com**

Published and printed in the United States of America
ISBN: 978-0-9891681-3-7
Fiction, Historical, Christian

BOOKS BY MARY ANN KERR

A WOMAN OF ENTITLEMENT SERIES:

Book One
LIBERTY'S INHERITANCE

Book Two
LIBERTY'S LAND

Book Three
LIBERTY'S HERITAGE

CAITLIN'S FIRE

DEDICATION

This book is dedicated to the Father, Son, and Holy Spirit,
Who has given me the creativity and opened the
doors for a dream to become reality.
I thank You for giving me the stories and the ability to write.
I also dedicate this book to Philip, my husband, for
supporting me every step of the way.

ᴬCKNOWLEDGMENTS

ᴬ NOVEL IS NEVER WRITTEN without the experiences of life coloring the words. I've found that relationships are the quintessence of life…our relationship to Jesus and our relationship to others. Nothing else matters. The writing of this book has been a journey some special people have taken with me. With a grateful heart, I'd like to acknowledge the following. My relationship to them is a treasure, and they have gone out of their way to help or encourage me.

I want to especially thank, in loving memory, my sister Jeane Wagner for listening, almost every day, over the phone to what I had written that day. Fran Dual, you're the first person who read part of the manuscript and encouraged me to continue—thank you. A huge thank you goes to my son Stephen, who preedited the entire manuscript. You gave much helpful advice, especially the line, "Mom, you need to keep a bit of tension throughout the book. You're solving everything as you go." Thanks to John Dunn, who played an instrumental role in getting me to start writing. Marla Gill, my prayer partner, prayed with me through the entire process —thanks, girl! I want to especially thank Karen Lange, who supported my writing and has been an encouragement to me…few have such a friend… Craig, you're a lucky man! A big thanks to Earl and Arlene Engle, who made me laugh and prayed for me throughout the process. Jean Hawkins, thanks for being a mentor and friend. Randy Craker, your words of encouragement have given hope to my heart—thank you. Thanks to my precious niece, Elida Roy, whose knowledge and ideas were very helpful. However, I did put the prologue back in! Most of all...your love is cherished.

Besides my son Stephen, with a grateful heart, I thank my sons and their wives: David and Rosie, Peter and Rebecca, and Andrew and Shari, who all believed I could do it. Thank you for being the kind of children who delight God. To Rosie, Rebecca, and Shari, thanks for being the daughters I never had...I treasure our relationships. David, thanks for your enthusiasm and encouragement via e-mails from Papua New Guinea. You are an awesome example of living Christianity. To my son Peter, owner of KerrComm, and author of two books, *Adam Meets Eve* and a sc-fi, *The Ark of Time*, I am blessed by the wisdom and helpful ideas you have given me about writing and communicating to my audience—thanks. To Andrew, owner of Relevant Studios and author of *Ants on Pirate Pond*, thanks for setting up a website, designing and printing my business cards, helping me with Facebook, and creating awesome covers for my books besides doing the interior design. God has given you amazing talents. Thank you so much for your time and efforts.

To my *favorite* and only brother, Peter Brown, and his wife, Regina, thanks for the retreat time and fun I have at your house every spring, laughing, relaxing, treasure hunting, golfing, and writing in the evenings.

Dori Harrell of Breakout Editing, what a treasure you are! I am so thankful for us connecting. Your attention to detail is amazing. God has given you great talent for editing, girl! And I don't know another single person in my life who never tires of talking shop!

Most of all, and best of all, I thank my husband, Philip, for his unending patience, encouragement, prayers, and love.

List of Characters

Our Inheritance

In *Liberty's Inheritance*, some thoughts became a book.
I hope you read it with some joy, but take another look.
People seem to come alive; there's some who love the Lord.
They don't rely upon themselves; they're daily in the Word.

I hope that I have made it clear that life can be quite tough.
It's simply that we're not alone, our Savior is enough.
Though trials try to beat us down and life itself seems bleak
The burdens, heavy on our back, we lay them at His feet.

As prayer and time we spend with God, fulfilled in every day
We come to learn to seek His face, to please Him, is the way.
Enjoy the reading of this book, but readers can you see?
Our inheritance is Jesus, and Jesus sets you free.

MARY ANN KERR

Prologue

Hearken, O daughter, and consider,
and incline thine ear;
forget also thine own people, and thy father's house
PSALM 45:10

"**No! A THOUSAND TIMES NO!** You cannot make me! Would you care to see Jacques dragging me up the aisle in front of all your high-society friends?" Liberty was crying but trying not to. At nearly sixteen, she was considered an adult. She should be allowed to make her own decisions.

Winged eyebrows arched over almond-shaped eyes as green as her mother's. Her lips were full but pressed tightly together in an effort to keep from crying aloud. Tears poured from her eyes, wetting her cheeks.

Violet stroked her coppery curls. "You look just like your father," she said.

"I don't. I don't look like him at all." Liberty raised her voice, angry that her mother never stood up to Jacques. She never crossed him or argued with him.

Violet walked over to the window, not bearing to see her daughter's anguish, with arms crossed and pressed against her abdomen as if in pain.

Having returned from finishing school in Switzerland two days earlier, Liberty found her parents had arranged a marriage for her. She'd arrived home in the spring of 1869 full of plans, but her father had chosen a man for her—no coming-out ball, no debutante parties, no freedom to choose for herself. She was to give up everything she'd dreamed about. Betrothed to marry an up-and-coming lawyer ten years her senior, she didn't even know him.

Liberty had met Armand Francois Bouvier only one time. Although he could be considered handsome by some, she found him not at all to her liking. Reeking of cologne and cigars, he was hardly taller than she, his looks dark and secretive. He seemed a man of the world, his look too knowing. She shivered thinking about him.

Liberty wanted time to live and enjoy life before she was married off. She had returned home wanting to renew old friendships, and she'd had hopes of meeting the right young man and making her own choice. Her dream was crumbling because of Jacques.

Violet turned away from the window as tears coursed down her own cheeks. "My darling, I am so sorry, but your father has made some bad investments, and we stand to lose everything. I'm not talking simply our bank account—I'm talking about the house, the carriages, the horses, everything."

Stunned, Liberty stared at her. She'd never known about her parents' financial situation but had always assumed there to be plenty. Attending the best schools money could buy, she'd never wanted for anything. Jacques made sure all his friends knew he had the best of everything. Liberty was aware of Jacques spending huge sums of money but had never thought about it running out.

Her mother had been a Browning, Violet Ann Browning, a Boston Brahmin, the highest and best of society. Violet's father had been wealthy, and he'd doted on his only child. He'd sent her to an artist's finishing school in London. She'd met and married Liberty's father, Jacques, who was French. Jacques Betrand Corlay had been on holiday to London, and her mother had been living there with friends. The two of them had met and were married within a month. *They must have fallen in love with each other, but I see very little love between them. In truth, they barely speak to each other.*

"Mother, do you agree to this, that I should marry this man to satisfy all Jacques' debts?" Liberty had always called her father by his first name. He'd insisted on it when she was a toddler.

Violet's eyes slid away. Taking a deep breath, she looked back at her daughter, carefully formulating her answer.

"No, Libby my dear, I don't. You know, however, that Jacques will cut you off without a cent, no support at all. When you turn sixteen, you'd have no money, no income. My own papa's money has been held in trust for you until you are twenty-five. Your father has gone through all the money Papa willed to me, and there is nothing left. Libby, I shouldn't say this, but Jacques has looked into how he can break the inheritance trust your grandfather set up for you. He couldn't do it…my papa made sure of that."

Startled by her frankness, the import of her mother's words hit her. Hopes of escaping an unwanted marriage began to crumble. Liberty sank slowly down upon the stool of her dressing table. There was little recourse for a young woman in 1869. Liberty knew nothing of children or of being a governess. She knew no one who'd hire her.

"So, I am being sold to the highest bidder?" Her tone was scornful, and she regretted the words once they left her lips as new tears sprang to Violet's eyes.

"Oh, Mother, I'm sorry. I know this isn't your fault. So many times I speak without thought." Putting her arms around her mother, she said again, "Mother, I truly am sorry." Liberty had become a Christian while at boarding school and neither of her parents knew. This was no time for rebellion against her mother but a time for quiet words and a time for her to fast and pray.

With her arms still wrapped around her mother, Liberty pulled back and looked into eyes as green as her own. "How long do I have, Mother?"

CHAPTER I

A gracious woman retaineth honour:
and strong men retain riches.
PROVERBS 11:16

STREET LAMPS SPUTTERED FITFULLY as gusts of wind forced their way into the meager shelter of glass. Orbs of light gleamed around their stemlike posts, swaying to and fro, tossed by the blustery wind. No other light shone from a sky laden with snow. Looking like upended tapers of glass, icicles hung from eaves. December 1882 was unusually cold in Boston. Dusk crept in quietly. The ground, covered in its blanket of white, drifted ghostlike as the wind tossed spits of snow here and there.

Standing in the deepest recess of shadow, an older man stared across the street at an office building. He tugged at his cravat, yanking it higher, wrapping his woolen scarf tighter around himself as the wind's icy fingers clawed their way down his neck. He could see another man across the street, quite young, standing in front of the office building, hawking his wares of shoelaces and polish. As he stood there, he saw a third man start down the side stairs of the building. Watching from the deep shadows, he saw the shoelace vendor turn as if he'd heard a noise. He couldn't tell if the vendor, who was looking straight at the stairs, saw the man who was descending them. The vendor stared for a moment, turned back to his box, and began to pack up. Finishing his task, he walked quickly down the icy street. It was nearly dark.

The man hidden in the shadows looked around and, seeing no one, crossed the street hurriedly. The man who'd come down the stairs stopped when he saw him.

"It's done."

"You sure?"

"More than sure."

"I want to see for myself." Pushing past his accomplice, he gained the stairs. The man with the scarf climbed the icy steps, using the railing. Unlatching the door, he slipped into the office.

Armand Francois Bouvier lay dead on the floor beside his desk. The man bent closer to be certain. At that moment he decided to take care of the shoelace vendor as well just in case he'd seen something. Looking up, he saw the man he'd hired paused in the doorway, his coat unbuttoned, revealing splatters of blood on the front of his shirt.

"See, I told ya he was dead. Now, let's get outta here." He looked down, seeing in the feeble light the blood on his shirt. With gloved hands he clumsily buttoned up his coat. The older man rose slowly, a smile beginning to spread out over his face. It wasn't the first time he'd paid a man to get rid of someone for him.

"Keep your mouth shut—I'll pay you generously. I think we'll get rid of the street vendor as well. I'll let you know," the older man said.

Descending the stairs together, they parted ways. They had nothing in common but their crimes.

Looking like the background of a Monet landscape, snow blurred the street outside Liberty Alexandra Bouvier's parlor window. The ground was covered, leaves hidden by a pristine coat of white, blanketing out the world. It was December of 1882, and the Boston winter had begun in earnest. The scene looked like a wonderland, and Liberty would have entered it and never turned back if she could. She stood watching as huge snowflakes floated randomly downward, feeling chilled. The fire had died down, and Pierre had not stoked it. Everything seemed like a dream. Her eyes burned but she'd shed no tears. Why should she? Everyone said she was so brave. Deep in her heart she knew she wasn't brave but feeling guiltily relieved… thankful for the untimely death of her husband.

The constables had come three days ago to inform her that Armand had been killed in his office in the city. Armand murdered. She could scarcely take it in. There had been a great cry of outrage among the populace. *The Globe* had published a long article about the increase of crime in Boston.

Libby picked up a shawl, wrapping her arms in its warm woolen softness. She knew life would not be easy in the future. Women had few privileges, but she looked forward to the freedom from pretense, shame, and admittedly freedom from the fear. In truth, it was the fear she would be glad to part with most of all. Every day for the past thirteen years she'd dreaded the appearance of her husband. *Thirteen, unlucky number, but not for me.* The shackles of a loveless, arranged marriage were over.

Liberty sank down onto the uncomfortable divan. She looked around the room that was depressing with its heavy dark furniture and walls painted a mustard color. Armand had commissioned the most prestigious sellers of furnishings in Boston and even Europe to decorate the premises. Nothing was comfortable, not even in her own rooms…every item stiff and formal.

Libby's father had heartily approved of everything Armand did. She had no doubt he would soon be knocking at her door wanting to take charge. He certainly had been made wealthy through her most advantageous marriage that he had arranged. Jacques Corlay was a very wealthy man. Armand had been his mentor, teaching him the way to handle business affairs.

Liberty thought back over the past thirteen years. They'd been more difficult because of the loss of her mother. Violet had died within a year of her marriage to Armand. Not complaining much, she had endured constant acute pain in her abdomen. The doctors had given her laudanum to ease the agony she was suffering, but nothing had helped. Liberty still missed her dreadfully.

She thought back to the day she and her mother had shared with one another their faith in Christ. What a joy that had been. Violet became a Christian while Libby had been away at boarding school. She'd said she never could have survived Jacques if she hadn't found Jesus as her Savior. Liberty knew where her mother was now and that she was well out of the sorrow and hardship her father had caused her.

There had been whisperings about him all the time, other women, gambling, illegal dealings and… Liberty, too, was acquainted with that kind of grief. Although Libby and her mother had been sheltered from much, still the rumors never ceased. There was always something that caused heartsickness and a constant uneasiness.

Liberty pulled the shawl closer around her shoulders. The room was cooling off. She needed to get Pierre to come feed the fire. She dreaded the meeting that was sure to take place this very day. She'd had enough of being dominated. Free from Armand, Liberty was now her own mistress. Even though he was not yet buried, she needed to make plans. *What can I do to thwart Jacques?* she thought. *Surely he will seek to take over the estate.* Liberty bowed her head, slipping naturally into prayer as she whispered to God, asking for guidance.

Startled, her prayer was interrupted by the discreet cough of Armand's butler. *My butler,* she corrected herself. Armand had called him an import from Germany.

"What is it, Sigmund?" Liberty asked.

The butler bowed slightly and replied, "A gentleman to see you, madam."

"Who is it? Is it Jacques?"

"No, madam. I believe it's monsieur's lawyer, Mr. Humphries." Sigmund had a strong German accent, but his diction was perfection itself. Armand, who'd been French, had taken much pleasure in baiting Sigmund, yet he'd been glad for what he considered the prestige that came with having a German for a butler. Sigmund was impeccable in his taste, and Libby found him to be unerring in deportment.

"Show him in please," she whispered, her throat suddenly dry with apprehension. Swallowing, she added, "And tell Pierre to come stoke the fire, please. It's cold in here." At the word naturally slipping out of her mouth, Libby thought of Armand and how he would mock her for saying "please" and "thank you" to the hired help.

The man entered the parlor as Liberty stood up, straightened her back, and lifted her chin.

Mr. Humphries had taken off his frock coat in the foyer but looked thoroughly chilled. He was unusually short for a man and had a huge paunch for a stomach. His watch fob chain strained across his middle. His hair was nonexistent except around his ears. Libby looked him directly in the eye and was startled. She'd had no previous dealings with him, but unexpected tears blurred her vision as she saw sympathy and concern for her in his bright-blue eyes. Care for her as a person was not something she'd seen in the last thirteen years among her husband's peers. The lawyer cleared his throat, and she remembered her manners.

"Mr. Humphries, welcome." She proffered her hand. The lawyer took it in a firm grasp and let go. His hand was cold.

"Good morning, Madam Bouvier. We've never met formally. I'm Elijah Humphries, your deceased husband's lawyer. I extend my condolences to you, madam, for your loss. I also must apologize for the early hour, but I happened to be near here and wanted to meet with you." His voice was pleasant, his manner easy. Pierre entered with a coal scuttle and began feeding fuel to the spluttering flames in the fireplace.

"Would you care to be seated?" Liberty asked.

He eyed her from under shaggy eyebrows, smiling gratefully as if surprised by the invitation.

If he'd had much to do with Armand, she could well understand his surprise. Armand would have kept him standing. His smile lit up his face, his teeth even and surprisingly white. As he took a seat on the uncomfortable winged-back chair, Liberty sat down facing him on the divan.

Pierre stood up, finished with his task.

"Thank you, Pierre, that will be all." Turning to Mr. Humphries, she asked, "Would you care for some refreshment, Mr. Humphries?"

He looked at her closely and smiled his pleasant smile again. "Oh yes, yes, I would, thank you. A cup of tea would be just the thing on such a bitterly cold day."

Liberty rang for Matilda and after instructing her, the maid scurried away to set about doing her bidding. Mr. Humphries and Libby made small talk until the tea service arrived.

As she poured, she glanced up. "So what brings you here at such an early hour, Mr. Humphries?"

He cleared his throat again before speaking. "Madam, before the reading of the will, I felt I should inform you of your late husband's wishes concerning the estate."

CHAPTER II

Bear one another's burdens,
and so fulfil the law of Christ.
GALATIANS 6:2

LIBERTY CAREFULLY SET THE PORCELAIN teapot down. A sudden coldness came over her, knowing whatever Mr. Humphries was going to say was not going to be of benefit to her. She took a deep breath, but her stays felt overly tight and dizziness ensued from the corset that constricted her breathing. The fire had caught and was blazing. The room, now feeling too warm, stifled her.

Mr. Humphries spoke as if from a distance. "Madam, I know this will come as a distinct shock to you. Your late husband, Monsieur Armand Bouvier, has left the bulk of the estate to your father. He has ensured that his will is unbreakable."

Liberty gasped. *Oh Lord, help me,* she cried silently in her heart, *help me!* She should have expected it. Her breath whooshed out, and she gasped again for air. She felt foolish as she was not one given to vapors. She swallowed and took as deep a breath as her stays would allow.

Armand can strike at me even from the grave, she thought. The depth of hatred and disdain her husband had felt for her must have been an all-consuming fire burning within him. He'd wanted an heir, and she'd not produced one. She'd never shown to Armand her own anguish over her barrenness. Liberty had wanted a baby above all things but, later, had found a certain gratefulness to God that she did not have any children. She was convinced that having Armand as a father would have birthed evil into their very veins. Liberty reached a semblance of control. She looked at Mr. Humphries, embarrassed by her gasping about like a fish for air.

"Mr. Humphries, please continue."

He gazed at her for a moment before speaking. "I advised your late husband against changing his will, but he wouldn't listen. He decided everything should go to your father, Monsieur Corlay."

She looked at him, the blood draining from her face. She was shocked and could not find her voice.

He continued, "You and Monsieur Bouvier were both young. I assumed you to be a woman of schooling and intelligence, quite able to handle an estate, should the need arise."

Liberty stared at him, the color slowly returning to her face.

"Frankly, Mr. Humphries," she said drily, "my husband and I did not agree on most issues, but I never thought he would go so far as to leave the entire estate to my father."

He shifted his weight on the uncomfortable chair and replied, "No, it's not the entire estate, madam. There is a large holding in the state of California. My understanding is that it's a house with acreage."

"California! Armand has property in California?"

"Yes, yes he does. I've never been there, but Monsieur Bouvier bought land, sight unseen, several years ago. It was a special land purchase. He paid a legislator who saw to it that he was given a land grant requiring improvements on it within a year, or the grant would be revoked. Monsieur Bouvier hired a man he'd never met and paid him a very small amount to make improvements. The man has been reporting to Armand these past three years. It's this property he's willed to you. I understand that the property is located in a large valley."

"California," Libby repeated. "Why would Armand leave me a property he'd never even seen?" She bit her lip, lowering her lashes to escape the pity she knew would be in this kind man's eyes. Liberty could not even begin to understand Armand's motives other than he'd never wanted anything to be easy for her. Armand leaving everything to her father would please him to no end. She knew of Jacques' greed. She knew, too, that his evilness would prevent her from ever asking anything of him. She stood up and so did the lawyer. Liberty began to pace the room, kicking at her skirts as if she could kick away the problems that faced her.

"Is there any money at all to pay for my passage to California and to get supplies to this valley?"

"Yes," he said, smiling a little ruefully. "Yes, there is. I know it's not much considering the vastness of this estate. You'll receive a stipend of twenty dollars per month, which should cover basic needs. However, my understanding is that prices are astronomical in California because of the shortage of supplies. Also, many things we take for granted here are a luxury there."

She looked at him and then down at the beautiful Aubusson carpet. Armand had taken the inheritance money her grandfather had held in trust for her, investing in mining when she'd turned twenty-five.

She turned in her pacing, stopping to ask, "Mr. Humphries, would I be entitled the amount taken from my own inheritance that Armand invested in mining?"

Before he could answer, the double doors swung open, and she looked over to see Sigmund fast approaching with her father at his heels.

"Sorry, madam, Monsieur wished to see you immediately." Libby glanced at Sigmund, who looked almost flustered, blocking her father's figure from her sight.

"It's all right, Sigmund. Thank you." As Sigmund left, she turned to see her father staring at Mr. Humphries. The will had not yet been read, so he had no knowledge that everything was going to belong to him. She was thankful he didn't know yet.

"Good morning, Jacques. I've been expecting you." Turning to Mr. Humphries, she made the introductions. "Jacques, this is Mr. Elijah Humphries, Armand's lawyer. Mr. Humphries, my father, Monsieur Jacques Corlay." The men shook hands, but she could see near hatred sparking from Jacques' eyes. She wondered at it, until she looked at Mr. Humphries. He was a gentleman, yet she could see and sense the distinct dislike in him for her father in the tightening of lips, the gleam in his eyes, and a stiffening of his back. They both seemed to bristle. *What have we here?*

she wondered. *Jacques looks as if he hates Mr. Humphries. My goodness, they seem so full of animosity toward one another.*

Jacques spoke first. "I've heard of you, Humphries."

"And I you, Monsieur Corlay," Mr. Humphries bit out.

He turned to Liberty, smiling slightly, his tone radically changing. "Would you have me stay? Frankly, I don't believe we're quite finished with our conversation."

"If you would be so kind. I do need your counsel," she replied demurely. Despite the atmosphere, she knew she would be supported and encouraged by Mr. Humphries. Liberty was in a tight spot and could use this unexpected source of help.

Her father snorted and said in a sarcastic tone, "Mr. Humphries, I wish to speak to my daughter...alone."

"And I would like him to stay, Jacques. He's now my lawyer, and anything you wish to say to me can be said in front of him. Truly, I prefer it." She lifted her chin, looking directly at her father.

He glared back at her, his lips pulled back, reminding her of a wolf with bared fangs. Liberty was startled into realizing she had always feared her father.

"Please be seated," she said stiltedly to both of them. Mr. Humphries sat at once in the winged-back chair. Jacques rudely placed himself in the middle of the divan, so Libby pulled a side chair forward and sat looking at both men.

"What do you want, Jacques?" she asked bluntly. Her eyes were veiled by her lashes. Liberty had learned from the best. She concealed her thoughts, keeping her voice flat and expressionless when she spoke to him.

He turned to her with a sneer on his lips, his almost-black eyes inimical. Adept at guarding his thoughts and motives, he was a successful businessman with his fingers in many pies. Liberty's father and dead husband had put many men out of business by their devious scheming. Armand had initially supplied the money to her father, as if it were a dowry in reverse. With the capital invested and diversified following Armand's suggestions, he'd made an enormous success of it. He'd profited by other men's downfall, providing the slide by which many came to be destitute.

Both Armand and her father colluded together, acting as if they would help an unsuspecting businessman. When the man used their loan to improve his company, the loan was abruptly called in by a banker in the pay of Armand. The small business owner could not pay back the loan and *voila*, the company became Armand and Jacques'. She had read in *The Globe* that several businessmen had committed suicide and knew it was because of her own father and husband. She also knew instinctively that Mr. Humphries was cognizant of these facts, which explained what she'd seen in his eyes.

Jacques, the sneer still in place, said condescendingly, "I know, daughter, how devastated you are over Armand's unexpected demise. I'd like to help you. I don't think it proper, nor are you capable of handling this vast estate. I will take the responsibility for you. Beginning tomorrow, after the reading of the will, I'll handle all of Armand's affairs." Libby glanced at Mr. Humphries and saw the slight nodding of his head. She thought quickly, glancing back at her father.

"I have delayed the reading of the will until the day after tomorrow, three o'clock in the afternoon to be precise. Mr. Humphries and I have just been discussing these affairs. So, in two days' time I'd be very grateful, Jacques, for your assistance." She smiled demurely at her father's stunned expression, concealing her small victory of an extra day before the reading of the will. Liberty peeked through her lashes at Mr. Humphries. His expression was benign, but she could see the gleam of approval in his eyes.

Liberty stood abruptly and Mr. Humphries, every inch the gentleman, also stood. "Now, if that is all, Jacques, I have much to do to prepare for the funeral. I'll see you there tomorrow afternoon." She rang for Sigmund, who must have been hovering nearby. "Sigmund, please show Monsieur Corlay out." She dismissed her father with a nod of her head.

Jacques' lips tightened in anger. He turned on his heel and strode across the room. "Good day," he bit out without looking in Mr. Humphries' direction. Liberty inclined her head and her father was gone.

After Jacques left the room, Liberty sat down a little shakily. Mr. Humphries also sat.

"Well done, Madam Bouvier," he chuckled. "You've bought yourself another day."

She looked across at him and laughed outright. "Thank you, and you may call me Libby."

He smiled and said, "Short for Liberty. I saw your name on the legal documents."

"Yes, my name is Liberty Alexandra, a name my mother insisted upon. I've never heard of another person named Liberty—have you? The Alexandra, I've always wondered about too. Do you think that's for Alexander the Great?" She smiled at her jest.

"I like your name." Mr. Humphries smiled back at her. "It's unusual but it fits you. I think you'll experience some true liberty once you leave Boston. Now," he continued, "you've gained yourself an extra day, and we have much to do. First, I need to tell you that as Monsieur Bouvier invested your inheritance into his own mining company, it'll be part of the estate and will go to your father. I'm very sorry for that. As for arrangements for you, I will book your passage to California. The trains are very reliable and will be the best mode of travel for you. Next, you must gather items from this house that you feel will be of use to you in California."

Libby looked at his face. His easy confidence gave her strength.

"Yes, I can do that, but just now I feel in need of refreshment. Would you care to join me for some of Cook's famous scones?"

CHAPTER III

But I trusted in thee, O LORD:
I said, Thou art my God.
PSALM 31:14

LIBERTY FELT OVERWHELMED BY HER new set of circumstances, and yet, something seemed to be percolating deep within her. The thought of the unknown, the freedom from what had been virtually bondage came near to choking her with excitement. She rang for a fresh pot of tea and asked Matilda to bring scones. As Matilda pulled the door shut, Liberty glimpsed Sigmund waiting for her outside the door.

Sigmund grabbed Matilda by the arm. "Do you know what's happening? Have you overheard anything at all, Tilly?" Matilda looked up at this big blond man and felt her heart turn over.

"No, Sigmund, I've heard nothing. Have you?" She laid her hand on top of his and gave it a caress. His eyes warmed, their blueness rivaling the skies on a clear day.

"No, I've heard nothing, but I don't like the feel of it. Madam's had a bad time of it, that's certain. I fear worse is to come, with her evil father always panting after money." Matilda started to move away. "I must get the tea and scones for her and her guest. Who is he, anyway?"

"He was Monsieur Bouvier's lawyer, but I believe him to be a good man. Hurry now and I'll help you." He swatted Matilda on her bottom.

She pretended to glare at him but ended up giggling. They both headed toward the kitchen.

When the door closed behind Matilda, Liberty spoke from her heart. "Mr. Humphries, I'm so grateful for your help. I'm humbled by it, knowing you represented Armand's interests and not mine."

He looked at her with a tightening of his lips. "I represented your husband because my associates delegated him to me, not because of personal choice. In truth, we drew straws and I lost." He smiled at her. "Now, let's get down to business. I'll try to find a suitable chaperone for your trip. I want you to take your jewelry and personal belongings. You'll need trunks packed with rugs, curtains, bedding, and whatever else you'll need to set up house. Assume the place you're going is empty—it might very well be. I'll make every effort to get you out of here before the reading of the will the day after tomorrow."

Liberty looked at him in shocked surprise. She could be gone before the reading of the will! She wouldn't have to endure her father's gloating eyes and comments. Her eyes filled, tears spilling down her cheeks. She was appalled, for she never cried in public. Her stiff back unbent, and she put a hand up to shield her eyes from his gaze. Mr. Humphries stood up, gently pulling her into his arms, patting her as if she were a child.

"There, there," he said. "You may not know it yet, but I'm predicting a lot happier life for you in California than you've ever known here." He lifted her chin, dabbing at her eyes with a pristine white handkerchief.

"Do you know I've seen you at the little chapel on Rice Street?" Liberty, her green eyes swimming with tears, was startled that he'd recognized her from the chapel and surprised that he'd been there himself.

"Are you a believer?" she asked in a whisper. Her voice almost cracked, still choked by tears.

"Oh. Yes, yes, I am, have been for years, and you?"

"Yes, since my last boarding school in Lucerne. I made a wonderful friend who kept telling me about her relationship with Jesus Christ. I was so bereft of love, and Jesus came into my heart filling me up. I'm so very thankful for my friend, Marissa Reed, who led me to Christ. I've never felt alone since, even through the travesty of my marriage…I don't know why I'm telling you all of this. I'm babbling. In truth, I feel closer to you than my own father, and we've only just met. Thank you very much for being here today." She reached up and touched his cheek.

He took her hand. "Let me pray for you. Lord Jesus, we are so thankful for Thy love. How good Thou art to us, and we praise Thee for Thy faithfulness. I now lift Liberty to Thee, asking Thy precious Holy Ghost to guide her and protect her. Grant her Thy wisdom and strength for the days ahead. May, by Thy provision, people be brought into her life to help her. We thank Thee and give Thee praise for what Thou art going to do in and through her life. In Christ's peerless name we pray. Amen."

He turned to leave. "I'll talk with you again tomorrow, after the funeral."

"I thank you, Mr. Humphries. And thank you for your prayer."

Liberty walked him to the front door, where he took her hand. "I was not jesting when I spoke to you about your future. It will be good, and you are in God's hands." He donned his overcoat with the help of Sigmund and jauntily walked down the front steps.

As Liberty watched him go down the walk, she saw that a carriage awaited him. She stood there thoughtfully for a moment. Giving Sigmund a huge smile, Libby quickly took the steps two at a time up to her rooms. It was something she hadn't done in thirteen years. She grinned to herself. Looking around at her belongings, pictures on the wall, beloved books in the case, lamps, and throw rugs, she rang for her maid, Maggie, who came right away.

"I'd like to borrow your clothes."

Her maid looked stunned, totally taken aback.

"Ma'am, I have only my maid uniforms and my own set of clothes I wear when going to visit the children at the orphanage." Maggie was Irish with dimples so deep one could fit their thumb into them. Her red hair was like a halo covering her well-shaped head. Bright and shining, it made Liberty feel as if her own coppery curls looked drab.

"Maggie, have you any more maid's clothing?"

"Yes, ma'am, I do."

"Get them and please hurry." Liberty began undressing.

"Yes, ma'am. Right away, ma'am." She hurried off to gather up her things.

Libby quickly undid her hair, pulling it straight back and rolling it tightly into a bun. Some curls sprang out, softening the effect she wanted.

Maggie returned with her extra maid's clothing, dumping them on the bed.

"Oh, ma'am," she said, "you're so beautiful!"

Libby was scantily clad with only her corset and chemise, but she unconsciously straightened, smiling at Maggie's compliment.

"Oh, Maggie, what'll I do without you?"

Maggie stared in amazement. "What are you talking about, ma'am?"

Libby paused, staring at Maggie as she quickly made a decision. She was definitely going to need Maggie's help anyway.

"Maggie, I've always trusted you. Now, I'm going to trust you as a friend and confidante rather than my maid. I'm going away—I must go away. My father will be taking over the estate. Indeed, he's taking over everything. That's why the lawyer came this morning—to tell me Armand cut me out of the entire estate except for a property in California." She hurriedly began to dress in Maggie's clothing. The servant halted a moment in helping Libby dress. She looked into her eyes.

"I've nothing to keep me here, ma'am. I've no family, no man, and you're the only person on this earth I care about. May I come with you? I've a bit of money saved up for a rainy day. Oh, please say yes!" Tears stood out in her dark-grey eyes. They fell into each other's arms, hugging.

"Oh, Maggie, I don't know what I'd ever do without you! Yes, yes, and yes! You may come with me, and I'll pay your passage, at least I think I will." She smiled as she spoke, hoping she would have enough funds. Maggie helped Libby with the buttons on her maid's dress. The length was fine, covering the tops of her shoes, but the waist was loose.

Maggie looked at Libby and giggled. "You look the part, ma'am. With my mob cap, you'll be perfect." Liberty laughed for the second time that day. She could not remember the last time she'd laughed, and now she'd laughed two times in one day. *Freedom*, she thought. *Perhaps Mr. Humphries was right in saying life is going to get better.*

The two women slipped quietly down the back stairs. Maggie had a heavy shawl wrapped around her sturdy shoulders and lifted its twin off the hooks by the service entrance, handing it to Libby. Liberty waited until they were outside to put it on, feeling exposed by the large kitchen just behind the swinging doors.

The sharp air sucked at her lungs and was bitterly cold. Trees, newly decked out in dresses of white, stretched laden fingers toward the sky. It was midmorning, and no one seemed to have ventured out. Snow crunched beneath their feet as they set off the few blocks into the city proper.

Sigmund turned to Matilda and Cook. "Did you see them? That was madam with Maggie!" he exclaimed. "Madam dressed up like a commoner. This does not bode well for us. I think we're going to be looking for other employment. Monsieur Corlay has his own staff, and I've no doubt that he'll be taking over Monsieur's estate, from the looks of it."

His words scared Matilda. Her chin quivered. "Will we be separated, Sigmund? Where will we go?"

Sigmund took her chin gently in his large hand, lifting her head to look at him. He gazed down into her sweet face, vowing that nothing would separate them.

"*Mein liebling*," he said, "we'll find a way. Somehow we will find a way."

Outside the skies were gray, heavy with eiderdown clouds ready to burst their ticking. Branches on the birch trees were dropping powdery clumps of snow, looking like the fine sugar powder Cook used to top her German pancakes. Maggie and her mistress wrapped their shawls a little tighter, walking quickly. They covered the few blocks in just minutes. Little puffs of smoke floated into the atmosphere from their breath as they spoke to each other.

Entering a textile shop, Liberty conferred with the proprietor to order bolts of material for Madam Bouvier. Libby thought it great fun being disguised. She smiled in wonder. *People don't really look at the hired help,* she thought and was surprised at the ambiguity she had achieved by her clothes. Amazement sparkled in Maggie's eyes at the types, colors, and textures as they strolled through the shop ordering bolts of rich and varied materials. They chose some beautiful fabrics but also added calico and muslin to the growing amount of cloth. Libby thought the lighter-weighted materials might be more suited for California's climate. They added to their purchases anything they could think of that might be needed in an area that had little to offer by way of textiles: large bobbins of thread, needles, scissors, ribbons and laces, trims and more trims. When they were finished, they thanked the proprietor and asked that the goods be sent to Madam Bouvier and be put on her account.

Once outside they began to giggle, careful not to let the passersby have reason to stare. It was difficult not to burst into a full-bellied laugh.

Although Libby had on Maggie's clothes, she'd been wearing deep black as befit a widow the past two days. Wearing black, but her heart was beginning to wear a variety of colors, bright and happy. She couldn't begin to feel guilty for her attitude—to do so would have been a deception.

Maggie asked, "What next, Madam Bouvier?"

"We have no need to go to the milliner. I've a large number of hats, gloves, and dresses as you well know, enough to last us a long time. I think the next stop will be the luggage shop. We'll need a vast amount of trunks to hold all our belongings."

"Ma'am, I don't need a trunk. My things will fit into a large satchel."

"That may be true at this moment, but you're going to need a wardrobe." She turned to face Maggie "We'll not be going to California as employer and employee. We'll be going as equals, as friends. You're my best friend, Maggie."

Maggie looked dumbfounded before her eyes began to sparkle, a huge smile spreading across her lips, her dimples looking larger than ever.

"I'll be the best, most loyal friend you've ever had, madam!" she exclaimed. They hugged each other, smiling into each other's eyes.

"Let's continue on, Maggie. We still have much to do, and we must be back before long. I am beginning to long for luncheon."

They visited several more shops. Liberty didn't know much about tools yet knew, somehow, to purchase them. She ordered nails, hammers, crowbars, saws, much rope, several shovels, pitchforks, and anything else the clerk helping them thought fit for sending to men in California. Libby felt sure he included more than they needed, but they didn't tell him the items were for their own trip west. Libby found a large butter churn and a pestle for grinding grain.

She smiled to herself when she thought how shocked her father was going to be when these bills were sent to him. Hopefully, by then she'd be long away from here and on her way to where his evilness couldn't touch her.

CHAPTER IV

THEY WENT TO A MERCANTILE store and ordered large amounts of staples: flour, cornmeal, sugar, salt, spices, dried fruits of lemon, lime, orange, prunes, dates, figs, and apricot. There were grains and all kinds of beans. Liberty didn't know there were so many types of beans. They noticed a large assortment of nuts and included pounds of each kind they saw. There were sacks of rice, and the merchant kept asking if they were sure Madam Bouvier wanted so much. They assured him that she did and that she was sending the goods somewhere out west.

Maggie whispered, "Ma'am, we'll need molds plus string and tallow for making candles and soap."

"What else, Maggie?" she asked, humbled by the thought that Maggie had more knowledge about their needs than she.

"Well," Maggie continued, "we'll also need lye for making soap, and flint for fires. I think we should revisit the leather shop and order lengths of leather for replacing worn harnesses and buckles and the like."

"That's a good idea." She'd thought about asking the leathers and luggage shopkeeper if the other merchants could send their wares to him and they could be loaded into the trunks and put onto the train of Mr. Humphries' choosing. She decided to leave the matter up to Mr. Humphries. Libby didn't want her father to get wind of Mr. Humphries helping her or having him aware of her plans. She decided to send a note to Mr. Humphries that afternoon, informing him of her purchases and letting him take care of the details.

Asking that several trunks be sent to her residence for packing, she was grateful that Mr. Humphries' clerks were taking care of the funeral preparations. All she need do was make her appearance, stand in the receiving line, and attend the reception following the service. She'd be glad for the veil that would cover her face from all inquisitive eyes. Libby decided she'd keep a stiff back and her chin well up.

She spoke to the clerk. "Madam also wants me to order two hand guns and two rifles with a lot of bullets because where she's sending this stuff is wild with outlaws." She smiled sweetly. The request seemed strange to her, and she swallowed, hoping he wouldn't challenge it. He took it in stride, showing her what was available. Libby had absolutely no idea what they would need; she'd just thought it might be a good thing to include.

"Could you please pick it out? Whatever you think would be the best for men in the West that need protection? Madam Bouvier doesn't know what's needed, but she thought it a good idea."

Her eyes slanted over to Maggie's, and it was all she could do to keep from laughing. Maggie's eyes had rounded in astonishment that madam would want guns.

The clerk helped the two women. "This is a Smith & Wesson New Model Number Three revolver. It's a fairly new model and came out a few years ago. Shoots seven bullets without reloading. I think this is what'd be best. As for rifles"—he walked over to another case and picked up a rifle —"the best'd be this lever-action firearm, it's a Henry-Winchester." He picked up two of the rifles and asked, "About how many bullets were you thinking you needed?"

Liberty glanced at Maggie before replying.

"I've no idea what madam has in mind. Probably enough to last for a year?"

Both Libby and Maggie were thoroughly chilled yet elated by the time they walked back to the Bouvier manse. A hansom cab was just pulling away from the curb, and a man was standing at Libby's front door. He glanced at them, but Liberty kept her head down as the two made their way quickly through the snow to the back entrance. As they turned the corner of the house, a bird flew out of a bush toward them. Startled, Libby lost her footing on a patch of ice, falling heavily onto her backside. Maggie leaned over to help Libby get up but ended up slipping. She fell beside Liberty, and they lay there for several minutes freezing, yet unable to get up because of their hysterical giggling. They rolled away from each other, got onto their knees, and tried to stand, still caught in the grips of uncontrollable laughing. Maggie helped Libby dust herself off, and Libby dusted her maid down. They entered as quietly as they could, trying to stifle their laughter as waves of it kept bubbling up from within. Once inside the door, Liberty saw that Sigmund had been waiting for her. He seemed anxious.

She forgot all about her attire, asking, "What is it, Sigmund?"

His eyes widened as he fully took in her clothing.

"A detective to see you, madam."

Liberty stared at him for a moment, and as the import of his words sank in, she took the back stairs two at a time. This was no time for decorum. She called back to Maggie. "Maggie, please hurry. I need your help!"

Maggie, close on her heels, hurriedly grabbed a dress from the clothespress. It was unrelieved black suitable for mourning. Libby quickly divested herself of Maggie's clothing but felt deceitful donning the black dress, because she was definitely not mourning.

"Maggie, you do my hair."

Maggie reached for the silver-handled brush given Libby by her mother as Liberty slipped her hands through the arms of the dress. Tiny buttons lined the front, and she buttoned quickly as Maggie combed. Maggie was deft in her movements and soon had her presentable. Libby ran to the top of the stairs, took a deep breath to settle her thumping heart, and heard her stomach growl but tried to ignore it. She was very hungry.

She descended with the utmost decorum. Entering the parlor, she found the detective gazing at the Rousseau hanging over the fireplace mantel. It was *Hoarfrost*, one of his better works. She felt Rousseau's paintings to be too dark and preferred the Ruysdael in her room.

She had entered quietly, yet the man heard her. He turned and smiled.

Liberty looked at him gravely, proffering her hand. She spoke softly. "Good afternoon, Mister…"

"Baxter, Chief Inspector George Baxter," he said with a slight smile. "I'm a detective investigating your husband's murder. Nice Rousseau you have there." He nodded to the picture over the mantel. He had a deep groove in his left cheek and a little quirk at the top of it when he smiled. His skin looked almost as white as hers. He was clean shaven except for a thin black mustache above his well-shaped mouth. He was dressed as a gentleman, and his cravat was impeccably done.

Liberty was surprised an inspector would know the artist and immediately felt ashamed. *Don't be so uppity*, she thought, berating herself for thinking like a snob.

"I'm so sorry for your loss, madam."

Libby made no comment. She felt guilty she could not mourn and felt deceptive in acknowledging any remorse. She inclined her head.

"Have you noticed anyone unusual on the street or at your service entrance?" he asked her in a gentle voice.

"No, I've seen nothing out of the ordinary. May I ask why you're inquiring here? I would think my husband's office and surrounding areas would be what needs investigating."

"That's being accomplished as we speak, madam, but we need to search out every avenue of possibility."

They were standing and she offered him a chair, trying to grasp why he would investigate here.

"Am I a suspect then, Mr. Baxter?" she asked incredulously.

Mr. Baxter leaned forward in the very uncomfortable winged-back chair, returning her stare a minute before replying.

"No, madam, but we must talk with everyone who had some sort of relationship with Monsieur Bouvier. I'd like to question your staff. Would that would be acceptable to you?"

Her stomach rumbled again, and she felt a headache would not be long in coming if she didn't eat soon.

"Yes, yes, of course. I know this may sound inappropriate, but have you eaten luncheon, Mr. Baxter?" She smiled engagingly. "I've not and I'm famished. You may join me if you wish, and then you're most welcome to interview my staff."

Surprise showed in his eyes at her hospitality.

"I'd be delighted, madam. I knew your mother back in the day. We attended the same social functions. She was a beautiful woman."

Startled at his comment, she replied, "Thank you. I still miss her even after all this time."

They went to the dining room, but Liberty proceeded to the kitchen to let the staff know to set another place at the table.

Mr. Baxter regaled Liberty with stories of her mother, and she felt much better after eating. Eager to start packing, she called her staff together and asked them to be as helpful as possible in talking to the inspector. She introduced Mr. Baxter, who wanted to talk to them one by one. Libby bade him good-bye as he called Sigmund into the parlor first.

"Thank you for your generosity, and your cook is superb. May I return if I find I have more questions?"

"Of course…although tomorrow is the funeral."

"Then the day after?"

Liberty was at a loss for words. She answered hesitantly.

"I plan to be out of town the day after tomorrow. Would it be amenable to you if you talked to Mr. Humphries, my lawyer, or perhaps my father?"

He eyed her closely, seeming to read her thoughts. Libby's face began to burn as he looked intently at her. She felt guilty, lowering her eyes as she sought for some excuse she could give him.

"Perhaps you could come tomorrow after the reception. Mr. Humphries could be here and assist you."

Mr. Baxter seemed approving of that suggestion and shaking her proffered hand, bade her a good day.

Libby left him with Sigmund. She went into Armand's study, finding paper on which to write a note to Mr. Humphries. Writing quickly, she explained her purchases and the trunks she'd bought. She sent for Pierre to ride over to Mr. Humphries' offices. She didn't care to ask Rufus, her driver. She didn't trust him.

She felt a great curiosity about Armand's desk. She knew she needed to get upstairs to pack, but she started opening drawers. Swallowing hard, she began looking through Armand's papers. There was a great deal there that would interest Mr. Humphries and even the constabulary. Since her father would be virtually left with everything, she decided to tell Mr. Baxter he was free to peruse anything in the desk he might find interesting. She felt no sense of ownership. As far as she was concerned, it was not hers and might give the detective some knowledge of Armand's dealings and with whomever he was in contact. Libby went back into the kitchen and delivered her message to Cook to give Mr. Baxter when it was her turn to be interviewed. Finally, she made her way upstairs.

Maggie was already sorting things out. The trunks had arrived up the service stairs, being lugged in by the shop's assistants with little fuss. The two women worked diligently until dinner.

Libby had few day dresses she thought might be appropriate for California. She wondered how formal the dress was there.

Maggie was thrilled with the clothes Liberty gave her. They sewed busily as they let out some of the waists. Libby emptied drawers, packing the trunks. She put in all her underclothes and told Maggie to get all hers as well. Those were the types of things that they would probably find difficult to get in California: corsets, chemises, slips, extra stays, and rags for their monthlies. They made much headway, and Libby was pleased with their progress.

"Maggie, could you please tell Cook to have two meals brought up to my rooms?"

"Two, ma'am?" she asked.

"Yes, two. Do friends eat at different tables? We need one for you and one for me," she said, lifting one eyebrow.

Maggie grinned at Liberty and skipped down the back stairs to the kitchen. She could tell things were going to be a lot different from now on. As she pushed through the swinging doors, she was surprised to find Matilda, Sigmund, Pierre, Cook, and Rufus sitting around the scrubbed table together. Their dishes had not been removed, and it was evident that they had been deep in conversation.

Maggie gave her message to Cook. "Madam would like two dinners sent up," she said. "Why have Madam Bouvier and I not been interviewed?"

"Dat man Baxter," Cook snorted. "He say he doan haf to be talking to you until ta'morrow." She wiped her chin on her apron.

"That's good news." Maggie grinned hugely at Cook.

"*Ja*, dat Baxter man, he still in monsewer's study."

Cook started to say something else, but Maggie forestalled her by saying, "I'll be happy to take the dinners up." She smiled, a bit cheekily, at Cook.

"So what's happening above stairs?" Sigmund asked. "Rumor has it, Monsieur Corlay will be taking over after the funeral."

Rufus sat up a little straighter and questioned. "Where'd you hear that bit of information?"

"It's just a rumor, Rufus. I don't remember where I heard it." Sigmund spoke a bit shortly. He did not like nor trust Rufus. The big blond knew Rufus was an informant for Monsieur Corlay and told him everything about the happenings in the Bouviers' household.

Matilda's mouth drooped at the corners. "Madam hasn't a chance against that evil man." Her chin quivered. Sigmund pressed her shoulder with a gentle squeeze.

"If he is taking over," Maggie announced, "it'll not be until the day after tomorrow. Madam has delayed the reading of the will until then." All sets of eyes were upon her. She didn't want to elaborate, so she added, "Now, I really must get back with some food." Maggie started dishing up her food as Cook waddled over to dish up madam's.

Maggie went up the stairs with both dinners on a tray. "Mr. Baxter is still in the study, ma'am," she said as she entered the room.

Libby grunted back a reply. She was on her knees in the clothespress trying to reach all her shoes, but she was surprised that the inspector should still be here. Liberty backed herself out of the clothespress, throwing half the shoes she'd dug out back in. They were too flimsy for where they were going. Sitting on her heels for a moment, she thought, *I wonder if Mr. Baxter's found anything interesting? I hope he finds something that will help him solve the case.* Liberty did not wish anyone dead and certainly not her husband. Still, she could not help being elated at the freedom she felt and the relief of not having to see him always watching her. Liberty hoped they could get away before her father caught wind of their plans.

The two women ate while they continued to pack.

CHAPTER V

But ye, brethren,
be not weary in well doing
THESSALONIANS 3:13

BY THE TIME LIBERTY AND MAGGIE had eaten, it was getting late. Libby knew she had another big day on the morrow.

"Maggie, thank you for your help. I'd never have gotten half this far in packing on my own, even had I labored all night."

She walked over to Maggie, who was standing by the window overlooking the gardens. The moon had risen, a bright orb in the starlit sky. Branches heavy with snow made long-fingered shadows across the heavy white drifts, the entire landscape serene. Libby stood next to Maggie, gazing at the beauty outside her window for a few minutes without speaking. A cloud partially covered the moon. *It's beautiful, Lord. Thank you for your peace.*

"This is not going to be easy, Maggie. I don't know what we'll find at the end of this long journey. We'll experience much, I believe, but we'll make it. With God's help, we'll make it."

Maggie turned toward her, the serenity of the scene outside the window reflected in her beautiful gray, luminous eyes.

"What will be, will be, ma'am."

"Yes, *lo que será, será,*" Libby quoted softly.

"What does that mean, ma'am?"

"Just what you said, Maggie—what will be, will be. It's a Spanish saying. And yet without God's guidance, that is a fatalistic attitude. I surrender what will be to Him."

Maggie looked at Libby with new eyes. She'd always known madam was special and had enjoyed caring for her and her things. She'd never seen her work as she had today. She'd been more like a companion, a real friend.

"Good-night, ma'am. I had a good time with you today. I'm excited for this new adventure, but we still have much to do to be ready the day after the morrow."

"I'm thankful for your friendship, Maggie. I, too, am very excited. I keep thinking this is too good to be true and that my father will find out and somehow prevent it. Let's pray that doesn't happen…I don't think I could bear it. Good-night, my friend."

Later, as she snuggled under the puffy duvet, questions ran though her mind at lightning speed, and her head whirled with no answers. She felt frightened by what the future might hold for her and yet elated at the same time. What would her life be like? Where was she going? Would she be happy? Could she, indeed, get away from her father? This one thing she knew, the dear girl, Maggie, would be going too. Best of all, Liberty knew God would lead her and guide her if she allowed Him. She fell asleep praying.

Liberty woke abruptly, thinking it was still night. She'd closed the heavy curtains before retiring to block out the bright light of the moon. It was dark in the room, and there was no sound. Lighting a taper, she looked at the ormolu clock. Her mother had told her that her grandfather had specially commissioned Jacques Caffieri, the Frenchman who was the best in his family specializing in ormolu. It had been a present to her mother on her sixteenth birthday. Violet had loved that clock. She'd given it to Liberty several months before she had passed away. Her mother told her the gilded clock was something she must never part with and to be sure to have it cleaned every few years. Libby had never had it cleaned, but it worked fine. The hands showed half past the hour of six. Liberty blew out the taper, pushed back the covers, and got up. She made a mental note to pack the clock and a few other things that she enjoyed. She would take Mr. Humphries' advice and not pack only the necessities.

Wrapped in her yellow satin robe, she walked to the window. Pulling back the heavy drapes, she saw that the clear evening sky of the night before was gone. Tiny lacy puffs of cotton drifted lazily earthbound to land unseen upon a heavy covering of white. The world was silent with drifts deeper than last evening, lying virginal across the sweep of lawns. *How difficult is it going to be for a train to plow through this snow? How do men clear the tracks? Do men clear the tracks, or do the trains themselves keep the tracks clean?* Questions bubbled up within her. She thought of the funeral and came near to panic as she thought of the day that lay ahead of her.

She gazed again at the tranquil scene before her. *I'm sorry, Lord. This is the day You have made, and I will be glad and rejoice in it. I'll do my best to be the light You want me to be and touch others this day with Your love. I know, Father, this day is not about me. It's all about You. I pray You help me to remember that every single day. And when I'm confused, help me remember to turn to You for answers. Help me, please, to have patience with every situation that presents itself this day. May I always give You the glory and honor You so deserve.*

Liberty lifted her head, looking out on the beautiful landscape with an unruffled heart…knowing that the God of her salvation held her in His hands. She stood there for a few more minutes thinking about her day but not anxious about it. Anything that came her way was filtered by the hand of the Almighty. He would guide her path. All she need do was figure out if she was listening to His voice and not her own.

Liberty remembered hearing a message at the little church on Rice Street. The minister had said everyone has three voices in their heads: God's voice, our own voice, and Satan's voice. *One thing I need to do*, she thought, *is distinguish which voice is talking. I know Your voice will never tell me to do anything contrary to Your Word, Father. Satan's voice may use part of Your Word, but it will be twisted and not Your best for me. The more I involve myself in Your Word, the more I'll be able to know Your voice.* Libby got out her Bible and read a few verses about Jesus talking about His sheep knowing His voice.

"Lord," she spoke aloud, "help me to know Your voice. I desire to please You."

Matilda entered with a tap on Libby's door, laden down with a breakfast tray. The aroma of coffee was tantalizing, and Matilda poured Liberty a cup.

"Good morning, Matilda."

"Good morning, madam." She set the heavy tray down, but her eyes filled with tears.

"Madam, are we to be let go?"

Libby felt sadness, looking at this young woman who'd been so faithful to her, but she couldn't endanger the plans Mr. Humphries had set in motion.

"Tomorrow will be the reading of the will, and I'm sure we'll all be provided for by my late husband. You know, Matilda, this house will need staff to run it, and I can't imagine my father letting anyone go should he take over the management. If I'm to be in charge, everything will go on as it has in the past. I hope all will be well, but if my father takes over, Sigmund will surely take care of you."

Matilda had been looking at the fire burning warmly in the grate, but slowly she became aware of the trunks scattered about the room. She looked back at Libby, her eyes hardening a little. Liberty colored slightly, feeling the heat in her face.

She looked her maid squarely in the eyes. "I'm preparing for the worst scenario, Matilda. If my father takes over the estate, I don't plan to sit around and have him fix me up with another man to marry. I'm going to leave here if that happens."

Matilda dropped her eyes. "I'm sorry, madam, that I doubted you. Now it's my turn to be frank. You know I love Sigmund, and I don't know if we'll be able to stay together. He doesn't like your father, not at all, madam." Her lips drooped and her eyes filled with tears.

Libby reached out, pulling Matilda into her arms. "I wish I knew the answer for you. If you do decide to leave here, please talk to Mr. Humphries. He is very kind and will find a good position for you. Now, you'd better get below stairs, but, Matilda…"

"Yes, madam?"

"Please don't say anything to anyone except Sigmund about my preparations. I wish to keep my plans secret from my father. If Rufus finds out…" Her voice trailed off.

"Of course, madam, and I do understand." She left the room, closing the door quietly behind her.

Libby sighed deeply. She began to eat her breakfast. The second cup of coffee tasted even better than the first.

The morning passed too quickly. Liberty and Maggie packed the entire morning. Liberty took the ormolu clock and her jewelry box, carefully wrapping them in a couple shawls. She placed them in one of the trunks, and taking the inkwell from her desk, she blotted the trunk front so she'd know later where to find them. Libby also took a few pictures down and packed them, including the Ruysdael, her favorite. Her mother had been an artist before marrying her father and had taught her much about different artists and how to look at paintings. Jacob Ruysdael had been trained by his own father and uncle, who were both landscape artists. He'd lived in the Netherlands. The poor man had died a pauper. The painting that was Libby's very own was *Tower Mill*. She loved the picture that depicted a windmill. The colors were intense but not dark, and the water looked so real.

Armand had given a party for her twenty-fifth birthday and made sure all his sycophants were present. The presentation of the painting was one of his best performances. Libby didn't care—she'd fallen in love with the painting as soon as she'd seen it. It had cost him a great deal of money. Libby hadn't known that the next day he'd gone to the bank and collected her inheritance money. She found out when she had gone to the bank herself to draw on it. It'd already been withdrawn, emptied out by Armand.

Time was passing, and Liberty needed to dress for the funeral. Maggie was indispensable in helping and fetching things for her. Libby's gown was unrelieved black, but it was beautiful. The bodice was cut low in the front and back, but she was covered from the bosom to the throat with velvet-flecked netting ending in a short Chinese collar around her neck. The waist was snug, showing off her incredible figure. Tiny jet buttons ran down the back to the skirt. The combination of velvet and taffeta was stunning. The hemline was gathered up in bows all around the skirt with ruffles of black lace peeking out. The shawl matched the skirting.

Maggie swept up Liberty's thick hair and fixed it in place with a tortoiseshell comb. Coppery curls sprang around her face, softening the look of deep mourning. Maggie looked at Libby's reflection in the mirror over the chiffonier and grinned at her.

"You look perfect," she said.

Libby took a deep breath. "You have made me able to face this day in style, and I thank you."

Rufus had Madam Bouvier's carriage ready. Riding to the cathedral with heated bricks under her feet and a lap robe for warmth, she was not cold. Her hands were encased in a fur muff.

Liberty couldn't seem to concentrate on anything. Her mind kept leaping from one thing to the next. She thought of how she would need to learn to do things for herself…no servants. Looking back, she wished she'd watched Cook make her magic. *I wonder if Maggie knows how to cook. What is Mr. Humphries going to say to me? Was he able to buy the tickets for tomorrow?* Libby tried not to think of her father and his smug grin. She thought of Matilda and Sigmund and wondered what would happen to them. Armand had seen to it that Liberty had no close friends. His business dealings and the type of social functions she attended allowed for many acquaintances but no truly deep friendships. Yes, there were women she liked, but she was surprised by the lack of feeling for anyone. There was no one she'd miss more than her own staff. Liberty looked at the scenery, trying to concentrate. The Bouviers lived only a few blocks from the huge church where her father wanted the funeral. She prayed, thanking God for the beauty and serenity around her, asking Him to give her serenity in her heart in order to face the next few hours. Liberty dreaded making small talk with Armand's friends.

The skies looked leaden as if they were mourning. Looking guiltily at the heavy grayness, Libby wondered to herself at her lack of sorrow. She felt none. Armand had caused her grief, much fear, and heartache. Her real sorrow was that things could have been good between them but never were. Her hopes of him becoming a Christian were dashed. He'd made his evil choices. Never again would he have the chance to repent, to know the fullness of forgiveness, and love for a Savior who willingly died for him.

The carriage began to slow as it approached the spired cathedral. Jacques had his own family pew there. It was the largest Protestant church in Boston. The roofline was steep and reminded Libby of some houses in Switzerland. The red brick of the edifice stood in stark contrast to the snowy white landscape. As the carriage drew closer, Liberty could see snow-covered headstones lined in humps behind the church. The carriage stopped, and Jacques' liveried footman opened the door. He held out his hand, and Libby took it as she stepped down. She drew another deep breath, carefully strolling up the icy walk to the large doors. As one attendant opened the door, another took Liberty's arm, leading her to Jacques' pew.

Nodding to her father, she entered the pew and sat looking at the stained-glass windows. The apse was beautiful with a rich darkly stained wooden altar that was intricately carved. The ceiling over the apse was arched, painted with scenes from the Garden of Eden. She saw that the upright columns were richly carved, depicting Bible stories from Genesis. It was a beautiful church.

She bowed her head, praying silently as she sat waiting for the service to begin. Liberty suddenly opened her eyes, startled, realizing Armand was lying only a few feet from her in the closed casket. She wondered, *Where is he now? Does one go straight to hell? I don't think so, since there is to be a Judgment Day for nonbelievers. The lost are judged for their sins, and the believers will be judged for their works.* Her pondering was interrupted by the rector who had come out and was standing at the lectern. He began to speak. *What can the man say about someone such as Armand? It must be difficult to officiate at a funeral where the deceased must surely be going to hell.* Liberty listened, but the basic message was about some of the charities to which Armand had contributed money. There were few scriptures and a most uninspiring eulogy.

Jacques Corlay sat musing to himself. He knew Armand left him everything and that Liberty would be under his domination once again. He stared at the casket, thinking. What a fool Armand had been. He liked the way the minister lauded the charities to which Armand had given and that he also praised him, Jacques Corlay, and his deep friendship with his own son-in-law. He decided he would donate some money to this church. It would make him look good in the eyes of society.

CHAPTER VI

Therefore, thou son of man, prepare thee stuff
for removing, and remove by day in their sight;
and thou shalt remove from thy place to
another place in their sight
EZEKIEL 12:3a

THE SERVICE FINALLY ENDED. Liberty stood to exit the pew into the middle aisle where an usher was waiting. She was to start the procession, going up to the casket and then exiting to her left. She was thankful it was closed casket. She'd wondered what Armand looked like now and yet didn't want to know. She didn't know where he'd been shot or if he'd been shot. Perhaps he'd been strangled or stabbed. Libby simply did not know nor did she care to ask. She kept her eyes fixed straight ahead, making her way to the rear of the church, thankful for the black veil.

Jacques was right behind her. "We'll stand here and greet people as they go out," he said to her back as if it was an order. She turned, glancing his way with a surge of relief. Soon she would not be under his cold gaze anymore. Libby tried to analyze her feelings, but the first in a long procession of people took her hand, offering his condolences. Under the circumstances she didn't have to smile, which was a blessing. Libby shook hands, receiving the sympathetic murmurings of hundreds of people. This was an event at which to be seen. She hated being so cynical, but most of these people were high echelon seekers. She saw Mr. Humphries look at her father. They did not shake hands, merely nodding to one another.

"Madam Bouvier, so good to see you. You're looking very lovely." Mr. Humphries had to move on for the press of mourners behind him, but one eye had imperceptibly drooped in a half wink, and she looked down, glad the veil helped to hide her amusement.

Mr. Humphries stood waiting for her until the last person had passed through the line.

Liberty said to her father, "I'll see you at the reception." The lawyer proffered his arm, and she took it. They strolled out together through the huge double doors held open by attendants, leaving her father talking to the rector. Mr. Humphries handed her into her carriage, and she invited him to sit beside her.

He stepped up and sat facing her.

"I've arranged for your passage, but I'm sorry to say I have not yet found a suitable chaperone."

"I meant to write in my note to you that Maggie, my personal maid, wants to go to California with me. We've packed for her also."

Mr. Humphries' shoulders sagged a bit in relief. He looked incredibly reassured. "I couldn't find anyone on such short notice, but I purchased two passes from Boston to Sacramento in case I did. You'll make connections in Chicago to the Union Pacific Railroad. This afternoon, while we're at the reception, the trunks that are ready to go will be loaded onto the docking area for tomorrow's train. I'll have the rest loaded early tomorrow morning, so the trunks you are packing must be ready to go tonight."

Liberty's face expressed thankfulness that he'd taken care of all the details for traveling.

He continued talking. "I've been in contact with Mr. Baxter. He seems to have some interesting information to share with me tomorrow."

She looked at him in surprise. "Did he find information in the desk or hear something from our staff?"

"I do not know yet. I've had a note from him setting up the meeting for tomorrow. Have you told him of our plans for you?"

"No," she answered slowly. "I did say you might talk to him today after the reception. I didn't know how much to tell him nor if he'd be speaking to my father, so I decided to tell him nothing."

He nodded his head and murmured, "Very wise, I'd say." He looked down at his gloved hands and then back at her.

"Madam Bouvier—"

"Libby."

"Libby." He smiled as he said it. "You and your maid will be traveling to the Napa Valley in California just north of San Francisco. I have telegraphed ahead so the man who staked out the property can meet you and take you to your new home."

Libby's eyes widened as she looked into his kind blue eyes. "What's his name and will he welcome us?"

Mr. Humphries' eyes crinkled at the corners when he smiled. "His name is Matthew Bannister. I do not know what kind of man he is, and I must say I have become quite fond of you. You need to take great care. He should welcome you...after all, you own the property. He shouldn't resent you. I do not like sending you on such a trip with no man present, but my wife is very fragile. In truth, she is quite ill, or I would accompany you myself. We've never had children of our own, and had I a daughter, I'd want her to be just as you are."

Libby's eyes misted with unshed tears as he spoke. She blinked them away, grateful that in such a short time she'd made a lifelong friend. She reached across and squeezed his hand, too choked for words. Things had moved so quickly in the past few days that she felt overwhelmed. He patted her hand as the carriage drew up to the curb. Mr. Humphries handed her down, and they stepped up the walk together.

"Courage, my dear, courage."

Liberty lifted her chin, stiffened her back, and they entered the reception building together.

The huge hall was already filling up with Boston's best. Tables were laden with fruits, cheeses, caviar, cold cuts, and all manner of enticing delicacies. There were salads: tomato aspic, lettuce, potato, vegetable, and jellied. Cakes dripping with icing, petits fours, scones, and pies of every kind were plentiful to tempt every palate, and the wine and punch flowed freely. *Armand is going out in style; he'd like this. My father has spared no expense. It's all about impressing others. Jacques' confident he's taking over Armand's business affairs, and the cost of this funeral will come out of Armand's coffers.*

Mr. Humphries seemed very much at ease, but Libby felt out of place. It wasn't that she was unused to these large gatherings—she didn't want to waste the time. She was eager to be away and finish packing. She felt as if she had a million things to do and no time to accomplish them. She'd never felt a sense of belonging around Armand's acquaintances. She hoped the time passed quickly. They gave their outer clothes to the cloak attendant and received a chit with a number on it. Libby handed it to Mr. Humphries.

"I've decided to tell Cook I'm going away. Maggie and I will need food for our journey."

"I don't think that's wise, my dear. Your father could easily ferret that information out of your cook. You'll have no need of food as you travel. There's a dining car on the train."

"Truly?" She'd never heard of such a thing as to dine on a train—that was a marvel.

"Yes, it's true. Most railways began offering dining services about thirty years ago, especially trains leaving Chicago going west. I understand the food is quite good.

"Now, are you packing only essentials, or will you be able to live in a bit of style? Since the will's not yet been read, I have authorized myself," he said, grinning, "to draw on your late husband's account—enough to see you out to California and get you started. I have a large amount of greenbacks to give you tomorrow. Be sure your satchel is safe and with you at all times, and don't use a little reticule to carry very much of the money. You'll also need to pay Mr. Bannister, as Monsieur Bouvier was negligent in that area. The man has essentially done the improvements on the property with no money and no support from your late husband. I'll give you the cash funds to pay him on the morrow at the train station."

He turned, looking at the people filling the building. "Enough for now. I suggest that we mingle a bit. We'd not like to start any speculation." He turned as he spoke and added, "I see your father has arrived. Let the festivities begin." He took her hand in his. "Be very careful, Liberty. Don't trust your father. I have reason to believe he may be involved in Armand's death." He left and Liberty felt bereft of support, then hot and cold as the comment sank into her consciousness.

Several women came up to her and began making pleasantries. They talked inanely for several minutes. Libby despised vacuous conversation.

Victoria Woodhull walked up to her and pulled her from the group.

"I'm rescuing you." She laughed sweetly. Victoria had run for president ten years earlier. She was probably the only woman there Libby greatly respected. Liberty knew she was a great reformer of women's rights and was well educated. She encouraged women to stand up and be counted. Men were allowed to beat their wives if they so desired, and Mrs. Woodhull was outspoken against this inhumane treatment of women. Many people felt she had been dealt with unfairly when she ran for president, because no man would debate her. They snubbed her. It was a man's world, and many men had attacked her character.

Libby greeted her warmly, and Victoria spoke to her bluntly. "You must be so relieved, Madam Bouvier."

Bright color flushed Libby's cheeks. Her face felt hot as a poker.

Mrs. Woodhull continued. "I know it's not proper to speak disparagingly of the dead, but I could never understand why you ever married that insufferable, evil man!"

Liberty looked at her, the flush ending abruptly. "It was not by choice, madam. I was a bartering chip used to keep my father from debtor's prison."

"I suspected as much." She took Liberty's arm in her own as if by the closeness she could strengthen this woman who'd suffered so much. Libby felt no remorse confiding in her. She'd been so circumspect in her conversation for so many years that it was a relief to speak freely to another woman. Victoria saw Libby's father bearing down on them. "What will you do with him?" she asked under her breath, nodding in Jacques' direction.

Jacques Corlay, without even a semblance of greeting, asked, "Why did you delay the reading of the will, Liberty?"

"I felt it to be too much in one day, Jacques. Having the funeral and the reception claiming much of the day, I decided to delay it." She looked him squarely in the eye. "Why, Jacques? Why do you care?"

"No reason." He spoke glibly. "I just despise putting off till tomorrow what can be done today." The quote rolled off his tongue.

"I think it is too much to pack into one day." Victoria spoke stiffly to Jacques. "I fully support your daughter's decision, and good afternoon, Monsieur Corlay. Pleasant as ever, I see." Her smile was brittle as she looked up at Liberty's father. He, in turn, glared at her.

Liberty looked covertly at Jacques with veiled eyes, wondering if he was capable of outright murder. *Could he have murdered Armand? He's certainly unscrupulous, but murder Armand? I'm surprised I can ask that question of myself and not know the answer.*

"I'm tired, Jacques. I shall ask Mr. Humphries to see me home. I'll expect to see you tomorrow at three o'clock. Don't be late," she said unnecessarily, smiling at him sweetly. Libby bade Victoria good day and turned to leave, but her father grabbed her by the arm. Liberty, not wishing to make a scene, looked at his hand surely bruising her arm, then at his face.

She hissed, "Get your hand off me, Jacques, or you'll be sorry!"

He stared at her, clearly surprised by the venom in her tone. Promptly removing his hand, he glanced at Victoria and turned back, scrutinizing Liberty's face.

Libby didn't want him guessing her plans, so she quickly said to him in front of Victoria, "I know you and Armand were partners, Jacques, and I have no doubt he's left you a considerable amount of the estate. You can wait until the morrow before you claim it. Good day." She swept her skirts across his knees and turned to leave, seeing Mr. Humphries rapidly approaching.

Libby took his proffered arm and nodded good-bye to Victoria, who nodded in response. She could see the gleam of approval in her eyes. Mr. Humphries collected their wraps from the attendant. Libby rubbed her arm surreptitiously before stepping into her cloak held courteously by Mr. Humphries. She saw his lips tighten.

"I'm fine, sir." Grateful for this man's concern, she added, "I'm delighted this is over and I can be away. I have much to accomplish before this night is over."

They waited for her father's liveried servant to tell Rufus to fetch her carriage.

She shivered in the frigid air and, glancing left at Mr. Humphries, stated, "In response to your earlier question, I'm taking things from my own rooms with me. I'd like to take the good silverware and crystal, but I'm afraid my father would hunt me down if I did." She lowered her eyes, thinking how horrible if he did hunt her down.

Mr. Humphries replied sagely, "He may hunt you down regardless. I can get those things packed up for you." Rufus arrived with the coach, rolling to a stop in front of the Great Hall. Mr. Humphries handed Libby up the step. He followed, sitting across from her.

He continued the conversation. "I'll send a couple of men out as soon as I'm able. We'll just act as if it is part of Monsieur Corlay's doing." He smiled broadly.

"I can pretend it is Jacques' doing, Mr. Humphries. Let's just hope Cook doesn't take a rolling pin to them."

They laughed, chatting together as if they were old friends. The ride took only a few minutes to the Bouvier manse that was soon to belong to Libby's father. She would miss the conveniences she was sure, but she wouldn't miss the house, only the staff she had grown to love.

CHAPTER VII

Now the LORD had said unto Abram,
Get thee out of thy country, and from thy kindred,
and from thy father's house,
unto a land that I will shew thee
GENESIS 12:1

MAGGIE WAS WAITING FOR THEM in the front entry as the
carriage drew up to the walkway. Snow was piled in drifts, and a wind had
picked up that was bitterly cold. The sky, again laden with heavy clouds,
looked dark and foreboding. Dusk had fallen suddenly as it was wont to do
in winter. Wind had driven the snow back over the walk Pierre had recently
cleaned. The lamplighter had already been this way. Glass lamps shed their
sparse light, causing the snow to sparkle and glitter, making a rainbow
prism of beauty around themselves.

The carriage had drawn up to the curb, but Mr. Humphries sat, not
getting immediately out.

"You know, Liberty Alexandra, I would love to come with you as a
chaperone to California. It's simply not possible at this time, because my
wife is becoming more frail every day. I've taken her to the best doctors
money can buy, but she is wasting away, and they cannot find a reason for
it." His eyes glistened with tears. "She's not in much pain, which is a
blessing, but I'm so worried about her."

Liberty squeezed his arm. "I'm sorry, Mr. Humphries. If she's half as kind as you are, she's an amazing woman. I'll be sure to pray for her." Mr. Humphries descended from the carriage, lifting Liberty down. He held her arm as they carefully walked up the steps to the front door. Ice crusted the walk, steps, and stair railing. Gusts of wind plucked at their clothing. The lawyer stepped gingerly back down the steps, holding the railing. He turned, looking up as Liberty spoke to him.

"Will the snow keep the train from leaving? Will the tracks be cleared off?"

He laughed, wrinkles crinkling the corners of his eyes. "No, no, it won't. Trains try to run on time, but there are factors that can change arrival and departure times. I believe the tracks should be fine." The train's departure time was ten past seven.

Mr. Humphries admonished her again. "You must be there on time. I'll pick you up myself at three quarters past five along with several wagons to take the remainder of your belongings to the station. It'll take about ten minutes to get there, but I want plenty of time to get the baggage loaded. The earlier the better, because anyone who might question you will probably not be up and about yet." He bade her good-bye with the promise of seeing her off in the morning.

The front door opened, and Maggie called down the steps, "Mr. Baxter is waiting for you in the study, sir."

With surprise, Mr. Humphries came up the steps with alacrity.

"Should I accompany you?" Liberty asked politely. She wanted to begin packing.

"No, if you're needed, I'll have a maid come get you."

Maggie showed him to the study as Libby ascended the stairs, taking off her wrap as she went. She looked with longing at her bed. She'd love to have a nap, but time was of the essence. Opening bureau drawers and checking the chiffonier, she needed to make sure she was not leaving anything she would later regret.

Maggie entered the bedroom, exuding vigor, and Libby sensed she was bursting with news.

"What did Mr. Baxter want?" Libby asked.

Her eyes were rounded in excitement. "He's found a secret compartment in the desk, ma'am!" she exclaimed. "I don't know what's in it, but Mr. Baxter felt Mr. Humphries should know about it."

"If he feels Mr. Humphries should be apprised of it, it must be of some importance." Libby was curious, but she had much to do before she could lay her head down on those feather pillows. *Pillows*, she thought. *We need to take bedding and pillows and bedclothes and...* Her mind began a jumble of thoughts.

"Maggie, bedding, bedclothes, a few of these carpets, that picture—we have much to pack."

"Yes, ma'am," she responded with a grin.

They hugged each other, chatting happily as they began to fill the rest of the trunks, working until very late. Finally they were finished. Both women had let out the waists on several more of Libby's dresses and one traveling suit so Maggie would have some suitable clothing for the trip.

The suit for Maggie was a beautiful bombazine twill made of silk. Libby had treasured it, because it was not the usual black of bombazine but a watered silk of dark gray, perfect for Maggie. It set off her deep gray eyes beautifully. Liberty found a saucy gray hat to match.

"You'll look fabulous, Maggie," she said as she laid out another traveling suit, in defiance of acceptable conventions, for it was not black. She felt it a sham to continue dressing in mourning clothes when she was anything but mourning. Also, no one would know her on the train. She wasn't likely to meet anyone who knew she was recently widowed.

Mr. Humphries had sent two men over earlier to collect some of the silver and crystal. They'd also taken one of the fine sets of porcelain, the Blue Willow one by Josiah Wedgwood from England. Years ago, Wedgwood had taken the pattern from Japan and made the beautiful dishes of blue and white. Cook had been so upset, thinking they were taking Madam Bouvier's porcelain to Mr. Corlay's house. Libby had calmed her down with a hot cup of tea after the men carted out the heavy trunk. She was happy to be able to take such lovely things with her. She knew many women had to leave everything behind when they moved west. Mr. Humphries had helped her immensely. Libby owed him a great debt. He was enabling her to start a new life.

She and Maggie hugged good-night. As Liberty climbed into the bed, pulling the fluffy duvet over her tired body, she prayed, *I'm ready to go on this long journey, Lord. I'm thankful to be able to start a new life. I never thought I'd ever be free of living with such an evil man, Father. How thankful I am to You. I want to lift up Mrs. Humphries right now, Father—she's so ill. I pray for Your healing touch. You are such a comfort to me, I pray You comfort Mr. Humphries. Father, grant him peace.*

Thank You for sending him my way. Good-night, Father. Good-night, Jesus, and good-night, Holy Ghost.

Her prayer quickly turned into dreams as sleep overtook her. She slept fitfully, her legs becoming entangled in the bedclothes. She decided to give up trying to sleep. She'd heard the term for people who couldn't sleep before going on trips. It was called journey proud. She was journey proud. Deciding to pray through the rest of the night, she fell into a light slumber two short hours before she was to get up.

Libby awoke slowly, her head feeling groggy. Opening her eyes, she sat up and lit a taper. The ormolu clock wasn't on her bedside table—she'd forgotten she'd already packed it. Lighting a candle and fitting it into its holder on the small table, her mind felt fuzzy. The grandfather clock in the hall chimed. One, two, three, four chimes. It was four o'clock, time for her to be up. She lay back, closing her eyes for a moment, praying for God to guide her steps. She felt herself slipping into oblivion, so she sat up abruptly. Wrapping her robe tightly around her, she lit the bedside lamp and the sconces beside the door. *The sconces*, she thought, *I need to add those to one of the trunks.* She had packed all but the bedside lamp. She lit several handheld candles, blew out the sconces she'd just lit, and hurriedly packed them. Libby blew out the beautiful leaded-glass lamp beside her bed and packed it, wrapping it in a coat. The lighting was dim but sufficient.

She entered the hall, the floor cold on her bare feet, and climbed the steps to Maggie's room. She tapped on her door, and Maggie opened it fully dressed.

Libby sighed in relief. She put her finger to her lips, but Maggie shook her head.

"Cook hears nothing at night...listen." She giggled. Cook was snoring so loudly, Libby was amazed she hadn't heard her before. Maggie grabbed the few things left in her room, and they descended to Libby's rooms. Opening cupboards and drawers, they looked around at what was left. It looked stark with almost all of the pictures removed, lamps and bibelots packed away.

"I wonder what Matilda will say when she comes up with my tray later." Libby had her clothes out ready to dress, and Maggie helped her.

"Probably nothing. I don't know if you are aware of how much your staff loves you. They're so loyal. I'll miss them."

"Yes, I'll miss them too. Only yesterday I was thinking how all the staff are closer to me than any of my acquaintances. Now, we'd better hurry. Is there anything else you can think of to take? Cook will be up shortly, and we need to get a bit of food to sustain us this morning." They descended the back stairs. Liberty ran into Sigmund as she pushed through the swinging doors, startled he was there.

Sigmund chuckled at her look of suprise. "I have some coffee and leftover croissants ready for you."

Libby looked at him in shock. "How did you know?"

He smiled an enigmatic smile. "I make it my business to know everything that goes on in this house. After Matilda talked to me, I assumed you, madam, would not care to be at the reading this afternoon when your father stands to gain everything. I've a little saved and will soon marry Matilda. If you'd care to have us, we'd like to join you in California. We'll not relate any of this to Monsieur Corlay, madam, but we'll not be in his employ for long. Speaking frankly, we'd never have stayed here under Monsieur Bouvier but for you. All your staff care about you, madam. We know you'll not be able to pay us, but Matilda and I would like to call someplace home."

Libby, the tears flooding her eyes, put her hand on his arm. "I could not ask for more. Maggie and I are leaving shortly, but you're most welcome to join us whenever you can." She took a cup of the delicious brew. Maggie was already drinking her coffee. They ate the croissants, having a second cup of coffee, when a knock sounded on the back door. Sigmund opened the door on Mr. Humphries, who looked up, surprised and then relieved. Libby directed the two men who were behind him where to go upstairs to get the trunks.

"Well, I can see the secret is out." Mr. Humphries smiled at Sigmund, glad he was aware the two women were leaving.

Sigmund looked back at him stoically. "The secret's not out very far, sir. I haven't even told Matilda that madam is leaving today. Would you care for a cup of coffee?" Mr. Humphries pulled out a watch from the little pocket in his vest.

"Yes, yes, I'd like that very much. It's quite early and I've not had my coffee yet."

Libby related to Mr. Humphries all Sigmund had imparted to her about wanting to go west too. Mr. Humphries stared at Sigmund.

"I wish I'd known this earlier. I'd prefer a man traveling with these two. I'd feel more at ease about the entire situation. Whenever you feel ready to go, please let me know. I'd be happy to help you myself."

Libby glanced his way, blowing on her coffee, trying to cool it down. "We'll be fine, I'm sure." She didn't know if that was true, but she didn't want this kind man to worry about them. She sipped and almost spilled her coffee as she heard a great thump.

It was only the men coming down with the first of the trunks. It didn't take them long to load them onto the waiting wagons. They were directed by Elijah to take the wagons to the station.

Mr. Humphries urged Libby and Maggie, "We must be going before the entire household is awake." Maggie and Libby made their way to the little toilet located under the stairs. *Chamber pots*, Libby thought. *We didn't pack any chamber pots.* She giggled, telling Maggie what she was thinking. They were both laughing as they emerged from the little room straightening their skirts. They donned their cloaks, and Libby took Sigmund's hand.

"We'll be looking forward to you joining us, Sigmund. Also, I'm glad to know our secret is safe with you. My father doesn't know where we're going, and we wish to keep it that way."

He squeezed her hand gratefully. She was amazed that she'd ever thought him cold and unfeeling.

Maggie smiled at the big blond man. "We'll see you soon, Sig, and by then you'll be an old married man."

"You have always been a cheeky redhead, Maggie, but it will stand you in good stead where you are going. I am solemnly charging you to take good care of madam." He gave Maggie's shoulder a gentle squeeze, and they filed out the door.

The air was frigid, and Libby wondered if Boston would have record-breaking cold this year. *It seems colder than I ever remember it.* She turned to look back at the house. *Will I ever come back here? I certainly hope not.*

Mr. Humphries took Maggie's hand, helping her into his carriage, then Liberty's. He stepped up, settling himself across from the two women. It was difficult to see, as it was still dark. The carriage lamps brightened the interior of the coach, and the streetlamps were still lit. Libby didn't look back again at the house in which she'd been so unhappy. She didn't think she'd ever long for its comfort. She was excited yet anxious at the same time. *What an adventure we are embarking upon…Lord, please guide us. How glad I am that Mr. Humphries picked us up. I don't care very much for Rufus. He's been Armand's man with no heartfelt courtesy for me at all. I'm glad he doesn't know we're leaving. He'd probably have told Jacques. I wonder if Mr. Baxter found anything.*

"Mr. Humphries, did Mr. Baxter find anything of importance in the desk?" It was so cold that as Libby spoke, puffs of smoke floated into wisps of nothing. Mr. Humphries cleared his throat, seeming to think before speaking.

"There was a secret compartment that Mr. Baxter found in Armand's desk. He found papers in there, not pertaining to the will, but important papers nonetheless. We didn't have time to go over all of them, but some of them have to do with Armand's and your father's business dealings. Detective Baxter and I will be meeting this very morning, after I see you ladies on your way. The detective's given me some of the paperwork that was found, and I'll be going over it very closely. Meanwhile, he'll be subjecting your father to what amounts to an interrogation on his activities involving your late husband. They've been very close in their dealings, and both were unscrupulous scoundrels, sorry to say. You're not to worry. I will keep you apprised of any developments."

CHAPTER VIII

And the LORD went before them by day
in a pillar of a cloud, to lead them the way;
and by night in a pillar of fire, to give them light;
to go by day and night:
EXODUS 13:21

MR. HUMPHRIES REACHED INTO HIS TOPCOAT and handed Liberty a great amount of money. She'd never handled much money and knew he'd be appalled at her ignorance. She glanced at Maggie, whose gray eyes were round as saucers. Mr. Humphries reached into another pocket and handed Maggie a much smaller amount, but still, more than Libby had ever come across.

"I know neither of you use money very much. You must be very discreet and not let anyone know how much you're carrying. I suggest you keep a small amount in your reticule and then spread the rest out on your person and in your satchels. California's an expensive place to live, and I wouldn't want you to lose any of this. A good rule of thumb is to never keep all your eggs in one basket."

Mr. Humphries reached across the carriage, taking Maggie's and Liberty's hands. "Things are going to be a bit hectic once we arrive at the

station. I'd like to pray for you before you embark upon this long journey."
Maggie took Libby's other hand and squeezed it as Mr. Humphries began.
"Dear Lord, how grateful that we have Thee to turn to in our despair and
in our delights. Thou art a most awesome God. I thank Thee in advance
for watching over these two precious children of Thine. Keep them safe, I
pray. Protect them from harm and may this journey go smoothly for them.
May they find happiness and comfort in their destination. Lord, I place
them in Thy great hands, knowing that Thou carest for them more than I
ever could. In Thy precious Son's name we pray. Amen."

They walked into the station house, and even at this early hour it was
busy. Maggie and Liberty sat down on the pew-like benches while Mr.
Humphries went to take care of their luggage. Libby wondered how far
they'd have to travel from this train station to the place in California that
belonged to Armand. *Not Armand's*, she corrected herself. *My place. I am now
a woman of property.*

Libby had decided to wear a traveling suit in a grass-green taffeta
trimmed in forest green velvet. She wondered how long she'd have to wear
it before she could have a change of clothes. It was narrowly cut and
complemented her figure and her eyes, so Maggie had told her.

We're wearing clothes that match our eyes. Libby gulped, feeling laughter
bubbling up as she looked down at her lap. *Outfits that matched eyes…whoever
heard of such a thing.*

Maggie wanted to know what was so amusing.

"I was just thinking about our outfits matching our eyes. Whoever heard
such a thing?" She laughed and Maggie laughed with her.

Libby was tired and knew that some things might seem more humorous
than they normally would. She was thankful they'd be able to sleep on the
train, but it must be so uncomfortable sitting up and trying to sleep, and for
at least six nights if not more. *I don't like the idea of sleeping in view of other
people's eyes, and what if I fall asleep and am robbed?* She felt extremely nervous
and tired.

Mr. Humphries came back to tell them he must make sure their
luggage was kept together and count the trunks. He walked hurriedly away
toward the back of the train.

Libby and Maggie sat quietly and watched the people around them.
Libby was surprised at the amount of bustle in the train station. Many
people were traveling west. Libby supposed a few would leave the train by

the time they arrived in Chicago. The entire trip would take less than a week...barring any difficulties.

"What's wrong, madam? You look concerned."

"I'm sorry. I'm wondering if we'll be all right, two women traveling such a distance. I suppose I'm borrowing trouble again. We'll care for each other, Maggie, you for me, and I for you. I am no longer your employer. I am your friend, Maggie, and my name is Liberty. You may call me that or Libby, but not ma'am or Madam Bouvier any longer."

"Yes, ma'am...I mean, Libby. Thank you for your friendship. It means everything to me right now. And I offer you my friendship and loyalty. Do you know my real name is Margaret and not Maggie? I prefer to be called Maggie, but if you introduce me to someone, you may use Margaret." She smiled that deep dimpled smile. "Margaret Regan O'Neill is my name. Regan was my mother's surname. She was a teacher and taught me proper English. My father was a professor, but he died on ship coming here to Boston. Mother and I had a few funds but only enough to keep us for a short while. She looked for employment and taught school for about three months but contracted lung fever and died. I went into service at age twelve. The Jamisons had me until their household fell apart. You do remember Mr. Jamison's death? Afterward, I found work with you."

Libby had been looking at Maggie's face while she spoke, but her eyes dropped to her lap. She thought of all the people her father and Armand had damaged by their thievery. Mr. Jamison had committed suicide, and his wife and children had to move into her sister's home because Libby's husband had cheated him out of his money. Until now, she'd never thought of how all the Jamison staff would have had to find new employment. How damaging it had been and to so many people. She was extremely thankful to be going away and hoped her father never found out where she was. *I hope from the bottom of my heart never to see him again.*

Liberty looked up at Maggie. "I cannot thank God enough for your coming to work for me. You've been a treasure, and now you're my best friend."

Mr. Humphries came striding up with a smile on his face. "Ladies, it's time for you to board. All your trunks are together, and we need to get you settled in."

The three of them climbed the steps of the passenger car. The porter led them down a narrow aisle to show them their comfortable traveling accommodations.

"This entire area is ours?" Libby was pleasantly surprised.

"Yes, this is all yours," the porter said. "These seats both make into beds. It's called a Pullman, car after George Pullman. Even the color is called Pullman green."

Mr. Humphries said, "This one is top of the line, and you'll not be sharing with any strangers. Other types have only curtains separating the rooms or no curtains at all." Libby viewed the compartment. They had a clear wide window and seating that was padded and comfortable. Reassurance flooded over her. She wouldn't have to worry about falling asleep in front of strangers or having to constantly be on the lookout for someone who might rob them. She straightened her shoulders, which had begun to sag in relief.

The porter added, "This can be seating too," and he patted the west side of the car already made into bunk beds.

She smiled back at him. "I'm thankful for such clean accommodations." She'd been dreading riding the train but was finding that it was going to be so much better than she'd dared think.

"If there's anything you need, madam, please pull this rope. Someone will be with you shortly." He smiled and left with a wave of his hand.

"There's usually only one porter per train car," Mr. Humphries said, "but this one is really top of the line, and you'll have two porters on this car to help you in any way you need. Also, you'll need these." He handed Libby a small stack of tickets, each one bearing a number. "These are the tickets for all your trunks. The trunks and kerosene are all marked bearing a Sacramento stamp on the tags. I've paid a porter to oversee the transfer in Chicago to the Union Pacific. There should be no difficulty, but I think you should both be there just to make sure everything is transferred with no problem." Libby thanked him and felt relief for his thoughtfulness. She stuffed the tickets carefully into her reticule. She certainly didn't care to lose any of them.

Walking across the cubicle, she was curious about the door she saw. It was a narrow one and opened into what looked like a tiny clothespress but was instead a small toilet room. The toilet sat low to the floor. Opening the lid, she could see snow lying beneath. She closed it hastily as cold air swept upward. There was a sink with a pipe running through the floor of the train. A jug full of water sat next to the sink. Clean towels were hanging on a rack, and a narrow mirror hung over the sink. *It's very cold in here, but everything's clean.* Libby drew a deep breath. They'd travel in comfort, barring any accidents or holdups by bandits, which she'd read about, or by Indians attacking the train. *I'll keep my worries to myself.* She reentered the main cabin.

They heard the conductor yell loudly, "All aboooard!"

"I'd better go, or I'll be joining you on your trip." They all laughed, but Mr. Humphries' eyes looked a little misty. Libby put her arms around his waist and leaned in to kiss his cheek. He wrapped his arms around her and said, "Liberty Alexandra Bouvier, you will write and keep me apprised of your situation, won't you?"

"Mr. Elijah Humphries, I certainly will." Tears made their way down her cheeks, and Mr. Humphries patted her back.

"How can I ever begin to thank you? I—"

"There, there now," he interrupted, "no thanks is needed. You know God will guide you and give you a wisdom you never knew you possessed. Just rely on him, my dear." The "All aboooard!" sounded again and Mr. Humphries said a hurried good-bye.

The great train started with a big jerk, beginning to slowly roll westward. Maggie and Libby looked through the window at the station, and there was Mr. Humphries, walking alongside the train, smiling up at them. He put his hand up in a sort of blessing. They both waved back as the train began to gather speed, and then he was gone from their view.

Liberty and Maggie sat quietly, looking at Boston slipping away, each wrapped in her own thoughts.

How rapidly we passed that park where I strolled for so many hours, trying to work out tensions that living with Armand brought. I was relieved when he stopped seeking my bed and found solace elsewhere. I knew, even the first week of our marriage, that he brought women home to spend the night. I smelled the cheap perfume on him and loathed our times together. He didn't love me nor pretend to. I was simply chattel. He'd been brutal when we were first married, then indifferent. I couldn't respond to his rough pawing. I feel so guilty that I have no sorrow for his death. The only real remorse is that he had never accepted my Savior as his. He'd scoffed, making fun of my beliefs. I know Maggie doesn't have much in the way of a personal faith. I'll have plenty of time, on this journey, to share the love of Christ with her. If people knew the depth of love God has for

*them there'd be a lot less anguish and hurt. I don't know how I could ever have gotten
along these last thirteen years without having a personal relationship with Jesus. What a
comfort to know I'm deeply loved not based on anything I do but simply because I am
God's creation.*

Liberty knew she didn't have to earn God's love. There was nothing she
could do to earn it. She could just relax in it, revel in it, and know nothing
she did could destroy it, either. Sure, she could turn away, but why would she
ever do such a thing? What she did was to delight God with her actions. She
tried to live the way God wanted her to because it was the best and most
satisfying way to live.

Maggie interrupted her thoughts. "Libby...I like calling you Libby."
She smiled a deep dimpled smile. "Libby, I'm beginning to feel very hungry."

Libby pulled out her grandfather's watch from a fob pocket she had
specially made in all her clothing. It was a beautifully engraved pocket
watch. Opening the face cover, she looked at the time. "It's only a little
after nine, but I know what you mean. I, too, feel hungry. What's that
basket Mr. Humphries brought in here?" She remembered he'd set a basket
down in the corner when he had come in to say good-bye. She opened it
and was surprised at the contents.

"Look," she exclaimed, "it's a luncheon with everything we need."
There was a flask she opened, smelling of coffee. Little porcelain cups and
plates lay protected in cloth napkins along with glasses. There was a small
jug of cider. Liberty unwrapped a large packet of brown paper to find fried
chicken, at least six pieces, and the smell made her mouth water. A Waldorf
salad of apple, celery, raisin, and walnuts nestled in a bed of lettuce leaves,
and she could see little cakes for dessert. Maggie unwrapped another little
packet, and there were four large cookies that looked to be coconut.

"Well," Maggie said, "I thought Mr. Humphries said we didn't need to
take any food. My goodness, he must have a fantastic cook."

"He did say we didn't need any food," Libby replied, "but he probably
didn't want us to tell Cook what we were about, nor did he want us to start
out empty handed. What a wonderfully kind and thoughtful man he is."

"Yes," Maggie agreed, "wonderfully thoughtful, and...my goodness, I
am thankful for his thoughtfulness!" She giggled and started to reach for a
piece of chicken.

"Maggie, let me pray first. Is that all right with you?"

"Yes," she answered. "Just make it quick, Libby." She grinned.

"Father, we are thankful for this food. We pray for protection on this journey, and we ask that You guide us, Lord. Amen." Libby grinned at her. "Was that quick enough for you?"

"Yes," Maggie said, sinking her teeth into a large breast of chicken, "and I am truly thankful."

Libby laughed as she poured steaming coffee into the charming demitasse cups.

"Mr. Humphries, may the Lord bless you for your thoughtfulness." She too took a big bite of chicken, and it was as delicious as it smelled. They finished their repast feeling happy and sated. Libby felt drowsy and could see Maggie's eyes beginning to droop.

"Get comfortable, Maggie. Stretch out on the berth or on this seat." Maggie lay down on the bottom berth. "I'm so tired," she mumbled, and she was asleep.

CHAPTER IX

For the ways of man
are before the eyes of the LORD,
and he pondereth all his goings.
PROVERBS 5:21

THE TOWNS PASSED, EACH ONE looking somehow the same. The scenery hadn't changed much either, as snow lay like a mantle over the landscape. It looked cold and desolate out the window, but it also had a certain beauty to it. Trees' frosted fingers pointed to a sky that had changed from Boston's cloudy overcast to a bright blue. The sun shone on the glittering blanket, making it hard to look at for very long. Libby's eyes watered at the brilliance of it. Closing them, she stretched out with a blanket on the bench seat.

When Liberty awoke, several hours had passed. Maggie was still asleep. She went to the little room and opened the lid of the toilet. Cold air swept up and into the little room, and the clack of the train wheels was loud. She giggled. *I will certainly make this quick!* Washing her hands from the jug of water, she splashed a little on her face, drying herself on one of the linen towels. She straightened her hair a little and thought, *How lucky I am to have curls. Neither Mother nor Jacques had curly hair.* She looked at her reflection in the little mirror and felt her mouth was too wide and wondered again, as she had many times before, why her hair was this coppery-red color. Her mother, who'd had light-brown hair and her father, who had jet-black hair, had no red highlights in theirs at all. *I must take after a grandparent, like Mother told me. Well, whoever I take after, I'm very glad for the curls.* Libby smiled at her reflection, returning to the compartment.

Maggie had awakened to an empty room. She sat up and stretched, feeling a bit groggy. Libby reentered the compartment, pulling the door shut behind her.

"Does the receptacle in there work all right?" Maggie asked, a question in her dark-gray eyes as Liberty began to laugh.

"Oh yes, it works…and believe me, it'll wake you up!"

Maggie started laughing. "Oh, we're going to have such an adventure and such fun. I want to enjoy every ounce of it!"

"I know. I'm so excited and yet a bit apprehensive at the same time. I'm excited to be away from the last thirteen years of my life. I can't begin to tell you how glad I am to be finished with it. All I had looked forward to for so many years was unhappiness for the rest of my life. I never thought I'd be free of it. How quickly our fortunes can change. Within five days, I'm beginning a whole new life. I keep pinching myself to be sure I'm not dreaming!" Libby sat down on the bench seat and continued talking.

"I'm apprehensive about what we'll find when we get to California. From all my reading, I understand it can be civilized and quite uncivilized. We may encounter some rough individuals, and yet, I keep thinking to myself there's no bigger scoundrel than my father. We'll have to keep a sharp eye on the trunks when it's time to change trains to make sure they're kept together. I keep wondering what kind of improvements this Mr. Bannister has made on the property, and will he resent us?"

"Well, he's been paid for his work, and it's your property. I should think he would have no grounds to resent us."

"That's just it, Maggie. He hasn't been paid much at all, according to Mr. Humphries. He received money from Armand for the survey of the land, and that's about all. Whatever improvements he made were supposed to be funded by Armand, but they weren't."

Maggie's eyebrows climbed up her forehead. "Oh, Libby, now I see why you're worried. I guess we'll have to go back to that Spanish saying you have—what will be, will be." Liberty stared at Maggie, surprised that her few words could calm her so.

"Yes, Maggie, you are right—*que será, será.*"

The rest of the day they sat chatting, looking at the changing landscape. Both women had brought knitting in their satchels.

At dusk, they left their compartment for the first time. The hallway in the train was narrow and lined with windows. They looked for the porter to ask him about the dining car, and he pointed them in the right direction.

They saw a few other travelers in the narrow passageway and had to squeeze up to the wall to let them pass. It was quite uncomfortable when a portly gentleman needed to go past them. When he finally squeezed by, both Maggie and Libby looked at each other, embarrassed. They continued on their way, passing through several cars. Finally they entered the one for dining. It looked wider because it extended the full width of the train as well as the length of the car. Tables lined the windows on both sides with a center aisle. Libby admired the way the tables looked like a regular dining room with pristine white tablecloths.

She and Maggie were shown to a table about midway down the car. There was a gentleman across the aisle from them with a woman dressed like none they'd ever seen before. Her bosom was quite full and quite exposed. Her hat feather curled around her face, and Libby was sure she had color on her cheeks and mouth. All this Liberty had taken in at a glance, quickly looking away...embarrassed by the woman's daring exposure. *One would think she'd catch her death of cold with all that skin showing.*

Maggie glanced over at the woman and started coughing to cover her sudden onset of giggles. She sounded like someone having the hiccups and snorting at the same time. Libby daren't look at her and bit her lip to stop the laughter that started to bubble up. She took a deep breath, and to her horror something like a snort came from deep in her throat. Her eyes flew to the gentleman who was eyeing her quizzically, one eyebrow lifted in amusement at her discomfiture. Libby quickly lowered her eyes, looked down at her lap, and swallowed. She used a technique she'd taught herself when Armand would embarrass her, and she would blush. She would just imagine him sneering at her, his lips curled in disdain. It would always help Libby keep a semblance of decorum and kept her from coloring up. *There, no flush and no blush.* She was successful in overcoming the unwanted color in her cheeks. She could act as if nothing had disturbed her.

Liberty glanced again at Maggie, taking in her snorting, hiccuping form sitting across from her and lost all of her disciplined, hard-won composure. Libby started laughing. She and Maggie went into gales of laughter. The pent-up emotions of the last few days made their debut in uncontrolled, gut-wrenching laughter. They laughed so hard tears rolled down their cheeks and just when they thought it was over, one of them would start again, and both of them would laugh and laugh.

Finally, they were able to stop. Libby felt exhausted but cleansed. It had been a catharsis, cleaning out years of self-control and pent-up emotions. She took her napkin and wiped her eyes. Maggie did the same. They kept their eyes on each other or on the table, totally ignoring the couple across from them. Looking out the window was useless, as their own reflected faces appeared. It had become dark.

They chatted until a waiter handed them menus. There was a choice of entrée but the rest was the same for either order. They could have beef Wellington or chicken Kiev. Maggie decided on the chicken. Libby, upon ordering the beef, was struggling to keep her eyes averted from the table across from them. The woman's attire, what little there was of it, was a bright canary yellow. In truth, except for the bodice, it was a beautiful dress. Libby glanced quickly at the man and thought him quite nice looking too. He was dressed fashionably and caught her glance. His eyes were a dark brown. He smiled at her. Libby was at a loss, because she'd been the one to look at him first. She nodded solemnly and turned to look at Maggie. Berating herself for looking across the aisle at the man, her cheeks became a rosy red. Maggie and Libby made small talk until their salads arrived. Libby said a prayer for their travels and the food.

Liberty had ordered small glasses of wine and after sipping it, commented, "This is a Beaujolais, grown in southeastern France."

"A what?" Maggie asked.

Liberty looked into her gray eyes, smiling. "It's a region in France that produces a particular type of wine." Libby, raised in a French home so to speak, had learned her wines in boarding school. She and her friends had laughingly called it "drinking and deportment."

Maggie said, "I've never tasted wine in all my life." She took a sip and pushed the glass away. "Ugh...how can you drink that? It's horrid."

Liberty replied, "Goodness, I was drinking wine mixed with water when I was five years old. I was raised in a quasi-French home, you understand. Then I went to several different schools. My primary grades were in Boston, but I've lived in France and Switzerland. I evidently have a discerning palate, at least that's what Jacques calls it. I can tell the different types of wine in France. I'm not so good at the wines of Germany, but I somehow know a Merlot from a Cabernet. I also can tell you in which area of France the grapes are grown because of the taste."

"My goodness, I would call that a gift."

Libby was surprised at her comment. "I've never thought of it that way, but yes, I suppose you could call it a gift. I had a friend in Switzerland who thought drinking wine was evil, but I don't believe it is. I think that perhaps for some people it probably is wrong. I was raised with it. If people can't control what they do, then anything they do could be considered wrong, such as overeating. Moderation is the key." Libby smiled, thinking of Marissa. They had stayed in contact through the years but didn't write as often as they should. Libby would have to write Marissa and tell her about this new adventure and her change of circumstances.

"I think it would be a good idea for us to keep journals. Don't you think recording our travels and new experiences would be fun?"

"Oh yes, that's a wonderful idea. I've never kept a diary. I started working at twelve years of age, so I never had time to write. Journaling would be a fun way to pass the time on the train. My first entry will be, I shall never drink wine." They laughed together.

Dinner had been cleared away, and they were offered crème brûlée and coffee in beautiful demitasse cups, which they accepted. It had been a wonderful meal. Maggie and Libby lingered over their coffee.

Their neighbors across the aisle departed and Maggie laughed. "This is going to be an interesting adventure, to say the least. I'm sure we're going to see and hear all manner things we've never experienced before. Weren't you embarrassed by our laughter?"

"Yes, it was embarrassing, but I can't help thinking it was good for us. It wasn't that we were making fun of her clothing. I wouldn't do that. I think it was the shock of seeing so much skin in a dress that revealed too much. I wonder if she's one of those women of ill repute. I thought her eyes looked sad, almost sick. I hope we didn't hurt her feelings. I didn't mean to if we did. I simply couldn't stop laughing after taking a look at you."

Maggie grinned, her dimples sinking deeply into her cheeks. "I think she's probably had to grow thick skin. I feel sorry for her too."

They picked up their satchels containing, among other things, their reticules. The two of them chatted together, making their way slowly back to the compartment. It was starting to get late, but since Maggie and Libby had such a long nap, neither was sleepy. They entered their compartment. Mr. Humphries had carried the large satchel with their necessities onto the train. They'd been so excited, neither one had noticed he'd carried the basket and the large satchel.

The interior of their car was lighted by compressed gas, according to the porter. He'd lit the lamps for them, saying they were Pintsch fixtures. Libby and Maggie were duly impressed with them. In Boston, Maggie had lit many lamps every evening, but they were kerosene. Mr. Humphries had sent three twenty-gallon drums along with their trunks. He thought it wouldn't be easy to get kerosene where they'd be living. That was one of the reasons they'd taken so many candles and the molds and paraffin, so they'd have ample lighting.

There are so many things we enjoy every day that we take for granted. Libby was amazed at how brightly the lamps glowed.

Maggie was still thinking about the compressed gas. "It's amazing that we can have light, just as if we were in a real room."

"Yes," Libby replied, "truly amazing. I was just pondering how many wonderful innovations we enjoy because someone has invented them. Just think of this Pullman car, a dining car, and the lighting in these cars by night. Whoever thinks up such ideas?"

"I believe a great many of them are invented because someone thought of the need for it, or perhaps imagined how wonderful if we had such and such a thing. I've often wondered what it'd be like to have a machine that could carry you places without having to use a horse and carriage."

"Oh, Maggie!" Libby exclaimed. "There is such a thing. I saw it when I was at boarding school in Switzerland. It was the most amazing sight. This man was driving a carriage called a Hippomobile. It was invented by a man from Belgium. I learned that there have been many such vehicles invented by different men from different countries for over a hundred years. I wonder if anything will come of such inventions."

"See? That just goes to show you. I thought of something that could make life easier and someone else has thought about it and made it." Her gray eyes sparkled. "Can you imagine, going home and not having to brush down your horse or feed it?"

"That would be nice, but then a groom would be out of a job." Liberty smiled. "I'm wishing someone had come up with an easy way to transport our enormous amount of belongings from the station in Sacramento to wherever this Napa Valley is located. I'm also beginning to worry how we'll get everything packed onto wagons and taken to our final destination. We have a great many supplies and trunks. This Mr. Bannister is going to be mightily put out of good humor when he sees the amount of luggage we have."

"I know. I've thought about that too. It took Mr. Humphries several wagonloads to get all of our purchases and the trunks from the house to the station. We'll look like a caravan from Arabia." Maggie giggled.

"I'm thankful Mr. Humphries foresaw the necessity of having someone oversee the transfer of the luggage to the Union Pacific in Chicago. What a trial that would have been if it had been strictly left up to us." She yawned and then Maggie yawned. They both decided it was time for them to retire.

CHAPTER X

*He that followeth after righteousness and mercy
findeth life, righteousness, and honour.*
PROVERBS 21:21

AS THE TRAIN PULLED ITS GREAT WEIGHT and began to gain momentum, Mr. Elijah Humphries held his hand up to bless the two women. "Lord, I pray Thy protection on those two. Mayest Thou grant Liberty a life full of the happiness she has so lacked these last thirteen years. Mayest Thou also reveal Thy great love to Maggie. May she find Thee as her personal Savior." Elijah turned away feeling, somehow, bereft. Liberty could have been his daughter for as close as he felt to her. He made his way off the platform, through the station, and to his waiting carriage.

"John, take me to Chief Inspector Baxter's residence please." He climbed into the rig and they set off at a good clip. Elijah sat thinking, *I wonder if Baxter's found out any more information about the murder. No one except Corlay is going to miss Armand Bouvier.*

He thought about how important relationships were. So many people, caught up in their own selves, failed to realize that life was all about relationships. *So tragic to live a life that could have been full and useful instead of one that sought power and more money.* He mused over the papers Baxter had found in the desk the day before. He didn't think it had been necessary to worry Liberty any more than preparing for this arduous journey and the uncertainty of her future. Time enough to relate what is necessary...when more details come to light. He'd gone over some of the paperwork last evening and was ready to collaborate with the inspector.

John had made good time. He was an excellent driver, and Elijah felt grateful for finding him. As they drew up to the curb, Elijah breathed a prayer to have wisdom in relating what he knew to Baxter.

He alighted. "Please wait. Perhaps you could go around to the back and wait inside. It's too cold to wait out here. I'll probably be a while. If you're fortunate, you just may get something to warm your insides. I'll send for you when I'm ready to leave." He smiled up at John. Turning, he made his way up the snowy walk.

The sun was trying to push its way through the bank of clouds in the eastern sky. It was still bitterly cold, and the wind seemed to cut right through his layered attire. He walked up the four brick steps using the railing. The stairs were slick with ice, and he didn't care to slip. He knocked on the door and waited as the wind snatched at his clothing. He held his hat in place lest it blow away.

A little maid, standing not more than five feet tall, answered his knock. She opened the door and bade him enter, closing the door hurriedly to shut out the weather.

Elijah spoke kindly. "Good morning, lass. What's your name?"

She dipped a curtsy. "My name's Tabitha, sir, and you must be Mr. Humphries. Mr. Baxter is waiting for you, sir. Please, sir, let me take your frock coat."

Elijah smiled down at this tiny woman. It wasn't often he towered over someone. "It's nice to make your acquaintance, Tabitha."

Her eyes widened, as she wasn't used to the gentry speaking to her, let alone speaking so kindly to her. She smiled widely, taking his coat and hanging it on the ornate coat tree standing in the foyer.

"Right this way, sir." She curtsied, leading him to Mr. Baxter's library. She tapped softly on the door, opened it to let Elijah in, and closed the heavy door quietly behind her.

He walked toward the large desk, his feet sinking into the deep Belgian carpet. *What a beautiful library this is*, he thought with pleasure. It was a man's room. Books lined the walls from floor to ceiling except for the outer wall, which was mostly windows. Beautifully bound volumes lined either side of the fireplace, and above the mantel was a picture of George

Washington at Trenton, praying before Valley Forge. Elijah smiled a little when he saw it. A world globe sat on a round pedestal table made exclusively for that purpose. Fire burned warmly in the grate. Four deep, dark leather chairs sat two by two, facing each other comfortably in front of the fire. Inspector Baxter sat at the gigantic mahogany desk covered with papers. Elijah took all this in at a glance as he strode across the room, thankful that it was warm. He felt thoroughly chilled.

"Welcome to my abode, Mr. Humphries." George Baxter smiled, standing up. He came around the desk to greet Elijah.

"You may call me Elijah," Mr. Humphries said.

"And I am George." He shook Elijah's hand warmly. "Now tell me what have you found?"

Elijah had a fleeting thought of how a man on an inspector's pay could afford such an opulent house. He looked George in the eye.

"I haven't had time to peruse the entire stack of papers, but it looks as if Armand Bouvier found out that his wife, Madam Bouvier, is not Jacques Corlay's daughter. Now, whether his source is correct or not, I cannot ascertain at this time. It looks as if Armand was blackmailing his own father-in-law about the information."

George's left eyebrow climbed upward.

"A good motive to do away with someone, don't you think? Let's get comfortable. It's still early yet. Would you like some breakfast? My wife passed away several years ago. She was a Cunningham and always did things properly. I've done away with the formalities. I eat in here more likely than not. It's comfortable, and I find it more amenable to my work."

Elijah murmured condolences about the dead wife. *Ah, Cunningham money…no wonder he has such a beautiful home.*

He said aloud, "Yes, that would be most pleasurable. I saw Madam Bouvier and her maid off this morning. They're taking the train to California. I've not had time for anything, save a cup of coffee at the Bouvier place earlier."

George looked up, surprised. "I was thinking of talking to Madam Bouvier again and her maid. California, eh? You don't say… She told me she planned to be out of town, but I didn't realize she was moving. Does Corlay know of this?"

"No, no, he doesn't," replied Elijah. "No one knew… We wanted it that way. That poor woman has suffered enough at the hands of her father and late husband. I sent her on her way in style. Corlay will not know until the reading of the will this afternoon. He'll have a conniption fit." Elijah looked down at the fire burning cheerfully, reflecting how angry Corlay was going to be when he found his daughter had eluded him, vanishing into thin air.

"I know Corlay to be evil. Years ago he murdered a man or had him murdered, but I couldn't prove it." George tugged on a bellpull, and Tabitha responded, coming into the room.

"Tabitha, Mr. Humphries and I would enjoy having some coffee and a bit of breakfast brought in. Tell Mrs. Roos, will you? There's a good girl."

She did a brief curtsy. "Yes, sir, right away, sir."

"Please, sit down." George invited Elijah with a gesture toward the leather chairs by the fire.

"Thank you." Both men sat, Elijah leaning forward. He asked abruptly, "So, George, what have you found?"

The chief inspector paused a moment before responding by leaning back deeply into the chair and crossing his legs. He stared at Elijah, collecting and organizing his thoughts.

"Not much yet. Bouvier was brutally stabbed...repeatedly. Things were a real mess with blood smeared everywhere. Papers were scattered all over the murder scene. Files had been emptied, and everything looked as if it'd been rifled through. The murderer was looking for something, that's for sure. My bet would be that Corlay did it, and yet that seems to be too easy of a solution. You and I both know there have been far too many victims of Bouvier and Corlay. Perhaps there's someone out there wanting revenge for what those two did to them. A man would gladly kill either Corlay or Bouvier, I should think. Both of them were the worst sort of crooks. Evil and wicked doesn't begin to describe the pair of 'em. I've had several friends who were caught in their clutches and have lost everything. It's a tragedy and I cannot mourn the death of Armand Bouvier. He was a greedy, hateful man, and this world is well shed of him."

Elijah sighed, sinking back into the comfort of his chair, lost in thought. The fire crackled cheerfully.

"Have you found the murder weapon?"

George looked up quickly. "Did I not mention it? It was a knife. A thin stiletto, but we've found no traces of it yet. Grizzly business to be sure.

Over seven stab wounds to his chest and then his throat cut." George looked as if he'd like to erase the memory.

Elijah cleared his throat and said, "After the reading of the will this afternoon, I'll go over that stack of papers with a fine-toothed comb. What's your next move?"

"I have my best men on the case. They're looking to see if someone in the area saw anything unusual. There's a man who sells shoelaces and polish on the street there in the late afternoons. He must have another job and works after hours. He's usually hawking his wares every day, selling right in front of Bouvier's office. To date, we haven't been able to locate him. Someone must know who he is."

Tabitha entered with a tray far too heavy for her to carry. *She's a tough little gal*, Elijah thought. His hunger took over as delicious smells wafted his way. The inspector and the lawyer enjoyed a delicious breakfast, speaking only of trivialities as they enjoyed their repast. They sat back to enjoy a second cup of coffee.

"Well," said Elijah, "that was delectable. I'd like to stay and simply talk with you, Inspector, but we both have much to do this day and—"

He was interrupted by Tabitha tapping on the door, announcing that Mr. Baxter had another visitor. *It's evidently someone who's a friend or else she would have asked permission of Baxter beforehand*, thought Elijah, who leaned back in his chair.

"Tabitha, fetch another cup and more coffee please." Both men stood as a man entered the room behind Tabitha.

"Yes, sir, right away, sir." Tabitha quietly closed the door as she had done before.

"Good morning, Inspector." The man was of medium height, perhaps about five feet ten. He was dressed in a brown wool suit. Thick brown hair was cut short and neatly parted on the side. He had a groove in one cheek that women would probably think fascinating. Bright, sharp brown eyes glanced at Elijah curiously. He looked every inch the gentleman. He seemed young, early twenties perhaps.

"Mr. Elijah Humphries, meet Mr. Cabot Jones, my right-hand man and the best detective I have on the force. Mr. Jones, Mr. Elijah Humphries, a lawyer friend of mine." Both men shook hands.

"I am pleased to meet you, Mr. Jones," Elijah said, smiling. "I've heard about you. You've quite a reputation for getting your man and solving incredible mysteries."

"I'm pleased to make your acquaintance, Mr. Humphries, and please...don't believe everything you hear," he said modestly. Everything about the detective seemed clean and neat, yet nondistinguishing. It was as if this man could fade into any background and not be noticed. It was probably one of the reasons he was so good at what he did.

"So what brings you here this morning, Cabot?"

"Bad business, sir," he replied. "I've just left the morgue. Our missing shoelace vendor is on a slab. I received a wake-up early this morning. The police hadn't touched anything, but Jacobs and I have found nothing yet. We do know from the mortician that the man has been dead since dusk last night. He wasn't stuck through though. He was strangled in the alleyway, his body found at the foot of those outdoor stairs just to the right of Bouvier's offices. So far, we don't have anyone saying anything, sir."

George's eyes had narrowed, and his mouth tightened as he listened intently to the detective's report.

"Another innocent man," he reflected grimly. "I think we'd better bring Jacques Corlay in...see if he has an alibi for the time period of Bouvier's and this shoelace seller's death. Let's see if we can put some pressure on him and make 'em squeak."

Elijah bent his head, saying a silent prayer for God to comfort any loved ones of this man who'd been murdered in such a violent manner. He decided it was time for him to be on his way. He stood, and both George and Cabot stood also.

"Sorry to say, I must be on my way. Thanks, George, for a delightful breakfast and stimulating conversation. It was nice meeting you, Mr. Jones. Good day, gentlemen."

In the foyer he asked Tabitha, "Could you please inform my coachman, John, I'm ready to leave?" He donned his overcoat and neck scarf, and pulling on his gloves, he made his way out the front door.

As the door closed on Madam Bouvier, Maggie, and Mr. Humphries, Sigmund went back into the kitchen to clean up the mess he'd made before Cook made her way downstairs. She was due any minute now. He rinsed out the pot used for coffee still sitting on the stove and made some fresh. He quickly washed the dishes used for the croissants, making sure everything was tidy. Waiting for the coffee to brew, he wanted to think over the events of the morning.

Madam Bouvier and Maggie are well out of it. She must be very glad Mr. Humphries saw them onto the train before the reading of the will this afternoon. One thing's certain—I'm not going to stay around working for the monsieur...he's a bad one for sure. I don't want Matilda being exposed to the man's wickedness. Monsieur Corlay has leered at Tilly more than once, and I'm quite sure it was the presence of Madam Bouvier that's kept the man in his place.

Sigmund suddenly realized there was nothing for him to do today other than ready the study for the reading of the will. He'd performed his duties well. Besides being the butler, he had been monsieur's man. A man's man, they called it. He'd never been Bouvier's man. He'd performed the duties punctiliously but had despised his employer. He had walked a fine line. He thought of monsieur's murder. *Who did it? I've certainly felt like it more than once. Bouvier had been evil through and through. How had madam stayed with him all these years?*

Sigmund's mind swung, inevitably, to Matilda and his love for her. He had a beautiful ring to give her. He knew that most people didn't use rings, but he was going to give her the opal that had been his grandmother's. It had been handed down to him from his own mother. What a beautiful fire opal it was...set round with tiny diamonds. He'd wait to give it to her when they stood in front of a minister. No justice of the peace for them. No, he wanted to be married in the large Lutheran church he attended when he could. He'd hoped to have Madam Bouvier at the wedding...that was a huge disappointment. He'd talked to the rector and knew it would cost him a bit to use the church. Sigmund had lived frugally and saved as much as he could. It wouldn't be a big wedding. He and Matilda had a few friends and, of course, Cook. Sigmund poured himself a cup of the new brew as Cook entered the kitchen, smelling the coffee.

CHAPTER XI

He that hath no rule over his own spirit
is like a city that is broken down, and without walls.
PROVERBS 25:28

MAGGIE AWOKE EARLIER THAN LIBBY. She was always up at the
crack of dawn, making sure Libby's clothes were pressed, buttons sewed on
properly, and that shoes were brushed or sponged off if needed. She lay
quietly on her pillow thinking of Liberty. *She's one of the most beautiful women
I've ever seen. I wonder if I think that because I love her.* She thought back to their
first encounter.

Maggie had been fourteen when Mr. Jamison had committed suicide.
It'd been the most horrifying experience of her young life. When her
mother died, Maggie had known death was on its way and had braced
herself for it. When she had found Mr. Jamison hanging from a beam in
the basement of the Jamison household, it'd been a horrendous shock. She
wondered if she'd ever be able to erase the terrible image from her brain.
She moved quickly on, not wanting to dwell on Mr. Jamison.

Mrs. Jamison's lawyer had informed the staff they needed to find
employment elsewhere. The Jamisons' cook told Maggie that the Bouvier
household was looking for a personal maid for madam. It was difficult for
people to find personal maids, as most people wanted someone who spoke

proper English. Most servants didn't. She'd gone over to their beautiful manse, knocking at the service entrance.

Cook had already been employed there for quite some time and was firmly entrenched. Knowing a good thing when she saw it, she kindly asked the poor girl to come in and have a cup of tea. Cook sent Matilda to find Madam Bouvier.

Madam Bouvier sent for Maggie to come to her sitting room. It was painted a dark green color, and the room looked dark, stiff, and uncomfortable. The paintings on the walls were dull and unremarkable, but Maggie remembered looking at Madam Bouvier and thinking she was the most beautiful woman she'd ever seen. The beauty, Maggie now realized, was not only external but also came from within. Just fourteen, Maggie had known, even then, she was looking at a person who was good. Madam sat in that darkly painted room with her shining coppery curls swept up from a neck that was perfect. Her face was gorgeous with green, almond-shaped eyes fringed by dark, curling lashes and arched by brows that winged upwards. Her full lips were made for smiling. Maggie would have died to have a figure like hers. Her bosom was high and full, her waist tiny. Not many women could boast of such perfection.

Maggie thought of the internal beauty. She knew Libby was religious but had thought it a way of mentally escaping her husband. Maggie had taken an instant dislike to Monsieur Armand Bouvier. She was glad he was dead. She'd been afraid of him but had never let him know it. He was the type to take advantage of every situation. He'd despised her because of her loyalty to Libby. Maggie wondered again about that inner beauty. She was beginning to see that Libby's faith was not an escape but something deep and precious to her. Maggie thought back to everyday life in the manse. Libby would be gone every Tuesday, leaving early morning and coming back just before dinnertime. She always seemed tired and for a long time, Maggie had thought madam had a lover. As she grew to know her better, she knew that wasn't true, but where did she go? As a maid Maggie had never asked. Now as a friend, perhaps she could. Maggie loved Libby as if she were a sister. She'd care for her and do anything to help her. Liberty was not her employer but her friend. Tears sprang to her eyes just thinking about it.

Maggie heard Libby stirring and whispered, "Are you awake?"

"Yes, I am," Libby answered. "I have been lying here not wanting to disturb you, but I need to go to the toilet."

Maggie giggled. "You'd better hurry or I'm going first."

Libby climbed down from the top berth, making her way into the little room. Her nightgown billowed around her as she used the drafty toilet. She washed her hands and face, brushing her teeth with the minced mint leaves and soda paste Cook had made for her. She reentered the sleeping compartment, which was a lot warmer.

Maggie grinned as she passed Libby. "I'm having the most wonderful time. This is an adventure we'll not soon forget."

"I agree. We're doing something that most people will never experience. I looked out that window yesterday and thought of all the women who traveled this great distance, sitting on a bumpy wagon or walking beside a Conestoga wagon. It made me grateful for how easy we have it on this comfortable train. We traveled a great distance while we were asleep. Those women had to cook for the men and children and sleep in a wagon or under it. I can't imagine the hardships they endured."

Maggie nodded her head in agreement. "That's true. I've never thought of the hardships before, but you're right." She pushed open the small door and disappeared.

When they finished dressing, they made their way to the dining car. The coffee was excellent and breakfast was delicious. They sat for a time watching the scenery. Now, passing through the state of Ohio, they'd be getting into Chicago sometime later that night.

"We'll be transferring to the Union Pacific once we arrive in Chicago. That's where we'll need to be sure all the trunks and kerosene drums are loaded onto the right train. I know Mr. Humphries paid the porter to oversee the transfer, but it wouldn't hurt to have us there, counting out the trunks and the kerosene drums. The longest part of our journey will be from Chicago to Sacramento. After that, I don't know what's going to happen. I don't know if we'll connect with another train or if the distance isn't very far and we go by wagon. I suppose this Mr. Bannister will send someone to help us."

Maggie nodded her head in agreement. She was enjoying the beautiful landscape. Was that a lake she saw? The snow went right up to the water.

As one of the waiters walked by, she stopped him. "Excuse me, is that a lake or an ocean?"

"That, miss, is one of the Great Lakes. It's Lake Erie, named by the Iroquois Indians. The name means Long Tail." Then he added, "There're five Great Lakes, and each so big they're like small oceans. There's Lake Erie, of course, Huron, Superior, Lake Michigan, and last but not least, Ontario."

"Thank you. That's interesting. I suppose there are all kinds of facts you learn for a trip you do two times per week." She smiled at the waiter, and he almost tripped over his own feet.

Libby's gaze swung from the waiter to Maggie. She looked beautiful in the gray traveling dress. *I wonder what will happen in a female-starved environment such as the West?* Liberty felt protective of Maggie. *I'll do anything in my power to make sure she'll be happy. I'll never let her get into the kind of marriage from which I've just escaped.* After the waiter left, she spoke to Maggie.

"I wonder how the reading of the will went yesterday. I prayed for Elijah last night. He told me I could call him that. It seems a little improper, but he's such a dear man. I'm so thankful he got us out of Boston before the reading of the will. I couldn't have endured watching my father gloat. I know he wanted to do that quite badly."

Maggie wrinkled her nose in distaste. "I'm sorry you have such a wretched father. I could never abide the man. I think he is just as evil as Monsieur Bouvier was."

"I know. I feel guilty that I feel nothing for Jacques, just sorrow that he has the opportunity to be good and yet has chosen an evil path." She looked out the window, sipping her coffee. "All right, no more sad thoughts. Let's think of things that are happy, and we'll begin writing in our journals a detailed account of our trip."

They strolled back to their compartment. Sitting down, side by side, they set out their ink, found their steel-nibbed pens, and opened their journals.

I'm entering the study belonging to a dead man...an evil dead man, Elijah corrected himself. Matilda had shown him into the study. *What is Jacques Corlay going to think once he finds out Liberty has left Boston?* Elijah smiled grimly at the thought. He was early. It was only one o'clock. The reading would not be for another two hours. He'd wanted to have time to get everything in order. He also wanted to have a look at the desk on his own.

He sat down on the fine oak chair. It was a very good one. It swiveled, leaned back, and had armrests...*very comfortable*. He began fiddling with the small panel built into the right side of the desk. It was undetectable to the eye, because the back and sides of the desk were similar to parquet flooring, little pieces set together. The only reason George Baxter found the secret compartment was because he was looking for discrepancies in sizes and realized the top right drawer began several inches lower than the top of the desk. *Ah*, he thought, *there it is*. The first little panel at the top closest to the front corner pushed in, triggering a spring that slid a flat drawer out to the side. He thought it a very clever hiding place. The front of the hidden desk panel was made of the little pieces of wood, making it blend in even more as if it were part of the side panels.

The contents had been removed by George and given to him the day before. He closed the secret compartment, sitting a few moments thinking about those papers. He and George had been so excited about the find. "I wonder..." he said aloud to himself. He got up and went around to the back of the desk. *What if there's another secret compartment?* Elijah pushed the last top piece of wood on the diagonal corner of the desk from where he'd just been. It too pushed in and another panel, identical to the one he'd just opened, sprung out. A sheaf of papers lay in the compartment. He withdrew the papers, hurriedly closing the flat drawer. He sat down, rather excitedly.

My, oh my, Elijah thought. *This is a veritable gold mine of information.* The papers contained a thorough account of all the people with whom Corlay and Bouvier had dealings. An itemized record detailed how the two of them had connived with each other, falsifying documents and contracts, cheating men out of their companies. It also named a banker who'd been collaborating with them. Names, dates, and details of all the victims were listed. *George will be able to use this to put Corlay away for a long time.* He perused each sheet of paper rapidly for the general information.

As he neared the bottom of the sheaf of papers, he found an envelope. It was addressed to Violet Ann Browning Corlay, Liberty's mother. Very curious, he carefully pulled the letter out of the envelope. The missive was from Burma, dated December 28, 1852. Elijah skipped down to the end and saw the signature ...Alexander Liberty. *Ah*, thought Elijah, *so that's it. Corlay must have given Armand Bouvier this letter. He probably did it out of spite, not knowing that Armand would turn it into blackmail against himself. Never trust a liar; never trust a thief.*

The letter read:

My darling Violet,

I cannot begin to express my sorrow upon hearing of your marriage to Monsieur Corlay. I thought you would have waited for me, my darling. I know the mail is not reliable, but my own mother has written to me of your marriage. This war is hell. I was wounded in one of the many battles. We have not yet taken Burma and really don't know why we're fighting, but it is only a matter of time now. You're not to worry, Violet, my precious. I'm now well. I had temporary amnesia from a shell that blasted quite near me. I was injured and knew nothing for several weeks. I can only pray you are happy and that you will enjoy America. May you find every happiness with Monsieur Corlay. I have only and ever wanted what is best for you, my love. Please remember, I will always love you and say a prayer for you each night for the rest of my life.

I promise, my darling,
Alexander Liberty

Such a sorrow. He considered Liberty. Liberty Alexandra, she'd said. He remembered she was twenty-nine, nearly thirty years old. Violet had been pregnant with another man's child when she married Jacques Corlay. She probably had no recourse. Alexander was in the war in Burma; she was pregnant. What was a woman to do? She hadn't heard from him for weeks on end, so Violet had done the only thing open to her—she'd married.

CHAPTER XII

Yet man is born unto trouble,
as sparks fly upward.
JOB 5:7

ELIJAH SAT CONTEMPLATING...*somehow, Jacques Corlay had found out. He must have intercepted the letter meant for Violet. It accounted for his cruel treatment of his supposed daughter. Ah,* Elijah thought again, *Sir Walter Scott was right, "What a tangled web we weave when first we practice to deceive." Violet had deceived Jacques Corlay.*

How sad life is when we don't do it right, Elijah thought. *God has laid out guidelines for us to follow. Waiting until marriage to claim all that it holds in store for us is part of the plan. People make so many mistakes and then blame God for them. To blame Him for our free choices is wrong. God's love is so deep for each one of us; we cannot even begin to comprehend the depth of it.* Elijah bent his head, saying another prayer for Liberty and Maggie. He knew they were in the best hands possible. Carefully putting all the papers in his satchel, he pulled out the last will and testament of Armand Francois Bouvier and began reading over the contents again. The time passed quickly, and he was surprised by Matilda poking her head into the study.

"Would you like some coffee or tea, sir?"

Elijah answered with a smile. "Yes, yes, I would. A cup of tea would be just the thing."

"Sir," she said hesitantly, "Cook's been crying since she found out Madam Bouvier's left us. I didn't know myself that she'd leave before the reading of the will. Sigmund didn't tell me because of Monsieur Corlay perhaps trying to get information from me before madam got away. I do wish they could have said good-bye to all of us. I will miss madam and Maggie."

Elijah murmured sympathetically, "I know, I know, my dear, but I think you have plans to join them shortly—is that not true?"

"Yes," she replied, "but I doubt it will be soon enough. Sigmund will probably want to help out here for the next few weeks. You do know Sigmund and I will be getting married very soon. We still have arrangements to make, but I speak for both of us when I say we'd like you and your wife to attend our small gathering," she said impulsively.

Elijah, surprised, replied, "I'd be delighted to attend, but my wife is ill and will not make it to your wedding. Now, I'd like that cup of tea." He'd pulled out his watch and looked at the time.

He began thinking about some of the paperwork he'd looked at. He would bet, except he was not a betting man, that Armand had not been able to break the trust Liberty's grandfather had set up for her. He would bet anything that crooked banker had a hand in Armand's getting the funds from Liberty's trust. He knew one thing for sure—no lawyer at his firm had handled any trust breaking for the Bouviers. He knew, too, no other firm had ever represented the Bouviers. This was definitely something to look into.

Jacques Corlay was finally realizing a plan he'd set in motion months before. He stood before his mirror, talking to himself. "Jacques Bertrand, my good fellow, you are going to double your fortune today. Because of that fool, Armand, you'll not only have your dead son-in-law's estate, you'll also be able to wreak a bit of havoc on Violet's illegitimate brat. Violet, my dear, dear, dead wife, you were no challenge at all. You were weak and insipid. Liberty, on the other hand, is full of spunk. Libby, my dear girl, I'm going to break you. I'm going to make your life a living hell. I've never considered you my daughter, nor will I...ever." He smiled at his reflection, ringing for his man to help him dress.

After enjoying a robust breakfast, Jacques sat at his desk, reading *The Globe*. He found the article he was looking for. *They've not caught Holbein yet.*

He, too, is a fool. Jacques sat musing over whether he should get rid of the banker. He was a loose end to be sure. Hans definitely knew too much, besides being too sure of himself. Perhaps that was what he needed to do this morning. Jacques could smell blackmail in his future if he allowed that mincing-stepped banker to live.

Putting the paper down, he picked up some bank receipts, beginning to peruse his companies' accounts. He felt satisfied with the incomes. By the end of the day, he'd add his new companies to the ledger, more than doubling his worth.

Jacques decided he needed to have a good chat with Rufus. The man was a wealth of information, relating to him all that occurred in the Bouvier household. Paying Rufus well for the knowledge he gained about the inner workings of the manse, he felt satisfied with the facts given him. He'd leave early today for the reading of the will. First on his agenda was to pay Holbein a last visit before seeing Rufus.

He walked for two blocks, catching a hansom cab, and had it drop him off three blocks from Holbein's residence. It was cold, but he felt quite warm. He had a hat pulled well down over his ears not only to protect him from the weather but to protect his face lest anyone should see him.

Jacques entered the foyer of the apartment house, climbing the stairs quickly. He knocked but no one answered. Jiggling the doorknob, he realized Holbein was out and the door securely locked. It upset him that he couldn't accomplish his mission. He'd come to kill Holbein, and the man wasn't home. *Well, there's always tomorrow as long as Holbein keeps himself out of the clutches of the police.* He laughed.

Elijah entered the study after a brief break for some of Cook's scones and was more than a little taken aback. Jacques Corlay was already there at the desk, nonchalantly looking at the will.

Elijah scooped up the papers. "Have you no integrity at all, Corlay?"

"No, I don't. I don't think I ever have that I know of. I should think you'd have known that by now the way you've cozied up to my daughter."

His insinuations were those created by a fetid brain, Elijah knew, and he didn't deign to answer them. He simply looked at Corlay, knowing he was evil and out of his mind. Elijah sat down, staring at him. They sat for a few minutes, simply staring at one another, neither saying anything. Elijah sat observing and seeing the darkness of this man's soul, he prayed for him.

The staff quietly filed into the room, as they'd all been asked to be present for the reading of the will. Sigmund had lined chairs into several rows, and they were beginning to fill up. Rufus came in, sitting next to Jacques.

"Where have you been? I looked everywhere for you. I wanted to talk to you," Jacques hissed into Rufus' ear. He softened his tone. "I've been quite pleased with the information you've given me. There's more money for you if you become my man, Rufus, a lot more money. Have you seen Madam Bouvier this morning? I don't see her here yet."

Rufus replied, frustrated, "That big dolt of a German sent me on errands all morning. I haven't even been in the house till now." They continued whispering to each other as more people filed into the room.

Sigmund had let in several of Armand's sycophants. Three women entered, talking volubly, all dressed inappropriately. The dresses, meant for evening wear, exposed too much. One man entered wearing a beautiful gray suit with a silk cravat. He wasn't very tall and walked with small, neat little steps. He was sharp faced with deep-set eyes and looked slick. All four sat in the back row. Inspector Baxter walked in with two other detectives, one of whom was Mr. Jones. The two detectives stood with their backs against the rear wall, but the chief inspector sat down in the back row next to the banker. Mr. Humphries cleared his throat and began.

"This is the last will and testament of Armand Francois Bouvier." He was interrupted at this juncture by Jacques Corlay.

Corlay stood up, looked around, and began to talk in a very loud voice. "Where's Liberty?"

Mr. Humphries calmly said, "Please calm yourself, Monsieur Corlay. Sit down and do not interrupt again, or you will be asked to leave the room."

Corlay shouted, "Where is Liberty? Where is the woman? She must be here for the reading of the will. I demand it!" No one else said anything.

Matilda's eyes rounded in fright. Sigmund took her hand and patted it comfortingly. He gave it a little squeeze, knowing she was apprehensive.

Mr. Humphries nodded to Inspector Baxter, who stood and, along with his two detectives, walked up to the desk. He looked Elijah in the eye, who nodded to him again. He turned to Corlay, saying, "We were going to allow you the time to hear the reading of the will, but now, Jacques Bertrand Corlay, you're under arrest for your suspected involvement in the murder of one Armand Francois Bouvier." There was a concerted gasp from those sitting in the rows of chairs.

"You have nothing!" Corlay shouted as the two detectives gripped him by arms and wrists. "Nothing, I tell you." The two men took Corlay out of the room as he shouted obscenities, and the door slammed behind them.

The inspector turned to the gathering. "I'm sorry for this interruption. I'm Detective Baxter, chief inspector for the Boston Police Department. Mr. Humphries will now continue with the reading of the will."

He started to leave, but Elijah called him back, saying to him quietly, "George, you need to see these." He handed him all but the letter from the second secret drawer.

"There was another hidden drawer in the opposite corner, and even if Corlay didn't murder Bouvier, there's enough in there to put him away for a long time," he said, his voice low. "And, George…thank you."

The inspector replied, "You're more than welcome. By the way, if you're not too tired, please drop by for a chat." He nodded to the waiting rows of people and left, quietly closing the door.

Elijah Humphries read the will. It went pretty much as everyone who lived in the house expected. Each of the servants received a small pittance. The three women who were dressed so unseemly received three hundred dollars each, and the man, who was a banker, received one thousand dollars. The rest of Armand Bouvier's estate went to Jacques Bertrand Corlay. In the event that Jacques Bertrand Corlay was not able to execute the demands for the estate, the entire estate would revert in its entirety to the deceased's wife, Liberty Alexandra Corlay Bouvier. This said wife was to inherit—and here Elijah supplied his own wording—a piece of property in the western part of the United States.

After the reading, the friends of Armand hurriedly walked up to Mr. Humphries and demanded to know how they were to collect their monies. Mr. Humphries directed them to appear in his office the next day at one o'clock, and he would distribute the amounts to them in greenbacks. All four of them filed out noisily, talking about their windfall. The staff milled about talking for a bit and headed for the kitchen, except for Rufus and Pierre, who went outside. Elijah sat for a moment, collecting his thoughts. He held his head in his hands, elbows on the desk. I *Thank Thee, Almighty*

Father, I thank Thee Liberty didn't have to witness the scene with Monsieur Corlay. Elijah stood, stretched, and went to the kitchen.

As he neared the door, he could hear a cacophony of noise, but when he opened it, all talking ceased abruptly. He smiled at all of them. *Liberty would want me to care for them, so I'll do my best.*

He cleared his throat. "I know the sum of money each of you received amounts to a slap in the face. Believe me when I say that Madam Bouvier would have each of you receiving an amount due your service, which to her was great. I believe that just might be done, with Monsieur Corlay going to jail. Each of you will receive a greater amount than that stated in the will. I can't tell you at this time whether or not Monsieur Corlay will be your new employer, but for the time being, please continue on here as usual until notified by me. Mrs. Jensen, your services are still required here until I hear from Madam Bouvier. Sigmund, please contact me about the details of your wedding. I understand Madam Bouvier has rented the church and provided flowers for the event."

Sigmund and Matilda were shocked with delight as the import of his words sank in. Elijah thought to himself, *It's the least I can do.* Then he bade them all good-bye, donning his heavy overcoat, hat, scarf, and gloves.

Liberty and Maggie passed several hours writing in their journals and comparing notes. There was much laughter and jesting with one another. The morning passed rather quickly, and lunchtime approached.

"It's interesting that you've written from a maid's perspective and then from the perspective of my friend. It makes your journal more interesting."

"No, yours is more interesting…dressing up as a servant and batting your eyes at the clerk in the mercantile store." Maggie giggled.

"I did no such thing."

"You did. You enjoyed dressing up as a maid, didn't you?"

"Yes, I suppose I did." Libby pulled out her grandfather's watch and saw it was a little after the noon hour. Time for lunch.

"Are you hungry yet, Maggie?"

"Not very hungry, but I'd enjoy the walk, and perhaps by the time we order, I'll feel more like eating. I'm not used to so much sitting. I've usually done the stairs a dozen times by now."

They went toward the dining car, meeting the couple from the previous night. The woman must have had on a twin of the dress she'd been wearing last evening— the only difference was that it was a green watered silk. Her bosom nearly fell out of it, and both Maggie and Libby concentrated on squeezing past without the hysterics of the night before. Libby felt uncomfortable edging past the man, nearly pressed up to the wall. He seemed to slow down, and her cheeks were uncontrollably red by the time she and Maggie could proceed to the dining car. One thing she knew for sure, although he dressed like one, he was not a gentleman.

They were seated toward the back of the dining car. Snow still blanketed the ground, and the landscape had changed to a flatter plain. There were forests but not much in the way of pine trees. Tall oaks, birches, elms, and maple stretched out leafless fingers, their branches covered with a fine white powder. The sun still shone brightly, making their eyes water at the dazzling scene. The two women decided to have turkey croissants with coffee.

Maggie said, "I had to bite my tongue to keep from giggling when I saw that woman again. Just remembering last night was enough to set me off." Libby's eyes sparkled with laughter, but she didn't reply. She scrutinized Maggie. *They say that clothes make the man; Maggie looks every inch a lady in my clothes.* The waiter arrived with their lunch, and they talked about their childhoods. *I know one thing for certain—I've never had a friend like this before.*

CHAPTER XIII

He heals the brokenhearted,
And binds up their wounds.
PSALM 147:3

ELIJAH **DECIDED TO FOREGO THE INVITATION** to stop by
George Baxter's house. He would dearly have enjoyed talking to him about
the papers, but it could wait until the morrow. He'd been so busy keeping
all hours at work that he knew he needed some time for his dear, beloved
Abby. Also, he was bone-tired. He'd done much arranging in the last few
days. He wanted to go home and get some needed rest. Perhaps his mind
would allow him to sleep tonight. He'd been so caught up in Liberty's
plight that he lay far into the nights thinking of all that needed to be done
for her and her arduous journey to California. He knew, too, he'd bent the
law a bit by giving her so much money from the estate before the will was
read. *Ah well, what's done is done. She's going to get it all now anyway.*

He entered his front door, and his man was there to aid him. Thomas
Feurst was ready with slippers in hand. Ten years Elijah's senior, his face
was still smooth, only wrinkled around his eyes and mouth. Elijah sat on
the seat of the oaken coat tree and let Thomas pull off his heavy brogues.
Thomas Feurst had been Elijah's father's man before entering Elijah's
service. When Elijah's father had died, Thomas had wanted to stay on with
the Humphries. He'd always loved Elijah as if he were his own son.

Thomas had come north on the Underground Railroad, that secret route allowing Negroes to go from house to house safely to escape the South and slavery. Long before the war broke out, he'd stolen away to Boston. He'd lost a brother and sister, sold to other slave owners with no way to find them. He remembered being out on the streets of Boston and Mr. Humphries Sr. had seen him and brought him home. He'd fed him and clothed him before sending him on his way...only Thomas didn't want to go. He'd begged Mr. Humphries Sr. to let him stay on in the household and work not for pay but for servitude. Mr. Humphries paid him far beyond the normal amount. Thomas missed the long evening talks with Elijah's father. He'd taught Thomas how to read and write, and Thomas felt himself to be part of the family, which indeed, he was.

Elijah's shoulders slumped in weariness, the lines of his face more pronounced. "How's the missus doing today, Thomas?"

"Not so well today, suh. One o' her bad days. She doan complain, but I kin sees the pain etched in her face, an' she doan leave her bed this whole blessed day."

Elijah straightened his shoulders. "Thank you, Thomas. Think I'll go on up. Could you please have Bessie put a tray in the study? I feel I should eat, although I'm so tired, I don't feel like it." He climbed the stairs slowly, praying as he went that God would see fit to touch his wife and restore her health. The nurse was coming out of the room and held the door for Elijah to enter. She shook her head, and Elijah knew it was not good.

She whispered as he passed, "I'm sending for Dr. Miller." She closed the door behind her to cut down on any drafts. He walked over to the bed. Abigail's eyes were closed. He hated to disturb her but took her hand gently in his. It felt cold.

Abigail's voice was weak. "Elijah, my dear, so glad you're home. I'm sorry about all this and the worry I've caused you. I'd thought to grow old with you, but it's not to be. I'll be waiting for you, my love." Her eyes closed, and she swallowed with difficulty. Elijah sat down on the side of the bed next to her.

"Hush, Abby, we know you're in the Father's hands. I just wish he'd bring healing to your body." He laid his hand on her forehead, which seemed cool to the touch. *At least she's not burning up with fever.* Her eyes closed and she lay still.

"Lord, I ask, again for Thy healing touch. I pray for Thy Abigail and mine to be able to live out her days with the health Thou has designed for each of us to have, Father. We know our days are written in Thy book, but Father, please heal Abby. Let us live out our days in good health together. Not selfishly, Lord, but so as a team we can minister to those in need. I ask this, beseeching Thee, Lord, in Your precious Son's name. Amen."

"I pray He will." Abigail attempted a smile. "Remember, Elijah, 'For my thoughts are not your thoughts, neither are your ways my ways, saith the Lord. For as the heavens are higher than the earth, so are my ways higher than your ways, and my thoughts than your thoughts,'" she said, quoting from Isaiah 55. "I'm in his hands."

"I love you so much, Abby. You are my heart's companion, the love of my life. We've had so many wonderful years together, and I'm not ready nor prepared to go on by myself. I want you by my side for many years to come. Rest now, my sweet." He left her room with tears clouding his vision. He found the nurse and told her that Annie could spell her whenever she needed a break. He'd installed a bellpull right next to the bed so that if Abby had need of anything, it would ring in Annie's room. Annie was devoted to Abby and had served her for thirteen years.

Elijah descended the stairs, making his way to his study. He found a tray of food and ate sparingly, but he didn't feel at all hungry. *At the rate I'm going, I'll lose this paunch.* Elijah opened his satchel and retrieved the letter written so many years ago. He reread it as he ate and thought of all that had transpired in the past few days. Amazing that so much could happen in such a short time. He went to bed early.

The next morning dawned with heavy clouds threatening more snow. The wind tore at the shutters, and branches scraped against the sides of the house. As he descended his front steps holding the railing, Elijah looked over at the branches. *I'll have Donald cut those back.* Abigail loved the flowers Donald cut from the sunroom. They'd added the room to the back of their house a year ago. Donald's selection of plants and flowers made it a lovely place to sit with greenery and blossoms all around. There was a small pond in the middle. The gardener had designed it with three fireplaces, one centered on each wall, and the fourth wall had French doors leading into the parlor. Elijah had ordered a daybed put in so that Abigail could lay and enjoy the scenery even though it was so cold outside.

Abby was no worse this morning. The doctor said she was stable, just weak and in need of eating more. He'd suggested the cook make some tempting broths instead of plates laden with food that made her stomach turn. Bessie, he was sure, could make something to pique Abby's appetite.

John was waiting with the carriage, a warm wooly hat pulled over his ears. Elijah was glad to enter the interior and be out of the bitterly cold wind. He'd make sure John was received into Baxter's kitchen. It was far too cold for anyone to be out. He wondered what the temperature was. The wind made it seem colder as it cut through his clothing.

The Baxter servants welcomed John into the kitchen. Any news service was slow compared to the way news could travel from kitchen to kitchen by way of servants. A different voice was welcome anytime to give out new pieces of information. It was thought about and carried on to another household if it was deemed interesting enough.

Elijah, ushered in by Tabitha, entered the Baxter library. George told Tabitha to get some fresh coffee, greeting Elijah warmly.

"Quite cold out there this morning. Heard we're due for another six inches or more of snow before nightfall." Elijah welcomed George's invitation to sit in the deep leather chairs close to the fire, but first he stood with his backside to the flames, warming his thoroughly chilled body.

George continued talking. "That was some piece of information you gave me yesterday. Can't begin to thank you enough." He smiled hugely and said, "Jones came in, and we went over the entire documentation. Bouvier did a fine job keeping track of every deal they made. Poor buggers. Some of those men are in the poorhouse or dead. Ruination of families… what a mess those two made of so many lives. Yes, a sorry mess. Corlay will be put away for life, we'll make sure of that—unless he killed Bouvier. Then, of course, he will most certainly hang."

Tabitha entered with a tray of coffee and sweet biscuits. The two men helped themselves. Sitting back into the deep leather chairs, enjoying each other's company and the taste of good strong coffee, they talked.

What a pleasure it is when you find a man that's a kindred spirit. Elijah surprised himself with this thought, looking sharply at George.

"Are you a Christian, George?" He felt a little chagrined that he had been so abrupt with his question. He couldn't for the life of him think why he had asked such a personal thing, and yet he was glad of it. George was in the middle of a sip of the hot coffee. Putting his cup down on the side table, he looked closely at Elijah.

"Yes, why do you ask?"

Elijah breathed in deeply. "I don't really know, George, except that I was thinking we're kindred spirits and then wondered if we really were. That's why I feel so at home here and as if we've been old friends instead of new acquaintances."

George responded, "It's amazing. Yesterday when you came into the library, I felt as if you'd done it before. You know, a kind of 'this feels familiar to me' feeling. I am glad we met."

"Me too," Elijah replied with a smile. "On a more serious note, have you found anything more about Bouvier's murder? Has anyone come forward?"

"No, not yet. Now that we have a list of names, we can pursue looking at these men and see if they have alibis for the time of the murder. I worry because the longer it takes, the harder it will be to find the real killer."

Elijah nodded in agreement. "I think the little banker at the reading of the will is the one Corlay and Bouvier used to call in the loans. He was just too smooth to be honest. He couldn't look me in the eye when he asked for his money."

"Yes, I sat next to him for a few minutes, and he squirmed. I thought he looked the part of a shady character for sure. Couldn't look you in the eye, eh?"

"No. I've never trusted a man that can't look you in the eye—or a woman either, for that matter. If you'd like to take a closer look at him, he's supposed to be in my office today at one o'clock to pick up his money."

"I've an appointment, but I'll send Jones over…might even have the man brought in for questioning. In truth, I think that's a good idea."

Elijah stood up with reluctance. "I guess I'd better get started on my day, but I appreciate your company. I've quite a full agenda, but this was a wonderful way to begin it. Thanks, George, for your hospitality." He reached over and shook George's hand in parting.

CHAPTER XIV

For I know the thoughts that I think toward you,
saith the LORD, thoughts of peace, and not of evil,
to give you an expected end.
JEREMIAH 29:11

ELIJAH'S NEXT STOP WAS to visit the Bank of Boston.

"John, sit inside the coach, out of this wind. Use the lap robe, and warm your feet on the bricks." Elijah alighted the carriage and hurriedly made his way into the building. He slowed down once he was out of the cold. Elijah always enjoyed walking into the beautiful anteroom that led into the huge lobby. The bank had an impeccable reputation for over a hundred years. He was a little early for his appointment. Sitting in one of the comfortable chairs, he waited.

Miles Edwards walked up and shook Elijah's hand, welcoming him to the Bank of Boston. Edwards was a young man who'd stepped into his father's shoes. His hair was trimmed and looked as if he had just combed it. His brown eyes were serious but with a touch of humor in their depths. He appeared sharp and efficient. As they walked toward Edwards' office, the two men spoke inanely of the weather.

When the door closed behind them, Edwards said, "Please be seated." He went around the desk to his own chair. "What can I do for you today, Mr. Humphries?"

Elijah admired his get down to business right away attitude. "I need to get more funds out of Bouvier's account for disbursement in accordance with his will."

Miles Edwards smiled. "How much, and in what type of denomination, and do you have the will with you for verification?"

Elijah responded by pulling the will out of his satchel and a sheet of paper scribed with people's names and the amount of money for each next to the name.

"You're a very efficient young man, Mr. Edwards, and here's all the documentation you'll need."

"So are you, Mr. Humphries, a very efficient man. I always enjoy doing business with you. You keep me on my toes and quite busy with your many clients." His eyes gleamed with humor. He got down to the business at hand, perusing the will quickly. He glanced at the names Elijah had written down and the amounts.

"Please excuse me while I get the funds for you." Edwards left Elijah sitting in his office while he went to a cash box and filled out a receipt for the denominations he was removing.

Elijah waited for Edwards, going over in his mind the meeting he'd have this afternoon with Bouvier's friends. He was glad Liberty had not been at the reading of the will the day before. What an embarrassment it would have been for her. Those women of the street had inherited more money than the hired help. *It's despicable.* He couldn't imagine a woman of Liberty's character living day in and day out with the likes of Armand Bouvier. He had no doubt that Bouvier had not broken her spirit, because she was a child of the King. *Thank Thee, Lord, for working out the details so Liberty could be gone. Thou art such a faithful God.* Elijah thanked God often for working things out.

Entering the office with the tray of money, Miles set it on his desk. The two men counted it out together and individually to be certain the amounts were correct. Elijah signed a receipt for withdrawal, putting the money into his satchel. He shook hands with Miles, knowing they would be seeing each other soon.

Elijah had John drive him to his offices. "I'd like you to come back for me at five o'clock, John." He watched John pull away from the curb. It was so cold that Elijah saw no one about on the street. He never entered the front door unless he was with a client. The building was a two-storied affair. He had three other partners, and they kept extremely busy with clientele from all over Boston and some outlying districts as well. Elijah quickly walked to the outside stairs facing the alleyway. Slipping around them to the side door located underneath the steps, he reached for his key in an inner pocket. It was difficult with his layered clothing. Pulling off a glove, he sensed a movement behind him.

He turned just in time to avoid a club aimed at his head. It caught his left shoulder, and he grunted with pain. The man had a mask covering his face. With gloved hands, he made a grab for the satchel. Elijah had the presence of mind to yell and held on to the satchel tucked under his arm and the injured shoulder. The man raised the club again, and Elijah, whose right hand was gloveless, socked the man in the chin. The door opened and the masked man, surprised by this unexpected source of help, dropped the club and ran away. James Berkley had been about to enter the men's room when he heard the yell come from outside.

"Elijah! Are you all right?"

Elijah leaned up against the wall of the building, breathing heavily. The pain in his shoulder was excruciating, and he needed to collect himself.

"Yes and no," he gasped. To move at all was painful. "Please send for Dr. Miller and Inspector George Baxter."

"First, I'm getting you inside." James gently put his arm under Elijah's good one and aided him up the one step and inside. He kicked the door shut behind them, leading Elijah to a leather waiting chair by the front entrance.

Elijah sat breathing heavily. He was quite sure his clavicle was broken. He bowed his head and thanked God for protecting his head and the large sum of money in the satchel. Perhaps he should have had someone with him since he was carrying over two thousand dollars. He'd not thought it was needed, because John had been with him right up to his office.

James strode over to the reception desk, talking to one of the clerks, who sent the office boy on the errand of delivering the messages. He returned to Elijah's side, kneeling.

"Do you have any idea who that was?" he asked.

"In truth, I do," Elijah replied. "There are not too many people who knew I'd be visiting the bank this morning and removing a large sum of money. I'll talk to Chief Inspector George Baxter before I make any accusations." He tried not to groan as he shifted his weight in the chair.

Dr. Phineas Miller arrived first. He had Elijah move into a private office with James trailing behind. The doctor gingerly removed Elijah's outer coat, suit coat, and shirt. The area was already bruising up a bright red and purple and felt pulpy to the touch.

"It's definitely broken," he said. "What happened?"

"I was attacked, Phineas, just outside the door." Elijah was trying not to groan as the doctor poked around. "I'd probably be lying out there in the snow if James hadn't heard me yell."

As James started out the door, Elijah said, "Thank you for your help, young man. I have no doubt you saved my life!"

George Baxter was ushered in by a clerk, who looked curiously at Elijah's shoulder, clucking his tongue. The clerk left to inform the rest of the office that Elijah had been hurt.

George asked abruptly, "What happened to you, Elijah?"

Elijah related the story, wincing in pain at the doctor's probing fingers.

Inspector Baxter went out and spoke to the clerk. "Send for Detective Jones immediately." He reentered the room. "I'll ask you to relate this one more time for Cabot. He'll need to hear all the details."

They waited for the detective to arrive while Dr. Phineas Miller finished up his bandaging.

"Now, I don't want you doing any lifting or anything strenuous. That shoulder needs to be as immobile as possible to heal correctly. I'm giving you a little laudanum powder for the pain."

"I don't want to take anything just yet," Elijah responded. "I need to keep a clear head for this afternoon."

As the doctor started to insist, Elijah forestalled him by saying, "I'll take it as soon as I get home this afternoon, Phineas. I had planned to work until five, but I'll go home early. It hurts like the dickens, and please believe me, I'll take your laudanum when I'm home and comfortable."

The doctor closed up his black bag. "I'll check on you when I come to see Abigail in a few days." He looked at Elijah closely. "You need some rest, old man. You look very tired." With a nod to the inspector, he took his leave.

After the doctor had departed, George asked, "Do you have any idea who did it?"

"Yes, yes, I do. I am quite sure it was our little banker friend from yesterday. I could see his eyes quite plainly, and they were sharp and deep set. He was of the right height, and I'm becoming even more convinced he's also in cahoots with Bouvier and Corlay. According to the will, his name is Hans Holbein." Elijah sat back gingerly, not wanting to disturb his shoulder any more than necessary.

The clerk tapped on the door, showing Cabot Jones into the office. He closed the door discreetly behind him.

"You sent for me, sir?" Cabot looked as neat as ever, his hair in place even as he removed his hat.

"Yes," the chief responded, "I want you to get a statement from Elijah. He was accosted outside the premises and has a broken collarbone from a clubbing." Elijah related everything that had happened since John dropped him off. He told the two men he was meeting with the banker and the three women from the day before at one o'clock. Baxter pulled out his watch and saw that it was now twelve forty.

George turned to Cabot and said grimly, "I want you to take over here, Jones. Stay with Elijah, and if that rat of a banker has a mark on his chin, arrest him before he gets his money. In fact, arrest him anyway, and we'll search his premises." He looked over at Elijah. "I want you to go home as soon as the meeting is over."

Elijah started to nod his head, but the pain stopped him. "I will…and George…thank you."

George nodded. "I am sorry I have this other meeting. I think attending yours will prove to be a lot more interesting." Eyes twinkling, he left while donning his overcoat.

Elijah spoke to Detective Jones. "I need to go upstairs to my own office. Would you mind carrying the satchel and my coats?" His shirt was buttoned over his arm, the sleeve hanging empty. They climbed the wide stairs together. Elijah reached for his key, suddenly feeling drained of energy.

Gently taking the key from Elijah's hand, Cabot Jones unlocked the door. Elijah involuntarily straightened his shoulders and winced inwardly. Both men entered the office.

Elijah said, "Thank you, Mr. Jones, and won't you please be seated?"

Cabot was curious. "What exactly is this meeting you're having?"

"It's a disbursement of Bouvier's estate, a very minute portion, to be sure. He was a real scoundrel, and I'm quite sure that my attacker was the banker from yesterday. Not many people knew I was withdrawing funds from the bank. I'm almost positive that Mr. Hans Holbein is the third partner mixed up with Bouvier and Corlay—the one who called the loans in early on falsified contracts."

"How sure are you, Mr. Humphries?"

"I'd bet my rose garden on it, but I'm not a betting man." He smiled tiredly at Cabot, who smiled back.

Elijah's office was painted in two shades of brown and looked neat and clean. Two pictures of sailing ships graced the walls, but his desk was the centerpiece. Elijah loved his huge oak desk.

There was a tap on the door, and the clerk admitted a woman into the room. Her dress was for evening, her hair disheveled, and her eyes looked sad. She was young with color on her mouth and cheeks.

Another one of Bouvier's victims, thought Elijah grimly. He seated her cordially, then sat himself. He wanted this day to be over. He felt so tired, and his shoulder was beginning to throb. The clerk ushered in another woman.

"Howard, could you please have a message sent to my residence notifying John I'll need my carriage in a half hour?"

"Yes, sir," Howard replied.

Elijah thought, *As soon as this is over, I'm heading home, taking some of that laudanum, and going to bed.* He sat talking quietly to Cabot Jones until one o'clock.

Finally, all three women were present, and Elijah stood. He started to reach for the satchel to distribute the money when Howard began to open the door, but it ended up being banged open by the banker. He shoved hard against the clerk, pushing past him. Howard, bewildered at the man's behavior, regained his composure and started to leave, but Elijah stopped him.

"Howard, do you have a minute? I need some help distributing this money."

Howard, rubbing his arm where he had been shoved hard against the doorjamb, said, "Yes, Mr. Humphries, I'd be happy to help you, sir." As he said it, he warily kept his eyes on the man who'd been so rude.

Detective Jones witnessed the behavior of the banker and looked intently at his chin. He had the beginnings of a fine bruise. Cabot stepped up quickly and said, "You're under arrest, Mr. Hans Holbein."

Chapter XV

Why art thou cast down, O my soul?
and why art thou disquieted in me?
hope thou in God: for I shall yet praise
him for the help of his countenance.
PSALM 42:5

HANS HOLBEIN JUMPED UP, RUNNING toward the door, but Detective Jones was faster. Quicker than anything, he had the banker down, pinned to the floor. He asked for a rope from the clerk, Howard, who hurriedly ran out of the room to retrieve one.

Holbein started wriggling, shouting obscenities at Jones, who was straddling him at this point. Cabot pulled out his handkerchief and stuffed it into Holbein's mouth. He nodded at the three women sitting wide eyed and quiet against the wall. "We're going to get this whole nest of Bouvier's cleaned up here shortly."

The clerk returned, and Jones expertly tied up Holbein. He hauled him to his feet, leading him out of the room. He called back over his shoulder, "If you need anything else, Mr. Humphries, just send for me." Howard rubbed his shoulder again, looking on with a bit of satisfaction in his eyes.

"Howard, could you please extract three hundred dollars for each of these women from my satchel?" Elijah opened a cupboard behind his desk, spinning a dial on the safe within the cabinet. He opened it. Turning, he watched Howard counting out the money into stacks of three. Howard recounted the stack of bills slowly, handing the money to each of the women.

Elijah admonished them. "I'm going to warn you to be careful with this and don't let anyone know you have it. If you've already told people you're getting it, be doubly careful."

They left quietly, in stark contrast to their behavior the day before.

"Howard, would you mind putting the rest of those greenbacks into my safe? I'll have to decide what to do with them. There should be a thousand left that was supposed to go to Holbein."

Howard replied, "Of course, and I'll count it to make sure of the amount. I'm glad that man didn't receive this money. What an awful person. Why was he arrested?"

"He's the one that broke my collarbone," Elijah replied drily, "among other things. Thank you for your help. And one more thing—would you please check to see if my driver has arrived?"

The train began to slow down, but the two women paid no attention until they heard, "Next stop, Chicago! Next stop, Chicago station!" They were at the outskirts of the big city.

"We'd better collect our things and be ready to get off and back to the baggage cars." Maggie was excitedly putting things into her satchel.

"I concur!" Libby grinned, her green eyes sparkling. "I'm so excited!" She started gathering her things. There wasn't much to collect. They'd already put their nightclothes into the large satchel and had dumped the remains of the chicken lunch from the day before. All they had were their satchels, the large satchel, and the wicker basket Elijah had given them. They were ready as the train slowed even more. Leaving their compartment, they headed to the car's rear entrance. The train finally halted and they alighted, going straight to the rear of the train. Libby saw the porter that Elijah had pointed out to her, and she quickly approached him.

"Are you overseeing the transfer of our luggage, sir?"

His eyebrows rose at her courtesy, and he smiled. "Yes, ma'am. That'd be me." He called out to the man offloading, who began throwing bags off the train.

"Y'all be careful of dese heah bags, man!"

Maggie and Libby stepped back out of the way, watching and counting as their many trunks and the kerosene drums were taken off the train. Libby was surprised at the efficiency and quickness of it all. Several men trundled it down the cobbled station platform and began loading it onto their next train. Both women thanked the porter profusely, and he smiled hugely at them.

"Your Mr. Humphries, he done paid me well ta do a good job, and that's what I be doin'. I'm also seeing you onto dis heah train, makin' sure your 'commodations is 'ceptable."

He ushered them up the steps, looking closely at their tickets. Going down the narrow aisle, he led them to their new compartment. Except for the location of the toilet, it was exactly the same as the last train, but a bit newer…less worn. Liberty thanked the porter.

Maggie stowed her satchel into a little cupboard. Libby didn't know if it was proper, but she handed the man two bits. He grinned widely. "Thank you, ma'am." He left, walking jauntily, whistling a merry tune.

"Whew, that was so much easier than I'd anticipated. Elijah thought of everything. He must have lain awake nights getting everything planned out for us like this. He's an unbelievably kind and thoughtful person. I've never known a man like him in my life. I may have to revise my opinion of men." She grinned at Maggie. "The only men I've known are my father and husband, both of whom were selfish, unkind, and evil."

"But not all men are like your father and husband, Libby. I'm thankful for Mr. Humphries too. Transferring the trunks was easy. I think the next debarking is going to be rough. Mr. Bannister will likely leave us and our luggage on the platform! I wouldn't blame him—we have a tremendous amount of luggage." They were excited to be on the train and settled.

It was dark when the train pulled out of Chicago. Libby and Maggie were hungry and decided it was time to head for the dining car. They found a porter and asked him where the dining car was located. He smiled at them and told them that the porter on the previous train had threatened his life if he didn't take care of the two sweet ladies in cabin number twelve. He laughed and pointed the way to the dining car.

Maggie appreciated his friendliness. "People seem so nice on these trains, don't they, Libby?"

"Yes, I suppose so. I'm not trying to be sarcastic, Maggie, but they're paid for it."

Maggie looked at her in surprise. "They don't have to be friendly to be efficient. These people are friendly because they are nice."

Liberty was embarrassed. "Yes, you're right. I think I've become distrustful of most people's intentions. I've been around Armand's friends for too long. Thank you for reminding me people can be nice without expecting anything in return. I guess I'd forgotten that."

As they proceeded to the car, Maggie grabbed Libby by the arm and whispered, "Look at that...look who's in front of us."

Libby looked up and started to groan. "Oh, I thought they would stay on the other train. Let's be sure we don't sit near them, lest we start laughing again. Look at that dress—it's a beautiful shade of red, isn't it?" The two women stopped to look into each other's eyes, laughter sparkling as green met gray.

Entering the dining car, they saw the couple ahead of them were being seated. A waiter came up to the two women, and they asked for a table in the rear of the car. As they followed the waiter down the aisle, the woman in the red dress stuck out her foot and tripped Maggie. She stumbled and caught herself on the back of the diner's seat, wrenching her shoulder.

Maggie straightened up and glared at the woman. "Why you....you trollop!" she hissed. Maggie was so angry she grabbed for the woman's hair, but Liberty gently pushed her from behind. They continued to follow the waiter to their table—he'd missed the entire incident.

Maggie was livid. "Why, I'd like to tear her hair out!" she whispered to Libby. "That...that wench had no right to do that. It was just plain meanness!"

Libby murmured soothingly, "I am sorry, Maggie, but I'm afraid we both deserve it for our behavior last night. Her feelings are probably hurt. That was her way of retaliating. In truth..."

She rose from her seat and walked back to the couple. Ignoring the man and with high color in her cheeks, she said to the woman, "I want to apologize for our behavior of last night. It was wrong, and I'm sorry. Please forgive us."

The woman looked stunned, swallowed, and replied in a husky voice, "Course I'll forgive you, honey." Her eyes were a light gray and looked tired, almost feverishly bright. She looked surprised that Libby would speak to her. "Y'all run along now, honey. You don't want to be seen talking to the likes of me."

"I don't mind anyone seeing me talking to you," Liberty said with dignity. With her head held high, she walked back to her seat feeling much better. The waiter was waiting for her order, and she quickly perused the menu, ordering the roast beef, as did Maggie. Liberty looked closely at Maggie, who totally ignored her. Maggie was livid.

Liberty spoke gently. "Maggie, we were in the wrong. It wasn't nice for us to laugh at that woman last night. I've no doubt we hurt her feelings. I know much of our laughter was pent-up feelings being released, but she had no way of knowing that. She most likely thought it was all about her. I'm sorry if you think apologizing to her was the wrong thing to do, but I'm not responsible for what you think. I am responsible to do what I know to be right, whether you approve or not."

Maggie said sullenly, "She had no right to trip me, and now my shoulder hurts."

"I'm sorry your shoulder hurts. She shouldn't have tripped you, but that's for her to ask for forgiveness from you. I know that apologizing for our behavior was the right thing to do," Libby said firmly.

Maggie's temper flared quickly and just as quickly was over. She began telling Libby all she knew about Sigmund and Matilda, about their romance, their engagement, and their wedding plans. The meal was tasty…although the roast was a bit tough. The two women stayed in the dining car long after the meal was finished. They talked together over the coffee and Black Forest cake, which was delicious. The rest of the evening was uneventful, for which Libby was thankful.

John drove Elijah home. He hated to tell Abby about the attack, not wanting to worry her, but it would be fruitless to try to hide his shoulder from her. It was bitterly cold, and his overcoat had been thrown over his shoulders but not buttoned up. Elijah was miserable with the cold and pain.

Thomas helped him, gently taking off Elijah's coat when he entered the house. He clucked like a hen while Elijah told him what had happened. Elijah sat down on the oak seat, and Thomas had his slippers ready. After relating the story to Thomas, he sat for a few moments.

"Mistah Humphries," Thomas said with concern in his eyes, "I'm thinking y'all be needin' ta be taking a few days off and rest up. It'll do you good, and the missus too."

Elijah looked up, surprised. "I hadn't even thought about doing that. I'll write a note after dinner. Please see that John takes it to the office first thing tomorrow." Elijah, getting up from the coat tree, felt better mentally. He'd stay home and get caught up on a few things.

"Thank you, Thomas. I'll go up and see Mrs. Humphries now." He climbed the stairs wearily.

Thomas said, "I'll have a tray sent to your rooms, suh." Elijah didn't reply, just nodded his head tiredly as he continued up. He wasn't hungry.

Thomas clucked his tongue again, heading for the kitchen. He told Bessie all that had transpired, and she set about putting together a tray from the tantalizing smells she'd concocted earlier. The word traveled throughout the household about the attack on the master.

Elijah climbed to the top of the steps and, without thinking, started to straighten his shoulders before entering Abigail's room. He winced in pain. *I'll be glad for that laudanum this night,* he thought as he entered Abby's room. The nurse looked a bit nonplussed at his shoulder but left to give them some privacy. She'd be leaving in just a few minutes to go home. Annie would then take over Mrs. Humphries' care until tomorrow. Elijah walked over to the bed, sitting down quietly on the side of it. Abby's eyes flew open. Looking closely at his face, concern etched itself in her eyes as she saw him looking so utterly drained.

"Elijah, are you all right?"

"Yes, Abby, thanks be to God, I am." Abigail saw his sleeve hanging empty and tried to sit up, but Elijah forestalled her with his right hand on her shoulder.

"What happened, Elijah? Whatever happened to you?" She put out her hand and touched his tired cheek.

"I'm fine, just very weary and sore and tonight, feeling a bit old. God protected me today from a vicious attack on my person. I'd gone to the bank and someone must have followed me. They intended to rob me of the money I was carrying. The man is now in jail. He aimed for my head, Abby, but somehow I sensed he was there and turned enough that he got my left shoulder instead. Dr. Miller saw me and said my collarbone's broken, but I'll be as good as new in a couple weeks, I'm sure."

"Oh Elijah, I am sorry," she said, her eyes filling with tears.

"Hush, Abby, I'll be fine. I'm going to take a few days off and stay home with you. I need to get caught up on some things, and I will rest up. I do need it." He kissed her cheek. "I love you so much." He stood up, smiling down at her.

"Now," he said, "I'm going to eat a bit, take some of your magic powder, and go to bed." He kissed her, his shoulder throbbing almost unbearably. "Good night, my sweet."

She caught at his hand. "Would you mind sleeping in here tonight? It won't disturb me and once you take the laudanum, you won't wake up anyway."

He looked at her, surprised by her request. He knew he'd awakened her quite often, which is why he'd started sleeping in his own room. Prior to that, the two of them had never slept apart since being married, as was the custom of many.

"Of course, of course, if that's what you'd like. Let me eat, and I'll be back shortly."

Once in his own rooms, a tray waited for him. He sat down tiredly at the desk. He preferred the one in his study, but this one was adequate and served him well to sit and eat a bit of his dinner. He decided to write his note first. Pulling the ink well out, he wrote a short missive to his partners. Thomas came in and helped him into his pajamas.

Chapter XVI

For I will restore health unto thee,
and I will heal thee of thy wounds,
saith the LORD
JEREMIAH 30:17a

BESSIE HAD MADE AN EXCELLENT meal of stuffed capons with potatoes and gravy. It tasted delicious, but Elijah didn't feel hungry. He felt discouraged. Much of it was probably due to his pain. Elijah knew, too, he was overtired. He reflected on the evil he had encountered this past week— Bouvier, Corlay, Holbein, and the suffering they had wrought upon innocent people. How many had the three men hurt? Not only the victims, but their families, staff, friends…it seemed endless. He hated the fact of so much suffering. Elijah remembered the verses in Ephesians 6, where it talked about struggling not against flesh and blood but against the dark forces of evil. He knew that righteous choices bears good fruit.

Both Corlay and Bouvier made the choice to do evil and thus what they put their hand to bore badness, hurt, and sadness. Exactly what Satan wants for us, he thought.

Elijah's mind swung to his Abby. She was so good and yet her life was seemingly ebbing away. *Why, Lord?* he asked. *I know that because there's sin in the world many people suffer as a result of it. It's not necessarily our own sin. I know that Thou, oh Lord, are in control and that everything that comes my way is filtered by Thy hand because I've asked Thy son, Jesus, into my heart. Maybe this trial isn't even for Abby, but for someone else that's watching. Maybe it's for me.* He bowed his head and prayed aloud.

"May I be ever faithful to Thy will, oh Lord, and not my own." He wasn't going to eat anything else, so he picked up the tray, feeling pain even in that movement. He set it on a side table in the hall, the note to his partners propped on it for John. He didn't want anyone coming in to disturb him once he'd gone to bed. He took the laudanum and going back into Abby's room, crawled into bed. He took her hand in his, kissed it, and went to sleep.

After his meeting, George Baxter looked in to see if Jones was back from Elijah Humphries' office. Cabot was sitting at his desk, filling out a report of all that had transpired before arresting Holbein.

"So, Cabot, what happened at the meeting?"

Cabot told him everything that had transpired, and as he spoke, the inspector's eyes glowed.

"I knew I was going to miss out on an interesting encounter," he said regretfully. "That Holbein looked like one shady fellow yesterday. How would you like to go check out his premises?"

"I'd like that very much, sir. I can fill this report out later. I'd like to snoop around a bit. I'm pretty sure that man was in it up to his neck with Bouvier and Corlay. Mr. Humphries thinks so, and I fully agree with him. I'd be very pleased to accompany you, sir." He stood up, stretching as he walked over to the coat rack.

The two men took a hansom cab to Holbein's residence. It was located in a nice apartment area, and they entered, climbing the wide stairs together. The entire second floor was part of Holbein's apartment. The detective rapped on the door to ascertain if anyone might be inside, but there was no answer. The chief pulled out his ring of skeleton keys and after trying several of them, the lock clicked open. They entered the wide foyer of a good-sized apartment.

As they entered the living room, the chief commented, "He must not have a servant, or they're very much overdue." Clothes were strewn on the sofa and in piles on the floor. The place was a disaster. The kitchen looked like a hovel and stank of rotten food. The dining table had papers and leftover plates of food scattered across its width. Cabot Jones had entered the bathroom.

"Look, sir!" He held up a shirt with blood spatters all over the front. Bending over, he picked up the trousers that had been lying under the shirt. As he did so, a knife fell out—a thin stiletto.

"Ah," Jones said to the chief inspector, "here it is. What a he fool he is to not rid himself of the evidence. Now we have our murderer."

The chief smiled widely. "Yes, I do believe we've got our man. Let's just check out the size of his trousers to make sure someone hasn't planted this in here." He held up another pair and measured.

"You're right, Jones. What a fool." The trousers were the exact size of the bloodied ones. "He was too confident for sure, and now we have our man." The chief quoted Proverbs 14:16, "'A wise man feareth, and departeth from evil: but the fool rageth, and is confident.'"

Cabot Jones asked, "What is that, sir, Shakespeare?"

"No," the chief replied, "it's from Proverbs in the Bible…a lot of wisdom in there. Sure wish people would read it. Cabot, I want you to get Coulter over here to collect anything that might be interesting, especially the papers on the table. I noticed a couple of them are bloodied as well."

"Yes, sir," Jones replied. "I'll get right on it when we return to the department. Holbein was Bouvier's murderer, and I'm thinking he most likely murdered our shoelace seller too. That man was always standing out on the street in the late afternoons. Perhaps the vendor noticed Holbein enter the building. I'll bet Holbein suspected he'd been seen and decided to get rid of the poor man. So many times it's someone in the wrong place at the wrong time. It's a sorry business, isn't it, sir?"

"Yes," the inspector replied sadly, "it's a sorry business all around. So many innocent men have died because of Bouvier and Corlay's avarice, as well as Holbein's, and many, if not dead, are ruined. Yes, Cabot, it certainly is a sorry business."

Both men left the apartment, glad to be out of the filth. As they rode a hansom cab back to the department, they spoke of the whole sordid affair. There was a lot to do and much information that needed to be clarified.

"Cabot, be sure to have Henry notify *The Globe* of the arrests and the details of the whole affair. It's always good business to let the public know the police and detectives are doing their jobs well." George thought about dropping by the Humphries' house when he was finished with work, but then thought better of it. Poor Elijah had looked done in, that was for sure. The man had certainly had a busy week. He mused over how quickly they had become friends. He knew Elijah was a good man. He admired him and his sharp wit. Probably wouldn't be a lawyer if he weren't so sharp.

Abby awoke, thinking she'd heard a sound.

Elijah stirred, opening his eyes. *What is that? Is that a bright light at the foot of the bed?*

"Who is it?" he asked, taking Abigail's hand in his. He could tell she was not frightened. He was curious. The room seemed full of peace, and he wondered if he were dreaming.

They both sat up slowly, and looking over at Abigail, Elijah could see an incredible peaceful look come over her face. He'd never seen such a look.

"Am I dreaming?" she asked aloud.

They both heard a melodic voice say, "No, my child, you are not dreaming. You have suffered much, but I have given you the grace to overcome. Your faith has made you well." The light became brighter and brighter, lighting up the entire room. The voice spoke again. Elijah could feel Abigail trembling beside him, but he could not take his eyes off the light that radiated a peaceful, bright glow.

"You are healed, Abigail. In the name of Jesus Christ, arise from your bed!"

Abigail gasped. She could feel a warmth flow from the top of her head all the way down to her toes. She suddenly felt strong and whole.

"Oh my Jesus, oh my Lord, thank You, thank You. I praise You with my whole being. May I be of real use to You, my Savior!"

Elijah felt her hand gripping his in a firm clasp and he watched as she stood up strongly beside the bed and quoted from Nehemiah 9. "'Stand up and bless the Lord your God for ever and ever: and blessed be Thy glorious name, which is exalted above all blessing and praise. Thou, even Thou, art Lord alone; Thou hast made heaven, the heaven of heavens, with all their host, the earth, and all things that are therein, the seas, and all that is therein, and Thou preservest them all; and the host of heaven worshippeth Thee....' I worship Thee, my Lord...I worship Thee! I thank Thee, my Lord and my God. I thank Thee."

Elijah felt as if he were in a dream. At first he'd wondered if it were the laudanum...*am I hallucinating?* It seemed so unreal and yet, the truth of it was in his soul.

Abigail laughed out loud, still standing. She raised her hands in praise and said, "Oh glorious Lord!" Elijah started to bow his head, but instead, he looked up, staring at the light. It seemed to penetrate his entire being, and he felt an indescribable peace flood through him.

He listened and prayed along with Abby as she said, "I'd thought I was going to join Thee in heaven...I didn't have the faith that Thou wouldst heal me. I know Thou canst do all things...I just didn't think Thou wouldst do that...for me...I'm sorry for my unbelief...but I am so glad...so glad."

Elijah watched as the light faded from the room, but the incredible feeling of peace lingered. Abby lit a sconce to see the mantel clock. It was four thirty in the morning...glorious morning. They both knew sleep was impossible. Abby threw a piece of wood onto the fire and crawling back into bed, they held hands. They didn't talk to each other, but they took turns praying aloud. Tears of thanksgiving trickled from Elijah's eyes. Over an hour later they fell asleep in each other's arms.

Elijah awoke quite late. The crack in the curtains let light into the room. He was surprised at the late hour but suddenly remembered he wasn't going to work that day. His shoulder hurt like a toothache but felt better than the night before.

Memory came flooding back into his consciousness. He turned his head, and there was Abigail, her head on the pillow next to him. *Had it all been a dream? Was Abby healed?* It had seemed so real, but his thoughts were jumbled. He'd dreamed he quit his law practice in Boston to go to California. He remembered dreaming that he and Abby had opened a mission in California for...he couldn't remember who it was for. *One thing I know...I am positive Abby's healing was not a dream.*

Libby and Maggie felt the days beginning to merge. The two women were becoming bored with the little compartment and the restrictions of being on the train. They continued to update their journals and took long walks, going from car to car, to stretch their legs. The scenery was taking on an altogether different look. The flat plains of Nebraska had turned into huge mountains in the distance like none they'd ever seen before. When the train had crossed into Wyoming, they'd stopped in Pine Bluffs, and then, just twenty miles farther at Hillsdale, they caught their first glimpse of the Rockies, with the Laramie Range coming into view. It was unbelievable to Maggie. Libby had experienced the Alps in Switzerland and had some knowledge of different terrains. Maggie had never seen such peaks and was mesmerized by their beauty. Further along the line, they saw huge, weird formations of rock and wondered in awe at their stark beauty.

Turning to Libby, Maggie exclaimed, "I never dreamed the world was so beautiful!"

"I know…it's so awe inspiring, isn't it? God made it, you know. His ways are unsearchable and His love so powerful. I came to know Him while I was at boarding school, when I felt so unloved. I've never felt alone since. God helps me in so many ways. Oh, Maggie, I wish you knew Him as I do. I could never have survived living with Armand without the strength of God leading me day by day. I would've been crushed by Armand's treatment of me. I know I'd never have developed into the woman I am. I give God all the praise for it, and now I'm free."

"You're a beautiful woman, Libby. I've seen your beauty, inside and out. I have so much wanted to be as you are. I was incredibly angry with you for going up to that woman in the red dress and apologizing for us, and yet, I knew deep down it was the right thing to do."

"I'd never have apologized if Jesus hadn't spoken to my heart and told me it was the right thing to do. So often, people do things because they feel like it, or they don't do things because they don't feel like it. I've learned that it is not about how I feel—it's about what God's Word says to me and me wanting to please my Savior. If I went on my feelings, I'd do very little the right way. I look at Jesus as my King… Maggie, my King. I'm a servant, and I do the bidding of my Master, just as you served me so faithfully and did everything I asked you to do." Libby gave Maggie a big hug. "I wish you'd ask Jesus into your heart. It's really living."

"I'll think about it—I truly will. It's a big step, and I have never given much credence to religion. I used to think it was a crutch for you to be able to escape Monsieur Bouvier's attentions."

"Oh, Maggie, it is a crutch. I lean on it because I can never walk the way I was intended. I know that I need that crutch the same way I need air!" She laughed at Maggie, giving her arm a squeeze.

After the town of Evanston, the train passed into Utah. A virginal white landscape glistened in the bright light. The blueness of the sky right down to the horizon was in startling contrast to the pristine whiteness of snow. The two women decided it was time to eat. They walked to the dining car arm in arm.

CHAPTER XVII

Sing, O heavens; and be joyful, O earth;
and break forth into singing, O mountains:
for the LORD hath comforted his people,
and will have mercy upon his afflicted.
ISAIAH 49:13

ELIJAH STAYED HOME AND WAS resting in his study from a night
that had been so busy.

George Baxter decided to call on Elijah midmorning. He'd been to the
office and checked on his men. Jones was his favorite. He was young but
extremely dependable. He had a sharp wit and sharp eyes as well. He saw
clues that many times other detectives missed. His next favorite was Simon
Coulter. He too was a good man. George was proud of his department.
The detectives were efficient and got down to business. He ran a clean
organization. He knew that some sections of the police department had a
few men of dubious character but not his. He made sure all his detectives
were men of integrity. He remembered back...when he was a young
detective. His chief, Detective Christopher Belden, had been a model that
he had always wanted to emulate. He hoped in his heart he measured up to
Belden's standards. He'd retired some years back, but George still kept in touch.

The sun shone brightly and was a welcome relief to the heavy clouds
and snow they'd had all week. He was thankful that over forty years ago

men had begun to invent snowplows. The main streets of Boston were cleared enough for travel. It was the side streets that were a problem. The city hired men to clear out the blockages the horse-drawn plows created.

His hansom cab pulled up in front of Elijah's house. It was a stately looking brick residence with a large bay window. He started to rap on the door, but it opened before he could do so.

Thomas had been crossing the parlor, and seeing the man coming up the walk, he'd waited for him.

George Baxter smiled at the servant, who seemed so welcoming and was grinning from ear to ear.

"Thank you. That's certainly service. Although the sun's out, it's cold out here!"

"Please step inside, suh." Thomas bade him enter. He could not stop smiling this morning. He kept thinking about the miracle and Mrs. Humphries being healed.

"I've come to visit Mr. Humphries. I don't have an appointment. My name's Inspector George Baxter."

"Welcome, Inspector Baxter. If you'd care to wait a moment, I'll tell him you're heah." Thomas quickly tapped on Elijah's study door.

Elijah said, "Please enter!" He was sitting on a love seat by the fire, holding hands with Abigail. They were talking about Elijah's dreams and her healing. Abby was glowing. Her face was almost ethereal as she sat next to Elijah.

"Inspector Baxter to see you, suh."

"Send him in, Thomas, send him in—and please tell Bessie we'll need coffee and a little something to eat. Thank you, Thomas."

Elijah saw George grin as he entered the study. He'd had the same reaction when he'd entered George's library. Both men had the same picture over the mantelpiece…George Washington at Trenton. Elijah rose to greet his friend and so did Abby. Making the introductions, Elijah was glad the detective had stopped by. Abby graciously held out her hand to George Baxter.

"I've heard so much about you, Mr. Baxter. Elijah esteems you highly." She turned her head to smile at Elijah and then turned back to George. "Thank you for arriving so quickly at his office and arresting that horrible man. He could've killed Elijah with that club!"

George had been given to understand this vibrant woman was ill.

"I didn't arrest the man, Mrs. Humphries. Mr. Jones, my detective, did."

"You ordered him to be there," she said with a smile. "At any rate, Mr. Baxter, I appreciate you watching over Elijah and responding so quickly to his need."

"Glad to be of service, madam."

"George, please have a chair." Elijah gestured to a comfortable chair. There were two done in needlepoint, depicting beautiful rose gardens in greens and rose colors with splashes of cream. A small, round oak table separated the two chairs facing the love seat.

George took the one farthest from the fireplace and looked around the room with pleasure. It was a comfortable study with books and bibelots on oak shelving. The room was done in green and cream with touches of rose for accent. His eyes came to rest on Elijah and Mrs. Humphries, who'd seated themselves on the love seat.

Thomas came in bearing a tray of coffee service and hot scones filled with apricot jam. He quietly set the service down and left, closing the door behind him.

Elijah said to George, "I've kept Abigail abreast of all that has happened these past few days. She's well aware of Bouvier and Corlay and even Holbein attacking me, so anything you have to say can be said in front of her." He smiled wryly. "I can't seem to keep much from her." Abigail kept quiet, but she patted Elijah's knee.

George first looked at Elijah and asked concernedly, "So, my friend, how are you feeling? How's the shoulder?"

"Oh," said Elijah, "I still have one, I know that. It's bearable. I'm not the first person to have their clavicle broken, but, George…Abby would like to share with you what happened during the night. We're a rejoicing household this morning—I can tell you that. Did you notice my man, Thomas? He's not able to wipe the smile from his face this morning. I'll let Abby share her story." He turned to her and said, "You do know that George is a brother in Christ, Abby."

Abigail replied serenely, "It doesn't matter whether he knows Jesus as his Savior or not, a miracle is a miracle." She proceeded to tell George about her encounter with the power of the Holy Ghost during the night. She thrilled to it, little goose bumps making their appearance on her arms as she related how she was healed. She got up and twirled for George, laughing all the while.

"I'm not sorry I can't be a little more sedate. I feel so alive and joyful and thankful and so very happy! I can barely contain it!" she exclaimed. She seemed to emanate life.

George stood and grabbed her hands, overcome with emotion. "Oh, Mrs. Humphries, I can't begin to express my joy at your words. God is so good. He is good all the time, and we comprehend Him so little. We just don't open our eyes and begin to see the good He does for us every day, but when something like this happens, we're so surprised, and yet we shouldn't be."

Still gripping her hands, he bowed his head and said, "Oh Father, how unsearchable are Thy ways. Thou art so good, and we thank Thee for Thy provision for this, Thy child, Abigail. May, by Thy hand, she live out her days in an abundance of good health. Not for herself, Lord, but that she may serve Thee. In Thy name, the name that is above all other names, we do thank Thee with rejoicing. Amen."

He released her hands and looked at Elijah. "What a wonderful miracle that God has brought to your wife, and you too, Elijah, you too." Elijah wiped his eyes with his handkerchief. He sat down, as he'd stood up when George had started praying. He spread his handkerchief out on his lap, trying to fold it back up again with only his right hand.

He looked up at George. "Thank you for your prayer. Yes, we are thankful for the miracle God has given us. We'll be giving Him thanks for this all our days."

Abigail said, "I'll leave you two now, for I know you have much to discuss. I'll tell Bessie to make a new pot of coffee." Abigail turned to George, holding out her hand. "George, thank you for your prayer. I can't begin to tell you of my gratitude to our Lord. You're welcome to drop in anytime. I'm happy to have made your acquaintance."

"And I you, Mrs. Humphries." George gave her hand a pat.

"Now, if you'll please excuse me." She left the room with a youthful stride as George sat back down.

Elijah leaned forward, his lips pressed tightly against the pain in his shoulder. He swallowed down a moan.

"So, George, do you have some good news for me? Did Jones tell you about the arrest? I supposed he did…very efficient man your Jones is."

"Yes, Elijah, your attacker was Holbein, as you suspected—not only your attacker but Bouvier's murderer. We got 'em, Elijah, we got 'em. Jones and I went to Holbein's residence after he was jailed. His apartment is in a good neighborhood and the layout quite nice, but it was an absolute sty. Why, a pig would probably be cleaner!" He wrinkled his nose in distaste. "We started looking around, and Jones headed into the bathroom, which was a mess. He found a shirt covered in blood and then under the shirt lay a pair of bloodied trousers. As he picked them up—what do you think—a stiletto dropped out onto the floor."

"He hadn't bothered to get rid of the evidence? The man must be insane!" Elijah said.

"Jones and I believe he was overconfident. Thought he couldn't get caught, I suppose. Yes, the man was a real fool, and insane? Yes, I think anyone who takes the life of another is insane. So, now we have Corlay and Holbein. We have enough on Corlay to put him away for a very long time. I'm wondering who killed the shoelace vendor—Holbein or Corlay? I'm quite sure Corlay killed a man years ago, but I could never prove it. Corlay's made a disaster of so many innocent men's lives. It's a shame the way some people live such lives of destruction, destroying all they put their hand to. Such a waste of a God-given life."

"I agree with you there. I keep wondering about Bouvier and how evil he was. His wife is a wonderful Christian. She put up with him for thirteen years. She didn't say so, but I imagine she's relieved he's dead. It must have been like prison, living with a man day in and day out, knowing his evilness and never thinking you could ever be shed of it."

Thomas came in with another tray of coffee. He quietly set the tray down and asked, "Is there anything else, Mr. Humphries?"

"Yes, yes, there is, Thomas. I want you to meet my friend George Baxter. He will most likely be coming by on a regular basis. He's a brother in Christ, Thomas."

"I'm happy to make your acquaintance, suh."

George, a little surprised that Elijah would introduce him to a servant, said gamely, "I'm glad to meet you, Thomas." The two men shook hands.

After Thomas left, Elijah said to George, who was helping himself to a scone, "I don't believe in class distinction, George. I believe God made us all equal, and the very fact that we are each a creation of the Almighty warrants honor and respect. As part of the human race we all have value."

George looked at Elijah with respect. "I'm quite sure that we're going to have some really good talks together." He sat down after pouring Elijah and himself coffee.

Elijah felt awkward having someone else pour in his own home, but he was thankful for George being thoughtful of his shoulder. The two men sat talking, and the time flew by. George, regretfully, needed to get back to work. He thanked Elijah for a wonderful break in his day.

As the train had entered the Valley of the Great Salt Lake, Maggie and Liberty saw a fantastic site. It was called the Devil's Slide, according to the porter. The snow was not heavy there, and the two women saw what looked to be a full slope of rock. It was as if the lava had hardened as it had run down the side of the steep, high promontory. The formation was incredible with jutting rock, and yet the downward slope of the hill made it look smooth. The train had passed through Wells, which had been an important supply town for the people traveling west in covered wagons. They'd also seen Devil's Peak rising straight up from the edge of the Humboldt River, which the train had followed for miles and miles. Now they were heading into Reno, Nevada.

Neither Liberty nor Maggie had ever heard of it, but it was the train's last stop in Nevada before they headed into California. They could see a mountain range ahead and wondered what it was. Liberty and Maggie had awakened before their normal time and were eating an early breakfast in the dining car.

Liberty said, "As soon as the train starts up again, let's ask the waiter what range of mountains we're heading toward. It's a fantastic view, isn't it? Don't you wish someone could paint it just as we see it, or that there was some way we could have a picture of it?" Maggie nodded her head. She was too awed by the picturesque site to say anything.

When their waiter returned, Maggie asked, "Please, sir, can you tell us the name of that mountain range?"

"That, ladies, is the Sierra Nevada Mountain Range. It begins in Canada and extends all the way into Mexico. We're heading straight for it. Colfax, California, is our next stop. It's a hundred miles from Reno, and it's incredibly steep going. You'll almost want to get off the train and help push it up the grade, it's so steep. Once we reach the summit, we have just one hundred five miles all downhill to Sacramento. We'll most likely be there early this afternoon."

Liberty and Maggie were ecstatic. It was their last day on the train! Maggie went around the table to give Liberty a hug. When their breakfast of bacon and eggs was finished, they ordered more coffee. The train had started its arduous climb up the rails toward Colfax. The sun was shining, but the snow had deepened as they climbed. It lay in deep drifts, but it hadn't snowed all week. It was a beautiful time to travel up the Sierra Nevada Mountains.

Maggie gave Liberty a long look. "What if Mr. Bannister doesn't meet us? What will we do? We have so much stuff, I guess we'd have to sit up all night watching it, wouldn't we?"

"Let's not go borrowing trouble. We need to just hold tight and see what happens. Remember our motto for this trip." Libby grinned at her.

"What motto?"

"You remember, back in Boston when we were packing—*que será, será*," Libby said with a smile.

"What will be, will be," Maggie quoted with an answering smile.

Chapter XVIII

Wherefore they are no more twain, but one flesh.
What therefore God hath joined together,
let not man put asunder.
MATTHEW 19:6

THE DINING CAR WAS EMPTYING quickly. Liberty and Maggie decided to go back to their compartment and straighten up all their things. Poking their hands into the little cupboards, they made sure all their belongings were removed. They pulled their nightclothes out from underneath the pillows and stashed them in the large satchel.

The train was climbing up the steep incline, chugging away at a slow pace. Libby sat looking at the unbelievably beautiful scenery. Maggie joined her and they both were silent, gazing at cliffs piled with snow. An eagle was circling lazily in the distance. Liberty wondered, *What does an eagle eat with snow seemingly covering everything?* Their view was suddenly cut off, and it was pitch dark. This had happened several times already, and they were not alarmed. The waiter had told them they should hurry to their compartment, because sixty-two miles of the hundred-mile run to Colfax was all tunnels.

The train was slow but sure. It took a very long time, seemingly endless in the dark, but they eventually made the summit. Finally leveling, the locomotive rolled into Colfax. It felt good to be back in the sunlight, and Maggie stood up and stretched.

"Another hundred miles, and all downhill!" Her dimples dipped into her cheeks, her dark gray eyes glowing with excitement. Libby stood looking at the platform of Colfax. It was interesting—every platform wasn't the same. At first, every station had looked nearly identical, but then she and Maggie had decided to point out the differences. They found that there was always something unique about each one.

She glanced over at Maggie and responded, "I think it's time I start earnestly praying about the platform in Sacramento. I'm not trying to borrow the trouble you mentioned this morning, but I can't seem to help it. So, if you don't mind, I'm going to do some earnest praying about meeting Mr. Bannister in Sacramento."

Maggie sighed. "That's fine with me. I need to do a bit more writing in my journal anyway." Both women sat, their heads bent in concentration, one praying and one writing.

Sigmund and Matilda were married two days before Christmas, on a Saturday. The sky, which had been overcast all week, cleared, the clouds swept away during the night. It felt like blessings from God as the sun, which had hidden itself for over seven days, peeked its way into the day. Growing stronger by the minute, it shone brightly in a royal blue sky as if ordered to be present for this special occasion. Its rays diffused on the roof of the church, and the unmelted snow glistened in its bright light. The church was beautiful, decorated with flowers from Madam Bouvier. Red and white bouquets in green bottle glass graced the windows, and loose petals were strewn across the altar railings. Candles lit the interior of the church, causing a worshipful atmosphere.

Elijah was wearing a sling, but his shoulder felt much better. He'd overseen everything, but his interest was in representing Liberty. *This is what she would have wanted,* he thought. He made sure the flowers and church rental had Liberty's name on the invoices.

Elijah had asked the couple for a guest list, but because both of them spent their time working, guests were few. He and Abigail arrived a bit early to make sure everything was ready.

"Sigmund, this is my wife, Mrs. Abigail Humphries, and this, Abby, is Sigmund, Sigmund…" His voice trailed off, and he looked embarrassed. He thought quickly back to the Bouvier will, but it had only stated "the staff of the Bouvier household shall each receive…"

"Sigmund, I'm sorry. I don't believe I know your last name."

Sigmund smiled. "It is Hintz. My name is Sigmund Henrik Hintz."

Sigmund shook Elijah's hand and then clicking his heels together, he took Abigail's hand to his mouth but did not touch it to his lips. It was a cultural thing from Prussia. He'd seen the same gesture several times at parties and balls.

Elijah turned to Abigail. "If you think this is one fine-looking specimen of a man, wait until you see Matilda." Turning to Sigmund, he said, "She's a beautiful woman, Sigmund, and I'm going to give you some unsolicited advice. If you love Matilda, you need to let her know it in different ways every single day. If you can do that, you'll have a most happy marriage."

Sigmund looked grateful for the advice. "I think I would be able to learn much from you. I'd be most happy for you to share anything in your vast knowledge that will make my marriage a good one. This I know…I love my Matilda with all my heart. This I don't know…how to keep it fresh and new. I know so many guests who have come to the Bouviers', and were not happily married. I'm willing to learn all you can teach me, Mr. Humphries."

Abigail laughed delightedly. "Sigmund, listen to anything my husband tells you. He's kept me happy for twenty-six years!" She patted Elijah's arm, and they made their way up the stairs.

Elijah was surprised to see his new friend, Chief Inspector Baxter, at the wedding. He supposed Sigmund had made his acquaintance the several times he'd shown up at the Bouviers' manse. He nodded to George who scooted over to make room for the Humphries to sit.

The music began and everyone stood up, looking back at the bride. She was a vision in white, and Elijah had never seen her look lovelier. Dark hair was a shining, braided crown. Her chocolate eyes glowed so that he could see them from where he was standing. He looked at Sigmund, who waited with the rector, standing so erect. Sigmund looked proud of her. Elijah could not only sense his love for her but could see it in his eyes.

As Elijah watched, Pierre, dressed in his Sunday best, held out his arm to walk Matilda up the aisle. Step by step, she walked toward her blond giant. Pierre handed her off to Sigmund and sat down in the front row.

The rector, a youngish man, was making some comments about marriage being a commitment not an emotion or feeling, and Elijah's ears perked up as the rector was finishing his talk before the exchanging of vows.

"Folks, we have always heard the quote, 'The grass is always greener on the other side of the fence,' but I would say to you the grass is not greener on the other side of the fence. The grass is always greenest where you water it. Sigmund and Matilda, take care to water it. Take care about each other's feelings. Take care, when you have an argument, and you will have them, to stay on the subject of the argument. Don't get personal and call each other names. You may be sorry later, but the name you said will never be erased. Take care to water the love of your marriage."

Elijah squeezed Abigail's hand. He was thankful that he'd learned by his own father's example how to treat a woman.

Elijah witnessed Matilda's shock when Sigmund produced the opal ring set with diamonds. She fairly gasped when he slid it onto her finger. Sigmund took her hand, holding it close to his heart, as they finished their vows. His vows said to love, honor, and cherish. Her vows said to love, honor, and obey.

The rector pronounced them man and wife. Elijah could see the joy flowing between them. He smiled and thought, *I will be sure to have regular talks with Sigmund. He seems to be an upright man of integrity.*

Elijah and Abigail had asked Sigmund if they could host a little reception for them. Elijah had Pierre take the flowers out of the chapel, and they lined a path through the Humphries' parlor, through French doors to the most beautiful sunroom. Plants and blooms were everywhere, and fires burned in three fireplaces. There was a little lily pond in the middle— it was a dream made into a room.

Bessie, with help from the kitchen staff, had produced delicacies to please the eye and tempt the appetite, and there was even a large wedding cake. Liberty's chef, Cook, checked over all the food and made her approval by taking a petit four and biting into it, nodding her head in satisfaction all the while.

Matilda and Sigmund couldn't thank Mr. and Mrs. Humphries enough for all they had done.

Mr. Humphries replied blandly, "You need to thank Madam Bouvier." When no one was looking, he winked at Abby.

There were toasts to the bride and groom and happiness all around.

He'd told Sigmund that Madam Bouvier needed him to continue on at the Bouvier manse until the will was completely settled. Madam Bouvier would be handling it since the estate had reverted to her. He encouraged the newlyweds to move into one of the large guest rooms until Liberty could be located and apprised of the situation. Perhaps she'd want to travel back and take up residence again. Until then, the manse needed to be kept up and ready for whatever situation arose in the future.

Elijah was glad that Sigmund and Matilda wouldn't have to pay for a place to live, as he knew money was an issue.

When the festivities were over, Elijah asked Pierre to haul the flowers to the Bouviers'.

He was pleased with the day's work and decided it was time to put his other plan into action. He'd have to do some real planning before presenting the idea to Abigail. *I should also write a couple letters first. I don't know why I have this deep-seated feeling that I shouldn't tell Liberty that she's inherited everything yet. The will had read that if, for any reason, Corlay was unable to manage the estate, it would revert in its entirety to Liberty. She is a wealthy woman, because Corlay is going to prison for a long time.* He thought about the families upon whom Bouvier, Corlay, and Holbein had wreaked their havoc. He had the lists of them.

When the train pulled into the Sacramento station, both women were ready to get off. The friendly porter, whom they had spoken with earlier, had promised to help them offload their luggage. The train was slowing down. Libby and Maggie stood next to the exit with their satchels and the basket, both chattering excitedly.

The train would have a long stop because it had to take on more fuel for the steam engine. There'd be no immediate rush. It finally came to a complete halt, and the two women alighted. They walked quickly toward the back of the train, the same as when they'd stopped in Chicago. How long ago that seemed!

The cobblestone platform seemed solid under their feet, and the lack of a swaying floor seemed strange. The porter, hurrying before them, knew exactly which luggage was theirs as the porter from the first train had written everything down for him.

The two women split the tag numbers between them and were checking to see if everything was there. All was offloaded and wheeled to the front side of the station with the utmost efficiency. Libby had pulled out fifty cents to tip the porter, and he was grateful to her. Both women looked around. The platform was full of people getting on and off the train. Some were saying their good-byes, while others were greeting the new arrivals.

Matthew Bannister had received a telegraphed message from the Bouviers' lawyer, Mr. Humphries. The telegram asked him to pick up Madam Bouvier and her maid on approximately the eighteenth of December. It was a lengthy missive, informing him that Madam Bouvier would be coming west to check out the property. It asked him to prepare for extensive luggage.

Why would a man send his wife all the way across the country to check on a property? Why now? It'd been three years since he'd staked it out. *And why extensive luggage unless they planned to stay? Why had the lawyer sent the message instead of Bouvier himself? Were the Bouviers planning to move west?* Bannister had many questions and none of his own answers added up. He'd been asking them ever since the telegram arrived a few days ago at his place up in the Napa Valley.

Matthew Bannister had come to Sacramento early so as not to miss the women's arrival. He'd spent two days wasting time waiting for them. Sometimes the trains were delayed and sometimes they were early. It depended on the snow, the track, so many different things.

Matthew looked around the platform again—the place was crawling with people. He waited at the entrance to the station hall. The bustle was beginning to die down a bit, but the crush of people was still blocking any view he might have of two women waiting for him.

He leaned against the wall, arms crossed in front of him as he waited for the crowd to thin. Maybe they weren't on this train. He reckoned he'd just wait. He knew he was on edge. Usually he was pretty long on patience, but after two days of waiting, he felt he was on a short fuse.

CHAPTER XIX

I will seek that which was lost, and bring
again that which was driven away,
and will bind up that which was broken,
and will strengthen that which was sick:
but I will destroy the fat and the strong;
I will feed them with judgment.
EZEKIEL 34:16

MATTHEW BANNISTER SURVEYED the station again. Still no sign of the two women. He looked up to the front of the train…nothing. Then he looked at the other end where they were offloading. He saw two women standing together, and he strolled down the cobbles. He took in the pile of luggage and swallowed. He swallowed again, trying to get his temper under control, but he was seething under the skin.

Walking up to the two women, he tipped his hat.

"Name's Bannister," he said, "Matthew Bannister."

Libby and Maggie stared at him in surprise. Libby recovered first. "I'm Madam Bouvier," she said, proffering her hand. He took it in a firm grip.

"And I am Margaret O'Neill." Maggie dipped a quick curtsey.

Libby didn't know what she'd expected, but it wasn't this. Matthew Bannister was tall and lean. He had a gun strapped to his hip and was dressed in denim trousers. His plaid shirt was open at the neck, and a black leather vest completed his outfit. He was clean shaven with a small cleft in his chin. His dark-brown hair was covered by a cowboy hat.

He must be just about my age. He's quite good looking. I thought he'd be older, Liberty thought.

"Which luggage here belongs to you? We need to get it sorted out, because the train for Vallejo will be here soon. From Vallejo we'll head north up to Napa, by wagon."

Maggie looked at him, her eyes rounded, too scared to answer.

"It's all ours," Liberty said firmly, looking steadily at him. "All of it." Her green eyes sparked as she said it. She didn't even wait for a reaction but picked up the basket and satchel she'd been tired of holding, looking at the man expectantly.

"All right, Mr. Bannister, since there's nothing to sort out, where's this train of yours?" Libby could see his deep-set blue eyes were glittering with anger. Because she was used to seeing a man seethe under the skin, she could feel the tension in him ready to explode. She, in truth, didn't care. She was tired and just wanted this journey to be over.

Maggie said soothingly, "We didn't plan to bring so much, sir. It just turned out that way." She tried smiling at him winningly, but he didn't return the smile.

He turned on his heel and bit out the words, "Wait here!"

Liberty could see Matthew Bannister was worse than angry. He was in a rage. *Well,* she thought, *it can't be helped. We're here, and we need help moving our things into the house he built for Armand. Frankly, I can understand his anger…it is a lot of baggage.*

As he strode down the platform, Matthew thought about the luggage.

It looked as if they were moving in. How could two women need all that for a visit? He couldn't imagine the two city girls wanting to live in the place he'd knocked up for Bouvier. It was little more than a lean-to. He knew he could get all that stuff on the train, but he'd need a caravan to get it from Vallejo up to Napa.

Matthew went into the station and sent a wire up to Kirk, his brother, to bring all the wagons he could muster to Vallejo to meet this evening's train. That accomplished, he felt a bit better. He knew he was going to have to keep his temper in check. He didn't usually have a problem, but he'd already lost three days' work, and he wanted to get home. He wondered where those two thought they were going to store the stuff. It certainly wasn't going to fit into their little shack. He'd have to build something to keep it out of the weather. Napa Valley was a month into the rainy season, and it could rain for the next few months. He strode back to the trunks, ignoring the two women standing there. The train for Vallejo was arriving on another track.

He turned to Madam Bouvier and asked, "Would you have some money to pay a couple men to haul your luggage onto the Vallejo-bound train?"

"Yes, of course I'll pay them," she said, digging deeply into her larger satchel for her reticule. "How much do you need for them, Mr. Bannister?"

He looked surprised at her cooperation. Liberty thought, *He probably thinks I wouldn't pay him.*

He named an amount, and she dug it out, not knowing if it was correct or not but handing it to him without batting an eye. Again looking surprised, he handed back a couple large bills to her. A flush started in her cheeks and he saw it.

He found a man to help him from the Vallejo train. The man was an icon in the railroad business in Sacramento and the outlying areas. Jed rode the train round trip every day between Sacramento and Vallejo. He said he was happy to be of some use to Bannister and that he would find another man to help.

He looked at the drums and asked, "Do you know what's in these drums, Bannister?"

Matthew looked at the drums in surprise. "I've no idea, Jed."

Maggie and Liberty were both standing at the edge of the platform out of the way.

Liberty, watching everything closely, said, "It's kerosene. The drums are full of kerosene."

Matthew looked at her with a bit more respect than he'd shown thus far. Kerosene was not easy to come by. It wasn't that expensive, but shipping it was costly. It was a coveted item for folks living in the country. He looked inquiringly at Madam Bouvier. She could clearly see the questions in his eyes, but she said nothing. *What's going on here? Why all the trunks and even kerosene? They must be moving west.*

While they were loading, Matt turned to the two women. "Go buy three tickets to Vallejo while we're loading your stuff." He wasn't about to spend any more of his money on this venture.

The two women walked down the platform, and Maggie said, "He's rather short on manners, isn't he?"

Libby didn't reply to the question. She was doing some fast thinking about their situation.

"I'm getting the distinct impression that Mr. Bannister doesn't know Armand is dead. I think I want to keep it that way, at least until I'm acquainted with the situation here. No slip-ups Maggie. Armand's still alive as far as Mr. Bannister's concerned. It's a lucky thing I'm not dressed in mourning. Before I trust him, he's got to earn it."

Libby stepped up to the window and said to the stationmaster, "Three tickets to Vallejo, please."

The stationmaster asked, "One way or round trip?"

"One way, please." She glanced at the tickets he handed her. "Thank you." She stuffed the tickets into her reticule. They went back out the door, and as they headed down the station platform, a man stepped into Libby's path.

"Excuse me," Libby said, looking up at him.

The man leered. "Hel-lo, little lady, how'd you like to go an' have a drink with me, honey-girl?"

"No, thank you." Libby started to step around him.

He grabbed her arm. "Aw, don't go bein' so uppity, little girl."

Liberty tried to wrench her arm away, saying firmly, "Mister, kindly remove your hand from my arm, now!"

"Leave her alone!" Maggie hissed at the man.

He responded by grabbing Maggie's arm with his left hand. "An' now I got me a little spitfire. You're some redhead! I like a woman with a little spirit and spunk."

Maggie pulled back with her right arm and slugged the guy on the tip of the chin. He let go of Libby and grabbed Maggie with both hands, starting to slap her. When Liberty saw that the man was going after Maggie, she dropped her satchel, aiming a kick at the man's kneecap as hard as she could. She felt she'd broken her toe.

Matthew Bannister came running up, spun the man around, and with one smart clip to the chin, the man dropped like a ton of bricks.

"Sorry about that, ladies." He stepped over the man, picked up Libby's satchel, and handed it to her. "We need to be going, or our train will be leaving without us. It's getting ready to pull out in just a few minutes."

He started walking with long strides toward the train. Both women followed him quickly, silent and shaken to the core. He handed them up the step and jumped up himself.

"You'll meet all types of men here in the West," he said, his demeanor calm. "For the most part, women are well respected, but every once in a while you'll meet a character like that one." He jerked his thumb backward where the man still lay on the platform.

No one was paying any attention to him, and Libby was amazed that a man could lie there and people acted as if it was an everyday occurrence. Perhaps it was. Matthew Bannister led the women forward to leather seats that faced each other. He seated them facing forward and then sat across from the pair of them.

The train began to move with a big jerk. The wheels started turning, and they were on their way. Liberty felt drained of energy. She'd been tired before. After being waylaid by that man, she felt exhausted and her toe hurt.

Maggie, usually so full of vigor, slumped back against the seat. She was so tired she felt she could drop.

"Well, ladies, just exactly what are your plans?"

"Plans, Mr. Bannister?" Libby looked the man straight in the eyes. She tried her best to hold her gaze steady. Keeping her back ramrod straight, she could feel herself beginning to tremble. She didn't know if it was a reaction to the man on the platform or the man sitting before her. *Can I trust this man? I haven't had much luck with honest men.* Besides servants, Mr. Humphries was the only man she knew who was good and honest. She dropped her eyes, then looked back up at him.

"Miss O'Neill and I are planning to live in Napa for a while. I'm here to see the property and make sure improvements are made. I must apologize to you for my husband's neglect in paying you. It must have slipped his mind. Please write a receipt for the amounts you have paid out for supplies and include what you think decent for labor. We"—she glanced at Maggie—"we wouldn't think of cheating you, Mr. Bannister. I will certainly pay you whenever you're ready with those receipts."

Matthew Bannister looked shocked at the possibility of the money and tried to hide it.

"The improvements I made on the property were just the essentials, such as a well and a shack," he said to them. "I don't believe it's habitable. I'm quite sure it's not for you women. I don't live there. My property abuts yours. The shack might leak, and it sure isn't big enough to hold all your stuff. I did the minimum because your husband didn't send out any money. I didn't want him to lose the property I'd staked out for him."

"How big is it?" Libby asked.

"Well, it's one hundred sixty acres. That was the maximum the government would allow, so that's what I staked out for your husband. As I said, it abuts my property. I own another one hundred sixty acres myself. I staked it all out three years ago. I've been building a house on mine ever since." He sat back, deciding he'd talked enough.

The women looked totally done in. He supposed they'd be guests at his Rancho until something could be done with the shack on their property. "I reckon you'll be my guests till we get something fixed up for you. I'd no idea you planned to stay there. Reckon I figured you'd be visiting your property and then be going back East." He looked at them quizzically.

Liberty didn't have a clue as to how to respond to this invitation of his. "Are you saying the house you made is uninhabitable?"

"What I'm saying is, yes, essentially it's nothing but a shack. I stayed in it when I was staking out the property, but it's not meant to live in. I knocked it up to prove that an improvement had been made on the property if anyone came looking. I don't believe it's a place you could live in at all. It leaks and I'm sure it must be full of mice right now. It's very small," he replied.

Maggie, who'd been fairly silent until she heard the word *mice*, piped up. "Thank you, Mr. Bannister. Madam Bouvier and I would be very happy to accept your invitation. We're both exhausted and need a place to lay our heads."

Libby glanced at Maggie, surprised she had spoken up but relieved the matter had been taken out of her hands. *Maggie is now my equal, not a servant without an expressed opinion. I'd better remember that,* she thought.

"Well, you're more than welcome to stay at my Rancho for as long as you need. I've plenty of room." Matthew Bannister, too, was surprised. He had thought Mistress O'Neill to simply be the madam's maid, but evidently she wasn't just a maid. Two beautiful women sat across from him looking out the window. He scooted himself over into the corner. Matthew slid down the seat a bit and tipped his hat down over his eyes.

CHAPTER XX

God setteth the solitary in families
PSALM 68:6a

THE TRAIN CHUGGED ALONG along across a flat landscape, but there was no snow. Libby, after glancing at Mr. Bannister, turned to look out the window.

Maggie, seated closer to the window, turned to look at Libby once she wasn't being observed by Mr. Bannister.

She whispered into Libby's ear. "I've never been so scared, in all my days, as when that man grabbed you back there."

Libby rubbed her arm, which she sure was bruising up. She whispered, "I know. I was so frightened, but I was angry too. I think it'd be a good idea if we learned how to shoot those guns we bought, both the rifle and the handgun. Do you think he'd"—she waved her hand toward Matthew—"teach us?"

Maggie's eyes widened at the suggestion. "It's a good idea. I think we need to learn how. Would you even know how to load one of those things?"

"No, but we need to learn. I think I'd have pulled a gun out and made that man dance if I knew how to fire one!" Libby whispered. "I'd have made him jump and dance." She and Maggie started giggling, which turned into laughter.

Matthew Bannister knew they were whispering but couldn't hear for all the noise of the train. He heard their laughter and was glad for it. Smiling inwardly, he didn't let it go to his face. The women had been given quite a scare. He'd tried to make light of it but was amazed at their resilience. Maybe having the two of them around wouldn't be such a nuisance after all. The redhead had slugged the man. His eyes crinkled at the corners under his hat, thinking about it. *I saw her when I'd turned from loading one of the drums of kerosene. A real surprise, that, but what really shocked me was the way Madam Bouvier kicked the man when he'd grabbed Miss O'Neill. Better not tangle with those two,* he thought with a grin.

As the train pulled into Vallejo, Matthew breathed a sigh of relief. He could see a string of wagons and was glad to see his younger brother had rounded up so many. Kirk had been quite busy the last couple hours getting neighboring men to help. Matthew could see Diego, his right-hand man and foreman overseeing where the men were to halt all the wagons for off-loading from the train.

The train came to a full stop. Matthew stood up to help the two women, but they were ready to go, satchels and basket in hand. He handed them both down and told them to wait over by the offloading dock. He strode away.

"He's sure a bossy one, isn't he?"

"Hush, Maggie, we have so much stuff. I'm thankful he showed up. Can you imagine what we'd have done if he hadn't? We're probably one big source of irritation right now. The house we thought we could move into is a mess, and now the poor man has unexpected company as well as the irritation of taking the time to help us. I imagine he's got other things he'd rather be doing than taking care of us." They walked over to the offloading area.

Maggie nodded her head in agreement.

"You're right. I guess we should be thankful we're not stranded in Sacramento. That man on the platform was so horrible." She shuddered involuntarily, but after a moment, started to giggle. "Libby, I would have loved seeing you make that man dance. We do need to learn how to

156

shoot…and I'm going to practice until I'm not just able to shoot but am very good at it. I'd say to that man, 'Dance, man, higher…I said, dance!'"

Liberty's eyes slanted over to Maggie's, and they both whooped with laughter.

Matthew, hearing it, grinned at them.

They watched the men load the trunks and kerosene onto the wagons. When they were finished, Matthew walked over with two other men.

He introduced them. "This is my brother, Kirk Bannister, and this is my right-hand man, Diego Rodriguez." Both men politely lifted their hats to the women.

Kirk said, "Pleased to meet you, I'm sure."

Diego said, "Pleased to make your acquaintance," at the same time. The two men grinned at each other and turned away without even waiting for a response.

Liberty and Maggie trailed after Matthew, and he helped them up onto a large flatbed wagon.

He went around the other side, got up, and clucked to the horses, slapping them with the reins. "Giddyup!"

The three were crowded together on the seat, with Liberty sitting in the middle. She had never been this physically close to a man except Armand. Her thigh was jammed against Matthew Bannister's. She tried to scoot to her right, but Maggie wouldn't budge. Libby blushed a bright red and hoped the man wouldn't look at her. She pushed against Maggie, who wasn't moving; it looked a long way down to the ground.

The wagon pulled out and the road was not smooth. There were ruts and bumps in it, and Maggie held on for dear life. Libby just sat gritting her teeth, wishing the ride were over before it had hardly begun.

The ride seemed endless, and both women were silent.

Finally, Maggie spoke up. "Mr. Bannister, I'm trying not to fall off, but I'm so tired I think I could."

Matthew replied by saying, "Whoa," pulling on the reins. "Sorry, miss, I put the two of you here so you wouldn't have to eat dust. If you'd like, I can put you on Kirk's wagon. It's behind this one."

"If you wouldn't mind, I'd rather eat dust than fall into it." Maggie said with a little laugh. Matthew jumped down, went around, and lifted Maggie down. She followed him to Kirk's wagon.

"Kirk, Miss O'Neill would rather ride with you than try to hang on up front." He helped her up.

"That's fine by me," Kirk said, his voice full of admiration as he looked at Maggie with appreciation.

Maggie perked up and said teasingly, "Thank you, kind sir, for rescuing a damsel in distress. I thought I was going to fall off that wagon seat!"

Matthew climbed back up his own wagon, noticing Madam Bouvier had scooted way over to the side. He smiled at her and took up the reins again.

"Guess we'll ride off into the sunset together," he said.

Libby glanced at him. "What time does it get dark?"

"Oh, it'll be getting dark way before we reach my place I reckon. I haven't paid much attention to when it gets dark, but you can see the sun is nearly setting now. I'm too busy working to pay much attention to time, and when it gets dusk, I try to wind things up."

Liberty said, "It's strange—I mean, different, I suppose. Boston was so cold. This entire trip west, snow covered the ground the whole way until coming down from Colfax into Sacramento. It is so much warmer, and yet, it feels cold."

Matthew replied, "That's because it's a damp cold. We're just starting the rainy season. Doesn't snow here, or even freeze, although I reckon maybe once in a hundred years or so it might. You'll get sick of it raining, most likely. It rains steady off and on until about the first part of April, and all the sudden it's spring and you just can't believe how beautiful it is. Here, our summers are fairly mild. The days are dry, although we do get a little rain once in a blue moon."

"Boston can get rather warm during the summer too, although what I dislike is the humidity. You feel like you're breathing in water sometimes, it's so thick. The weather changes quickly from a very warm day to a pleasantly cool night."

"I've been in Boston during the summer, and I heartily agree with you. The humidity is the worst thing, but at least it does cool down at night. Here, the nights aren't too bad either." Matthew talked about the fruit and produce in the area, and Libby would talk about something in Europe or Boston. The conversation was easy and relaxing, making the time fly. Liberty, although extremely tired, enjoyed herself. It was interesting to learn a little about the area she was going to live in.

Innocently, she asked, "Are you married, Mr. Bannister?"

Matthew Bannister looked straight ahead and clipped out, "I was, but I'm not now."

Liberty felt as if the temperature had just dropped twenty degrees. All the easy camaraderie had evaporated. Neither spoke for a long time.

It was pitch black as they started up the long entrance to the Rancho. Liberty looked interestedly around her. She could see that the drive was lined with some kind of shrubbery, but it was too dark, and she couldn't see much farther. The drive swept around in front of a beautiful house. She'd read about haciendas and thought this must be how they looked. It was low and the roof was rounded red tile. The wide front was creamy stucco and had arches all across, which were painted a pale orange on their underside. A large flagstone walk spread itself between the arches and the actual front wall of the house, like a breezeway front porch, only it was level with the ground. The entire place blazed with light as if a party were taking place. Growing on either side of the entrance, orange trees with fruit in every stage of ripeness hung on neatly-trimmed branches.

Matthew jumped down to help Liberty.

"You must be exhausted," he said sympathetically as he reached up to help her down.

Sudden tears sprang to her eyes at the sympathy. She quickly looked away so he wouldn't see. Liberty was usually under control of her emotions, but she knew her composure was slipping...she was beyond exhaustion.

The two women followed Matthew into the house. It was beautiful, but before they could even look around, a plump woman entered the room and took over.

"I yam Conchita Rodriguez, Diego's wife. Meester Bannister, he own thees casa"— she waved her hand expansively—"an' me, I run eet." She laughed, and strong white teeth were startling in her swarthy face. She was a beautiful woman with long, black shining hair hanging in braid down her back. Her black eyes sparkled with delight at the two women.

"You hungry...you wanna eat now?"

Liberty looked over at Maggie. Both of them shook their heads in answer. They were too tired to eat.

"I haf the room for you. I know you tired... come...you come."

Liberty turned to Matthew. "Thank you, Mr. Bannister, for opening your home to us. I am certainly in your debt." She turned to follow Conchita.

The short woman led them down a wide hall of flagstone to bedrooms lined on either side. The first she showed to Maggie. "And your name ees?"

"Maggie, my name is Maggie. Oh my, this is a gorgeous room." It was a beautiful bedroom done in different shades of apricot. White organdy-lined silk curtains hung in the two windows, and all the trim was stark white. There was a white mantel over the fireplace that looked as if it hadn't been used much. A large picture graced the wall above the mantel, a painting of a terrace with delicate chairs and a lacy tablecloth and an ocean in the background. Maggie was delighted. A little room had been built between the two bedrooms, and Conchita led them both into it.

"Thees Meester Bannister's idea," she said. "He haf the leetle room for all guest." The room contained a large tub for bathing and a large commode containing two chamber pots, behind two different doors. A high window and a floor-to-ceiling cupboard for towels, soaps, and candles filled one wall. There was another door leading into the second bedroom.

"Thees room, eet ees for you. What ees your name" She looked questioningly at Libby.

"I'm Liberty, but you may call me Libby. Thank you for being so thoughtful, Conchita. We're both very tired. You've made our arrival here special by being ready for us. Again, thank you." She entered the room behind Conchita and was charmed by it. The room was painted an airy yellow, making the entire room look sunny. French doors—all glass—led to the outside. She'd never seen doors like these. A curtain on the door was pulled to one side, with matching curtains at the large windows. It was fresh and warm. The four-poster bed looked inviting. There was a fireplace in this room too, but the mantel above it was a dark mahogany. Above the mantel was a picture of a field of daisies. *Peaceful*, thought Libby. Such a stark contrast to the dark, heavy look of her room in Boston. Tears sprang to her eyes.

Conchita took Libby into her generous arms and patted her back, murmuring, "Oh, *niña bonita, es bueno*. Oh pretty girl, it's good. You one tired girl." She glanced over at Maggie. "Mees Maggie, I put her to the bed. You go now to the bed too. You tired."

"Thank you, Conchita," Maggie murmured gratefully. "I need my night things out of the satchel."

"There ees fresh nightdress on bed, Mees Maggie. Eet ees nice name you haf." She smiled a wide smile.

Maggie smiled tiredly back. "Good-night." She closed the door quietly behind her. She used the "leetle room," smiling to herself about having such a nice bedroom. Hurriedly undressing, she picked up the soft cotton nightdress, donned it, and turned the lamp wick down. It flickered softly then went out. Maggie closed her eyes and knew no more.

"Now, Mees Liberty, we get you in the bed," Conchita said as Maggie left the room. She took down Libby's hair. Picking up a brush from the bureau, she brushed it with swift, skillful strokes. She undid Libby's buttons and pulled off her dress. Kneeling down, she removed Libby's shoes and stockings. Conchita took off her chemise and corset, helping her into a soft cotton nightdress.

"Mees Libby, go use the leetle room."

Libby took her special tooth cream Cook had made and her Wadsworth toothbrush from the large satchel and went into the little room. It too was beautiful. The walls had been painted white, and there were hand-painted roses and leaves in a trim around the tops of the walls. She washed her face and hands and brushed her teeth. As she started to crawl into bed, she saw that Conchita had left but not before closing the curtains and turning down the bedclothes. She'd placed a pitcher of water on the nightstand and a glass. Libby was thankful and so tired.

She lay on her back for a few minutes, and tears began to course down her cheeks. She cried and cried. She turned onto her side, not knowing why she was crying, nor could she stop the gut-wrenching deep sobs that ripped through her. She couldn't remember the last time she'd cried like this. *Maybe when I knew I had to marry Armand? Why can't I stop?*

Finally the tears subsided, and she lay there spent as she had never been in her entire life. She heard the door open, but she didn't move. In the soft light from the hall, Conchita came to her bed, wiping her face and hands with a warm, damp cloth as if she were a baby. She kissed Libby on the forehead, whispered good-night, and was gone. Libby wondered again why had she cried like that. As she started to drift off to sleep, she realized she knew the answer. *I have come home.*

CHAPTER XXI

The wise in heart shall be called prudent:
and the sweetness of the lips increaseth learning.
PROVERBS 16:21

ELIJAH HAD DECIDED TO ENACT his next plan. He knew he should send a message by telegraph to apprise Liberty of the situation, but he didn't think it wise just yet. She should be in California by now.

Perhaps I should let her know she has some money. What if she got into a situation and needed it? He'd checked on the Bouviers' manse several times and everything was running smoothly. He'd given Sigmund quite a sum of money and carte blanche to keep things running for all the staff. He had every confidence in Sigmund's capabilities.

The days passed swiftly. Elijah's shoulder was feeling almost normal, and Abigail was blooming. How grateful he was to the Lord God Almighty! Bowing his head, he thanked God again. Having been hard at work, he had decided to walk home. Elijah was losing much of his paunch and felt the better for it. The exercise of walking home every day had done him some good. It seemed to clear his brain of problems related to work and gave him a sense of well-being. He arrived home, and as he walked up the steps, he began to whistle. It surprised him a bit. He used to whistle and sing a lot but hadn't done it in a long time. It seemed strange that because of Abby's healing, he felt whole. As he topped the steps, the door opened. Thomas was waiting for him.

Faithful Thomas. Before Thomas could even greet him, Elijah grabbed him, giving him a hug. Thomas was startled. "Mistah Humphries, what's gotten into you? You're not s'posed to hug me!"

"Thomas, what's gotten into me is the Holy Ghost!" Elijah laughed. "I don't know exactly what's going on inside me, Thomas. I know I'm thankful to be alive and have a wife who's healthy. I think God has plans for us, Thomas, but for now, please know that I love you, I value you, and I thank God daily for you and for your faithfulness to the Humphries' family." Without waiting for a response, Elijah hurried up the stairs, taking them two at a time. Abigail was coming down the wide hall that was open to the downstairs. The railing above spanned the width of the foyer below.

"Abby, my lovely Abigail, you're as beautiful as the day I married you!"

"Land sakes!" Abby exclaimed with a laugh. "I'm getting older by the minute and these lines around my eyes—they're not laugh lines. They're crow's feet, because nothing's that funny!"

Elijah laughed at her jest, pulling her to himself. He planted a kiss on her mouth.

"You're so witty, my sweet. You have always had the ability to make me laugh!" Looking deep into her blue eyes filled with love, he decided to share his plan.

"You know, my dear, our anniversary is coming up soon. Twenty-seven years married and to the same woman. Can you believe it?"

"Oh, I can believe it all right, but they've gone by fast, haven't they, my dear?"

"Yes, very fast. I have a plan, Abigail, my dear. Let's go sit in the sunroom and I'll tell it to you." They descended the stairs together and entered the sunroom. Sitting side by side next to the little pond, Elijah took Abby's hand in both of his. "How'd you like to go on a second honeymoon, Abby?"

Her eyes slanted a look of amazement his way. "You're serious? You really think we could do that? Where would we go? Okay, out with it. I'm already thinking you have an ulterior motive, Elijah Humphries! What's this plan you're thinking about? The plan isn't a second honeymoon, is it?"

Elijah got up, beginning to pace between Abby and the pond. "Part of it is a second honeymoon, a trip for you and me. I've been thinking for some time that you and I should go to Europe. While we're there enjoying the sights, we could perhaps find this Alexander Liberty fellow, the one who wrote the love letter to Violet Ann Browning Corlay some twenty-nine years ago. We could see if he's happily married and if he is, I think we'll leave well enough alone. It wouldn't do to spring an illegitimate child on him at this point in his life. But…what if he isn't, Abby? Then what?"

"Oh, what a wonderful idea! Just think, if your Liberty could know that Jacques Corlay isn't her real father and that her real father's a good man… Oh, Elijah, what an absolutely fantastic idea! When will we go? How will we go about finding someone from nearly thirty years ago?"

"Well, truth to tell, I wrote a couple letters and am waiting for the responses. We'll book berths on a liner and set sail as soon as we hear something."

"Where'd you send the letters?"

"I sent one to the Department of the British Armed Forces giving what information we have from Mr. Liberty's letter to Violet Corlay. I also sent one to the vicar in the parish from whence the letter came. The churches keep good records of births and deaths. If this Liberty fellow was killed in the army or has died since, it'll be recorded in the parish in which he was born."

Abigail looked at Elijah admiringly. "No wonder you're a lawyer— you're so organized in all you do. Most people wouldn't be able to accomplish half the things you do. You're so smart and I love you very much!" She stood and, reaching around his neck, kissed him. She started for the door. "Are you going to tell Liberty Bouvier about your plans?"

Elijah looked surprised at the question. "No, no, I'm not. I don't know why, but I am quite sure the Almighty has been impressing upon my heart not to tell Liberty anything yet, except that she has sufficient funds. She may need to know she has money, but I'm not telling her she's inherited the estate. She needs some time and if she knew, she would probably head back here immediately and take up the responsibility for the companies. No, I'm not even telling her that she's ended up with all of it. I think the good Lord is going to do something for that girl. She's had such an awful time of it… years of an awful time of it. She's going to need some healing before she has to take on all the responsibilities of the estate. The companies have fairly competent men running them, but there's one that's definitely doing some shady business. I'm going to have George look into that." He looked at his wife standing in the doorway. "Well, Abby, my girl, I'm starved. Are you ready for dinner?"

Maggie awoke and lay, lazily looking around her beautiful bedroom. Her attic room at the Bouviers' manse had certainly been adequate, but it was small, sufficient for a maid's needs. It had no fireplace and had been painted white. This guest room had been painted a warm apricot color. She thought about yesterday. Coming down from Colfax, the total landscape had changed, no more snow. Then, encountering that man who'd grabbed Libby and her. She'd been so scared but mad too that he would accost Liberty like that. Maggie knew she had a temper she needed to control, but that man had been horrible. He'd reeked of body odor.

Maggie had no experience with men. She'd only worked for them or worked with them. Mr. Bannister had come to their rescue. He seemed like an enigma, someone who would be difficult to get to know. And…there was Kirk Bannister. He was definitely someone totally outside her expertise. He'd been very nice, and they'd enjoyed talking with each other. She'd told him that she'd been Liberty's maid but was now her friend. It had been different acting the part of a lady, as she had the entire trip, instead of living the part of a maid. *People seemed to treat you differently, as if you were real people instead of being invisible.* Except for Liberty, she'd felt unnoticed since she was twelve going into service with the Jamisons, and later the Bouviers.

Maggie thought again about Libby. She'd seemed so composed when that man had grabbed her. She hadn't even acted scared, just irritated. When the man directed his attentions to Maggie, she'd gotten angry. Liberty was protective of her. It felt good that someone cared so much for her. She wondered if what Libby had said about God was true. *Does He really care for me, or is that something made up to try to make a person feel better?*

Swinging her legs over the side of the bed, she stood and stretched. She walked into the little room and quietly opened the door to Libby's room. She was still in a deep sleep, one arm flung over her head, her coppery curls spilling out over the pillow. Maggie closed the door silently. Dressing in the same thing she'd been wearing all week, she felt in dire need of a real bath. She looked longingly at the tub. *Later*, she promised herself, *later.* Filling up the tub now would probably wake Libby.

Stepping out into the hall, which was painted in two shades of green, Maggie again admired the color combinations. A grass-green wainscoting covered the lower walls of the hall. The wall above it was a mint green with white trim at the top of the wainscot, and the floor trim board was white. Pictures of what must be family members or friends lined the hall on both sides. The pictures were different sizes, but all were framed in white. The contrasts were beautiful and eye pleasing.

She entered the large room she'd been in the night before. It was lovely, homey, and comfortable. The impression she had was of natural woods and leather. The floor was a smooth red-brown tile with a huge braided rug. One wall was all windows, two walls were of some kind of beautiful wood, and the fourth wall was painted a rusty red. There were end tables, a large square coffee table made of varying shades of wood, and deep leather chairs.

Conchita came into the room with an armful of laundry. "*Buenos dias*, Mees Maggie. You haf comfortable bed? You sleep good, no?"

Maggie grinned widely and replied. "Yes, I slept wonderfully and feel as good as new."

"Come, come, breakfast waiting for you. Ees Mees Liberty up?"

"No, I peeked into her room, but she's dead to the world."

Conchita nodded, heading for the kitchen with the load of laundry still in her arms, Maggie trailing behind.

The kitchen was gigantic, at least twice the size of the Bouviers' kitchen. It smelled of freshly baked bread and bacon. Gleaming copper pots hung from a large rack over a wooden island, serving as a counter and cutting board. Dominating one entire side of the kitchen were windows with a huge scrubbed-oak table and chairs overlooking a courtyard. Another wall had large glassed French doors opened to the courtyard that extended past the end of the house. It was open, sunny, and cheerful.

There were two young women working in the kitchen, and Conchita introduced them.

"Thees ees my niece Guadalupe. We call her Lupe. An' thees ees Lucinda, an' we call her Luce," she said. "They twins, and eet take time to tell them from each other. Lupe, Luce, thees Mees Maggie." The two women smiled shyly at Maggie.

Maggie greeted them warmly. "I'm happy to meet you. Your breakfast smells wonderful!"

Conchita said, "Een the mornings, we haf everyone helping themselves to the buffet breakfast...eet be cooked early. Sometimes, Meester Bannister, he call an early meeting. He call eet the powwow breakfast."

Maggie simply nodded her head.

Conchita showed her the silverware, plates, and mugs for coffee, telling Maggie to help herself. She also showed her she could eat in the formal dining room or at the scrubbed-oak table or through the French doors and into the courtyard that let in the sunshine but blocked any wind. It was pleasant. Maggie chose to sit outside and think about her new surroundings.

Matthew and Kirk came into the kitchen to get coffee, taking a break from their labors. They went into the courtyard to join Maggie. Both were dusty from working out in the fields. Maggie looked surprised they would join her.

Matthew grinned. "Good morning, Miss O'Neill. Conchita says that Madam Bouvier's not up yet. Does she usually sleep in so late?"

"No, in truth, she's a very early riser. This has been a difficult trip. Both of us were exhausted last night, and I think it's good to let her sleep."

"Oh, I don't care if she sleeps. Why did she come instead of Monsieur Bouvier?" he queried. "For that matter, why'd you come?"

"I came because it was a chance to look at this great country of ours. I was Madam Bouvier's chaperone."

"You forgot one," he said softly. "Why'd she come instead of the monsieur?"

CHAPTER XXII

There is no peace, saith the LORD,
unto the wicked.
ISAIAH 48:22

MAGGIE DID SOME QUICK THINKING before she replied to Matthew's question. She did so with alacrity.

"Monsieur Bouvier's been quite indisposed and I, in truth, don't know their personal affairs. I think madam wanted to see the property. I believe it's to see if something can be done to make it a business concern, or perhaps they are going to move here. Do you know," asked Maggie, changing the subject to throw him off his line of questioning, "that Madam Bouvier has a discerning palate?"

"A what?" asked Matthew.

"A discerning palate," Maggie replied. "She's able to tell you, just by tasting, any wine grown in France and what region it comes from. The German wines are a little more difficult, she said, but she can tell a Chardonnay from a Merlot or a blend of the two. Quite a talent, wouldn't you say?"

Matthew's deep blue eyes had gotten a little rounder, and his eyebrows raised up.

"Are you serious? Can she really do that? I've heard of people who can tell by taste the wine and region, but I've never met one. I can tell the difference between wines, but not their place of origin. That really is something." He pushed his hat back off his brow and stared at Maggie.

"Yes, I'm serious, and yes, she really can."

"Well, I'll be darned," Kirk said. "That's an unusual talent." He grinned at Maggie.

Realizing he wouldn't get any more information from Maggie, Matthew asked, "How are you feeling this morning? Are you sore from your ride on the wagon?"

"No," Maggie replied with an answering grin. "I feel fine and have enjoyed a wonderful breakfast and delicious coffee. This"—she waved her hand to include the courtyard and the house—"is magnificent. Who designed this house? It feels homey and is comfortable and yet it's beautiful."

Kirk answered, "Matt designed the entire thing. I was away at school. I didn't start college until I was twenty-five. Matt had almost given up hope of me going." He grinned a little ruefully. "I finished up last year and came here to find this house almost finished. It *is* nice, isn't it?"

Matthew sat thinking while the two talked.

Well, little Miss O'Neill, you did a good job at turning the subject, didn't you? How is Bouvier indisposed…is he sick, or what? There're just too many questions and not enough answers. He knew he was going to get to the bottom of this. Before too long, he'd need the room in the barn where they'd unloaded the trunks. He wondered what Madam Bouvier had planned. He looked toward the kitchen and saw Conchita beckoning to him. He excused himself, but Kirk and Miss O'Neill were so engrossed in their conversation they didn't notice him get up.

"What's wrong, Conchita?" He could see she looked troubled.

"Meester Bannister, I doan know what ees happening here." She nodded toward Maggie. "She go right to sleep last night, like the baby. But Mees Liberty, oh Meester Bannister, she cries last night for the long time, the grand cries, as eef her heart be broken. I no can stand to hear it. I go back to her room, get dirty clothes to wash, but she crying, Meester Bannister. And me, I no want to embarrass her."

"Thanks for telling me." Matthew patted her shoulder. "I don't know what's going on either, but I'm determined we're gonna find out." He turned to his brother. "Kirk, I'm going back out. I'll be in the lower east field. You'll come help with the wire, won't you?" Matthew went back through the kitchen and out the door.

Elijah had received a letter. It was lying on his desk when he walked into his office. *It must have come in after I went home last night.* The letter was from the rector in Reading, Berkshire, England. It stated that Alexander Edward Liberty lived in Florence, Italy, and was an oblate at the Benedictine monastery Badia Fiorentina. More than that, he did not know. Elijah told Howard, the office clerk, that since he had no appointments for the day, he was going home. It was still early, and he had much to do.

Elijah ran up the steps in his house. "Start packing, Abby. Start packing! The post has come, and Mr. Liberty's living in Florence. I'm going out to purchase four tickets to Italy."

"Four tickets, Elijah? I don't need help and neither, for that matter, do you. We'll pack lightly and just the two of us shall go. I think the service we'll have on board will be adequate. Just the two of us, Elijah—no one else." Abigail was adamant.

"Are you sure, Abby? It would make it easier to travel without a retinue tagging along. I thought you might want Annie's help."

"No, Elijah, I don't. I would have before, but I'm trying to cut down on excesses. God wants me to be a good steward of my time and my possessions. Now, go buy those tickets, and I'll set about packing. Annie will help me."

She sat down at the little desk in her sitting room. It was a comfortable room painted the palest of turquoise and trimmed with white, which always seemed fresh and inviting. She started making out a list. Abby was an organized woman and found packing was much simpler when she knew exactly what was required.

Elijah smiled, knowing she was already lost in thoughts of practicality. He went back down the steps and made some mental lists as he went. *Let's see, I need to get the tickets, inform the office, talk to Sigmund, and stop by to see George Baxter.*

He went to the ticket office of Cunard Lines, a well-known ocean liner with magnificent ships, and purchased tickets for London, England. They would board a smaller ship to travel to Florence from London. Sailing in three days' time, he had much to do. The next stop was to Liberty's manse. Sigmund was right up to speed on all that needed doing.

He had John drive him to the police station but found that George had gone home before lunch. Thinking he should go home first to have a bite of lunch, he decided against it. His stomach rumbled as John drove him to the Baxter residence.

"John, you can wait in Baxter's kitchen." Elijah smiled at his driver. He walked up the steps, knocking on the heavy, ornate door.

Tabitha opened it and said, "Mr. Humphries, sir, how nice to see you. Could you please wait here while I tell Mr. Baxter you are here?"

"Certainly, Tabitha." He looked down at her, amazed that she was so tiny yet full grown. She looked a child until he looked into her eyes.

"I'm here without invitation, so if he is busy, there'll be no offense taken." He smiled at her, and she smiled back before entering the library.

She returned quickly. "He said you're more than welcome, sir." She opened the door leading to the library, dipped a small curtsey, and closed the door behind him.

George had already walked across the deep carpet to shake his hand and welcome him. Elijah smiled, grasping his hand. He liked this man. Suddenly, Elijah realized they weren't alone. Cabot Jones was already seated comfortably before the fireplace and stood as the other two shook hands. He walked forward, greeting Elijah also.

George, looking at Elijah closely, saw he was excited.

"Have you had lunch yet?"

"No, but I don't want to be a bother."

"No trouble, no trouble at all, Elijah." He walked out of the library, returning in a few moments.

"Lunch is almost ready and there's plenty. They'll just add another plate. Sit down and make yourself comfortable. What's going on, my friend? I can see you are chomping at the bit!"

The two older men sat facing Cabot. Tabitha entered with a tray of plates already dished up, chicken with rice and vegetables. She served each man a plate while George poured all three glasses of apple cider. After a couple swallows, Elijah answered George's question.

"Well, George, I've had news from England. Abigail and I will be setting sail in just three days' time. We're going to hunt down Liberty Bouvier's true father and see if the man even knows he has a daughter. If he is happily married, Abby and I will leave well enough alone. If he's single or childless, we're going to tell him about Liberty, his daughter."

George looked surprised. "You don't say. You, in truth, know where the man is? How'd you find out?"

Elijah grinned at his new friend. "You're not the only one who can do a bit of investigating. Alexander Liberty is, according to the vicar in Reading, Berkshire, an oblate of a monastery in Florence, Italy."

"An oblate," George asked. "What's an oblate?"

"An oblate is a person who's committed themselves to a life of dedication to God, to seek to be holy. In this case, I'd say he was Roman Catholic because of being in Florence. Oblates can be Orthodox or Anglican too. They live simply and renew commitments once a year. They reside outside the monastery but live out the values set by that order. I looked up the word *oblate* right after I received the letter. Otherwise, I'd have no clue either." He grinned again.

"Well, that is interesting. I believe I've learned something new today. How did you find the man?" George asked again.

"I wrote to the Department of the British Armed Forces and the vicar of the village from whence the letter to Violet Corlay came so many years ago. I was lucky to get a response from the vicar. It's interesting, but it's not the only reason I came by." Elijah leaned forward. "I've been going over Bouvier's papers. He had so many concerns going that it's taken me this long to find there's a definite problem with one of the companies."

George and Cabot both perked up because of the way Elijah spoke. They knew something was coming that would concern them.

Elijah said heavily, "There are seventeen companies owned by Bouvier. I think sixteen of them are on the up and up." He sat a moment and drank some of his cider. "I am quite sure one of the companies is just a front, George, a front for an unbelievably filthy business."

George exclaimed, "What is it, man...out with it!"

Elijah said, "I'm quite certain that one of the companies, George"— and he included Cabot in his look—"the one in San Francisco, is dealing in white female slavery. Bouvier was receiving money quarterly from the company, a lot of money. Supposedly, it's a salmon canning company."

Both George and Cabot looked shocked. George recovered first.

"We'd like to go over those papers with a fine-toothed comb. I hope you'll give them to us, Elijah."

"Of course, that's why I came by." He pulled a sheaf of papers out of his satchel. "Here are all seventeen businesses. The bottom one is the salmon canning company in which I think you'll be most interested. I think I'm giving you some more business."

"I'm glad that you came by today, Elijah. Cabot and I were just going to have a bite to eat before going to Corlay's trial. It's set for one thirty this afternoon. Would you care to join us?"

Elijah pondered the question for a minute. He still had much to do this day. "Yes, yes, I think I would."

All three men ate the delicious luncheon Mrs. Roos had made. They talked about Corlay, Holbein, and of course, Bouvier getting what he deserved. Cabot talked about what he'd heard about white slavery— that entire ships were coming from Scandinavia with women who were drugged and sold to the highest bidder. It was a despicable business to be sure. The three men finished eating and made their way into the city proper, to the courthouse.

As they entered the courtroom, Elijah realized this was the day of sentencing or acquittal. Corlay had the best lawyer money could buy to defend him. When Elijah saw it was Detrich Werner, his heart sank. Werner had a reputation for almost never losing a case. Elijah personally thought the man was as crooked as his client. His opponent was the state's prosecutor, a good man, Jedidiah Long, who was well-known for getting his man. *The Globe* had carried the entire story, and the courtroom was full.

They sat talking in low voices to each other, because the jury was out deliberating when they arrived. After a short wait, the jury returned with the verdict. Elijah was thankful the United States Constitution allowed a person the right to trial by jury. It wasn't the same in many other countries. He wondered if any of the men sitting on the jury had been bought off. It happened, he knew. He sat up a little straighter and listened intently as the verdict was given. Guilty. Corlay was found guilty of fraudulent business dealings and of hiring an assassin to murder Armand Bouvier. He was sentenced to three life imprisonments.

Elijah and his companions grinned at each other, and George held his thumb up. Liberty was free, Elijah rejoiced. She was finally free. The three men left the courtroom.

George said, "The man finally got what's coming to him. He deserves to hang, in my estimation. We still don't have the murderer for the shoelace vendor. I'm glad that justice won out and Werner didn't win that one. Werner is sleazy."

"That's true— I've heard of Werner paying off juries. I was quite worried there when I saw him. He's a man with unclean hands, that's for sure. I'm just so glad this verdict was guilty. I'd hate to see a man like Corlay go free," Elijah said.

Cabot looked with interest at Elijah. "Paying off juries, eh? That's something else we could have one of the men look into. I think the next step for me is the business dealing with white slavery. Why would two men who made so much money even need to be involved with such a sordid business?"

"Because," George replied, "their greed knew no bounds."

Jacques Corlay sat impassively, showing no reaction to the verdict of guilty. He had a backup plan. Rufus was his point of contact and had been in the back of the courtroom. Corlay had laid out his plans earlier, telling Rufus to grease a palm. There was always a guard willing to look the other way for greenbacks. Jacques' main plan was to escape and find Liberty. He blamed her for all his misfortune. She had his money…she was the real thief, and he was going to make her pay if it was the last thing he ever did.

CHAPTER XXIII

I know that there is no good in them,
but for a man to rejoice, and to do good in his life.
And also that every man should eat and drink, and
enjoy the good of all his labour, it is the gift of God.
ECCLESIASTES 3:24

LIBERTY FINALLY AWAKENED. She lay drowsily for a while before realizing where she was. A feeling of peace suffused her being, yet she was utterly exhausted. She opened her eyes as the day before came flooding into her mind.

"Oh Lord," she whispered, "what are Your plans for me?" She lay deep in thought and prayed for a while. "Thank You, Father God, for safety and protection throughout the long journey. I pray for guidance. I don't know what I'm supposed to do." She couldn't stay here—at least, she didn't feel she should.

"Lord, I pray for Elijah and his wife. Father, touch his wife's body, I pray. Lord, I thank You for Sigmund and Matilda, for Cook and Pierre, and for Rufus." She prayed for Maggie most of all. "Father, Maggie is such a wonderful friend. Help her to find You as her Savior. Lord, I bless You for

Your magnificent, wondrous love, and the knowledge that I'm in Your hands. I trust You, knowing that Your plans are right and just."

The peaceful feeling gave way to a feeling that she needed to get up and get on with the day. She was a bit excited at the thought of being a landowner. A plan had been percolating in her brain since yesterday, knowing that Matthew Bannister was growing grapes. *Perhaps that's what I need to do too. I don't know. I only want to get started on my life of freedom. No evilness, no depraved husband, no wicked, unloving father telling me what to do anymore... that's freedom!*

Liberty padded barefoot into the little room. She was surprised by the steam that enveloped her upon opening the door. *That Conchita is one wonderful woman.* Conchita had filled the tub with hot, hot water. Libby dipped her fingers into it to see how warm it was. It was perfect, and Liberty couldn't wait to soak in it. She went back to rummage through the large satchel, coming up with a clean chemise but no corset, as well as the muslin dress she'd packed. It was wrinkled, but she didn't care. Stripping off the soft cotton nightdress, she threw it on the bed and entered the bathing room, sinking down into the tub. There was a bucket of water nearby for rinsing her hair. Fragrant soaps and shampoo lay on a table next to the tub along with two towels on the second shelf of the table. Libby sighed, enjoying the relaxing heat.

Conchita, was in Maggie's room and heard Liberty in the bathing room. She went into Liberty's room and collected all her dirty clothes and stripped off the pillowcases so they would be fresh for tonight. She was wondering what would be a good dinner to welcome these women. She talked aloud to herself as she worked.

"Mees Maggie, she catched Meester Kirk's eye. He always going out with different womens... He the flirt, that ees for sure."

Kirk had left a string of broken-hearted women in his wake.

"I hope he no break thees Mees Maggie's heart. I doan know what thees redhead ees like. Perhaps she ees a siren or maybe she a sweet girl. She look young." Conchita thought about it a bit. "I surprise I feel some kind of closeness to Mees Liberty. When I first set eyes on her, I know here ees a good heart. When I show them the rooms, Mees Liberty, she thank me. That politeness weens my heart. Then, I hear her sobbing like that...I weel halp that woman eef I can." She crossed herself as if it were a vow.

Conchita had watched as Kirk took Maggie out to show her the grapevines and get her oriented with the property. She'd given Miss Maggie a brightly colored shawl to wear to protect her from the wind. She muttered to herself about Kirk needing to go out and help Meester Bannister.

Liberty was glad to be clean. Straightening up her mess in the bathroom, she'd hung her wet towel on a hook. Combing her curls out had been work. Usually Maggie did it. Her hair was thick, and instead of putting it up, she decided to leave it down until it dried. In this climate, it wouldn't take long. She exited her room, impressed with the freshness of greens and white in the hall. When she went into the great room, her first thought was comfort. *This is comfortable. My home in Boston is so heavy and dark, stiff, and uncomfortable.* She walked over to the large bookshelf and was intrigued by the variety of books and authors. She loved to read.

Hesitating in finding the kitchen, she could hear laughter but felt a little shy of Conchita, who knew about her out-of-control display of crying. *I feel different, purged, as if all that's gone on in my life before has been a precursor to being here. I have this sense of peace and belonging I haven't felt since before entering boarding school as a young girl.*

Her mother had adored Liberty, but once Jacques shipped her off to France at twelve years of age, she'd never had a sense of belonging. Certainly not when she'd returned from Switzerland to find she was being married off to pay her father's debts...certainly not being married to Armand. Being married to him, she'd always had to be on her guard, wondering what he was going to spring on her next. She'd never had this feeling that she truly belonged. She was glad she was here. The past would not haunt her. She took a deep breath and headed for the kitchen.

Conchita was there. "Oh, Mees Liberty, you sleep good, no?" She walked over to Libby and enveloped her in a big hug.

Libby hugged her back. "Yes, I slept and slept. I had the most heavenly bath, and I thank you for that. You're one very thoughtful lady. I appreciate it. Uhmm, it smells so good in here!"

Conchita patted Libby's shoulder and said, "Thank you, an' here ees breakfast. We deesh up food ourselves een mornings." Conchita also introduced Libby to Luce and Lupe. Libby smiled at them and helped herself to food but not too much, as it was nearly lunchtime. Conchita showed her where everything was located and poured her a big mug of the steaming coffee. Libby decided to sit at the big oak table by the window and listen to the women talk. They chattered and laughed as Liberty enjoyed a little breakfast. She was watching them and decided there was no time like the present.

"Conchita, I'd like to help."

Conchita looked at her seriously. "No, you rest an' feel at home, here. You no work."

Liberty smiled. Walking over to Conchita, she whispered in her ear, "I can't cook, Conchita. I need to learn how to cook, and I'd love to start today." She started rolling up her sleeves and went over to wash her hands.

"Okay, Mees Libby, you weel cook." She found a big gunnysack and tied it around Libby's waist for an apron. "Lupe, you tell Mees Libby all you do and why you do it. I choose you 'cause you never stop talking." She grinned at her niece to lessen the sting of her words.

Lupe laughed. "I tell you what I learn from Meester Kirk. 'I think the pot is calling the kettle black.'" Everyone laughed, and Lupe began to show Libby how to cut up an onion. Libby was enjoying herself, but she didn't know onions made a person cry.

Conchita said, "Mees Libby, if you breathe through open mouth, not nose, when you cut the onion, you no cry. We making the lunch now and almost feenish. If you wheeshing to learn, after lunch we making the deener and you halp. The secret to the cooking ees you cook, and the spices, uhmm, they make eet so good, of course the right amount of spices."

Kirk and Maggie walked into the kitchen, and Maggie gave Libby a hug. "I've been exploring with Kirk as a guide. This place is fantastic! What are you doing, Libby? Are you cooking? Is that an apron?" Before Liberty could reply, Matthew walked in.

"Where've you been, Kirk? I needed help, and you said before the coffee break you'd be out there to hold the wires."

Kirk replied laconically, "I was with Maggie."

Matthew's lips thinned, and he turned to hide his anger, but Conchita and Liberty saw it.

"I'm to blame, Mr. Bannister," Maggie said quickly. "I kept asking questions. I should've known he had work to do."

"Never mind. Diego came out and helped. Is lunch ready, Conchita?"

"Si, Meester Bannister, ees nearly ready. You tree go wash, an' eet be ready pronto." She clapped her hands, and Lupe and Luce started setting the large oak table. They set it for four.

Libby said a little shyly, "I'd like to eat when you eat, Conchita."

"Nooo, you weel eat now." There was apparently no arguing with Conchita, and she put her hands on her hips.

Libby could see the stubborn glint in her eyes and quickly acquiesced. "All right, I will eat now." She helped set the table.

Matthew returned to the kitchen first and noted the apron on Libby. He smiled as he spoke. "I didn't know I had a new cook. Welcome to Rancho Bonito."

Libby returned the smile. "Mr. Bannister, if I cooked for you, you'd be as skinny as a starved cat. I don't know how to cook, but I want to learn."

Conchita said, "I tell her, Meester Bannister, she cannot cook here, she ees guest. But she get down on her hands and knees, and she beg me to let her cook. 'Pleeese,' she say, 'Oh pleeese, Conchita, let me cook.' So what I do, Meester Bannister? I cannot have her down on a floor like that." Then Conchita laughed, a burst of explosive laughter that had everyone else in the room laughing.

Kirk and Maggie joined them, wanting to know what everyone was laughing about. "Oh," said Conchita, "ees nothing. You seet now an' eat. Mees Libby, she want to eat with me, but I tell her no, she must eat with you."

Matthew was surprised. First, because he didn't know she went by Libby. It had a nice friendly sound to it. The second surprise was that she wanted to eat with the hired help. He smiled inwardly at his huge mistake in thinking he would be hosting a couple of uppity Bostonians. He was glad to hear Madam Bouvier was friendly. He wondered if she wore her hair down often. It was beautiful, like gleaming copper.

Libby took a bite. "What's this? It's delicious."

"It's *tacos*," Kirk said. "It's nothing special, just tacos."

"It's delicious." Libby's green eyes sparkled as she took another bite. The sauce was making her eyes water because of its hot tang. "What's in the tomato sauce? Whew, that's hot!"

Everyone except Maggie started laughing. She hadn't started eating yet. She stared at Libby, wearing a muslin dress with her hair hanging down. *She looks as if she belongs here! That's amazing! My employer...new friend looks as if she's always lived here...as if she truly belongs. She looks very tired but happy. I've never seen that look before, not ever, in Boston.* Thinking of Libby and all the heartache she'd had over the years, Maggie's eyes teared up.

"Eet's the jalapeno pepper. We call eet salsa." Conchita laughed. "Look, Mees Maggie ees crying too."

Maggie took a big bite of taco to cover the fact that she hadn't even started eating yet, but it was a mistake. The salsa was hot—very hot. She was embarrassed as she started to choke. She walked out the open French doors into the courtyard. She was wondering if she could spit the whole mess out of her mouth, when Conchita came up and held out the peelings bowl in front of her. She spit it out and coughed and coughed. Her tears flowed in earnest now, and she wiped her eyes on her sleeve and started laughing...laughing at herself for making such a spectacle, laughing that they all thought initially that she had teared up because of the salsa, laughing that she really had teared up from the salsa, laughing for the joy of seeing Libby's look of contentment.

Conchita laughed too, with relief that this girl could laugh at herself. No fake snobbery here. She thumped Maggie's back and told her to raise both arms over her head.

Conchita wanted to plug her nose. *Whew, thees girl! She needs a bath.* And she laughed again. Lunch was a merry time with jesting and good conversation.

Matthew turned to Libby. "Are you up to going over to take a look at your husband's property?"

My property, Libby corrected him in her head. "Yes...yes, I'd enjoy that. I've been looking forward to seeing it for quite some time." She nodded to Kirk and Maggie. "You're welcome to come too, if you wish."

"Thanks, but no thanks. I've neglected some chores this morning." Kirk winked at Maggie.

Maggie beamed at him. "I'd love to come. We've been dreaming for some time about it, and now it's a reality."

"There's not much to look at, but it's in an excellent location and the view is beautiful."

"What do y'mean beautiful, Matt? It's just rolling hills with scrub oak and quite a few rocks, if you'll remember. There's a few eucalyptus trees scattered here and there." He looked at Liberty. "Some Australians introduced the eucalyptus and planted huge groves of it in the Sacramento Valley. They thought it could be used for railroad ties because it grew fast. It didn't work out though. The trees have to be really mature to not warp and twist when they're cut. Some of the trees were planted as windbreaks for orange groves. Some of them border your one hundred sixty acres on the west side. I suppose that was because sometimes the wind will pick up from the Pacific Ocean. We border your south side. Your property's due north of us, and yours and our eastern border is the Napa River. I guess you're right, Matt. It is beautiful, and I'm finished with my soliloquy." He took a long drink of water.

Chapter XIV

Better is the end of a thing than the
beginning thereof: and the patient in spirit
is better than the proud in spirit.
ECCLESIASTES 7:8

"**Mees Libby, you learn to cook** another day. We making the *enchiladas de pollo…enchiladas* made with the cheeken. You weel like the deener we prepare. The *tortillas* are specialty of Luce. You go look at the new property." She began removing plates, and both Maggie and Libby helped clear the table. When they were finished, they went to the bedroom.

"I envy you—you've already bathed. I stink to high heaven. Maybe I should stay here and get cleaned up."

Libby quickly replied, "No, I think you should go too. You can help me decide if there's anything to be lived in over there." Matthew made her feel ill at ease, and she didn't care to be alone with him. "I need you to help me make plans." She started to twist up her hair, but Maggie grabbed the brush out of her hand and expertly swept it up, fixing it with the tortoiseshell comb.

"All right, but I've never felt so dirty in my entire life!" She giggled. "I think I almost made Conchita choke when I raised my arms up to stop choking." They came out of the bedroom laughing.

Libby hadn't realized she'd been so full of tension for years. She didn't have to put up a front, or be strong, or hide her feelings so much here. How relaxed and easy she felt. It was amazing. She didn't have to wonder what her husband or her father were conspiring about together. It was a wonderful feeling. *Thank You, Lord. Thank You.*

Matthew waited for the two women with the horses hitched to the wagon. He wondered what Madam Bouvier would make of the land. Kirk was right…it wasn't much to look at, but he loved it. He liked the feel of the earth in his hands. Planting the rootstock was hard work, but rewarding. It sure beat working behind a desk, which is what he'd done for several years. He'd always wanted to please Jess, and money was the way to her heart—he'd found that out soon enough. He quickly shut out the memory. He was going to get a bit of money when he wrote out those receipts and gave them to Madam Bouvier. Not only would he buy some rootstock, he could also buy more acreage just to the south of his property. The government was offering it for a dollar seventy-five an acre. A person was allowed to buy up to one hundred sixty acres. He sure wished he had that much. He'd double his holdings if he could get his hands on that kind of money.

The two women came out of the house together, still giggling. Matthew swallowed looking at the pair of them. They were gorgeous women—Miss O'Neill with her bright halo of red hair and Madam Bouvier with her shining coppery curls and winged eyebrows.

The day was beautiful and clear. No wind stirred the leaves on the orange trees. Blue skies hugged the hills, giving them an almost hazy look.

Matthew had come around and grasped Maggie's hand and then Libby's to help them up. Libby blushed when he helped her.

"Since you're afraid of falling off, Maggie, I'm sitting on the outside." She sat down abruptly on the outside edge, and Maggie sat next to Matthew.

As the wagon headed down the long driveway, Liberty looked at the rows and rows of grapes lined up like an army battalion. The vines stretched endlessly over rolling hills as far as the eye could see.

"Mr. Bannister, have you planted in every direction? Are you planting more rootstock? Do you have enough workers?"

"Yes." He grinned at her many questions. "I've planted almost my entire property. When you give me the money your husband owes me, I'll be able to buy some more rootstock. I've been buying from a man down south. His vineyard grows a grape that makes a wonderful Merlot. He also has another type of rootstock that he's made into a very light Chardonnay. I've just started buying the stalk for Chardonnay from him. Last year was the first year of production for Rancho Bonito. We kept very busy, and selling is slow. But once it catches on, more people will buy. It was a decent Merlot, but I've tasted better. I've found that a south hill planting yields a much better grape...more sunshine, I suppose. I've been reading everything I can get my hands on about growing grapes. And, yes, I have enough workers. There are migrants who come north just to work as they are needed, and after the season is over, they go back south."

Maggie asked, "What kind of trees are those in the distance?" She pointed up at the surrounding hillside. The trees lined the top of a hill as if they were sentinels.

"Those are the eucalyptus trees Kirk was talking about. They have a very distinct shape and smell. They also drop bark, leaves, and branches all the time."

The sky was cobalt, so blue it looked like a painting. Not one puff of cloud marred its perfection. A faint wind blew softly. It was beautiful and Libby, used to the bustle of the city, reveled in the stillness and beauty of her surroundings. A hawk spiraled lazily overhead. *Gorgeous, Lord. Thank You for this beautiful creation of Yours.*

The wagon went over a rise. "You see those stakes there? That's the end of my property and the beginning of yours."

Libby could tell the difference without the stakes, because Mr. Bannister's property had all been tilled at one time or another. The demarcation was quite evident. Matthew stopped the wagon, and the three gazed into the distance.

Liberty prayed silently, *Father God, I can say this is my property, but all I have is Yours. Lord, I praise You for the beauty, and I pray this ground be dedicated to You. I declare right now, in the name of Jesus, that this place be one of peace and joy and bring comfort to all who come here. Thank You, Father.*

Leaving Matthew's land that had been worked, the wagon bumped over ground that was rough, uneven, and strewn with rocks. It, too, was rolling hills like Matthew's. Where his land was tilled, hers was untouched, and grasses dotted with wildflowers waved in the slight breeze.

Libby spotted a structure.

So that's my house, she thought. *It's little better than a lean-to.* She swallowed her disappointment and knew with a sinking feeling that she and Maggie would be Mr. Bannister's guests for quite some time. *Well, at least I'm a landowner.*

It was a beautiful area, and she could see the eucalyptus trees in the distance. Probably some people would think it was barren except for the scrub oak that grew everywhere, but Libby was from the city and this was nature, and it was hers.

Matthew drove the wagon down the slope, stopping at the shack. Libby waited for him to help her down. Behind the lean-to was an area thick with scrub oak. It was a mass of tangled weeds and bushes. She walked straight into the little shack. It was just that, not a house but a shack. Looking up, she could see the place leaked and the bare boards were weathered and warped. She went back outside, looking around. She found the pump he'd put in. Gazing up the valley, she saw a pool of water and looked questioningly at Matthew.

"It's a hot spring. I can't see much use for it, so I staked this area for your husband."

She nodded, listening with half an ear. Libby shaded her eyes with her hand. Looking farther up the little valley, about halfway up the hill was a beautiful flat area. *That's where I'd want a house, right there tucked against the side of the hill. The front facing south to catch the morning light.*

"Thank you, Mr. Bannister, for bringing us out here. Do you think you can bear the two of us as guests until we can get a house built here? Miss O'Neill and I'd be happy to help with whatever jobs you'd like, and I could pay you some money for room and board." She, in truth, had no idea how much anything would cost. She realized how ridiculous it was that she had rarely handled money. Here she was twenty-nine years of age, and now she was supposed to figure out how much she had and what could be done with that amount. She was going to have to swallow some of her pride and some of her reserve and have a real talk with Mr. Bannister.

Matthew was surprised by her question and her offer to help. He'd thought when she saw the condition of the property, she'd turn tail and run back to Boston, to her life of comfort and ease. He scrutinized her closely, and she blushed under his gaze. He looked away and out over the hills for a minute.

When he looked back at her, the blush had subsided but the look in her eyes was that of a wounded animal. Did she think he'd taken a long time to answer because he didn't want them here? He'd been giving her a moment to recover.

He said slowly, "I honestly didn't think you'd want to stay…that you'd go back home when you saw the condition of the property." He noticed the quick look the O'Neill girl gave Madam Bouvier, but then her eyes slid away. He also noticed the blush was back in madam's cheeks.

Matthew went on to say, "You're welcome to stay as long as it takes. If we need the barns, we'll knock something up to keep your trunks dry. So for now, I guess you'll just be family. I'd like both of you to call me Matt or Matthew." He smiled at them but still wondered why Madam Liberty Bouvier would move out here.

Libby looked at him with a smile in her deep green eyes. "I suppose it isn't proper, but I'd like you to call me Libby, and I'm sure Miss O'Neill would prefer Maggie." She was relieved that they wouldn't be booted out and thankful for his hospitality.

"Mr. Bann—ah, Matthew"—she held out her hand to shake his —"thank you very much for being so generous. Maggie and I are both grateful and indebted to you. We'll do our best to not be a nuisance. Maggie will have to promise not to keep Kirk from his chores." She smiled most winningly.

"You're welcome…and both of you can stay for as long as you need."

Abigail was tired. It was an extremely cold crossing, and the days seemed to have merged. She had no idea what day it was. She'd lost count somewhere in the middle of the Atlantic. She certainly wasn't interested in being outside at the rail. She spent her time either in their cabin, which was amidships, or in the lounge.

Abby had packed for winter weather, as she'd known it would be cold on the ship and in England. She'd also packed for Florence, which would be a bit warmer. At least there'd be no freezing weather there. It wouldn't be this damp cold that cut like a knife right through one's clothes. Abby had decided that she was old enough to be done with cold, freezing winters. She'd tried to pack lightly, but winter clothing took more luggage space. Abby thought, with envy, of Liberty Bouvier enjoying the milder weather in central California.

Elijah found his wife knitting a sweater in their cabin. The stateroom walls were beautiful, lightly stained wood paneling trimmed in a darker wood. There were twin beds with feather duvets for covers. It reminded him of a trip they'd made to Bavaria, in southern Germany. The Germans would hang the duvets out their windows every morning to air out the feathers. Elijah watched Abby knit for a few minutes before he spoke. She had knit sweaters all the time for children at the Boston Orphanage. She'd stopped several years ago when she became so weak that even knitting tired her. Elijah sat in a chair opposite her, and they began to dialogue about finding Liberty Bouvier's father.

"He must be a deeply religious Catholic to be an oblate at the monastery." Elijah shifted his weight to get comfortable. "I'm very interested in meeting him. It is, in truth, interesting to me what a person becomes. Is it because of one's environment, or is it from one's parents? How much is Liberty Bouvier like her real father?"

"Oh, Elijah, you're such a philosopher. I'm interested in meeting him too, although I've never met Liberty Bouvier. I do know she can't be like the man she's spent twenty-nine years calling father. If the oblate is happily married and we don't say anything to him about Liberty, I think we should at least let Liberty know that Jacques Corlay's not her father. I believe she'd take comfort knowing her intense feelings of animosity aren't for her own flesh and blood."

"You're right, Abigail, my dear. It must be confusing for her to have this deep-seated acrimonious feeling for the man she believes is her own father. He's been nothing short of cruel to her. Her husband was Corlay's best friend, and I believe the two of them worked overtime trying to make her life a living hell when they weren't too busy ruining honest men."

"I know this is a change of subject, darling, but I've been wondering… when are you going to retire?"

Elijah looked at his wife, shocked that she was thinking such a thing. "Abigail, being a lawyer is my life's work. It's what I do! Why would I even think of retiring yet? I love my work."

Abby looked at her knitting, realizing she'd dropped a stitch two rows earlier. She began unraveling the two rows of neatly done stitches.

"Well, Elijah, I suppose it has something to do with me being tired of cold weather. I also keep thinking about that dream you had of us opening a mission together. You couldn't remember what the mission was for, but I keep thinking about it. It's strange how, when you keeping thinking about something, it seems more and more plausible. I can't seem to stop thinking of it as real."

Elijah looked at Abigail in amazement. He'd forgotten that dream. He'd been so overwhelmed by her healing that it had driven the dream out of his mind. As she'd related it back to him, he could understand her fixation on it. It had been so vivid.

Elijah began to pace the small space of the cabin. "I'll start earnestly praying about this. I don't want to miss something the Almighty might have for us to do, but I need to be certain what His will is before I change our entire way of life. Liberty Bouvier will most likely come back to Boston when she finds she's inherited the entire estate."

"Elijah Humphries, this has nothing to do with Liberty Bouvier," Abigail said firmly.

The rest of the crossing went pretty much the same. They hit a bad winter storm, and Elijah was seasick for a half day. He felt miserable losing all his breakfast and then dry heaving. Abby wiped his face with a cold cloth and kept quiet. When the storm abated, so did the sickness, but it left in its wake a raging headache. He lay on his berth resting and sleeping almost all that day.

Abigail looked out through the little porthole and saw the waves had calmed and the wind was blowing but only fitfully. The rain beat a steady tattoo on the deck and rails of the steamship. The cabin felt snug and warm. When evening came, the rain had stopped. Elijah felt a bit weak but much better. Abigail found him some milk toast from a cook in the galley, and he ate it slowly.

"Did you know that the French have a jest about England inventing toast? It's that the English had to invent toast because it was the only way they could butter their bread in England's climate," Elijah said. He felt better than he had all day. He decided to take a short stroll to get some air, and Abby said she'd go too.

They walked the length of the ship, arm in arm. It was hard to hear each other, because the wind snatched the words out of their mouths. Smiling at each other, they enjoyed the buffeting wind to clear their heads. The walk was cold, but refreshing.

CHAPTER XXV

And I will be found of you, saith the LORD
JEREMIAH 29:14a

THEIR SHIP CAME INTO PORT on another cold, blustery day. The wind plucked at their clothing, and it felt bitterly cold with the damp of the Thames splashing whitecaps against the pier.

Elijah and Abigail felt wobbly—both knew it was called "sea legs." They had gotten used to the ship's roll and now needed to get their land legs back. They laughed as they leaned on each other.

"This must be what it feels like to be drunk." Abigail giggled. Elijah felt disoriented and tried not to lean on poor Abby. They claimed their bags and had a hansom cab take them to the Bull and Boar, an inn where they'd stayed years before. The rooms were safe, clean, and the food quite appetizing.

Elijah left Abby in the room and went out to purchase their passage to Florence. He wanted to waste no time and was lucky to book passage on a small steamer that would be leaving in three days' time.

They ate the inn's famous fish and chips and went to bed early. Elijah read, by the flickering lamp, the Bible he'd brought along. He was studying the second of Paul's journeys. Also, he read one chapter in Proverbs every day. There were thirty-one chapters, and so five times a year he read two chapters. He gained more wisdom every time he read them. It was the book he tried to follow in his life's journey. *So much wisdom in there,* he thought. He put the Bible down and blew out the lamp. He was weary. He rolled over, and spooning his body around his sweet Abby, Elijah slept.

The next day, they did the tour. They viewed the Tower of London first. *What a gruesome history this country's had—kings murdering their own children, kings beheading their wives, kings bleeding the people dry of monies, and yet, wasn't that the history of any country that had age behind it? If the United States ever turns its back on God, our country will disintegrate,* Elijah thought. After studying history and law, he knew the whole American system was built on God's laws.

England might have a bloody history, but it was also the leader of the world. Elijah knew the biggest contributor of the United States Constitution was the famous Magna Carta. England had also brought enlightenment and good to many lands that were oppressed.

"You know, Abigail, they say the sun never sets on the British Empire. It's because of the vast number of countries under their control, such as Hong Kong and India. England is truly an interesting country, and London has enjoyed hundreds of years of history." Elijah and Abby enjoyed the day. They walked a good deal, and both were exhausted by the time dusk fell over the busy city.

Two days of touring London and then they were on a steamer heading to Florence, Italy.

After looking over her property, Liberty worried all the way back to Rancho Bonito. *I don't want to tell Matthew Bannister I'm a widow. I don't know him, but I sense a deep-seated anger in him. I don't want to tell him I know nothing about money either. I've never trusted a man, except Elijah. I don't even know how much Elijah has given me, nor how much that amount is worth. I'm not going back to Boston, that's for sure. Perhaps I'm going to have to level with Mr. Bannister after all.*

Liberty was in a total quandary as to how she should proceed. She felt so uncomfortable around him. It was kind of him to open his home to them. Libby was quiet all the way back to the Rancho as she prayed silently for God to make his perfect way known to her.

Maggie chattered the whole way back, Matthew listening with half an ear, responding only if necessary. He, too, was wondering what was going on.

They pulled up in front of the Rancho, and Matthew lifted them both down. As they entered the front door, Conchita handed Libby an unopened telegram. Libby thanked her, knowing it must be from Elijah, but she didn't intend to open it in front of the others.

"It smells wonderful in here. Is it your *enchiladas?*"

"Si, Mees Liberty." Conchita smiled widely. "We make the guacamole and the salsa and many good things we eet. You weel like what your mouth tells you."

"It does smell good." Maggie's nose twitched. "I want to enjoy it, so I think I'll have a bath first. Where would I draw water for heating?"

Conchita said, "Luce, she feel the tub for you with hot water, Mees Maggie."

"That's wonderful…thank you for having it ready for me." Maggie left hurriedly to take advantage of hot water, looking forward to being clean again.

"I believe I'll lie down for a few minutes. I'm still quite tired." Liberty walked down the hall knowing two pairs of eyes followed her exit.

Once in her room, she tore open the telegram. The message read:

HOPE ALL IS WELL STOP
UNLIMITED FUNDS AVAILABLE STOP ELIJAH

She reread it, beginning to cry. *Oh Lord, sometimes it seems we wait forever for Your answer. I've prayed and prayed that my father could be a man I understand, a man I could love and who would love me. Father, you know that I prayed that even before I came back from boarding school, and yet he's so evil. I prayed for Armand to be a man I could love, and yet he hardened his heart against me, never loving me. Now, I have prayed about a need of how to proceed here, and look at this. I asked for help not more than half the hour past, and already my answer is here. How did Elijah get the funds, Lord? Not from my father, I'll wager. Thank You for answering my prayer so quickly.*

She slipped the message into the flyleaf of her Bible, wiping away her tears. She took off her shoes and undressed. She'd foregone her corset and had only her chemise to deal with after taking off the muslin dress. She slid between the cool sheets. Hearing Maggie splashing in the tub, she heard her singing, but the sounds faded as she slipped into sleep.

Maggie sang softly to herself, enjoying the bath immensely. She thought about Libby and wondered what was in the telegram. *My, this bath is wonderful. Life is certainly different not being a maid. In all my life I don't remember anyone getting my bath ready, except my mother when I was young.* She hummed to herself. *This is the life. I hope Libby never wants to go back to Boston.*

Maggie looked forward to seeing Kirk. *He's quite good looking and so easy to talk to.* She leaned back to soak a few minutes and closed her eyes. *I need to be careful. I don't know the ways of men, and I certainly don't want to be a nuisance or think there's more to this than just being friends.*

By the time Maggie was finished and dressed, Libby was awake and dressed also. If she took a nap, it was only for about ten minutes. If perchance she slept for an hour or so, she felt groggy and tired, whereas if she slept just ten minutes, she felt totally refreshed. Libby called it a "snap."

She tapped on Maggie's door. "Come on in, Libby." Libby entered, sitting down on a comfortable chair upholstered in a deep apricot color. Maggie was combing out her beautiful red hair. Liberty saw the bloom in her cheeks. *What a beautiful woman Maggie's become.*

"I'm curious, Libby, who sent you the telegram—or is it private?"

Libby blushed. "I don't quite understand it myself. It's from Elijah. I guess I have enough money to build or do whatever I want. It was pretty cryptic. Maggie, I have to tell you, after looking at that shack, I felt very depressed. I didn't know what I was going to do. I've never handled money. I don't know how much things cost, and I didn't even know if I had enough to pay Matthew for all his help in the past. I don't suppose what he invested was all that much, but I'm certain having someone come in to dig a well wasn't cheap. He also had to file for the property and pay for someone to survey what he had staked off. Also, he did use lumber and his own labor to build the shack. I'm quite certain that was for appearances only, to show improvements had been made on the property. Oh, Maggie, when I thought of all that, I felt we were going to be in a heap of trouble. I don't even know how much money I have or even if we have enough to pay for tickets back to Boston."

"Back to Boston! Why in the world would we want to do that? We just got here!"

"I know, I know. I'm simply making the point that we could have been helpless. While we were riding back from the property, I prayed that God would make his will known to me. It wasn't one half hour later that my prayer was answered, in the form of that telegram. I praise God that He knew I needed some real help before I did."

"That's just a coincidence, Libby."

"No, Maggie, it's not. I don't believe in coincidences. I know that God watches over me. And the more dependent I am upon Him, the more I see His help and care over me." With that statement, she started toward Maggie's door to the hall.

"I love you, Maggie." She pulled the door shut after her.

Maggie stood there, brush in hand, thinking about what Libby had said.

Is it possible that God is that intimate? I've always thought of Him as way out there, a stern God who just waited for you to do something wrong and then He'd get you good. Could it really be true that He loves each person as much as Libby keeps telling me?

Florence, Italy, what a glorious city! Abigail thrilled to the sights and sounds. *Lord, thank You...thank You for letting me enjoy this. How I rejoice that You love me, that You healed me, and I pray that I can be a delight to You.*

Abby was thankful to be in a city of history, beauty, and warmth. Spires stretched fingers heavenward and the Piazza del Mercato Vecchio was filled with people bargaining at the vendors' stalls. The intense colors of their wares, scarves, brightly colored satchels, carpets, blankets, and pots and pans hung from ropes strewn across the fronts of the stalls. There were stalls laden with every kind of vegetable, and others with fruit. The chatter of voices, the busy aliveness of the marketplace, lifted the spirits of the weary travelers.

They found a hotel just off the main square. It was Monday, the afternoon beginning to fade. Late that morning they'd disembarked the steamer and boarded the train for Firenze, or Florence, thankful to be finished sailing. If they couldn't find the oblate, they would do some sightseeing.

Elijah decided they should rest up before locating the monastery. He began unpacking some of his necessities.

Abigail was lying on the bed, crosswise, her feet dangling off the bed. "I've been reading some literature about Florence. Did you know the Badia Church is the oldest monastery in Florence? This article says the foundations date back to 978. Just think, Elijah, it's over five hundred years older than when Columbus discovered America! My goodness, The Marquis of Tuscana was the founder of many Benedictine abbeys in Florence, and his tomb is in the Abbey of Badia. Even if we don't find Mr. Liberty, we shall have a holiday. It's amazing how many buildings are made of marble. It's a beautiful city." Abigail was warm and happy.

Later that evening, the couple walked to the Arno River and ate at a small restaurant near the Ponte Vecchio, Florence's oldest bridge. It was lit, making a beautiful sight with the water reflecting the bridge's lights. They ordered a dinner of scampi, enjoying a leisurely meal. As they strolled hand in hand down the cobblestone streets back to their hotel, they looked into shop windows. Many of the shops had apartments above them where windows were dressed in lace curtains and lights glowed. Back at their hotel, they climbed the wide stairs together. The bathroom was located at the end of the hall, so Abby went first to prepare for bed.

Once they were settled, Elijah read a portion of First Peter to Abigail. He read a chapter in Proverbs to himself before blowing out the candle.

The next day dawned clear and bright. Elijah had been awake for some time thinking of how entrenched into the affairs of one Liberty Alexandra Corlay Bouvier he'd become. Jacques Corlay would never be out of prison, and Hans Holbein would hang for the murder of Libby's husband. What would her real father be like? He lay still, not wanting to awaken Abby. He prayed about many things, but most of all, he was full of praise for the Almighty God. What a miracle it was, healing his Abby. He lay thinking of all the Psalms he'd memorized dealing with praise, and he whispered them to his God.

Abigail heard Elijah whispering praise. She kept her eyes closed, echoing his praise in her heart. Finally, they both arose. Looking out the window at the skyline, they saw many red roofs topping marble and stone. They picked out a slender, pointed bell tower as the best most beautiful spire, rising into the sky. They didn't know it, but it was Badia Fiorentina's bell tower. They would shortly be at the doors of the abbey.

Enjoying fragrant coffee with eggs and sausages for breakfast, Abby basked in the warmth of the sunshine streaming through the window. Elijah asked the waiter for directions to the Badia Fiorentina. Helpfully, he took them out to the street, pointing to the spire they had admired earlier.

"*Badia, si, Badia si, Via Del Proconsolo.*" They were delighted it wasn't far. Thanking him, Elijah and Abby walked the distance, realizing it lay at the heart of the city. Elijah held Abby's hand and squeezed it in excitement. The day was bright with sunshine, and although it wasn't warm, it was pleasant. They came up to some old impressive-looking doors. There was a bellpull, and Elijah gave it a tug. Hearing the bell chime deep within the ancient walls, they waited. After a few minutes, a monk came to the doors, and they asked to see the abbot. He beckoned them to come in with his hand but did not speak. He pointed to a marble bench, and the couple sat down to wait. The monk left them, walking smoothly with measured steps, no sign of hurry in his demeanor. He returned fairly shortly and led them down a dim hallway. Tapping on a huge wooden planked door, they heard a voice from within.

"*Entrate, prego.*" They were ushered in by the monk, who stood quietly by the closed door. The atmosphere was one of peace and tranquility. The abbot greeted them, saying he was Giovanni Petroni. His hair was thick and white. Long indentations marked both cheeks. The habit he wore was faded and worn, his greeting softly spoken. He seemed gentle and kind.

"What can I do for you, sir ?" He looked intently at Elijah when he began to speak, as if he were concentrating on the words or translating them in his head. Elijah cleared his throat, as he was wont to do when nervous.

"Sir, my wife and I are glad to make your acquaintance. This is Abigail, and I am Elijah Humphries. We're from Boston, Massachusetts. I'm a lawyer, and we are in search of a man we believe is connected to this monastery. We believe he is an oblate here. His name is Alexander Liberty." At the mention of the name, the abbot's head jerked up.

"You are looking for Alexander Liberty. May I ask why?" The abbot looked at them expectantly.

"He's still connected here then—he's alive?"

"Oh yes, yes, he's very much alive." The abbot smiled slightly as he spoke. "Now, can you please tell me why you wish to see him?"

"We might not wish to see him," Elijah answered with a smile.

The abbot looked at them with surprise in his eyes, and it spilled over into his voice.

"You are telling me you came all this way to find a man, and after finding him, you might not wish to see him?"

Elijah replied, "Yes, that's correct. You see, if Alexander Liberty is married, we'll not want to see him. It is not our intention to disturb the man or upset his life. If, however, he's not married, we'd like to see him."

The abbot looked closely at Elijah, seeing honesty and openness in his eyes and face. He could sense the goodness in this man. He looked at his wife. She looked like a nun to him. Her face glowed with inner peace and contentment. He'd seen a number of Americans over the years and had never seen this look in any of them. It was the peace of Christ, and the abbot recognized it.

"I do not need to know the reason, but our Alexander Liberty is a good man. He's not American, you understand—he's British. He's hard working and dedicated to the cause of Christ. He labors here, and he also helps with the orphanage. No, he's not married. I know his past, but it's not for me to share with you. Come, you may see him. He's here now."

Chapter XXVI

ELIJAH AND ABIGAIL FOLLOWED THE ABBOT out into the hall, proceeding opposite the way they had come in. They entered a large courtyard. It was full of laughter. Children were everywhere, laughing and running, shouting to one another. There were several adults, all in habits except one man. Elijah drew in his breath and expelled it in surprise. He would've known this man was connected to Liberty if he'd seen him on a street without knowing who he was. It was uncanny! It was Libby's face, aged at least twenty years and, of course, masculine, but definitely her face.

The abbot said, "If you care to wait a few minutes, the children will be going back inside for classes, and Mr. Liberty will be free."

"Yes, yes," Elijah said. "We'll most definitely wait." They watched the children play, but Elijah could not take his eyes off Alexander Liberty. It was unbelievable, the likeness so unmistakable. Elijah began praying about how he should talk to this man. He asked God for guidance. A bell rang deep in the recesses of the building and the children screamed, laughed, and scrambled, running out of the courtyard ahead of the monks.

Only Alexander Liberty was left, the courtyard suddenly empty and quiet except for the echoes of children's voices as they ran down the stoned corridor.

The abbot said, "Alexander, do you have some time? There are people here who wish to speak to you."

"Yes, of course." His British accent was evident in his well-modulated voice. Alexander Liberty walked over to them. He wore a white shirt open at the neck, with ballooning sleeves gathered at the wrists. He was quite thin and yet had a look of strength about him, his face a replica in the shape of his daughter's.

"Alexander Liberty, this is Mr. and Mrs. Elijah Humphries. They are from the United States and would like to talk with you. You're welcome to use my office. The chairs there are the most comfortable."

Alexander Liberty looked with interest at the two people in front of him. He looked openly and curiously. He liked what he saw in their eyes and held out his hand.

"Welcome to Badia Fiorentina," he said, smiling a Liberty smile. He held out his hand and shook both Elijah's and Abigail's hands. His teeth were even and startling white in a darkly tanned face. His wavy hair, a coppery red, was sprinkled with gray. His eyes crinkled at the corners, and dark lashes fringed a pair of beautiful, clear gray eyes rimmed by a darker gray. His look was direct but questioning.

Elijah cleared his throat and said, "Mr. Liberty, we'd really like to talk to you for a few minutes, if you don't mind."

"That is fine with me," Alexander said smoothly. "Please follow me. We'll take the abbot up on his offer."

He led the way back to the abbot's office and offered them the most comfortable chairs. He sat down on a wooden one facing the pair of them. He smiled encouragingly, as he could see Mr. Humphries was very nervous.

"I'd offer you some refreshment, but it's not mine to give. So what is it you wished to speak to me about? Is it about the orphan children you just saw?"

Elijah cleared his throat. "No, no, it's not, Mr. Alexander. We came because we'd like to talk just a bit about your past."

Alexander stared in surprise, his look a bit wary.

"I am a lawyer, and I found this in a secret compartment of a desk." Elijah reached inside his coat pocket, removing the letter written so many years ago. He'd replaced the letter into its original envelope and could see that Mr. Liberty recognized it immediately.

"Yes, I wrote that letter to Violet Ann Corlay many years ago." His voice had softened to almost a whisper.

"It's my belief, and I might add this is purely conjecture, Mr. Liberty, that Violet never received the letter. I believe it was intercepted by her husband, Monsieur Corlay. Perhaps it arrived and was put on the salver in the front hall, but just recently, it was found in the secret compartment of a desk. Violet had no knowledge there was such a letter."

Elijah handed the letter to Mr. Liberty.

Alexander took the letter and held it without opening it, as if he had memorized it contents so many years ago.

He spoke quietly. "I thought she loved me. It was such a blow that she married another man. It was unthinkable that she would do so. To this very day, I still feel sorrow that she didn't wait for me, that she didn't care enough. I heard, some years back, that she died, and I stopped praying for her when I received that word." He looked down at his calloused hands.

"I firmly believe, Mr. Liberty, that Violet loved you with her last dying breath."

Alexander's head jerked up. "How can you even say that?" he asked vehemently. "I wasn't gone two months and she was married!"

Elijah responded gently, "Do you remember your shrapnel wound within the month of arriving in Burma? Do you remember she'd had no word from you?"

"Yes, I remember," he said softly. "She could have waited though, couldn't she?"

"No…no, Mr. Liberty, she couldn't. You see, she was carrying your child."

Alexander was dumbstruck. His eyes widened and held Elijah's, but he wasn't able to speak at all, his mind quickly assessing what had been said.

"Mr. Liberty, you have a daughter who is twenty-nine years old. She's recently become a widow and believes a very unscrupulous man to be her father."

Alexander jumped up and started to pace the room. "How do you know this to be true? Perhaps she is, indeed, Monsieur Corlay's daughter."

"Now I've met you, there can be no doubt. I was just thinking that if I didn't know you and saw you on the street, I would have known that you were a close relative. Liberty Alexandra Corlay Bouvier is the spitting image of you except she has the greenest eyes I've ever seen."

"Liberty? Her name is Liberty Alexandra? Lord! Oh Lord, I receive your blessing! I can hardly credit this to be true. Where is she? Boston?"

"No, no, she isn't. It's a long story."

Alexander Liberty stopped pacing. "Could the two of you come to my humble abode and have luncheon?"

Abby finally was able to say something. She'd been caught up in a life-changing drama and felt emotionally drained.

"We'd love to come, Mr. Liberty," Abby said.

"I can scarcely credit this. No wonder Violet couldn't wait. I could have been dead for all she knew, and her carrying our baby." He said it with awe and amazement. "Please, come." And he led the way out of the monastery.

They spoke little on the walk to Mr. Liberty's house. All three were caught up in their own thoughts, the drama of the past half hour at the forefront of their minds. Alexander pointed out a few landmarks and sites. There was so much history there that one didn't have to go far to find it. He gestured to some of the old buildings and gave little anecdotes about their history.

Flowers exploded in a riot of color in front of the houses. Window boxes and little gardens were bursting with an array of pinks, yellows, purples, and reds. Butterflies flitted from flower to flower. There were ivy, geraniums, petunias, nasturtiums, and other flowers that bloomed year-round in the temperate climate. The entire scene was gorgeous.

Alexander lived within a mile of the monastery. They took several turnings, and Elijah hoped he'd be able to find his way back to their hotel later.

The oblate lived in a little whitewashed stuccoed cottage with a red tiled roof.

Alexander opened the door, calling out, "Company for lunch!"

A woman turned from the kitchen sink, and it was Elijah's turn to be shocked. His eyes widened. It was Libby in another forty years! Her face was lined and worn but still beautiful. Her hair was a striking white, and her son had inherited those spectacular gray eyes from her. Liberty had a grandmother!

Alexander Liberty said, "Mother, we have some American guests for lunch. They have quite an incredible story to tell you, and I want to hear the rest of it but not until we've eaten. Elijah and Abigail Humphries, I'm pleased to introduce to you the most wonderful mother, counselor, and friend in the entire world, Phoebe Alexandra Liberty."

Phoebe wiped her hands on her apron and held out both hands as she clasped Elijah's hand in one and Abby's in the other.

"I am quite pleased to meet you, and you're most welcome to have lunch with us. It's not often we hear English spoken, and it'll be a joy to hear it." She smiled warmly at them.

Elijah's mouth nearly dropped open at the Alexandra in her name. Of course, Violet would probably not have known—or would she? Her daughter's middle name was that of her true grandmother.

Abigail smiled back at Phoebe. "I am delighted to meet you."

Elijah bowed slightly in respect and addressed her, saying, "I cannot begin to tell you what a pleasure this is."

Phoebe looked questioningly at him and then over her shoulder as she heard the hiss of the stove.

"Goodness!" She hurried to the stove, her pot of potatoes ready to boil over. She swiftly took the pot off the heat.

"Please, allow me help. It smells delicious in here." Abigail's mouth began to water from the tantalizing smells that permeated the cottage. There was a roasting portion of beef in the oven, asparagus   and potatoes on the sideboard, and a pie sat cooling on the drainboard.

"I've nearly finished making lunch, but you could set the table. You may wash up over there." She nodded toward a large pan with an ewer of water beside it.

As Abigail washed up, she looked around.

Flowerpots were lined in the little window over the sink, bringing the garden inside. Gleaming copper pots hung on hooks over the large, thick cutting board standing by itself on four sturdy legs. The walls were whitewashed, and gaily colored pictures were arranged in an artful manner. Abby began to set the table, picking up four large, bright pottery plates and placing them on a small square wooden table that was covered by a bright checked cloth. She related to Phoebe about her crossing of the Atlantic and then of their trip down on the steamer to Florence.

When the food was ready, the four sat to eat. The oblate bowed his head and prayed over the meal. *"Benedic, Domine, nos et haec tua Dona quae de tua largitate sumus sumpture. Per Christum Dominum nostrum.* Amen."

Elijah, who had studied both Greek and Latin, said to Abby, "His prayer was, 'Bless us, oh Lord, and these thy gifts which we are about to receive from thy bounty through Christ our Lord. Amen.'"

Alexander asked, "Would you like a glass of this excellent Merlot?"

"Thank you, no. We'll just take water," Elijah said.

Alexander poured the Merlot for both his mother and himself. Phoebe poured water into Abigail and Elijah's glasses.

The conversation was easy and relaxed. Alexander Liberty told them of the long history of the abbey and how he came to be part of the life there. He was grateful to his mother for joining him on this venture.

"I was blessed with two sons," Phoebe related to them, "but our oldest son, Christopher, contracted lung fever and died at the age of fourteen. My husband followed three years later from a heart ailment when Alexander was fifteen. After he entered the army, he did a stint in Burma while I continued to live in London. Alexander stayed in the military for several years. We lived a few years in London after his separation from the army and then moved here. We've been here for, let's see, nearly eighteen years. My, how the time does fly by."

"Mrs. Liberty, was it difficult for you to leave your friends in London and move here?" Abby's eyes slanted over to Elijah, as if to say, Listen, Elijah.

Phoebe looked contemplatively for a moment. "Yes and no. I've a brother, Ian, who lives in Scotland, and we still see each other regularly. I had friends in London, especially women, that I met at charitable functions. I'd also had people with whom I went to dinner or the theater. I don't miss them particularly. I do have two very close friends who were very difficult to leave. We have our faith in common and a heart bond that even distance and time has not been able to erase. The two friends in London are lifetime friends. We write one another regularly. Once in a very long while I'll go visit them for a fortnight or so, or they'll come visit me. Once we're together, the time apart seems negligible, as if we've never been away from each other. The most important thing in life besides my relationship with God is my son. I moved here because he's so dear to my heart. He has no close relative other than me. I wanted to support and be near him." She reached over and patted Alexander's hand.

Phoebe smiled that beautiful engaging smile that looked so like Liberty. Elijah was listening closely, knowing Abby was wanting to make the move to California. He loved his practice and the men he worked with. *I can't even imagine giving it all up. Lord, I'm going to need Thy total direction on this. I don't want to miss something Thou hast planned for Abby and me.* He kept praying about it, but he needed assurance that it would be in alignment with the Almighty's will.

CHAPTER XXVII

He that dwelleth in the secret place of the most High
shall abide under the shadow of the Almighty.
I will say of the LORD, He is my refuge and my fortress:
my God; in him will I trust.
PSALM 91:1-2

THE MEAL WAS DELICIOUS, the gravy perfection. Phoebe was an excellent cook. They ate heartily, except Alexander, who kept toying with his food.

"What's the matter with you, Alexander? Why aren't you eating?" When Phoebe saw his eyes full of tears, she was totally perplexed.

"Mother, these two dear people have brought us the greatest gift we could ever ask for in this entire world!" Phoebe looked at Elijah and Abigail, even more bewildered than ever.

"What are you talking about, son? What gift? I see nothing." Alexander gestured to Elijah to relate to his mother what had been told him earlier.

Elijah cleared his throat. "Madam, it is with the greatest pleasure that I tell you that you are a grandmother these past twenty-nine years." Phoebe looked dumbfounded. The blood drained from her face, and she looked at Elijah as if he were out of his mind.

"How can this be? What are you saying? Me, a grandmother?"

"Mother," said Alexander, "Mother, I never told you that Violet and I had been together, that we'd been intimate. I never told you because she married someone else so quickly after I left for the war. The reason she married was because she was carrying our child. I have a daughter!"

Phoebe looked at the couple who had come from America and said flatly, "I don't believe it. Why have you come here like this with some cock-and-bull story to dig up the past?"

Abigail said gently, "It's true, Mrs. Liberty. It's true."

Elijah added, "I found a letter hidden in a secret compartment of a desk, one your son had written to Violet so many years ago. Violet married because she was carrying Alexander's child and hadn't heard from him once he went to Burma. She—"

"That's because he was wounded and had amnesia!" Phoebe interrupted him. "She could've waited for my son to come home, couldn't she?"

"No, she hadn't heard from him. For all she knew, he could be dead. She was pregnant, madam. She could not afford to waste time. I can assure you that Liberty Alexandra Corlay Bouvier is, in truth, your granddaughter. The Liberty look is unmistakable. In time, she'll look just as you today. She's a beautiful woman, enduring much at the hands of her father and husband, who's now deceased. For the first time in her life, she's free."

Alexander bowed his head in remorse for the past. Phoebe threw her apron over her face and began to cry.

"She looks like me? Her name is Liberty Alexandra? Oh, what news you have brought! I can hardly credit what you're saying. How can you be sure she is not...what was his name? Monsieur somebody's child... I had to write Alexander the news that Violet had married. Do you truly think she looks like me? You have not only news, but life itself!" She raised her eyes heavenward and said, "Oh Lord, how can I thank You for the blessing of family... Thank You, Lord, thank You."

She pulled the apron down and asked, with tears streaming down her face and her voice quivering hopefully, "Does...does she have children?"

"No, no, she doesn't. It's a very long story, but the short version is that her husband was murdered just a few short weeks ago. He and Monsieur Corlay, whom she believes to be her father, were both evil men of the worst ilk. Monsieur Bouvier was murdered, and Monsieur Corlay has just been sentenced to life imprisonment. Libby knows nothing about Monsieur Corlay's sentence. She's gone to California, which is on the other side of the United States from Boston. She traveled with a servant who's become her friend. Her late husband cut her out of the entire estate, which, I might add, is quite substantial. She was willed nothing except a property in the state of California."

"Libby," said her father. "Libby—I like that." And he smiled through his tears.

Libby sat in the comfortable great room, marveling that every chair in the house was comfortable, made to enjoy. A suet ball covered with seed hung from a tree close to the window. There were several birds clinging to the ball, but many were pecking at the ground under it. She didn't recognize some of them. Loving the freedom of not having to be prim and proper, she wore no corset and her legs were curled up underneath her. Conchita had given her a pair of toeless espadrilles, which lay on the floor. She was sewing a split skirt for herself. Several women she knew in Boston had worn them for riding astride. As she sat there, she thought back over the past few weeks.

Liberty and Maggie had been at Rancho Bonito for more than a month. Just a few days after their arrival, it'd been Christmas. She and Maggie had been so busy with all their traveling that it had completely slipped their minds. Libby had rummaged through a couple trunks and found a small lithograph she'd always treasured of a vineyard in Tuscany. It depicted a few men and women harvesting grapes. She'd wrapped it for Matthew. She'd also found a soft yellow shawl for Conchita and two decorated combs for Luce and Lupe. For Maggie she got out a gray watered-silk dress and let out the waist. After she discovered he liked to lasso everything, she'd cut a length of the new rope for Kirk. Thinking for a while what she could give Diego, she decided on one of the shovels. She'd also dug out handfuls of the different nuts, filling a dish with a variety of them. She did the same with the dried fruits. Unpacking the handguns, she put them into her room along with some of the bullets.

When Christmas Day came, she surprised everyone with her gifts. Luce and Lupe exclaimed over the hair combs. Conchita loved the shawl and hugged Libby. Maggie was ecstatic over having a new dress. Kirk kept fingering the rope, expressing gratitude for it. Libby had loved Diego's response. He'd kissed the handle of the shovel, and turning it, he'd wrapped ribbon around the blade and danced with it as if it were a woman. They had all laughed. Matthew had opened his gift slowly and looked at the picture. She wondered at first if he even liked it, but when he looked at her, she knew he did. His eyes were warm and a little misty. He thanked her quietly.

Under other gifts was a small one for her from Matthew. She opened it and found a small green peridot brooch. It was a lovely piece, her birthstone, and nearly matched her eyes. Her eyes teared up, and she thanked him in a whisper, her voice choked with emotion. She'd never, since her mother died twelve years before, had a gift that was thoughtfully chosen. It touched her that a man could be so thoughtful.

As she sat in the great room, she blushed thinking about what had happened after they had all opened their gifts. Everyone headed for the kitchen, but she'd gone to her room to put away her few gifts. As she returned from her room, heading for the kitchen, Matthew had been standing, waiting for her in the wide hallway. He had grabbed her, drew her close, and planted a tender kiss on her mouth. As she pulled away, shocked at his behavior, his blue eyes smiled into hers. He'd grinned, pointing upward. Someone had hung a bunch of mistletoe. Libby had laughed and shrugged her shoulders, but she'd hugged that memory to herself. His kiss had been gentle and warm as his lips had moved over hers. She'd never been kissed like that before.

It was now almost February, and life had settled into a routine. Matthew had given Liberty the receipts, and she'd counted out the money carefully to match each receipt. Mr. Humphries had been generous. She still didn't know if she had a lot of money or little left. She decided to ask Matthew how to go about getting funds from Boston out here.

Liberty felt as if she'd escaped from prison. The freedom here was unbelievable. She knew her heart had been burdened for years. She'd been afraid of her father. She'd been afraid of her husband. She had despised the life of self-service, so little generosity going out to others.

On Tuesdays, because she knew Armand would be gone early and home late, she'd risen early and gone to the Boston School for Deaf Mutes. She had learned to sign and helped not only children but adults to cope with their disability. It had been rewarding but left her drained by the end of the day. In some small way, Libby felt that she could identify with those people, perhaps because she'd never been allowed to express how she felt about anything.

Here at the Rancho, I speak, and people are interested. I wish I could start building. We can't impose on the good graces of Matthew forever. What a hard worker he is, toiling from sunup till sundown. It's refreshing that he labors at honest work and does it well. His Rancho Bonito is aptly named…Beautiful Ranch.

Matthew told her that once she began building, it wouldn't take long to have a habitable house. Labor couldn't begin until the rainy season subsided, which wouldn't happen for at least another month or two. She'd have to wait, but she'd already begun sending requisitions out for wood, stucco, sinks, tubs, so many things, as well as ordering specialty woods for cupboards, closets, and whatever else was needed. Sketching in her journal was helping her visualize how her house would look.

Meanwhile, Liberty was learning what she could about vineyards. She'd begun avidly reading books Matthew selected for her from the great room in the evenings. Later, on her own, she was reading small volumes on accounting. As yet, she couldn't make heads or tails of the money factor. She was beginning to wonder if she was a dunce when it came to money. She brought herself up short. *I'm not a dunce. I am uneducated, and therefore I will educate myself.*

Matthew came into the great room, interrupting her reverie. He poured himself a glass of port and sat in one of the deep leather chairs facing her. Libby had become much more comfortable with him. She no longer felt threatened by him. They'd come to enjoy some great conversations, and he was teaching her how to play chess. She could beat him sometimes at checkers. A few times Kirk, Maggie, Matthew, and Liberty played Parcheesi or whist after dinner. There was much laughter, fun, and competition on those evenings.

"What are you up to?" he asked. "Still reading about vineyards?"

"Yes, I am. Although just now, I've been sewing and bird watching… thinking how wonderful this all is. It's so relaxing and comfortable. My house in Boston doesn't have one stick of furniture that's comfortable."

"Why is that?" Matthew asked curiously.

Libby blushed. "Armand liked things formal. He commissioned a French designer to decorate our home."

"Oh." Matthew immediately picked up on her use of "liked." *Liked things formal? Why did she use past tense? Because she's here now? Has Jess tainted my opinion of all women? Am I always going to be distrustful?*

"I think furniture's impractical if it's uncomfortable. What's the purpose of it—to look at it or sit in it and enjoy the sitting?" He smiled at her.

Libby smiled back. "Then, Matthew, your furniture is very practical." She uncurled her legs. "I know I'm supposed to stay out of the kitchen before dinner tonight, but I'm hungry, and I'm going to see if there is anything I can do to speed things up." She slipped on her espadrilles and headed toward the kitchen.

Matthew sat there for a bit, sipping his port.

Her husband had chosen to hire someone to decorate, not caring, evidently, about her wishes. He'd known before she'd ever come out here that he disliked Bouvier, and the more he got to know his wife, the more he disliked the man. In probably less than three months, Libby and Maggie would be neighbors instead of house guests. It couldn't be soon enough for him. She was a married woman, and that was that. It was becoming difficult to keep feelings in check. He'd been trying his best not to like that woman so much. It was a fruitless endeavor any way he looked at it. He finished his port and went to the kitchen.

The days passed quickly. Each day seemed to bring new adventure or some new pleasure.

Maggie was having a wonderful time. Kirk had taken her to a dance at one of the neighbor's homes the night before. She'd worn the watered-silk dress Libby had given her for Christmas. She'd looked every inch a lady and enjoyed meeting the neighbors. The only one she'd taken an instant dislike to was a girl named Consuelo, who was Conchita's cousin.

She must pad her top, Maggie thought resentfully. *She's slinky.*

That was Maggie's term for it—slinky. She had glossy black hair and little, very white teeth that flashed when she talked or smiled, which was all the time. Maggie thought Consuelo's dress was almost like the woman's on the train. Her lips were carmined, Maggie was sure, and she'd flirted with every man there.

Disgusting, she thought. *Purely disgusting.*

Consuelo had flirted with Kirk, and he'd eaten it up. It made Maggie a bit more wary of him. She didn't want to give her heart away to someone who was going to break it.

Perhaps it'd been good for me to see his response to slinky Consuelo. I wonder if I'm the jealous type? I don't want some man who likes everyone in skirts.

Working extra hard at her chores, Maggie was trying to help Libby all she could. She hoped never to go back to Boston. It'd been shocking when Libby had talked about it right after they'd arrived. Maggie did extra things besides her chores to show her appreciation for a place to stay. She didn't want to be a bother or an extra mouth to feed. Biting her lip, she worried a bit about not having her own money. She'd given the money Mr. Humphries had given her back to Liberty. What if something happened to Libby? What would she do?

CHAPTER XXVIII

Thus speaketh the LORD of hosts, saying,
Execute true judgment, and shew mercy and
compassions every man to his brother
ZECHARIAH 7:9

MAGGIE WALKED INTO THE KITCHEN with a basket. "Here are the eggs, Conchita."

"Thank you, Mees Maggie. I no like to get eggs. I never like the pecking birds. No, not me." She was plucking one while she was talking. Maggie didn't mind getting the eggs at all, but she did mind plucking chickens.

"I don't mind gathering eggs, but that!" She pointed to the dead chicken. "That's not anything I ever want to do!"

"You muss learn thees one, Mees Maggie. Ees good to know."

"I'll just watch, thank you. It's nasty, and putting your hand in that thing and pulling out the entrails...ugh!"

Libby came into the kitchen and started expertly plucking the second chicken.

Matthew had just come into the house and leaned against the doorway to the kitchen, watching the three women, unobserved.

Maggie looked at Libby in total surprise. "Where did you learn to do that?"

"Right here, a couple weeks ago. I'm going to learn everything I can about cooking. I may have to be the chief cook and bottle washer when we live in our own home. Conchita's been graciously teaching me how to cook. I don't want to be only proficient, but good!" She grinned at the astonished Maggie. She added, "You know, Maggie, there're many things in life we don't like to do. I don't imagine Luce enjoys emptying the chamber pots or that Conchita really likes plucking chickens, but they do it because it needs to be done. There's a verse in the Bible that says, 'Work heartily as unto the Lord.' It means that in all we work to do, we do everything as if we are doing it for God. That's truly the best way, because then if it's not recognized by anyone here, our feelings aren't hurt. We've done it for God, who truly appreciates us. Our reward is in heaven."

Conchita nodded her head sagely and murmured, "*Por Dios.*"

"That's right, Conchita, for God." Libby added, "I love it here! I'm enjoying learning to cook, and I love not wearing a corset. I feel free. No one makes fun of me if I have an opinion, and here, I'm allowed to voice it. I have never in my entire life been so happy. I plan never go back to Boston, never!"

Matthew slipped back out of the kitchen doorway and went outside. *So that was interesting. Is she leaving her husband? Is he planning to join her here?* He was no closer to any answers than he'd been when he first laid eyes on the pair of them. Conchita had said Libby cried that first night she was here. Did her husband kick her out? Had Bouvier left her for another woman? It'd been known to happen. He couldn't see why anyone would leave someone who had so much personality, seemed so very nice, and was gorgeous to boot. Matthew was frustrated not having any answers.

Sigmund was enjoying life. He loved Matilda dearly. Since the wedding, they'd been sleeping in one of the guest bedrooms. It was so much nicer than the servants' quarters. He wondered what the future would bring. *Perhaps madam will end up selling everything, or perhaps she will come back and take up residence here in Boston.* He didn't have much hope of that. She'd not been happy here. Although Mr. Humphries had reiterated to him after the reading of the will that everything in the estate was reverting to madam, she'd not ever live in this house again, of that he was quite certain.

Sigmund had talked about going out west, but Matilda was now against it. She said she was a city girl, and the thought of living in the country frightened her. He thought about how smoothly everything was running.

He and Matilda were keeping everything clean and shipshape, but it seemed a fruitless endeavor when there was no master or mistress to serve. He carefully doled out the money Mr. Humphries had given him. Every week, Sigmund had budgeted for everything: money for food, money for salaries, coal, and incidentals; but he had also gone out on a limb.

He'd talked it over with Matilda, and she'd thought him wise for doing it. He'd taken fifty of the dollars from the salary he'd saved, money he'd been going to use for the wedding, and invested it in railroad stock. It was risky, he knew, and if he lost it, he lost it. He'd gone to Mr. Humphries' office to get his opinion, to see if it would be a wise thing to do, but Mr. Humphries wasn't back from his trip yet. So he'd gone ahead on his own and done it. So far, the stocks had continued to rise. He was excited that he'd done something only people of wealth did.

Sigmund decided he was also going to invest in the stock of the new Bell Telephone. He knew several people who were buying the telephones, at least so their servants had told him. He'd painstakingly read everything he could find about the telephone. It'd been exhibited at the World's Fair a few years ago. He thought that it was going to change the face of communication, and he wanted in on it. He wanted his children to have some of the benefits money brought. He knew money didn't bring happiness. *Look at madam and monsieur—they'd tons of money, but it hadn't brought happiness.* It did, however, make life easier. He wanted the assurance that if anything happened to him, Matilda wouldn't have to worry. He wondered again what was going to happen to the Bouvier manse.

Rufus paid Jacques Corlay, who was in jail, a visit. Jacques was scheduled to be transported in three days' time to New Bedford Prison. Rufus was his only visitor. Jacques was surprised that all his friends had left him. Well, he'd show them…he'd show them all. Rufus brought him food from the Bouvier kitchen. The guards checked everything out before it was allowed to go into the jail. Jacques was glad for Rufus' faithfulness. Once he got out, he'd reward the man generously.

The two men schemed together, thinking of a plan to get Jacques out. Rufus was to grease the palm of one of the guards who'd be willing to look the other way during the transport to the prison. Rufus was to find someone who could use a bit of extra cash.

If everything went according to plan, Jacques Bertrand Corlay would be a free man in three days. He could hardly wait. He had a large sum of money stashed in a metal box in the garden maze behind his house. He'd sneak in there during the night, and he'd be set. It was enough to last him for a long time. It always paid to have more than one plan up your sleeve.

Rufus invited him to sleep in his quarters over the stables at the Bouviers' manse, but he doubted very much that he'd do that. It was a place the police would look immediately. There were plenty of places in downtown Boston where a man could lose himself. He'd pay Rufus well though. Perhaps he might need his help in the future.

Corlay was going to find out where Libby had gone. She was the source of all his troubles, and he was going to make her pay. *I'll bet she and that lawyer have cooked up this way to get rid of me, and then they will have all the money. I'll make her wish she'd never been born.*

Elijah and Abigail decided they would leave Florence. They'd been there a week and plans had been laid.

Alexander Liberty would finish up his work in another week. Phoebe would pack. Once in England, they'd stay with Phoebe's friends for a fortnight before sailing to America. In Boston, they would be Elijah and Abby's guests. Once in Boston, plans would be made to travel out west. Both Alexander and Phoebe had plied Elijah with questions concerning Liberty. Abby wasn't able to help because she'd never met her. She did, however, share her physical healing from the Lord with them. Alexander had taken her to the abbot so she could share her miracle with him also. All three of them praised God for what he had done for Abigail.

Elijah tried his best to describe Liberty to her father and grandmother. His heart ached for all the years they'd missed in her life. He was thankful he had made the effort to come, to let them know about her.

Alexander told Elijah that Libby's eyes must be just like Violet's. He thought back. Violet's eyes had been incredibly green. He remembered now how he'd made up a silly ditty that was very trite, but then, he was young. He'd say to her:

Violet should have violet eyes. Instead her eyes are green.
Violet eyes for someone else, But green eyes for my queen.

He felt as if he were walking on air, finding out he had a daughter. He couldn't wait to see her. Excitement percolated in his veins. He had a child! He and Violet had a child! He couldn't seem to stop exclaiming to himself about it. *Liberty Alexandra, my child. Oh great God and Father of all mankind, I thank You. I give You praise. I give You glorious praise, for You are good!*

He felt as if he'd been exiled and was now returning home. Alexander was also happy for his mother. She'd never said so to him, but he knew she'd sorrowed in her heart that he'd never married, and she had never held a grandchild in her arms. Well, the grandchild was now a reality. How thankful he was.

As Alexander walked to the abbey to finish up some things he needed to do, he thought about his good friend. They'd become close. The abbot had said God's blessing was upon him. He'd never confessed to him that he had been intimate with Violet. He'd done penance when he was young and had been given the Sacrament of Reconciliation by a priest in London. He'd never felt the need to bring it up again.

When he arrived, the abbot welcomed him warmly. Alexander told him all about Violet and how he'd found out that he was a father. The abbot was very understanding. He was also wise.

"Years ago, Alexander, you repented of your sin and God forgave you. Being sorry for sin is not the same as repenting of it. One can be sorry for their sin and turn around and do it again. Repenting of sin, ah, that is a different matter. Repenting of sin means you turn away from it. It's an active rejection of it. You give it to Christ and let Him absolve you of it. I've heard many confessions. So many people are sorry for their sin, but there are those who are sincerely wanting to please Christ, and they repent of their sin. Christ has taken upon Himself the sin of the world. We do well, who allow Him to do it in our lives. I wish you every blessing of our Lord and Savior, Alexander Liberty. I will sorely miss you."

Alexander would miss him too, but he also knew that God had things for him to do.

Phoebe was chafing at the bit. God had given her many years of good health, but she could feel in her bones she was slowing down. She was seventy years old. She'd had Christopher when she'd been eighteen and

Alexander when she was twenty. Alexander must have had Liberty when he was…what…twenty-one? *A granddaughter! What a blessing.* She was eager to be on her way to America. She'd leave tomorrow if she could. Patience had never been one of her strong points. If one prayed for it, it seemed the Good Lord always tried it. She chuckled to herself. She prayed often for it. The more it was tried, the more she gained it. Now, however, she knew she was impatient. She'd lost too many years of enjoying a grandchild. She was sorry Liberty didn't have children of her own. It would have been a solace for her to hold a baby to her heart that was bone of her bone and flesh of her flesh. *Adam had a way with words,* she thought wryly. *Genesis 2:23, "And she shall be called woman." Woe to every man.* She chuckled again.

How blessed I am in my old age. I knew Alexander would never marry. He'd loved Violet with an undying love. Loyalty is strong among the Libertys. She remembered the days of passion and sweetness with Alexander's father, William. *Sweet William, I laughingly called him, as if he were a dianthus. There I am going off on another tangent. I do that a lot nowadays. Where was I…oh yes, loyal Libertys. Well, from what Elijah told me, my granddaughter also has that loyalty…she'd stuck it out with that crook of a husband. I think I'd probably have taken a frying pan to him and realigned his face a bit.* She chuckled again at her thoughts. She knew she was an independent thinker. It was probably because she'd been educated. She was originally from Scotland, and her father had insisted she have book learning. She not only had book learning, but she'd sat alongside her brother, Ian, learning Latin and Greek, and she had learned it better than he.

That's another thing—I probably should write Ian and let him know that he has a grandniece. What a wonderful thing family is. I wish we were leaving tomorrow.

CHAPTER XXIX

Behold, I am the LORD, the God of all flesh:
is there any thing too hard for me?
JEREMIAH 32:27

ELIJAH, RIDING IN HIS CARRIAGE, sat thinking over the past few weeks. John was taking him to George Baxter's, having sent a note ahead of time that he would be dropping by.

The last four weeks had passed in a whirlwind of activity. Abby was finished sightseeing, and they'd come home after just a total of three weeks in Europe, not counting sailing time. They'd gone up to Switzerland for a week and a half, but it was just too cold to be enjoyable. They'd gone back to England and then sailed home. He guessed five weeks away was long enough. He'd spent the entire week at the office trying to get caught up, although he still had nearly two and a half months left of the break he'd asked for. He would work until the Libertys came.

He and Abby planned to accompany Alexander and Phoebe out to California. He was a bit hesitant to have Abby go. Once there, he was afraid she'd never want to come back. Much had been accomplished as far as the Liberty family was concerned. They'd soon be here. They were going to England for a week and Scotland for a week, and then were sailing for Boston. Given the time Elijah and Abigail had been in Switzerland,

Elijah figured they could be on board ship on their way to Boston. He was happy and excited for Liberty Bouvier, who had no idea that she had family who would love her and care for her. At first, he'd not contacted Liberty, because he hadn't been sure about finding Alexander. Now, he felt he should at least send her a telegram to let her know there'd be more than just he and Abby coming west. He didn't want to tell her about Alexander and Phoebe. He and Abby had discussed it at length, and both decided to surprise Liberty.

He knocked on Baxter's door, and Tabitha answered. *She's such a little thing*, Elijah thought again. He doffed his hat and coat and handed them to her. She hung them on the coat tree and asked how his trip was.

"We had a wonderful time in Italy," he answered. "It's a cold time to sail, that's for certain. We'll probably never again sail in winter."

"It's been a right cold winter here too, sir. My little brother took a bet he could lick the pump handle, and his tongue got frozen to it. They had to get warm water and pour it all over his face to get his tongue loosened up. He didn't talk for a few days after that! He won the bet, but he suffered for it!" She giggled, leading him straight to the library door.

"Mr. Humphries here to see you, sir. I'll get some coffee, sir."

"Hello, my friend!" George came around his desk to greet him. He shook Elijah's hand and clapped him on the back. "It's good to see you. I'm glad you came to see me, as I would have been knocking on your door as soon as I heard you were home."

"Yes, yes, it's good to see you too, George," Elijah responded. "I think Abby and I are getting old. We've seen so many sights in Europe when we were younger that now when we go anywhere, we can't seem to wait to get back home." The two men walked over to the chairs before the fire to sit comfortably.

They chatted about various kinds of topics.

"Have you heard Holbein was hanged?" George asked.

"No, no, I didn't." Elijah looked down at the carpet. An unconscious part of his mind took in the rich colors and thought, *How beautiful*. His conscious mind thought about the waste of such potential, and how God must hate it when people ruin their lives. He spoke softly.

"It's such a sad thing when a man's greed outweighs his conscience. We have principles and guidelines in which to live, and so often God is left entirely out of the equation. When He is, that's what you get, lawlessness, greed, hatred, murder, such corruption…a bankrupt soul."

George nodded in agreement. "Elijah, I've some very bad news besides Holbein."

Elijah looked at him questioningly, feeling in his gut a reluctance to hear what George was going to tell him.

"Jacques Corlay escaped. He's on the loose."

Elijah, visibly upset by the news, stood abruptly and paced for a minute. *I'll need to wire both Mr. Bannister and Liberty when I leave here. The sooner, the better.*

"That is, indeed, very bad news. I'm quite certain he'll try to get at Liberty somehow. He's a reprehensible man. Do you know exactly when he escaped?"

"Yes, it was the day he was being transported from the jail to New Bedford. As far as we can ascertain, Rufus Bertoli, Madam Bouvier's driver, paid a guard to look the other way. We caught Bertoli, and we also have the guard who took the bribe. They're both behind bars, but we haven't been able to trace Corlay. He's disappeared into thin air."

"Yes, yes, I understand. But when? What day?"

"He was being transported…ah, let me see." George couldn't exactly remember. "Yes, I remember—he escaped the day you left for Europe."

"Five weeks ago! He's been on the loose now for five weeks?" Elijah stopped pacing and sat down as if the air had been knocked out of him. *If he hasn't been caught by now, he won't be. Oh Lord, please protect Libby. Hedge her in behind and before with Thine angels.*

George tried to encourage him. "If he surfaces, we'll find him. I get so angry when a trusted guard will look the other way for a few greenbacks. To allow a villain to escape is despicable. I wonder if Corlay had money hidden away someplace. I've had detectives out looking for him, and the police have his description. He couldn't have gotten far if he'd been broke. Either he had money someplace, or he got help from someone."

"He's had time to find out where Liberty is. He'll go after her. I'm sure of it."

"Frankly, I think you're right. He'll transfer all blame to the one closest to him. You're going to need to send her a wire."

"I've already thought of that."

"There's another matter I have news about. The company you reported to Cabot and myself is definitely a front. It's operating under the cover of a valid salmon cannery. The company, located in San Francisco, has shipped some of the girls out to high bidders in Hong Kong." A shrill ring pierced the air, and Elijah jumped. George calmly walked over to the wall and picked up an earpiece off a wooden contraption on the wall, speaking loudly into a little funnel on the front of it.

"Chief Inspector Baxter speaking. May I help you?... Umm, yes... Hmmm, yes... Well, tell Coulter to get on it immediately!" George hung up the earpiece.

Elijah walked over as George spoke and marveled at the telephone he'd installed. He'd heard about them but had never seen one.

Bell had formed a company in 1877 and offered to sell the patent to Western Union for one hundred thousand dollars. The man who'd been president of Western Union considered the telephone a toy and had balked at the deal. Two years later the same man said if he could buy the patent for twenty-five million dollars, he'd jump at the chance. By then, the Bell company didn't want to sell.

Elijah could see the great benefit of having such a device.

George patted the box on the wall. "I'm in love, Elijah! I'm in love with a machine. This box"—and he patted it again—"is going to revolutionize the world. It's an amazing invention." He smiled hugely, quite proud he'd had the foresight to have one installed in his home. He received calls from the department and could give instructions without having to jump into a carriage and go to the office. Yes, it was amazing.

Tabitha came in with coffee and a plate of chocolate covered macaroons. The two men poured their coffee and put a couple of the small cakes onto little plates. Elijah took just two. He loved the almond paste and these little cakes were perfect. They drank and munched for a few minutes in silence. George put down his cup, looking at Elijah with a sudden thought.

"How long a break did you take from your office?"

"I took four months. We were going to do a lot of sightseeing in Europe, but Abby decided she was through and wanted to come home. Why...why do you ask?"

George asked excitedly, "How'd you like to go to California? What I mean is, for me...I need someone I trust implicitly to work with the San

Francisco police and be cognizant of what needs done with the salmon company. Right now, my understanding is the companies are under your jurisdiction, isn't that correct?"

"Well…yes, yes, I suppose it is since I am handling the estate, but it's a nasty business, and I don't like the idea that a company like that is under my authority."

"That may be true, but we need to round up any and all participants in the company's shady dealings. We need to know who is involved, and I think we'll have to have an inspector who can go in undercover. It's not as if we can just dissolve the company. If we did that, we'd be putting some honest people out of a job and end up with guilty people going scot free and perhaps setting the same type of thing up somewhere else. After all, they already have the connections in Europe—you understand, the people that are shipping the girls here."

Elijah wrinkled his nose in distaste. "I suppose I could go for you. On a lighter note, we located Madam Bouvier's father and found she has a grandmother as well. They'll be arriving any day now from Italy. We're to accompany them to California. You know, it's amazing, the family resemblance. Liberty looks so much like her father and grandmother, it's uncanny."

"You don't say! How glad I am that she will know her real father isn't a scoundrel of the worst sort! A grandmother too, eh? That'll be a boon to her, I'm sure. So, you were planning a trip to California anyway! My, God does work in mysterious ways, doesn't He?"

Elijah thought about their trip to California. "Yes, yes He does. I know Abby'd like to go tomorrow. She's tired of this cold, and she wants to meet Madam Bouvier… She has some idea of opening a mission there."

"A mission? For what purpose?"

"Oh my! Oh Lord! Oh my goodness! There's the answer I've been searching for. Oh my, George, sometimes when the Almighty opens your blinders, you feel as if you've been hit over the head with an answer you should've seen coming!"

"What are you talking about, Elijah?"

"The mission! I've been wondering if the dream I had the night Abigail was healed was simply that, just a dream, or was it a direction from the Lord? Now I know, George. Abigail and I are supposed to open a mission for battered women! Battered or abused, or homeless or whatever. I feel it in my spirit, George. I know Abby will feel the same way. We're to go to California and help those women who have been kidnapped by that company in San Francisco."

George looked at him in astonishment. "I'm thankful you're willing to go. I didn't know who I could send there to coordinate with the office here. We will, of course, pay for your passage and Abigail's, I should think. I'm going to be sending Cabot too, as he will be the person who will go under cover. I could hire Pinkertons, I suppose." He paused for a moment, thinking about that option. "No, I think Cabot would be the best for the job."

Elijah was a bit dazed from the rapid change in his immediate future. He thought back a few weeks to Florence and how his words had changed the entire future of Alexander Liberty and his mother. *What will Abby would think of it all? I'll need to inform Sigmund as well as distribute my clientele among the remaining lawyers. So much to do!*

He rallied quickly. "When would you like me out there, George?"

George replied, "In about three weeks' time or so, I think. That'll give you two weeks here to get your affairs straightened out. Will that be all right with you?"

"Yes, yes, I believe it would, my friend."

"Returning to our previous conversation," George said, "I'll be sending Cabot out immediately. I need him to get into that cannery. Perhaps, before you leave, we can set up a place where the two of you could rendezvous. Someplace safe for you, Elijah. I don't want you dragged into anything dangerous. You could telegraph me the developments of the case. We need to meet again and refine our plans, but I thank you again. It's a relief I can have someone trustworthy for this job."

The two men sat and chatted a while longer, wondering just what Corlay may have planned. With the decision to talk more later, Elijah left George's house with much on his mind.

I'd better wire Liberty right now. I need to get home and inform Abby what the Almighty has shown me. I wonder if any of the servants would like to go live out west. I'd sure hate to lose Bessie. I think she's the best cook in the entire world. I know Thomas will be going with us. Thomas is family.

Elijah had John drive him to the station, and he sent telegrams to Mr. Bannister as well as Liberty. Riding home, he thought about moving west. Perhaps they'd keep their Boston house, the way Liberty had, for a time and see how things went in California. Once the mission was built, they could move the servants out there, or at least the ones who would like to go. He'd have to see how the land lay.

Winter was fast disappearing in Boston. The wind was still chilly but not a biting cold. Elijah looked out of his carriage and saw skies that were clear. The sun was shining, but with no real warmth to it. It would be a lot nicer weather to be transporting trunks than when Liberty had left. He wondered about meeting up with Cabot. That would be an interesting venture—he was looking forward to it. He decided he'd say little to Abby about it. He didn't want her to worry. *Lord, I cannot begin to thank Thee enough for the healing of my wife. How grateful I am. I will be forever grateful for the time Thou have given us. Bless in this new venture, I pray. Lord, may Abby and I be used however Thou seest fit. May we be instruments of Thy peace.*

CHAPTER XXX

He is thy praise, and he is thy God,
that hath done for thee these great and terrible things,
which thine eyes have seen.
DEUTERONOMY 10:21

ELIJAH ARRIVED HOME TO FIND that Alexander and Phoebe had arrived. He was surprised but glad to see them. He hugged Phoebe and clasped Alexander's hand in both of his.

Elijah asked, "How was your crossing? How long did it take?"

Alexander replied in his English accent, that was such a delight to hear, "It was so cold, I felt I was in a crypt! I'd forgotten that damp cold that cuts though you like a knife. I haven't missed it, that's for sure!" He grinned a grin that was so like Liberty it made Elijah's heart clench.

He'd like to be her father himself. He'd be glad to see her again.

He turned to Abigail. "When is dinner?"

"We have about a half hour. Why?"

"Let's go into the sunroom. I should talk to you alone, Abigail, but I feel as if the Libertys are family."

Elijah felt discombobulated by his talk with George. It was not a feeling he experienced often. It made him feel everything was a bit off kilter. Coming home to find he had company had taken him by surprise. He hoped Abby would not mind him sharing in front of guests. They all walked to the sunroom. Phoebe and Alexander admired the beauty of it.

"Will you please be seated?" He paced while they sat down. When they were ready, he began to share with Phoebe and Alexander the dream he'd had the night Abigail had been healed.

"The dream had totally slipped from my mind. Abby had to remind me of it, because I told her in detail all about it the morning after her healing. I've heard that if you forget your dream, that's all it is, just a dream, but if it stays with you, it's a vision. I don't, in truth, know about that. I do know I remember it in detail. I've been praying for an answer ever since Abby reminded me. What was the mission for? I've been asking God that question for some time now. Today, I received His answer."

Abigail gasped and smiled because she knew in that moment they were moving to California. She wanted to get up and dance, feeling her heart soar.

Elijah continued his story. He shared all of it. He didn't think these two dear people needed to be kept from the truth. He was so excited and told them about Armand Bouvier's businesses. He'd not even shared with Abby about the sordid business because he'd known it would hurt her heart to hear about the abuse of women.

"I believe now," he told them, "that Abigail and I are to open a mission for abused women. I know our job will be to dedicate all our time and efforts toward helping women become whole."

Matthew had arisen before sunrise and was saddling up Piggypie. He smiled every time he said her name. Kirk had been upset when Matthew named his horse. As a filly, she'd eaten everything in sight, and since she was a piebald mare, Matthew had named her Piggypie. She was a good horse, and Matthew loved her easy disposition.

Conchita gave him a list of things she wanted from the city, but he wasn't about to announce to a bunch of females his intentions. He wanted no encumbrances today nor any distractions. He had things that needed done and planned to return late tonight. He was going to ride south to Sausalito and take a ferry across the bay to the city. San Francisco was only thirty-seven miles from Napa, and a day's jaunt to the city was fairly easy as long as you weren't dragging a harem behind you.

Conchita came out of the house to tell him to not forget the honey.

He slapped Piggypie's side and tightened the girth with a jerk. "Thanks again, Conchita, for making my breakfast. I told you, you didn't need to get up." He stepped easily into the stirrup, swinging his right leg over the saddle.

"I no send my boss out with the empty stomach, no, not me!" She grinned up at him.

"You tell Diego he'd better treat you good," he said with an answering grin, "or I'll be carrying you off into the sunset! Hasta luego!"

He turned Piggypie and rode out. He needed a day to think, get finances straightened out, and open that account for Libby. Both he and Libby had received telegrams over a week ago relating that Jacques Corlay had escaped. Libby didn't seem too upset about it. *I didn't even know her father had gone to jail for fraud. She told me that Bouvier and Corlay had been business partners. Is that why she's out here? Is her husband in trouble with the law?* Matthew didn't understand why Mr. Humphries had sent a telegram to him about Liberty's father unless there was trouble brewing. He wondered about that. Something felt wrong...very wrong.

He spoke aloud to himself. "What was it that palace guard said in *Hamlet*? Something's rotten in the state of Denmark. Well, something's rotten about this whole setup of Madam Bouvier living in California and her husband back in Boston and her father escaping from jail...something very rotten." He kicked Piggypie into an easy canter.

After Matthew rode out of sight, Conchita went back into the house. She started breakfast, beginning to make corn tortillas. As she stirred the batter, she thought.

I wonder why Meester Bannister no take these womens with heem. They would like a day in the ceety. I wonder much about Mees Libby's husband. I can see Meester Bannister he ees liking her more and more, an' I cannot blame him. Mees Libby ees not only very sweet, she ees beautiful. Conchita reached for more masa harina, adding several handsful. Stirring it calmed her thoughts.

That Consuelo, she comed here last night. Mees Maggee and Consuelo, they skirting around each other like the cats ready for the fight. Consuelo ees bad news. My aunt and uncle, they have spoiled her. She ees the last child of seex, an' only girl. She noh good. Her heart ees mean and she selfish. Eet's sad she turn out like that. Mees Maggee, she ignore Meester Kirk. He making the eyes at Consuelo, and Consuelo, she making the eyes back. I wonder eef Mees Maggee care. She didn't act like she care at all.

I love Meester Kirk, but he ees flirt and likes all the womens. I theenk someday the right one comes an' Meester Kirk, he weel be a goner, uh-hum, swept right off hees beeg feet. She chuckled at the thought. *He's always making the eyes at someone.* Conchita had thought perhaps Miss Maggie was the one.

Maggie stretched…she loved mornings. A new day to live and laugh and learn. She stretched again and thought about the night before. *That Kirk's sure a flirt.* He'd held her hand and made eyes at her out in the courtyard. Then along came a spider. She remembered that rhyme from her nursery book. *That's what that slinky Consuelo is, a spider. Black widow most likely. She'll suck the blood right out of Kirk, and nothing will be left but a husk of a man.* She giggled at the thought. She liked Kirk, but she didn't love him. They had long talks together and she was quite sure he liked her. *But look at what happened last night—Consuelo and Kirk left together.*

Maggie thoughts swung to Libby. *The longer she waits, the harder it's going to be to tell Matthew she's a widow. She isn't lying, is she?* Maggie liked things straightforward. She was not at all devious by nature…at least she didn't think she was. She knew she had a temper and she couldn't abide that Consuelo. Who'd she think she was anyway? She'd made huge eyes at Matthew, and he'd laughed at her and told her to grow up.

Maggie decided it was time to get up. She swung her legs over the side of the bed and sat there looking for the hundredth time around the room. It was beautiful and so peaceful. She stood up, stretched, and walked over to open the curtains. It looked like it was going to be a beautiful day. She was excited because she knew that soon they would begin building Libby's house.

Libby lay in bed thinking about her new life. *I love it here. I have a sense of belonging and relationship with others I've never known before.* She stretched, enjoying the feel of cool sheets. She thought about Conchita's faith. It was deep and strong. Her love for others showed in everything she did. Liberty had often wondered what God thought of all the different kinds of Christians. *Did God like it that there were many different kinds of Christians? Did that variety cause worship of Him in different ways, and so it was good? Or did Christians*

stay behind those denominational walls and not love each other the way they should and thus weaken the church? She thought most likely the latter was the case.

She did know love was the biggest key. She'd tried so hard to love Armand, but he had spurned all her efforts to attain even friendship. Libby had been stunned by his incredible selfishness. It was as if all of life revolved around him and for him. When it didn't, he destroyed it or turned his back on it. She'd felt sorry for him, and yet he'd made those choices that alienated even the nicest people.

Libby knew many people continued to make bad choice after bad choice because they had not given their lives to the One who could help them make good choices. *So Jacques is loose. I know I fear him, and yet I believe it is wrong to fear.* She remembered a verse from First John, "Perfect love casts out fear." *Dear Father, thank You that I can call You, Father, and know that You are good. I pray for my father here on earth. Lord, he is so evil, and I know that I still fear that somehow he'll be able to make me go back to Boston or harm me in some way. Lord, I pray for him that he would accept You as his Savior and turn from his wickedness. I also pray against the spirit of fear. Lord, Your Word tells us that perfect love casts out fear. I pray that my love would be perfected in You and that the fear would vanish. I don't want to fear Jacques coming after me. Thank You for the love I feel here in this house. Lord, please help me be a blessing this day. Through Your perfect Son I pray. Amen.*

Libby lay thinking it was time to come clean about Armand. She sat up and said a quick prayer for guidance. She stood and stretched. She could see sunshine peeking in between a crack in the curtains. *Yes! That's two days in a row.* Soon they would begin to build. *Yes! Yes!*

Conchita was singing a song in Spanish as Maggie entered the kitchen. "Good morning, Mees Maggie," she said. "How was the bed last night?"

"Good morning to you too! A beautiful morning, isn't it? And thank you—I slept like a baby." Maggie spun around in a circle and laughed for the sheer joy of living.

Conchita smiled widely, showing her strong teeth. She thought to herself, *Mess Maggie, she doan seem sad—no broken heart here.*

Maggie laid a corn tortilla on her plate, dished up scrambled eggs, beans, tomatoes, and onions, expertly wrapping it up. She got a dish of salsa and a cup of coffee. Going over to the scrubbed wooden table, she began to eat.

"Conchita," she said, talking with her mouth nearly full, "this is deeelicious!"

Liberty walked into the kitchen and over to Conchita. "Conchita, I love you!" Her eyes filled, and she blinked away the tears as she gave Conchita a big hug.

Conchita, surprised, felt a surge of warmth for this woman, hugging her right back.

"I love you too, Mees Libby!"

Maggie came over and got in on the hugs too.

Liberty said, "I cannot begin to tell you how much this feels like a real home to me. I'll be interested to see what it'll be like when I have my own home. Will I feel the same way in it? I've never felt this way before, and you're a big part of it, Conchita. You bless me!"

"Oh, Mees Libby, thank you. You ees so sweet. I almost forget...thees comed yesterday, when you at your property." She pulled a letter off a shelf, handing it to Libby. Liberty took the letter with dread, fearing it was from her father. She breathed a sigh of relief when she saw that it was from Elijah. Before she even read the letter, she walked over and poured herself a cup of coffee.

"Conchita, would you please sit down here with Maggie and me for just a few minutes? I need to talk with you."

Maggie first looked surprised and then relieved. Liberty was going to tell the truth about Armand.

Conchita looked serious. She knew whatever Mess Libby was going to say would be important. She poured herself a cup of coffee and sat down at the table.

Liberty took a sip of her coffee and, reaching across the table, took Conchita's hand in her own.

"Conchita, I didn't know what to expect when Maggie and I came out here. Maggie and I have become very good friends. In Boston, Maggie was my personal maid. We've shared many things together for the past four years. When she came to work for me, I was twenty-five and Maggie just fourteen. Even though she's been my servant, she was always a comfort to me. I have been all alone since my mother died twelve years ago."

Conchita interrupted. "But your husband...he been weeth you!"

"Yes, and many other women as well, Conchita. He brought some of them home at night. I was never enough, not even the first week of our marriage. I was so young, just turned sixteen. It's a long story, but the short version is that my husband was an evil man. He ruined many people's lives and caused some men's deaths. His will left everything we owned to my father, who's just as evil and was his business partner. I was given only the property here in California. My husband was murdered just five days before I boarded the train for California."

Conchita gasped. "Murdered!"

"Yes, Conchita, and I cannot mourn him—to do so would be a travesty. I tried to love him, and I tried to respect him, but I failed. Now the property is all I have. When I left Boston, I believed I would receive twenty dollars per month for necessities. The telegram I received told me, without any explanation, that I have unlimited funds. I don't really know what it all means. I do know that I've been praying I'd not be bitter, not be distrustful. The only good man I've ever known, besides servants, I only knew for little more than two days. He was my husband's lawyer and is a trustworthy person. That last telegram was from him to tell me that Jacques, my father, has escaped jail. He's supposed to go to prison for fraud and for hiring the man who killed Armand. So I'm here, and the property Matthew staked out for Armand is all I own. Now that I'm here, I'm finding it the home I've never known."

CHAPTER XXXI

Happy is the man that findeth wisdom,
and the man that getteth understanding.
PROVERBS 3:13

CONCHITA STOOD UP, DRAWING LIBERTY to her breast. She hugged her, stroked her hair, and murmured to her.

"I love you, Mees Liberty, and weel not tell your story, no, not eef you say no."

"I don't know why I kept it secret. I suppose it's because I didn't know what kind of man Matthew was. I've not trusted men so easily in the last few years. If you wish to tell it, then tell it. Elijah sent a wire to Matthew as well as me about my father escaping. It probably made no sense to him, since he thought I was a married woman."

Liberty started to drink the cooled coffee, but Conchita took the cup from her hand. She dumped it out, refilling it with fresh, hot coffee. Maggie took a deep breath, letting it out slowly. She felt as if she'd worked hard all day. She dumped her coffee as well. Pouring another cup, she sat back down at the table.

It was quiet in the kitchen that was usually so full of laughter. Conchita started cleaning up the breakfast clutter. Maggie sipped coffee while Libby opened the letter. It was dated a few days before she received the telegram telling her of Jacques' escape.

My dearest Liberty Alexandra,

I want you to know that my wife, Abigail, and I pray for you every day. We trust you are well and enjoying California. It would be helpful if you could send a telegram and let us know how you're doing. I'm writing to you to inform you of certain events here in Boston. First of all, as you well know, Monsieur Corlay was arrested during the reading of the will. We found papers your late husband kept of every transaction he and Corlay made. I suppose I should say I'm sorry, but I am not. He was sentenced to New Bedford Prison for life. Now that he's escaped, you must be very careful.

On a happier note, in the event that Corlay was unable to administer the estate, it reverted in its entirety to one Liberty Alexandra Bouvier. So congratulations, you are now a very, very wealthy woman.

After closer inspection of the companies owned by Monsieur Bouvier, we have found that one company is a cover-up for white female slavery. The girls are being shipped in from Europe and sold to the highest bidder. This company is located in San Francisco and is a valid salmon cannery. The women, once rescued, are going to need a place to stay until they go back to Europe or stay here. Abby and I want to help them. We will be opening a mission somewhere close to, or in, San Francisco. We feel called to aid these women once the *investigation is over. As owner of this company, and me representing you, please advise me as to your wishes in all these affairs.*

Sigmund and Matilda send their love. They're enjoying the house.

Abigail and I arrive in Sacramento on March 15, 1883. We're bringing two people with us that you will be very happy to meet. They will need separate rooms, if that is possible. So please prepare for four of us. We are so looking forward to seeing you again, my dear.

May our Lord watch over you.

Fondly and respectfully yours,

Elijah Humphries

Liberty wiped her eyes, looking up at Maggie. "Well, Maggie, Conchita, it looks as if I inherited after all." She read the letter aloud to the two women.

Maggie jumped up, upsetting her chair, and asked as she picked it up, "You won't go back to Boston, will you, Libby?"

Liberty looked up, surprised by her question. "No, of course not, Maggie. California is my home now. Do you think I'd want to go back where I have so many unhappy memories? No, Maggie, I may have to go back once in a while for business, but I think even that can be done out here. Perhaps I will open an office in San Francisco.

"Conchita, do you think Matthew will not mind having more company. Mr. Humphries probably thinks I'm in my own house on my own property."

"*Sí, es bueno.* Thees house hold many peoples."

Maggie wondered about the company Liberty now owned that Mr. Humphries wrote about. "Is Mr. Humphries saying women are kidnapped and then sold? How horrible! What a despicable thing! I've never heard of dealings such as that."

Libby's eyes teared up. "I know. Why can't they go expose the whole business to the police and let them arrest everyone?"

Conchita chimed in. "I haf heard of such things en Mehico. The womans ees sold to bad men. We just property, you know. Mees Libby, they must catch all thees mens who do thees thing. Sometimes we must wait for the good to come."

"It's horrible, and I don't want to own a company that does such ugly things." She picked up the letter and looked at it again.

"We'll have company in just six days!" Libby exclaimed. "I'll find out from Elijah just how much the companies are worth and what can be done about most of them. Oh, it'll be so good to see him again!"

Maggie's eyes sparkled in anticipation.

"I know you'll have much to talk about," Maggie said excitedly. "He'll probably bring news of Sigmund and Matilda. I want to hear all about their wedding."

Liberty announced, "I'm going to ride over to my place and sit for a while and think. It's a beautiful day, and I need to see exactly where I want my house. If I have unlimited funds, I'm going to build a house much like this one. I want laughter and joy to be a commonplace thing. You have no idea, Conchita, how dull my house was in Boston. Armand had it decorated. It was dark, heavy, and very dull. Maggie and I packed the things we liked but left many things we didn't. Thank you for being so sweet. See you both later. I'll be back in time for lunch."

Matthew arrived in San Francisco a little after ten. He was glad the ferry ran often; he'd timed it just right. He needed to make several stops and shop for things on Conchita's list. That was definitely last on his agenda. He didn't want to have to lug food around with him all day. The survey office was his first stop, and he had conversations with two men about surveying some more land connected with his property, setting up a meeting time. He visited the treasurer's office, paying taxes on his and Liberty's property, hers being assessed at a significantly lower amount.

Breaking for a late lunch, he ate Chinese rice at a hole-in-the-wall eatery. It tasted quite good, and he was pleasantly surprised. Matthew left the eatery and rode to the Bank of San Francisco, asking to see the manager. Not having an appointment, he had to wait a half hour before entering the man's office.

The manager came out of his office and greeted him cordially. " Welcome to the Bank of San Francisco. My name's Calvert Foster."

Matthew stood up, his hat in his left hand. He shook hands with the banker. "And I'm Bannister, Matthew Bannister."

"Yes," said the banker. "You have an account with us, isn't that correct?"

Matthew knew the man had looked up his file and perused it before seeing him.

"Yes, I do."

"Please be seated." The manager waved to a chair in front of his desk. "So, Mr. Bannister, how may I be of help to you today?"

Matthew looked him squarely in the eye, liking what he saw. An honest, straightforward look was directed his way by clear blue eyes. Foster's manner was easy and relaxed, putting Matthew at ease. A clerk entered, and Mr. Foster directed him to get some coffee, which was a welcome surprise to Matthew, who sat back into the chair.

"I need a couple things. First of all, I'm depositing some money, and then I have some questions for you."

The banker pulled out a ledger and wrote down Matthew's account information and proceeded to count out the money Matthew brought to deposit.

The clerk entered with the coffee, poured out two cups, and quietly left. Matthew sipped the brew. It was hot.

He spoke when Mr. Foster finished counting. "I wanted to get to know you personally as I have a feeling I'll be needing help in the future. I've started a vineyard and—"

"Mr. Bannister, I have heard of Rancho Bonito," the banker interrupted him. "As a matter of fact, a friend of mine gave me a bottle of your Merlot. I think you are going to have a fine future in the business. It was a pretty good bottle for your first harvesting."

"Who's the friend?"

Calvert Foster replied, smiling, "Ah, it's Jedidiah Sanders, the man—"

"On the train from Sacramento to Vallejo," Matthew supplied the answer. Both men smiled at each other. Matthew had given Jed several bottles of his Merlot last fall. It wasn't even aged.

"At any rate, we as a bank would like to help you in any way we can. I can see from your account that you'd perhaps like a loan?"

"No, not right now, but I may in the future. How would I go about transferring funds from the Bank of Boston out here?"

"Why, that's easy," replied the banker. "Do you have an account with them also?"

"No, not me, but I have a houseguest, Madam Armand Bouvier. She'd like to draw on her account at this time."

The banker's head jerked up, and he looked at Matthew intently.

"Horrible business, wasn't it? Have they found the murderer yet? We only got news that Bouvier'd been murdered, but not anything since. I know I shouldn't say this to you, but it certainly couldn't have happened to a better person. I have a close personal friend who was ruined by Bouvier."

Matthew bent down to fiddle with his bootlace to hide the shock he knew must be stamped on his face. Murdered! Bouvier murdered! So many things clicked into place as the fact of a deceased Bouvier filtered through his brain. Sitting back up, he knew his face was red. He hoped the banker would attribute it to his bending over.

"I am sorry about your friend. I've had trouble with Bouvier owing me money and not paying. I believe his widow is of a different ilk. She paid me the monies owed me by Bouvier. Besides making my own deposit, I'm here to help her. Can you help me to withdraw some funds for her?"

The banker looked embarrassed and said, "Yes, I can do that, but I need her signature or her present to do so. I can't just draw funds from her account and give them to you, much as I'd like to do so."

Matthew looked nonplussed. "I should have thought of that. She has property adjoining mine and is planning to build a house soon. I reckon I'll bring her here next time I'm in town."

The bank manager smiled. "I can certainly give you an application for a bank letter of credit. Madam Bouvier is a very rich woman, and her credit will be good anywhere." He handed Matthew a form.

Matthew stood up, feeling overwhelmed by the information he'd received this day. He thanked Mr. Foster and left the bank, still feeling dazed. He walked down the street slowly, trying to absorb all the information he knew thus far. He started cataloguing all the information from the time he'd first set eyes on Liberty Bouvier, with the added knowledge of a dead husband.

He decided he'd better do the shopping for Conchita while he could still think clearly. He entered a mercantile store pulling the list out of his pocket. He got the honey first so he wouldn't forget, as it wasn't on the list. Matthew shopped, pulling the items off the shelves, keeping his mind on the business at hand. After paying the clerk, he loaded the items, slinging them over Piggypie's back in two saddlebags.

Matthew led Piggypie down the street for a bit, feeling the need to stretch out his legs and his brain at the same time. His thoughts were unsettled.

Dead, her husband's dead. I wonder why she kept that information to herself. She must have loved him very much. Conchita said she'd cried that first night, huge racking sobs. How many other nights has she cried? Why did she come out here? Just to get away from all the wagging tongues? Why wasn't she wearing the traditional black, worn by every mourner I've ever known? Now that I have a few answers to some of my questions, I have another whole set. My brain feels tired. I've been up since four this morning and will be glad to get home.

Elijah had much to accomplish and found it difficult trying to entertain guests and close up a house. He'd decided to do with his house much as he'd done with the Bouvier manse. After much discussion, it was decided that Thomas would stay in the house until things were settled in the West. Thomas insisted he'd be of more benefit to Elijah by staying at the residence until things were established in California. It was a relief that the man had come up with such an easy solution.

Elijah still had not heard from Liberty and could only hope she'd received his letter. Abigail was in a whirlwind of activity, packing trunks and having John take many things to the mission for the homeless. There were some things she would not part with, but they were amazed at the number of things they'd amassed over the years that were simply dust collectors.

CHAPTER XXXII

For wisdom is a defence, and money is a defence:
but the excellency of knowledge is,
that wisdom giveth life to them that have it.
ECCLESIASTES 7:12

FOR ELIJAH, THE DAYS SLIPPED rapidly by. He met with George one last time to finalize their plans. They sat in George's office at the police station. Cabot Jones, who was already in California, had been hired by the company in question to a minor role of assistant bookkeeper.

Elijah and George talked together, formulating a plan as to how to get Elijah and Cabot to meet without inciting any suspicion.

Elijah said, "I have friends at Burbank and Hobbs. I'm sure I could have the use of one of the offices there. If you could send a telegram to Cabot's boardinghouse and let him know, perhaps we could meet at a designated time."

"Well, to use the offices it would have to be during the day, and he'll be working during the day. Are you close enough to someone that they'd allow you the use of an office at night?" George asked.

"No, no, I'm not that close to them." Elijah thought for a moment. "Perhaps we could meet at a church instead. While getting information on missions, I ran across the first cathedral built in California, which is San Francisco's St. Mary's."

"That's an excellent suggestion. I'll contact Cabot and let him know." He looked at Elijah. "Perhaps you could meet early before he goes to work and cause less suspicion. How about Friday mornings? Yes, I think that's a good idea, Elijah. Let's say seven o'clock on Friday mornings. Then, if there's information, you can send it by telegram. The less people who know about this, the better. There's a great deal of money in this nasty business. Now, you're leaving the day after tomorrow? I will expect your first report, whether you've heard from Cabot or not, three weeks hence. Will that do for you? I assume you'll be going to the Napa Valley before heading to San Francisco, is that correct?"

"Yes, yes, that's my plan," Elijah replied. "I sent Liberty a letter saying we'd be arriving, so they should expect four guests. Abby and I don't plan to stay long. We'll be staying in a boardinghouse a friend from Burbank and Hobbs rented for us. He wanted us to stay with him, but both Abigail and I would feel uncomfortable staying with them because we don't know how long it will be. We'd like, well, not we, but I would like to take Bessie with us. That woman is the best cook in all creation, and I don't look forward to boardinghouse food. Ah well, it is a small enough sacrifice, I suppose."

The two men shook hands and ended up giving each other a hug.

"I'll miss you, Elijah."

"As I will you, George." And then clasping George on the shoulder, Elijah prayed, "Dear Lord, how I thank Thee for relationships. I thank Thee that Thou hast brought this man into my life. I pray for his safekeeping and that Thou wilt watch over his coming in and his going out forevermore. Guide his steps, I pray, and may everything he puts his hand to be blessed by Thee. We both love Thee and I ask it, knowing that Thou art good. Amen."

George, his voice cracking, said, "Thank you, my brother in Christ, thank you." He walked Elijah to the front steps of the police station, waving good-bye as Elijah turned the corner.

Elijah stopped by the Bouvier manse to talk to Sigmund, who was grinning at him with enthusiasm.

The big blond was happy to see this man who had been so good to them. Matilda had a wedding day beyond her wildest dreams, and to be able to live right there in the manse in one of the guest bedrooms…she was one happy wife.

"Guten Tag, Herr Humphries." Sigmund pumped Elijah's hand. "I'm happy to see you. How was your trip? I told Matilda it would be so cold you'd come back looking like an iceberg. She didn't believe me, of course."

"Hello to you, Sigmund, and yes, it was a very cold trip. Abigail didn't enjoy it until we were in the middle of Italy." He rubbed his hands together, for he'd forgotten his gloves and it was still chilly.

"Sigmund, I need to speak to you about Madam Bouvier. I've not heard from her since she left. You haven't, have you?

At Sigmund's negative headshake, Elijah said, "I thought not. She most likely has to take some time to adjust to the situation there. I think the best plan for you is to continue on here until we hear from her. She may end up selling the manse. On the other hand, she may want it to be a place for her to stay when she needs to be at a board meeting or something. I don't know yet what her plans are."

"Mr. Humphries, I am, of course, quite content to stay here until we hear further. The rent is the right price!" He smiled at the lawyer. "I've been, however, a bit bored, so I've been reading stock reports and the like. I came by your office to talk to you about a little plan I had, but you'd already left for Europe. I decided to go ahead, and I invested fifty dollars into the Union Pacific and another twenty in Bell Telephone. I plan to add to the Bell Telephone stock as I'm able. I believe that it's going to be one incredible company. I find much satisfaction in knowing that I've made good choices." He looked extremely pleased with himself, but Elijah looked at him speculatively.

"Have you ever considered going into business? What I am suggesting is that should Madam Bouvier decide to close the manse, would you continue as a butler somewhere else, or would you perhaps venture out into business?"

The question startled Sigmund. He had, in truth, never considered himself anything other than someone else's manservant, but now the idea left him with a feeling of distaste. He was surprised that such a few words from Mr. Humphries could solidify what had been brewing inside him for quite some time.

Elijah could see his question startled Sigmund, who took his time before answering.

"If I have anything to say about it, I think I'll never be a manservant again. I'm a good manservant, probably one of the best. It's just that I feel energized looking at businesses and trying to guess which of them will succeed, and yes, if I have the money, I believe I'll definitely do something other than be someone else's servant. I don't wish to be indigent—I want enough money to provide for my family to live comfortably. Matilda doesn't like adventure, but me…I'm discovering I thrive on it."

"Sigmund, that's exactly what I was hoping to hear. You have a business acumen that's phenomenal for someone who's had no training. I'm quite certain, since I am her lawyer, that Madam Bouvier will be asking my advice. I believe you'll have a place in one of her companies. Mrs. Humphries and I are moving to California. We're starting on a new venture, even at our age. If you know in your heart it's the right thing, you're never too old for change. I'm giving you more funds to run the household." He reached into his satchel and pulled out a large envelope.

"Madam will be contacting you soon. Expect a telegram in a week or so. Oh, I nearly forgot, if you have money left from the last amount I gave you, I think you should try investing it. If it gains, you split the gain with Madam Bouvier. Would that be amenable to you?"

Sigmund grinned—he felt as if his whole body were smiling. "Yes, sir, it would be very amenable to me."

Elijah shook his hand, bidding him farewell.

Jacques Corlay was in San Francisco. He knew detectives were looking for him, but he'd decided to hide out in the big city. He was buying supplies, getting ready to do a little camping. Liberty was living in Napa, California, which wasn't far north of there. He'd known where Liberty would go from reading the will. He'd had a great opportunity when that fool of a lawyer was in the kitchen consoling the cook. He'd been caught reading the will, but Humphries didn't know he'd learned that Armand had left Libby property in California. It'd been a stroke of luck that Humphries had left the will out on the desk for him to read.

There was one thing Corlay knew he was good at, and that was not blabbing to others about his plans. That had been Armand's mistake. *He'd blabbed about changing his will to exclude Liberty and give everything to me. He owed me anyway, blackmailing me about Liberty's real father. I didn't know, before reading the will, about the property in California. That was a real stroke of luck, that lawyer leaving it out on the desk for anyone to see.*

He shuddered, thinking about spending the rest of his life in prison. Rufus Bertoli had been caught before Jacques had even paid him for his help. He was a fool too. Bertoli didn't know he was heading west, but he wasn't stupid and had probably figured it out. He wondered how much the man had told the police. Jacques needed a plan. One way or another, he was going to get Liberty back for ending up with what should have been his. He'd killed, more than once, and he could kill again.

Phoebe sat next to the window, the changing panorama looking like something out of a picture book. She listened with half an ear to Elijah and Alexander talking.

"Do you think your letter has reached Liberty?"

"It should have done by now," Elijah replied, "although I don't know how reliable the mail is in the West. It's very reliable in the East. Libby's supposed to have a house, but I don't even know if that's true. I sent the letter to Matthew Bannister's house because his address was listed in Armand's papers. Liberty should've sent a telegram, but perhaps she isn't able. I don't know how remote this place is. You do understand that Abigail and I won't be staying very long. Just long enough for you to get acquainted, and then I'll be going to San Francisco. I've written several letters, and I'm thinking San Rafael would be an excellent place for these girls. It's just a few miles north of San Francisco. There was a mission there at one time for Indians who were ill."

"I think I would like to help with this endeavor," said Alexander. "I'll have to see how the meeting goes with Liberty. I've been praying fervently that she won't resent the fact that Violet never told her about me. I would not have her becoming embittered."

Elijah agreed. "I hadn't thought of that possibility. I wouldn't like to see that either. Violet must have had her reasons. Perhaps she saw a breach in Corlay and Liberty's relationship already and didn't want to exacerbate the situation. Whatever her reasons, I would've thought that she might have told Liberty, at least when she knew she was dying."

"Yes, I've thought so too…why not tell her when she married? But as you say, she must have had her reasons."

Cabot Jones was worried. He'd entered the company under the guise of being a bookkeeper and been hired on as an assistant bookkeeper. He was supposed to meet with the head accountant, Mr. Saul Simmons, directly after work. Cabot was sitting in Mr. Simmons' office waiting for him to come. His knee bobbed as his heel tapped an impatient tattoo on the floor. *Where was the man?* He hoped he was not going to be terminated. He felt he'd done a decent job at the assigned work and hoped no one was suspicious of him. Cabot checked for his gun, which was safely tucked in his trousers in the middle of his back.

He'd been looking closely at the books. There were large discrepancies between what was coming into the business and what was going out. If he were in charge of the business, he would have fired Simmons.

So why hadn't Brooks fired him? Because Ethan Brooks, the president of the company, is as crooked as the day is long, that's why. Brooks is supposed to be making money for the owner of the company, Madam Bouvier. Instead, besides dealing in human flesh, he or Simmons, or perhaps both, are diverting large sums of money, but where? Into their own pockets? To pay for the women to be transported? This place reeks of corruption, and the whole setup has me on edge.

The door opened and both Saul Simmons and Ethan Brooks walked into the office. Cabot wondered what was coming next. Ethan Brooks had greasy-looking black hair and was always in need of a shave and, although dressed correctly, looked unkempt and disheveled. He was in stark contrast to Mr. Saul Simmons, who was tidy looking, with a neatly trimmed beard and an impeccably tied cravat.

CHAPTER XXXIII

Surely the churning of milk bringeth forth butter,
and the wringing of the nose bringeth forth blood:
so the forcing of wrath bringeth forth strife.
PROVERBS 30:33

ABOT STOOD WHEN THEY ENTERED, but Brooks waved him to be seated, although neither Brooks nor Simmons sat. Cabot knew the tactic, as he'd used it himself during interrogation of suspects. It aided in making the seated person feel a little inferior. Cabot tried to look as if he were entirely cowed by the two men.

Brooks spoke down to him first. "Well, young man, I understand you've been going over the books with a fine-toothed comb. Am I understanding that correctly?"

"Y-yes, s-sir, I have," Cabot stuttered, trying to act scared. It wasn't difficult. These two men looked as if they could easily do away with him, and who would know? *Stay on the subject, Cabot,* he told himself.

Brooks said, "So tell me…what have you found?"

"Well, s-sir, someone's been cooking the books," Cabot replied.

Brooks reached over, grabbed Cabot's cravat, and jerked him to his feet.

"And just who do you think did that, you little pip-squeak?"

"I don't know, sir!"

"I have," Ethan Brooks yelled at him. "And I'll continue to do so. And you aren't going say a word—you hear me?" He shoved Cabot back into the chair.

"No, sir….I mean, yes, sir!"

Saul Simmons stepped up and said gruffly, "So, young man, you're on a special payroll, and we're gonna pay you double what ya bin making. We want ya ta doctor those books so's the next person who sees 'em cain't find what you seem ta have found. I'll be givin' you a new ledger tomorrow mornin', an' you'll be copyin' it so's the monies coming in and a goin' outs th' same. Do ya hear? We needed a smart man like you, and now you work for us. Whatever you're told to do, you'll do…an' no questions asked. Do ya understand?"

"Yes, sir, I do, and I'll be glad for the added income and do whatever necessary to assist you," answered Cabot. He stood up, acting wary of the two men. In all truth, he was more than wary of these two men. These were two of the most wretched men of society. How anyone could deal in the bondage of people, Cabot didn't know nor understand.

Brooks walked up to Cabot and stuck his face into Cabot's own, jabbing his finger into his chest. "You make sure you understand, do you hear?"

Cabot backed up several steps, acting intimidated, but the man's breath was enough to make him sick.

"Yes, sir, I hear."

The two men looked at each other and Brooks nodded to Simmons. "Let's get out of here."

Cabot stood there for a few minutes to let the two men clear out before leaving the office. He went down the stairs and out onto the street. The wind was blowing hard, and he almost lost his hat. He walked for two blocks and then turned, looking into a storefront. His eyes slid sideways, and he confirmed that he was being followed. *I'll let the man follow me. If I lose him, it would definitely make me look guilty of trying to evade him. I only have another week and a half before I'm to meet Elijah.*

He strode down the street, not bothering to look behind him. *Wonder if I'm going to be followed on a twenty-four-hour watch or just until I enter my hotel for the night. Time will tell.* He whistled jauntily and turned into his hotel. Cabot had been visiting St. Mary's several mornings per week. He liked the peaceful feeling he had when he entered the beautiful cathedral. He wasn't really needing to be there except on Fridays, but he'd started going when he knew the organist would be practicing. It was the most beautiful sound he'd ever experienced.

Walking up the stairs to his room, he washed up and went down to get some dinner. The boardinghouse was run by a Mrs. Fender. She served dinner between five and six o'clock. If he was late, he missed out on dinner. The food wasn't too bad, and he enjoyed talking with the other boarders. The added bonus was the two girls who stayed with their aunt, Mrs. Fender.

Cabot entered the dining room with freshly combed hair and smiled, the deep groove in his cheek irresistible—at least Iris and Lily thought so. Cabot thought it silly to name one's daughters after flowers, but they were pretty as flowers. He smiled again as he sat down between them to eat.

Libby was in a quandary. What was she supposed to do anyway? She sat in the great room thinking over the letter from Elijah. One of Armand's companies was a front for white female slavery. She'd never heard of such a thing. She also knew that there was no way she would ever want a cent of the money earned by such sordidness. She sat with her legs curled up underneath her. "What can I do, Lord?" she whispered. "What can I do?" Elijah said he and Abigail were going to open a mission for those girls. Abigail must have made a rapid recovery. The way Elijah had talked, she'd thought his wife was dying.

Her mind jumped to Matthew. He'd come home late last evening from San Francisco and was definitely cool toward her. She wondered what was wrong with him. It was past time to build a house. She wanted a home of her own where she didn't have to worry about offending anyone, especially her host.

As she sat thinking about her new life, she gave God praise for it. What a difference in circumstances. She had a startling thought: Armand actually made this possible! If he hadn't left her the property, she'd be back at the manse in Boston, probably being controlled by her father. *I'm so thankful for Elijah helping me get away from there. He was right when he said I would probably have freedom. Goodness, in just four days' time he and Abigail will be here!*

She was glad Matthew had built a house with many rooms. There were six guest rooms in the Rancho, with a little room between each. With distances between houses being what they were, guests were invited to spend the night or even several nights. She heard laughter coming from the kitchen. *Conchita and Maggie are giggling like girls. Maggie is a girl,* she amended in her mind. She heard something at the door, or did she? There it was again. She uncurled her legs and padded barefoot to the door. She opened it, and standing there swaying was, of all people, the woman on the train with the obscene dresses. The woman looked at her, recognition dawning in her tired eyes before she fainted in the doorway.

Liberty yelled, "Help! Conchita! Maggie! Help me!" Both women came running, seeing the woman collapse to the floor.

"Oh my goodness!" Maggie yelled.

Conchita crossed herself, but when she got closer, she yelled, "Eet ees Jess! Eet ees Jessica. She not dead! Me, I no help that *mujerzuela,* no, not me!" She hurried out the door to find Matthew.

Maggie picked the woman up under the armpits, and Libby carried her feet. Somehow they managed to get the woman into a guest room and laid her on the floor. While Maggie disrobed her, Libby went to tell Luce and Lupe to heat some water. The woman stank of vomit and another sick, unidentifiable sweet smell. Maggie felt like retching from the rancid odors emanating from this woman. Libby got towels, soap, and washcloths. The woman was now naked, and Libby washed the woman's body down with soap and water. Then she repeated the process.

"She's lost a lot of weight since we saw her on the train. Look at her. Why, she's as thin as a scarecrow! Ugh, do you smell that? What is that wretched smell?"

Somehow, they got the woman into a soft nightdress and put her into the bed. Maggie threw out the water, and Libby gathered up the towels, washcloths, and the filthy clothing, taking it all to the kitchen to be boiled. She threw them down just outside the doors to the courtyard. She was washing her hands when Matthew came striding in, Conchita at his heels. He said in a low, furiously angry voice, "Get that woman out of my house! Now!"

Libby looked at him totally bewildered and shocked. "She's sick. She can't be moved now."

"I said I want her out of here—now!" he yelled.

Libby looked at him, beginning to get angry. "I am not moving her. She's very, very ill!"

Matthew turned and strode to the bedroom, bursting in with no thoughts of being quiet, but it didn't matter—the woman, Jess, did not stir.

Her breathing was quite shallow. He looked at the woman lying on the bed and the anger drained away.

"Who is she?" Liberty asked in a hushed tone.

"She's my wife," he replied in a tired voice. "I thought she was dead." He turned on his heel and walked out of the room.

Liberty was completely flummoxed. *Matthew…has a wife?*

Conchita opened a window, hoping to assuage some of the smell. "Ees long story, but we all theenk she dead. *Sí*, it be better eef she dead." She left the room, with Maggie and Libby staring after her.

Libby hurried out after Conchita. "Someone must get a doctor."

"I send Diego. Thees doctor weel come soon, Mees Libby." Conchita walked with head bent and shoulders drooping to the kitchen.

Liberty got some cool water in a pan and went in to bathe the woman's forehead. She was warm to the touch, definitely running a temperature. There was nothing more to do but wait for the doctor, who should surely be here soon.

Libby went to the kitchen to see if she could get some broth for the woman when she woke up. Remembering Matthew's anger that first day when she'd asked if he was married, she wondered about it. Why had Jess left him? Why had she lived the way she did? She couldn't be happy living like that. *Perhaps the glitz and glitter had been attractive, but it didn't last. The soul longs for a lot more than this world has to offer, poor woman.*

Matthew stalked out of the house, slamming the door shut behind him. *Jessica, back after all this time! I wish Diego would hurry with the doctor.* He felt in need of talking this out, and Kirk wasn't the right person. He went out to the stables and climbed into the loft. Matthew lay down on the loose hay and stared at the rafters. *What a mess it all is! I thought Jess was dead. Who'd sent that telegram I received, anyway?*

Now that he thought about it, it was just the thing Jess would do so that he wouldn't go out looking for her anymore. She'd probably heard he was hunting her down. He'd been going to drag her back and make her work off the money she'd stolen. Jess had taken every red cent he'd saved up and ran away with that tinkerer who repaired tack in the stable.

Matthew was left with staked out property and not a cent to build or plant on it. He'd worked on Daniel Hedley's place, his closest neighbor, during the day for wages. At night he worked on his own place. That was how he'd met Diego. He had saved Diego from drowning in the Napa River while working for Dan. Diego had been working for Dan too.

Matthew knew he was angry. It always simmered in his gut. What had been a real bitter pill for him to swallow was that he'd misjudged Jess. It left a bad taste in his mouth that he'd thought her to be something other than what she was. She was shallow and selfish, without a thought in her head for anybody but herself.

Well, now she was back, and he didn't want her. *She's a travesty of what womanhood is supposed to be*, he thought bitterly. *What am I going to do now?*

He lay there thinking about his past. Then he began to dig deeper into his emotions and realized that he was not only angry at Jess...he was angry at God. He lay—feeling stunned in that moment of realization. He'd been mad at God ever since his parents had died. They'd been vacationing in Mobile, Alabama, and had taken the ferry, *Ocean Wave*. The boiler had exploded and his parents killed. He'd been nineteen, and Kirk seventeen. That was more than eleven years ago.

He lay thinking about what he believed. He knew Conchita, Diego, and Liberty were all religious. As he thought about it, he amended his thinking. They were all Christians. One could be religious about going to work or religious about going to bed at a certain time. They all three were Christians, and he liked everything about them he knew. Did being a follower of Christ make them so kind and peaceful to be around? His mind jumped back to the present situation. *What do I do about Jess?* He listened— Diego was coming back with John. He'd wait and see what happened.

The doctor entered the bedroom and knew by the smell that the woman had diabetes. Many times it was difficult to diagnose, but he recognized the smell. Many times there was no smell, but this woman was in the advanced stages, and the smell was sickly sweet. *Poor soul*, he thought. As he drew back the covers, he realized it was Jessica. He was visibly shaken. He hadn't seen her for three years, but he'd heard she was dead. Well, she was going to be, and soon. Taking her temperature, he felt for her pulse, which was rapid and thready. He pushed on her stomach. It looked bloated and was sensitive to the touch.

Her eyes opened slowly, and she looked at him, knowing without asking that she was dying. She didn't know why she'd come back here. Her eyes wandered around the room. They latched on to the woman on the train, who had been so kind. She stared at the woman and saw love and pity in her eyes. She closed hers and tried to swallow.

Jess whispered, without opening her eyes, "How long, John?"

"I want you to swallow this," he said, giving her a large dose of laudanum. He added reluctantly, "A week at most, Jessica. I'm sorry."

She swallowed the morphine. "Don't be. It's for the best." She closed her eyes again and slept. The doctor left the room with Libby trailing behind. Once they were in the great room, he turned and spoke to her.

"I'm John Meeks."

She held out her hand. "I am pleased to meet you, Dr. Meeks. I am Madam Bouvier." She looked at him closely and liked what she saw. He was probably in his midthirties, and handsome. Quite tall, he had reddish-blond hair and blue-green eyes.

They shook hands, and then he questioned her. "Are you from around these parts? I don't recognize you."

"No, I'm not. I came from Boston last December. I own property adjoining Matthew's and am waiting for the rainy season to cease so I can start building. In truth, some workmen are coming tomorrow to get started." She smiled up at him.

Handing her the laudanum, he said, "Jess can have it whenever she needs it. It'll help to alleviate some of the pain, but she must be in a tremendous amount of it. Her disease is very advanced. I'd be surprised if she makes it through the next couple days. I'll drop by again tomorrow."

Libby walked him to the door, her mind on the woman in the guest room. Matthew was married. She'd had no idea. She was curious why Jess had left Matthew. She remembered how she and Maggie had laughed at her the first time they saw her, and hot shame filled her.

She bowed her head, whispering, "I'm sorry, Lord. Please forgive me and help me to remember we're all equal in your sight." She headed toward the kitchen.

CHAPTER XXXIV

Weep ye not for the dead, neither bemoan him
JEREMIAH 22:10a

CONCHITA WAS BANGING POTS, and Maggie was in the courtyard talking to Kirk.

"Conchita, may I help you?" Liberty asked.

"No, I do thees myself," she responded shortly.

"Conchita, I am not going to pry into matters that are none of my business, but no matter what people do, we are to love them as a creation of God. We all have value in God's sight. I don't know what Jessica has or hasn't done. I do know that I'm called to love her as one who was created by God. I'd like to share something I have recently come to learn. God has created all of us for a purpose. The main purpose is to worship Him and enjoy Him forever. Most of us never fulfill the purpose for which He designed us. He has a plan for each of us, and not many of us choose that path either. You serve people, Conchita. You make everyone feel special, and it's a gift God has given you to use. The only thing is…you are to use it for everyone, not just people whom you pick and choose. God loves you very much, Conchita, and I know that you know that. When you use your gift for Him, it delights Him. It brings Him pleasure."

Libby went back to the bedroom where Jessica was lying. She took a damp cloth and wiped her face. Sitting in the rocking chair, she closed her eyes and rocked. She hummed a hymn she'd sung in the little church on

Rice Street. How long ago that seemed! Libby rocked, thinking about Elijah and his wife opening a mission for abused women. She looked at Jessica. Would she have come here if she'd had someplace else to go? Elijah said the mission would help women who were victims of illegal white slavery. *That's it…that's it!* The money from that company could be donated to the Humphries to start the mission. It would cover building and maintenance fees for a long time. *Thank you, Father, for planting that idea into my heart.*

Jessica was sleeping, so Liberty decided to ride over to her property. She did that nearly every day now. She'd sit on a log and think about many things and pray for guidance. She always told Conchita where she was going.

Cabot had one more week before he was to meet Elijah. He was beginning to fear for his life. He'd received written threats. If he told anyone about the company's money discrepancies or that the company wasn't only about canning salmon, he'd be found in the deep, cold waters of the bay.

He wished it was next week already. He'd worked steadily at doctoring the books, but he didn't want to accomplish the task, because he figured Brooks would get rid of him once they were done. He worked painstakingly on making everything neat, legible, and wrong. He smiled to himself.

Cabot thought about the two girls at the boardinghouse. Iris and Lily were pretty…and pretty insipid. Neither could talk about anything but vapid notions. *I'm bored with the pair of them.*

He was still being followed every evening after work, but once he entered the boardinghouse, he thought they must quit. He'd gone out to the cathedral several evenings a week and had not noticed anyone following him. He'd have loved to be able to send his boss, Chief Baxter, a telegram and fill him in on all the information.

The girls were coming in on ships docking at the popular wharf area under cover of night. He'd sneaked down on several occasions and was surprised at the volume of human cargo. It sickened him that people could treat other people as if they were possessions. The women were loaded onto wagons and taken to a large warehouse located just northeast of the docks. It must be terribly cold and miserable inside the dank warehouse. He'd climbed an old fire ladder and scrubbed at a scummed-over window with his sleeve, peering in. The floor had been covered with women. Guards walked around groups of women, patrolling the area. Most of the women cowered down and some were crying. Cabot hoped all those men hanged for what they were doing. He just hoped he could stay alive long enough to testify.

Sigmund was pleased with himself. His stock in Bell Telephone had already doubled. He'd added the money Elijah had told him to use and everything was going well. Bell Telephone was not just a toy. It was a company that was growing by leaps and bounds.

He entered the kitchen and talked to Cook. Mrs. Jensen missed working for madam. She'd never liked Monsieur Bouvier, but he'd been her employer and she had faithfully dispensed her duties.

Sigmund decided it was time to have a talk. "Cook, are you planning to stay here in Boston, or are you thinking of going west?"

"I am tinking I go vest. I like cooking for madam, me. I am tinking she can like me to come. Zo, I go vest un be her cook, me!" Sigmund knew he was going to miss this wonderful woman, but he also knew she'd not been happy since madam had left.

"When I hear from her, I'll tell you, and you can make plans. I think Mr. Humphries' cook is planning to go to California too. Perhaps the two of you could travel together. What do you think?"

"I am tinking zat is da beste plan. I vill go vest, un again I vill be madam's cook, me!"

Elijah was weary with the constant inactivity of train life. He was usually active, and since he'd been walking to and from work, the inactivity grated on his nerves. He was happy the trip was nearly over. They should be pulling into Sacramento in another day. He was excited for Alexander and Phoebe to meet Liberty. *My, what a reunion that will be.*

Abigail was tired and Phoebe exhausted. Elijah wondered how it was that a person could get so tired doing nothing. He'd enjoyed talking about church history, and the exchange of ideas from Alexander was a stimulant to his mind. The man was like a balm to the soul. He was so full of peace, and yet one could feel energy exuding from him—a conundrum for sure.

Phoebe was a wealth of wisdom and very entertaining. Abigail and Elijah enjoyed the woman immensely. It was interesting that she was Protestant and Alexander Catholic. Elijah could see the love emanating from the two of them to each other. It was wonderful to watch. *That's how the church universal should be,* he thought.

Phoebe was an encyclopedia on flowers. She and Abigail had spent many hours discussing various species and how to grow and propagate roses. Alexander had told them all about grape stock and the great French blight, caused by the aphid, and how the only remedy was grafted stock.

The four would linger over coffee and talk about every subject they could think of. Elijah and Alexander even played chess, as Alexander had brought pieces and a chessboard. They'd walk from one end of the train to the other stretching their legs.

The beauty of the landscape never palled. The Sierra Nevada Mountains were now in view, thickly blanketed in snow, the sun gleaming on their peaks. The train wound its way through virginal forests, crossing rivers that raged with melting snow. Waterfalls dropped from great heights into deep green pools, mists of spray making rainbows of color. The vastness of the country was incredible.

Liberty was going to take a bath. The water was cooling. Lupe and Luce both had filled the bath with boiling water. Liberty was weary; she'd spent the last three days nursing Jessica. Dr. Meeks had come to visit each day, but he seemed to do nothing for the patient. He spent his time talking to her. Libby would get up five and six times a night to check on Jess. One time when she entered the sick room during the night, Matthew was sitting in the rocker, fast asleep. She quietly checked on Jessica without waking him. It was cool with the window open. Libby had gotten a blanket from the clothespress and carefully covered Matthew so as not to awaken him.

She sat many times with Jessica reading the Word of God. It seemed to bring some peace. She'd prayed for the sick woman, but she could sense there was a discomfort in the woman's soul, and Jess refused to pray a prayer of repentance. Jessica said she'd never loved anyone except herself. She hadn't liked living the way she and Matthew lived before he'd built this beautiful Rancho. She'd wanted the beautiful things without the drudgery of work. She wished she could begin over again with the knowledge she now had, but she felt she didn't deserve God's love.

Liberty could identify with some of that. If she had it to do over again, she would have gone into service as someone's maid before ever subjecting herself to a life with Armand. If her father went bankrupt because of her choice, it wouldn't have been her fault but her own evil father's. She wondered again at how different life would've been. *Ah well, I made my choices and now I am free of the constraints of marriage. I don't think I will ever marry again.* Libby felt an attraction to Matthew, but he carried too much anger, and he was probably burned out on marriage the same as she. Libby straightened Jess' blankets and went out to get fresh drinking water. She counted the days back. *Oh my! We are fast approaching dinnertime, and tomorrow Elijah and Abigail will be here.* She spilled some water as she counted again just to be sure. Reaching for a cloth, she wiped it up.

"Conchita! It completely slipped my mind—has anyone told Matthew about Elijah and Abigail coming tomorrow?"

Conchita threw up her hands. "No, I too forget about eet! Oh, I have work to do! You go to stable. Meester Bannister, he ees there—he take care of eet. Lupe! Luce!" She yelled out to the courtyard where the two girls were talking and laughing together.

"Dose girls...yes...I find work for, *sí*!"

Liberty walked out to the stables and found Diego mending a harness and Matthew pitching hay for the horses. She crooned to Piggypie and slipped her a piece of carrot she had filched from the kitchen. Piggypie nodded her head, and Liberty smoothed her cheek.

"Matthew," she said hesitantly. She was nervous to ask such a big favor of him. She would never have broached the subject had he been Armand. She'd never asked him for anything after finding he could go into a tirade over the most mundane requests. "In the confusion and busyness of nursing Jessica, I've forgotten all about a letter I received from Elijah Humphries, the lawyer in Boston. Conchita, Maggie, and I forgot that they will be arriving into Sacramento tomorrow. I'm so sorry I haven't told you earlier. I truly forgot."

She could see his eyebrow quirking upward, as it did when he was puzzled about something.

He grinned to put her at ease. "It's all taken care of," he said. "Maggie didn't forget, at least she let us know this morning, early, before she and Kirk went to Napa. It's the lawyer who telegrammed me about your arrival, isn't it? I'm not so fond of lawyers." He grinned at her again to take the sting out of his words.

"He's the most thoughtful man I've ever met. Both he and his wife are coming out west to live, and it sounds as if they're bringing two other people to visit too," she said, her eyes sparkling at his grin.

Matthew groaned, but he was grinning. "Not another whole move! Where are we going to put all the trunks? We're all filled up with trunks!"

Diego, looking at Liberty's face closely, said, "Eet ees a good thing you haf friends to come. You work too hard, Mees Liberty. You need to seet and veesit for a few days, not be up all the night."

Matthew, on closer inspection, agreed. Liberty looked tired, but she colored up at his close perusal.

"Can Maggie help nurse Jessica?" he asked.

Libby responded, green eyes gazing into deep blue. "No, there was a bit of an altercation between the two of them on the train coming here, and neither of them likes the other."

"What kind of altercation?"

"Oh, it is over and done with now. It's not my story to tell. You can ask Maggie about it if you want to know." Changing the subject, she asked, "So you plan to pick up Elijah and Abigail Humphries along with the two people they're bringing?"

"Yes, of course. Diego can round up some wagons for the luggage and organize the wagons to go to Vallejo." He turned around. "You will, won't you, Diego? He'll round up several, since the couple is moving west and probably will rival you with how much luggage they brought with them!"

"Thank you, I appreciate it. I cannot begin to tell you how excited I am they are coming." Turning, she went back to the house. She talked to Conchita, telling her that Maggie had remembered to tell Matthew and that Diego and Matthew would pick up the Humphries and their two guests the next day.

Libby went back into Jess' room. *I am so tired.* Last night had been a hard one as Jess had been in much pain and had run a temperature all night. Libby knew she was too tired and wondered if Maggie could spell her tonight when Jess wouldn't know who was nursing her. The smell was worse than ever.

She went up to the bed and felt Jess' forehead. She was dead. Although Libby had expected it, it still came as a shock. Libby looked at her and felt bereft. She'd thought something wonderful would happen and Jess would become the vibrant woman she must have been at one time. She went in search of Conchita.

"Conchita, Jessica's gone."

Conchita crossed herself. "The poor restless soul. Perhaps she rest now. You go to bed, Mees Libby. Luce, Lupe, and I, we weel take care of her. We weel wash her and get her ready for viewing. I tell you, please go get some rest."

"I am willing to help, Conchita. I've been caring for her. It's only right I should help prepare her body."

"No, I weel not allow eet, Mees Libby. You go to the bed now. I have water een the tub waiting for you."

Liberty felt a huge relief. She was exhausted, and she wanted to be fresh for tomorrow when Elijah and Abigail would arrive. She wondered who they were bringing with them. Elijah's letter had said two people she'd be happy to meet. She was looking forward to meeting Elijah's wife. Walking slowly to her room, she wondered if Conchita had already known Jess was gone.

Libby gingerly put her fingers into the water. It had cooled enough, though it was still quite hot. She stripped off her clothes, dropping them into the hamper. She stepped into the hot water, slowly easing her body down into the steaming liquid. She soaked for a while, not thinking about anything. Finally her brain began to work again, and she lay back thinking. It had been a shock to find Jess dead. In all her life, she'd never seen a dead person. Her father had no wake for her mother and a closed casket, so she'd never seen her mother. In a way, Libby thought it was good, because her mother was alive in every memory she had of her. In another way, she felt it wasn't right. *Death is a part of life.*

Her mind swung to her father, who was now loose somewhere. She felt no fear. It was a mystery to her that she didn't care more about him. Would he die too without ever recognizing what kind of man he was? Liberty tried to remember a positive memory of something good they'd done together, before she'd gone away to boarding school, but she could think of nothing.

She remembered hating the library because it was where Jacques had given her punishment for whatever he thought she'd done wrong.

After washing her hair, Libby finished bathing. She stepped out of the tub and dried herself, wondering when Maggie was supposed to get back. She was too tired to go find out. She put on a soft clean nightdress, braided her wet hair, and went to bed. Libby prayed for just a few moments before sleep enveloped her.

CHAPTER XXXV

And ye shall dwell with us: and the land
shall be before you; dwell and trade ye therein,
and get you possessions therein.
GENESIS 34:10

THEY WERE PULLING INTO SACRAMENTO! Hallelujah! They were finally getting off the train. The four were more than ready to disembark. Phoebe and Abigail had only their satchels to carry.

The sky was an intense blue, stretching itself right down to the horizon with no dimming of its cobalt color. The sun shining warmly, created a feeling of lightness. Large pots of flowers stood as sentinels by the doors of the station, a mass of rioting color. Ivy, twining its branches up the sides of the station, created moving shadows on the bricked wall, in the slight breeze.

Passengers descended the train, meeting with people eager to see them. The noise of voices and the hiss of steam dispelled the feeling of serenity the station building exuded. The platform itself seemed to come alive as people milled about.

Alexander was the first to alight, Elijah at his heels. They had planned what they were going to do when the train stopped. Alexander headed straight back to the luggage offloading area, and Elijah turned and helped the two women down the steep steps. Once everyone was on the ground, they headed directly to the rear of the train.

Phoebe felt her legs wobbling under her. "Oh, Abigail." She laughed. "I feel as if I've been on board a ship again."

Abigail chuckled. "Me too...I don't think it would help to lean on each other. I can see where it would lead. The two of us would go sprawling, and what a spectacle we'd make!" The two women giggled like girls.

Matthew was looking for two couples, so he did not take any notice of the one man or the other man with two women. He leaned back against the wall of the station much as he had over three months ago. *Now where are they?* He decided to head down toward the offloading area. He walked down the length of the platform, and as he did, he stopped dead in his tracks.

There was a man there directing the placement of trunks who reminded him of someone. *Who is he? Do I know him from some time long ago?* The fluid motion of the man's arm as he pointed to one of the trunks not yet offloaded clued him in. It was Liberty! The man reminded him of Liberty! Was the lawyer she'd mentioned just yesterday morning a relative? He moved closer and saw the man's hair was curly, a burnished copper peppered with a little gray. It was like Liberty's, only darkened by age.

He walked up closer and said, "Good afternoon! I believe I'm supposed to meet you. Are you Elijah Humphries?"

"No, I am," said a voice behind him. He turned to see a short, blue-eyed man with a charming demeanor smiling at him. Alexander hadn't heard Matthew with all the noise and commotion and kept working with two other men taking luggage and trunks from the men in the train car.

"I'm Bannister, Matthew Bannister." He reached out to shake the lawyer's hand, and then Matthew thought he was going to choke, his jaw dropping open. There, standing beside this man, was Liberty Bouvier! She was a much older version, but beautiful nonetheless. Her eyes were a clear gray ringed by darker gray, instead of the deep green of Libby's, but the likeness was incredible. Matthew couldn't believe it.

Elijah reached out, seeing the shocked look in Matthew's eyes, and shook the man's hand.

"It's a long story, but this is Liberty's grandmother, Phoebe Liberty. I think I had that same look of stunned surprise just a few short weeks ago."

Matthew swallowed, taking Phoebe's hand gently in his. "My goodness, you're granddaughter is the spitting image of you. It's a pleasure to meet you, ma'am. He's related too, isn't he?" He jerked his head toward Alexander, who was still too busy to notice what was happening around him.

Phoebe looked at the young man, liking what she saw. "I'm happy to meet you, too, and yes, he's Liberty's real father. She doesn't know yet that we even exist. As Elijah said, it's a long story."

"She doesn't know about you? I'll enjoy hearing this story! Your accent is British English, flavored with…"

Phoebe smiled and said, "Italy." She drew Abigail forward. "This is Abigail Humphries, Elijah's wife and my friend."

"I am glad to meet you," Abby said. "You're the man who staked off the Bouviers' property and built a house on it, are you not?"

"No," Matthew replied. "I mean, I didn't build a house. I only did enough so that the land would not be repossessed. Liberty and Maggie are staying at my Rancho. They have just started building her house now the rainy season is over. It's a pleasure to meet you, ma'am, and I'm happy to have you as my guests at the Rancho."

Elijah asked, "Do I need to get tickets for the ride up to Vallejo?"

"No, sir, I purchased them. Mr. Humphries, I'm glad you're here. I know Liberty admires you very much, and I'm looking forward to talking with you once we're on the train, but we need to hurry to get the next connection. We'll need to set about loading this stuff onto the Vallejo train."

He turned and looked about for Jed.

"Jed!" he yelled across the platform. "Hey, Jed, we need your help!" He strode off in the direction of the Vallejo train.

As Matthew left, Alexander finished unloading the last trunk. He turned, rubbing his hands together, trying to rub off some of the dirt.

Elijah said to him, "We don't have quite as many trunks as Liberty had. I told her to take all she could out here, and she did."

Alexander nodded. "You realize Mother and I don't want to be a bother to anyone. I wonder if there's a boardinghouse nearby where we could stay."

"Nonsense! I'm quite sure you'll be welcome to stay with Mr. Bannister, and I know Liberty will want you to," Elijah said.

Matthew came back to start loading the luggage, Jed with him. When he saw Alexander, he stuck out his hand to him.

"I'm Bannister," he said. "Matthew Bannister. I understand you're Liberty's father."

"Alexander Liberty, here. It's a pleasure to meet you."

Jed looked at the men and said, "Waal, if ya'll wantin' to be on the train to Valley Joe, we'd best get these loaded."

Matthew spoke to Elijah, a grin on his face. "Liberty and Maggie had more trunks than all four of you put together!"

"I recognize that fact, Mr. Bannister, as I had all their trunks collected and hauled to the station." Elijah grinned. "Liberty brought things that we didn't. She has supplies and food staples to last a year, besides all she could take out of her own rooms. The only thing she took from the main part of the house was a set of dishes, silverware, and crystal."

"She has food staples in those trunks?" Matthew asked.

"Yes, hasn't she unloaded the trunks?" Elijah asked.

"No, we've just finished our rainy season, and the builders are only now beginning to build her house." Her trunks are stored in a barn at my Rancho."

Everything seemed to be in good order, and the five made a beeline down the platform toward the passenger cars. There was no time for conversation as the train was to leave in just a few minutes. Alexander escorted the two women, helping them up the stairs of the train. The women sat together on one bench seat and the three men sat across the aisle from them. They heard the "all aboooard" only once, and the wheels began to move slowly…gaining speed.

Matthew spoke above the noise of the train. "I'm happy to have all of you as guests at my Rancho. We have plenty of room, and Liberty will be very happy to have you all close at hand."

Alexander replied, "If you're certain you have room, and we won't be a nuisance, we'd be delighted to take you up on your kind offer."

"I'm certain." Matthew smiled.

The three men chatted, and Abigail and Phoebe gazed out the window making comments about the indigenous flowers that grew all over the hillsides as the train chugged its way toward Vallejo.

Mr. Bannister, what kind of crops do you grow on your Rancho?"
Alexander asked.

Matthew responded, "First of all, here in the West, we're much more
relaxed with the formalities. You are free to call me Matt, or Matthew—
in fact I prefer it. As for my Rancho, this past fall we had a bumper
harvest and produced our first wine, a Merlot. It's not bad, even if I do
say so myself."

Alexander exclaimed, "You grow grapes?"

"Yes, I do. I planted the rootstock when I first took possession of the land,
three years ago. I planted and didn't even have a place to live."

Elijah spoke up. "Alexander is a vinedresser! He can distinguish the area
and type of wine grown by taste. A discerning palate, I believe it's called."

Matthew grinned. "Now that is interesting! I understand your daughter
has the same trait. It must be inherited. Libby's able to tell where any wine
in France is grown and what kind of wine it is. What a wonderful thing you
being a vinedresser, especially since Liberty is intending to plant grapes.
You and your vast knowledge will be invaluable to her...and me too, if
you'll share what you know with me. Libby and I have been reading
everything we can get our hands on. We're both trying to learn."

"Liberty's planning to grow grapes?" Alexander couldn't believe his
ears. He reached across the aisle for his mother's hand. "Mother, Liberty's
planning to grow grapes!" Phoebe's eyes widened as the import of Alex's
words sank into her mind. She smiled tremulously at him, her eyes welling
up with tears.

"Everything has a purpose, Alexander. All that poring over books
about grape rootstock, and reading everything you could get your hands on
about the different kinds of grapes and the best conditions for growing
them...nothing wasted, Alexander, nothing!" Phoebe turned to Abigail,
who was sitting next to the train's window. She patted her hand.

"Alexander was saying to me, before we left Italy, that all the studying
and working on the varieties of grape rootstock was going to waste, a
fruitless endeavor, if you'll excuse the pun."

Abigail smiled and nodded her head sagely. "God doesn't waste
anything, does he? If Liberty's going to start growing grapes, her father's
knowledge will be invaluable to her."

Matthew sat in a quandary. *What should I tell these people about Jess and
what's just transpired at the Rancho? There's going to be a wake tonight for my dead*

wife, and they're going to be there. What should I say about it? His stomach rumbled with nerves.

Matthew cleared his throat, swinging his legs around to the aisle so he could easily face the women as well as the men. He was not one to air his dirty linen, but these people needed to know what they were walking into. He had a fleeting memory of Liberty asking him if he was married. He hadn't even shared it with her.

"I need to say something here before we get split up on the wagons, something you need to know, although this is not my normal…well…" He cleared his throat again.

"Three and a half years ago, I was married to a woman named Jessica. It was before I'd staked out the property, and I didn't have much in the way of money. We were married only six months when I staked out the land. I'd saved up enough to buy rootstock and begin planting, but no extra, and we did without. I didn't realize how difficult that was for Jess. She lit out with another man and all the money. I received a telegram from a supposed bystander, who said Jess had died. I've been very bitter and have poured myself into my property and house. Just five days ago, Jessica appeared at the front door and fainted. Liberty's been nursing her. Libby was exhausted but wouldn't leave Jess' side, and Jess didn't want anyone else. Yesterday afternoon she died. My housekeeper, cook, manager, boss, Conchita"—he smiled—"made Libby go to bed, and she wasn't up this morning before I left. I just wanted you to understand that there will be a wake tonight, but we won't expect you to stay up. We know you're exhausted from your trip." Matthew used his hands a lot when he was talking, but they now dropped to his sides.

There was silence except for the rattling noise of the train. Abigail was the first to respond.

"Matthew, we cannot, as much as we'd like to at times, control another person's behavior. We can't even control their responses to things we do. We can pray to the Almighty and allow Him to conform us to the way He is, or we can go our own way and suffer the consequences. It's not your fault your wife chose to leave you, unless you beat her or were cruel. She must've been skin deep, or she'd have stuck by you through thick and thin.

"In contrast to your wife, look at Liberty. Her husband was unspeakably evil and cruel to her."

Matthew's eyes widened at the revelation as Abigail continued to talk, revealing much about Liberty Matthew did not know.

"She, however, stuck by him. She's not even shared the hurts she endured at his hands, although rumors, especially through the servant grapevine, have a way of making themselves known. A woman can stand by her man or she can choose a path of her own, which most likely leads to destruction. None of us can judge how you treated your wife. That's something you know and will live with, whether it was good or bad. The Almighty knows, and he cares about the way we treat others. Life itself is all about relationships, not things, just relationships. We'll support you in any way we can, and if you feel at all that we'll be a burden at this time, we can find another place to stay."

"No," Matthew said quickly. "I'd like it if you would stay at my place. We have plenty of room, and Conchita has been in a flurry, cooking and getting ready for you. Also, Libby has learned to cook and will be helping with the food preparation today, I'm sure. Jess won't have many attending the wake, probably just folk around the place and perhaps the doctor. He's taken a real shine to Libby." Matthew's face reddened a bit. *That John spent more time with Libby than with Jess. I feel as if being just widowed, I have no business interfering in Libby's life, but that John is a real flirt. He equals Kirk in his string of broken hearts.*

Liberty slept straight through dinner and the night. At nearly half past the hour of ten the next morning, she began to stir. Opening her eyes, she thought, *I need to get that ormolu clock out of my trunk.* She picked up her grandfather's watch off her night table and looked at the time.

Her head felt fuzzy, and she squinted at the dials. *It was after ten o'clock, but it was daylight! I couldn't have slept all night!* She sat up and leaned against her pillows for a few minutes, collecting and ordering her thoughts.

Jess had died and, after bathing, Liberty had gone straight to bed. *Oh my goodness,* she thought. *Today...today Elijah and Abigail are coming!* She threw back the covers, swinging her legs over the side of the bed.

Maggie had been helping Luce and Lupe make beds, clean, and dust. She liked to help in every way, except in the kitchen. She supposed she should learn to cook the way Libby had. She didn't think she'd marry some rich toff with a pocketful of money who'd be able to afford servants. That should be her next goal, she decided. She needed to learn to cook.

As she dusted, she hummed while she thought about the day before. Kirk had taken her to Napa. It wasn't much of a town by Boston standards. She'd done a bit of shopping, and they'd wandered around. They'd walked down by the river to eat the lunch Conchita had made them. It was delicious. Kirk had wanted to go to Consuelo's house, but she said she wanted to be dropped off first. He wouldn't drop her off, and they ended up at Consuelo's house. *That's the last time I'm going anywhere with Kirk. He's nice, but taking me to go sit and wait while he went off with Consuelo has certainly not endeared him to me.*

Maggie dusted the books in the great room and looked at the titles. Some of them she'd read, but there were a lot here she hadn't. Maybe she should read a little before bed every night since she had a lot more time on her hands than ever she did at the Bouvier manse. *I'm not wasting my evenings with Kirk anymore.*

Maggie could hear Liberty talking to Conchita in the kitchen.

Liberty entered the sunny kitchen and stretched again. She walked over and gave Conchita a big hug.

"You really must think me a bedbug," she said laughingly.

"No, I no teenk you bedbug, Mees Libby, I teenk you one tired girl. I glad for you to sleep."

"Well, I'd planned to be of some use to you since it's my company that's causing all the work."

"No! Eet ees not the company. I glad for company, *sí.*" Conchita smiled. "We haf the wake thees night. Meester Bannister, he haf many friends to come to eet."

"What time do you expect Matthew to be here with all the company?"

"The train, eet comed earlier now the weather better. They have better times een *Marzo* than *Diciembre.* I know thees true. They comed maybe for dineer, I teenk."

"What would you like me to do, Conchita?"

"You make tortillas. You no tell Luce"—her voice dropped to a conspiratorial whisper—"but you make better than hers, *sí*." She laughed her full, contagious laughter. Libby found herself joining in.

"I'll be happy to make them, Conchita, but first I need some coffee. I still feel groggy from so much sleep. I can't remember ever sleeping like that unless I was sick. Oh, Conchita, I'm so excited about Elijah coming and being able to meet Abigail! You will love them, I'm sure."

Jessica's body lay in a room waiting for the wake. They would all sit for a while with her. Some for just a little while and some perhaps all night. Candles would burn the entire night in her honor.

Conchita said, "Dare weel be refreshments een the kitchen for any who wants to eat or dreenk. Anyones can be talking loud een the kitchen but not een the room where Jess lays, no, only the quiet talk there. Lupe and Luce, you put chairs in leetle circle around the room. Mees Maggie, you halp."

The afternoon passed quickly with work for everyone. Libby was so excited to see Elijah that every once in a while she would go outside to spy down the road to see if they might be there.

When they finally did arrive, she was in the kitchen. Matthew pulled up the horses and sat as Elijah jumped down. Elijah thought he should prepare Libby for the arrival of her father, but she'd come running out the door when the wagon pulled up. She had no eyes for anyone except Elijah.

"Oh, Elijah!" She gave him a big hug. "I'm so glad to see you!"

Alexander just sat, gazing down at his daughter. No one had told him how beautiful she was. He sat motionless, held fast by the scene in front of him.

Elijah hugged Libby back and then held her away from himself, looking into her deep green eyes, he said, "I brought someone with me I want you to meet."

"Yes," she said quickly. "I've been looking forward to meeting Abigail." As she said this, she looked up and stood stock-still.

There was a man sitting on the flatbed wagon. She stared at him…he looked familiar…but who was he? He returned her stare, not looking away. His beautiful eyes held her like a magnet. She walked slowly, as if mesmerized, toward him.

She heard Elijah's voice ring out. "Liberty Alexandra Bouvier, meet your father, Alexander Edward Liberty!"

The man jumped down, containing himself any longer. "Oh, Liberty, my daughter!" And he enveloped her in his arms.

Liberty could hardly believe it, but she knew, she sensed within herself the truth. She hugged him as if she would never let him go. Then she started crying. *Jacques' not my father. Oh thank You, Lord!*

The two women had been helped down from the second wagon by Diego. They both stood, taking in the scene of father and daughter finally united. Both Alexander and Liberty were crying. Finally, Alexander pulled back and looked at his daughter with tears streaming down his face as he wept unashamedly.

"Liberty," he said. "Liberty, I have brought my mother with me." Turning, he said, "Liberty Alexandra, this is Phoebe Alexandra Liberty, your grandmother!"

Liberty put a shaking hand to her mouth and gasped as she looked at this old woman who looked so like her own reflection, and the tears poured forth again as the two women hugged each other. Liberty's shoulders shook with sobs. "I have a family!"

Phoebe could hardly stand it.

She held this precious young woman in her arms and said, "Bone of my bone and flesh of my flesh." Tears ran rivulets down her wrinkled cheeks.

Alexander came up and held the two most precious women in his arms. The three of them stood hugging each other. What a blessing God had bestowed upon them!

"Oh Lord, I praise you! Thank you!" Alexander said.

"Amen," Liberty said, the tears streaming down her face.

There was not a dry eye among all those who watched this incredible meeting of family.

Elijah drew Abigail forward and said, "Liberty, this is Abigail."

Liberty hugged Abby. "I can hardly believe this!" She held Abby at arm's length to better look her in the eyes and said, "I have *so* looked forward to meeting you." She hugged her again and dabbed at her eyes with her apron.

Abigail was so overcome by emotion, she could hardly speak. "I too have looked forward to meeting you. Elijah has spoken so highly of you. We have much tell each other."

Liberty nodded in agreement, but she turned to look at her father and grandmother. She stared at her father, for he stood straight and tall and looked wholesome and good. She teared up in wonder that Jacques Corlay was not her father. She reveled in that fact alone, besides the blessing of seeing this man.

He caught her eyes upon him and just stood, drinking her in. Green eyes looked into gray, and love spoke through both.

Taking her father's arm and then her grandmother's arm, Liberty walked them to the front door.

CHAPTER XXXVI

And my people shall dwell in a peaceable habitation,
and in sure dwellings, and in quiet resting places
ISAIAH 32:18

THE HOUSE DID NOT HAVE AN AIR OF mourning nor sadness. Jessica would go out with a party...something she always enjoyed. Everyone seemed to convene at the kitchen and spill out into the courtyard. The women were setting out food for dinner, and the men stood or sat around talking.

Alexander couldn't take his eyes off Liberty. He longed to tell her all about Violet. It'd been one of those all-consuming fires that never burned out, even after she died. Liberty's green eyes, so like her mother's, jerked his heartstrings and he was grateful, so very grateful.

Phoebe kept touching Liberty. She couldn't help herself. She too was thankful. Her mind had been put to rest about Libby's character when Matthew had talked about her selflessness in caring, these past few days, for his long-lost wife. She saw honesty and truth in those green eyes that were identical to Violet's.

Liberty could scarcely take it all in. She had a father who loved her and a grandmother. *Oh Lord*, she prayed as she set food out, *thank You, thank You. I cannot begin to tell You how thankful I am.*

Dr. John Meeks came and enjoyed the meal also. Tables in the courtyard were full, as some of the neighboring people came to show their respects. John flirted outrageously with Liberty, and she laughed at his jests. Her father could already get a sense of the woman she was and knew she was not so attracted to the man as amused.

Alexander looked over and caught a look on Matthew's face not intended for anyone else to see. *Now that one*, Alexander thought, *that one is a deep man, with emotions kept well hidden.* Alexander had seen the look Matthew gave Libby before he had schooled his face to a casual smile. *He's in love with her*, Alexander thought with a start. *I wonder if even he knows it yet.*

After the dinner, most people sat around talking and drinking coffee. Alexander slipped out and into the room where Jessica lay. He could not administer last rites, but he could certainly pray for her. After lighting a candle for her, he did so in Latin. He bowed his head and prayed for this poor woman who'd never found peace in this life.

Liberty had slipped in just behind her father and sat down quietly with bowed head when she heard him praying. She understood a little of the prayer. She knew Catholics believed in Purgatory and wondered what faith, if any, Jess had been. She hadn't shared any personal beliefs with Liberty, and she didn't want Libby to talk about anything Christian, although she said she'd enjoyed Libby reading the Bible to her.

When Alexander finished, he sat down next to her, and they talked quietly together until others came in to join them. There was so much she wanted to learn from him. He told her about meeting Violet and how they'd fallen in love at first sight.

"Did she still have the ormolu clock I gave her?"

"You gave the clock to her? I thought it was a present from my grandfather to mother on her sixteenth birthday—at least that's the story I was told."

"No, I bought it for her in London, at Aspreys on Regent Street, just before I shipped out to Burma."

"Yes, she loved that clock. She gave it to me a few months before she died. She told me I was to have it cleaned every few years, but I never did. It was still running when I packed it away. I was thinking only this morning that I need to get it out and use it."

Others began to filter into the room for the wake. Alexander and Liberty sat quietly next to each other, both thankful to the Lord for bringing them together.

The Napa Valley had many caves, some natural and some dug out specially, for aging wine. Located in a perfect spot, this cave had been a lucky find. Jacques had quietly moved some supplies and a couple bedrolls to one of the abandoned wine-aging caves. Bannister's ranch was not far away. Jacques was ready.

He'd bought two horses. The second one had been used for a pack horse, but Jacques intent was that it soon would carry Liberty. He had rope, a couple guns, plus food. It'd taken him two and a half weeks to find a place that was well screened by trees, close to water, and not in an area anyone would normally go. He hoped it was a forgotten cave.

It was located at the very top of a hill on a small plateau jutting out from the hillside. He had a view of the valley to the west, over the tops of trees, which acted as a screen to the cave's entrance. As well, he was able to look right over the top of the cave to the east. The entrance to the cave was low. Sagebrush hung over its edge, and he had to duck down when he entered it.

He had tea bags and coffee for drinking. He'd bought a box of the new safety matches, but wasn't sure he'd even use them. He didn't want smoke to give away his location. He thought after dark he could risk a fire without being detected.

Every day for two weeks, besides getting the supplies, he'd been scouting out Bannister's place. He watched, as nearly every day, Liberty went out riding on her horse to the same place. There was nothing special about where she went, but he assumed it must be the bit of land Armand had left her. She was a fool. She could've made Armand happy but instead, she had chosen to walk around with her nose in the air. She thought she was better than anyone else.

He'd show her. She had ruined his life. It was her fault he'd been caught. Somehow, he knew it was all her fault. She was in cahoots with that lawyer, Humphries. They'd conspired together to get the fortune Armand had left. Well, he was going to make her pay.

Liberty awoke early the next morning. Perhaps, it was because she'd slept so late the day before. She couldn't go back to sleep, so she climbed out of bed and padded to the little room. She quietly took care of her business, not wanting to wake Maggie. She washed, splashing water on her face. As she dried with a towel, she looked into the mirror and grinned. *Now I know why I have curly red hair. I do look so much like my father.* She giggled a little as she thought, *At least my name's not Liberty Liberty.*

She dressed in what was fast becoming her favorite attire, the split skirt and a blouse with full sleeves, open at the neck in a deep V. She pulled on her boots, loving the feel of the soft leather. Picking up her wide-brimmed hat, she jammed it onto her head, tightening the leather thongs around her neck.

Saddling up Pookie was easy because she stood so quietly. Waiting after she tightened the girth, to cinch it up even tighter was a must with Pookie. Libby knew the trick of a puffed-out chest. She'd seen more than one rider go sprawling who didn't recheck the girth before getting on. She walked Pookie until they were far enough away from the house so they wouldn't wake anyone. She gave Pookie a little kick with her heels, and they were off at a gallop that was smoother than a rocking chair.

Jacques was up early, watching the Bannister place while he munched on some beef jerky, washing it down with water. He'd lost quite a bit of weight in the past few weeks. Food didn't seem important. He sat up straighter. Was that Liberty? He strained to see. Yes! It was Liberty, and she was alone. *I've never seen her ride out this early. Well, well, well. This is it!* He quickly saddled up both horses and headed cross country to try to get there before she did.

Jacques rode hard, with the reins of the second horse tied to his pommel. He almost skidded to a stop when he got to the lean-to. He rode around to the back, hiding the horses from view. He'd already hollowed out an area on the back side of the bushes and scrub oak to hide. *I always plan ahead, and that's why I'm much more successful than anyone I know. Stupid fools, all of them.* He quickly hobbled both horses, putting feedbags on their noses. He'd carried the feed in the saddlebags. He didn't want them snorting or calling out to a strange horse. Jacques could hear Liberty's horse on the path leading to the lean-to. He was ready for her.

Matthew awoke suddenly, raising up on one elbow, listening. He'd heard someone go out into the hall. He lay back against the pillow for a few minutes. He heard the hinges on the barn door screech. *I need to oil those things.* He sat up as he heard the doors being shut. *Liberty must be heading over to her property. She does that almost every day. Think I'll ride over and talk with her in private. I want her to know that I know about her husband being dead.* He also remembered the telegram Elijah had sent and thought, *Until she learns to shoot, she needs protection.* He got up and stretched and grabbed his denims off the floor where he'd dropped them last night. Taking a clean checkered shirt out of the closet, he buttoned it as he walked over to get some socks. Soon, he was ready. He'd shave later. He strapped on his gun and walked out quickly to saddle up Piggypie.

The air, still brisk from a cool night, filled his lungs with its freshness. Matthew looked around as he trotted out of the stable area. Piggypie settled into a gentle stride, and they headed easily down the long lane. He was looking forward to talking to Libby.

As Liberty approached her land, she paused on the rise above the shack and surveyed again, with pleasure, her possession. She had hired workers, via Matthew, to begin clearing the area of rocks and sagebrush. She leaned on the pommel and looked down at the shack. It would be taken down as soon as improvements were made up the hill. She kicked Pookie gently and headed at a walk down the slope.

Dismounting at the shack, she tied Pookie to a rail by the pump. Reaching for the pump handle, her neck prickled as if she were being watched. She paused. *That's strange—I've never had this feeling here before. Lord, if I am not alone, I pray right now, in the name of Jesus, for protection and wisdom. You alone are in control.* She reached for the handle and began to pump it. Water streamed out, and she made a cup of her hands, drinking in its cool freshness.

She felt a hand grab her shoulder and spin her around. Her eyes widened. "Jacques!"

His grip on her shoulder tightened. Liberty tensed under the pressure but didn't flinch.

"Jacques, what are you doing here?"

"I've come to make you pay, you wretched little piece of garbage!" His grip tightened even more.

"That hurts! Take your hand off me." Instead of complying, Jacques grabbed the other shoulder too, spinning her. He took her wrist and hammerlocked her.

Libby tried not to moan with pain as Jacques pulled her arm up even farther behind her back. She felt as if he were going to wrench her arm from its socket.

He walked backward, pulling her with him. When they got to the horses, he grabbed a rope to tie her wrists together. As he reached for it, Libby spun out of his grasp. She began to run, moving quickly to the slope she'd just ridden down, but she wasn't fast enough. He caught her and pulled her backward by her hair. "Come here, you illegitimate wretch."

"I'm not!" Liberty cried out.

"You are. You were never my daughter. I knew within three months of marrying your mother that she was pregnant with someone else's whelp. Violet never loved me. I was a convenient sucker. I thought we loved each other, but I knew soon enough it was all an illusion."

"You could've made it work, Jacques. I considered you my father."

"Shut your trap!" He slapped her face.

Her eyes stung, but she looked him straight in the eye. "Do you know I pray for you all the time? I've prayed that you'd come to know Jesus as your Savior, Jacques, that you could find the peace that I've found."

"I said, shut up!" He yanked her, pulling her arm backward. He smiled when she gasped from the pain. "I never had much use for God, and he's never had much use for me. I don't believe in all that mumbo jumbo."

Liberty felt light headed from the pain. "Oh, Jacques, God has a lot of use for you, if you'd—"

Jacques slapped her again as he yelled, "I said shut up, and I mean it!" He dragged her back to the horses. Tying her hands together, he threw her up onto the horse whose reins were tied to the pommel of his. He wrapped the end of the rope tying her wrists around her pommel. Taking the hobbles and the oat bags off the horses, he quickly stuffed them back into his saddlebags. He got onto his horse, kicking its sides hard. They set off at a gallop. Cutting through sagebrush, they were up and over the hill, heading straight for the cave. Jacques didn't want to waste any time in case someone else had risen early at the Rancho.

CHAPTER XXXVII

For the wages of sin is death;
but the gift of God is eternal life
through Jesus Christ our LORD.
ROMANS 6:23

MATTHEW ARRIVED AT THE LEAN-TO having enjoyed a leisurely ride in the sweet morning air. The sun lay low in the sky, just coming up fully over the horizon. Matthew could tell it was going to be a beautiful day. He loved this time of year. He didn't see Libby, but Pookie was tied up by the pump. He went into the lean-to, but she wasn't in there either. Walking out, he started to head up toward the slope where she'd said she wanted to build her house. As he passed by the pump, he thought he'd have a drink. He saw turned-up dirt around the pump and squatted down to have a look. There were two sets of shoes— Libby's boots were easy to identify. He looked closely at the other prints. They were a man's boot, and it looked as if Libby's were dragged. He quickly followed the scoring of earth around to the back of the lean-to, where bushes grew thick and wild between the scrub oaks. Behind the bushes, two horses had stood. He ran back to Piggypie, jumping into the saddle.

He galloped up the steep slope, where not ten minutes before Jacques had led Libby. Matthew rode fast, tracking broken sage branches and glimpses of shod horse tracks. He reached down to his thigh, undoing the safety on his gun.

Diego had heard Liberty ride off and not long afterward, Matthew. He could tell the difference in the horses' hooves. Piggypie was a larger horse than Pookie. Diego got up carefully. He didn't care to disturb Conchita. She was one unhappy woman if he woke her earlier than when she needed to get up. He smiled to himself, satisfied that he was being quiet. *I do anything to make thees womans happy. When she happy…I happy.*

I teenk I scout around a beet and see what going on so early thees morning, not that Matthew would need any halp. He one self-sufficient hombre. Eet's just that feeling. I haf eet now for a couple weeks…thees feeling that someteeng's brewing. I learn not to ignore my gut, or maybee eet's my heart. Whatever eet is, eet not be Jess that cause it. I teenk thees feeling go away after she show up, but eet not. Dere ees malo storm coming soon. When…I doan know…but eet definitely coming. He dressed quietly, picking up his holster. He wrapped it around his waist, grabbed his sombrero, and left the room.

Jacques Corlay, eyes wild with hate, yanked Liberty off her horse, letting her free-fall to the ground. With no way to break her fall with hands tied together, she fell hard. Hearing a snap in her left arm, excruciating pain hit her like a hammer, and the breath was knocked out of her. Jacques grabbed her and drug her to the front of the cave. He pushed her down before the low-hanging entrance.

Squatting down, he rasped out, "What have you done with my money, Liberty? Where is it?"

Liberty looked at him but didn't answer. She was thankful he hadn't pulled her by her other arm. It was broken. Biting the inside of her cheek to keep from moaning, she could taste blood. She wouldn't give him the satisfaction of having power over her…he didn't, only Jesus. Her lips began to curve slightly at the thought.

Jacques saw the beginnings of her enigmatic smile and saw red. He doubled his fist and hit her on the chin. Her head snapped sideways, and she knew no more. He shook her, but she didn't wake. He hadn't meant to knock her out. *I need her to talk. I want to know how I can get at Armand's money. It's my money, not hers.* He stared down at her in a rage.

God, she's always ranting about God. I don't believe in heaven or hell, nor God for that matter. I believe you take what you can here and then you die. You're buried in a hole, and that's it.

He got up, bumping his head on the overhang of the cave. Jacques angrily rubbed his forehead. He'd hit it hard. Hungry, he ducked down to avoid hitting his head again and entered the cave. He rummaged around in one of his packs and found some hardtack. He went back out where the light was better and he could stand up, watching for Liberty to regain consciousness.

Chewing on the hardened biscuit at the low entrance of the cave, he thought about the situation. *It will take days for anyone to find us here. By then, we'll be gone to the city. I'll get her bank account and then I'll leave, but I want Liberty to suffer a bit first. She's always been aloof to me...acting as if she were better than me. Well, I'm going to show her who's boss.* He turned to look over the entrance to the cave. He scraped back some sagebrush he'd loosened when he'd bumped his head.

He heard a quick buzz and froze. He'd disturbed a rattlesnake. He stared at it, eye level, as it lay coiled just above the entrance, its tail straight up and buzzing hard. He panicked and started to turn, but the snake struck with lightning speed, its fangs sinking deeply into his neck. It clung to him, pumping its full store of venom into him. He screamed. Reaching for his gun to shoot it, he shot wildly. Pulling the snake from his neck, he shot it in the head. He dropped to the ground, the snake dead next to him. He writhed with burning pain in his neck, but the scream in his throat stuck there. He writhed again next to an unconscious Liberty, feeling excruciating, burning pain.

Matthew had tied Piggypie far enough down the hill that she wouldn't give him away. As he started to climb, he heard a sound behind him. He spun around, drawing his gun quickly. It was Diego, a wide smile on his face.

"You een good practice, Meester Bannister." He spoke with admiration in his eyes and voice.

Matthew put his forefinger to his lips and nodded to him. He nodded back and then, looking down, made sure he placed his feet where he wouldn't disturb the scree. The stones were small and could easily start a slide. Matthew waited for him to get across the rocky area. When he reached him, they whispered, Matthew telling him all that had transpired. Sound carried around these parts and they didn't want to alert Corlay. That it was Corlay was a foregone conclusion.

At that moment they heard a scream, low and ugly, and a gunshot, then another. Both men started running up the incline, rocks sliding under their feet. As they ran into the clearing, they both stopped dead in their tracks. Liberty was lying at the entrance to the cave, facing away from them, not moving. *Had she been shot?* Corlay lay next to her, writhing on the ground, a bloody swelling on his neck. He'd killed the rattlesnake, but not before it got him. It must have been disturbed. Corlay was already dying. The snake had caught him right on the jugular. Diego ran to the dying man, and Matthew ran to Liberty.

"He no make eet, Meester Bannister."

"I know." He gently turned Liberty to a more comfortable position. She moaned but didn't regain consciousness. The bruised swelling on her chin was turning dark. Her left arm lay crooked, and he knew it was broken. He felt down her legs and around her ankles, but nothing else seemed broken.

Diego went into the cave to get some water for Corlay. He picked up a flask, opened it, and smelled. It was water. He went back to the dying man and lifted Corlay's head up, putting the flask to his lips, but he wouldn't drink.

"What we do weeth heem, Meester Bannister?"

"I'm not sure. I was wondering whether we should take him with us, or just leave him here. Maybe we should put him into the cave and tell Sheriff Rawlins to get him."

Diego picked Corlay up and carried him into the cave, laying him down on the bedroll that had been spread out. He tried to make him comfortable, covering him gently with a blanket. Corlay, unconscious, was fading fast. Diego knew, had the bite been in another place, Dr. John could have fixed him up, providing he kept quiet and they got help within an hour. Corlay had pumped his blood hard by writhing and screaming. He could see the man wouldn't last but a few more minutes. He looked down at Corlay with sorrow in his eyes. This was the storm he'd felt in his heart. He crossed himself and went out of the cave. Matthew stood up as Diego exited the cave. Diego shook his head in a negative way.

Matthew picked up Liberty, as gently as he could, glad that she was still unconscious.

"Diego, I'll ride for the Rancho. You ride the other horse down and get our horses and ride over to Libby's property for Pookie. We'll never know where these horses came from unless Corlay has paperwork someplace. We'll let Sheriff Rawlins figure it all out."

Diego took Liberty until Matthew got on the horse and then lifted her up to him. Matthew started down the steep path, trying to ride smoothly so as not to jar Libby. Diego went back inside the cave, but Corlay was dead. He covered his face with the blanket and hoped Sheriff Rawlins would get up here before animals did.

Conchita had heard Diego get up, but she didn't open her eyes until after he left. She quietly got up and dressed, braiding her hair quickly. Entering the kitchen, she was surprised to find Diego wasn't there. Conchita sensed something was wrong. The normal pattern of Diego waiting for her to get him coffee was broken. She crossed herself and whispered a prayer of protection for him.

Making coffee always came first because it was what everyone wanted to start their day. Still feeling troubled, Conchita picked up the big kettle from the stove and began to fill it with water. She also filled a an extra pot of water to heat. Hot water would be needed if someone was hurt.

She began to beat some batter for pancakes. Luce had picked some fresh strawberries from her little garden the day before. *Spring strawberries, they ees the best*, she thought. Letting the batter rest, she sat down and had her first cup of coffee. It tasted wonderful and helped to restore her peace of mind, although she still felt uneasy. *Matthew ees usually up by now. Where ees everyone?*

She began to think about Maggie. *Mees Maggie, she ees not so much laughing with Meester Kirk anymore. Meester Kirk, he involved with that Consuelo. I hope he know what he do. Consuelo, she ees bad through and through. I hope he doan get her into trouble. If Consuelo end up pregnant, it no matter who the father ees, she weel say ees Meester Kirk.*

Where ees everyone? Something doan feel right, that's for sure. She got up and heated some maple syrup for the pancakes, pouring herself another cup of coffee. Lupe and Luce were taking the day to go to San Francisco to their aunt's house. While they were there, they'd pick up some supplies for the Rancho.

"Good morning, Mees Maggie."

Maggie was wide awake and ready for a strong cup of java.

"Good morning." Maggie was definitely an early riser. "Where is everybody? Mmm, that maple syrup smells good!"

Conchita looked mournfully at Maggie. "Someting no right, Mees Maggie. I can feel eet een my heart. I doan know where anyone ees."

They both heard horses' hooves coming right up to the front door of the Rancho. Conchita and Maggie ran to the door, throwing it wide open.

Matthew was trying to get off his horse without causing Liberty more pain. Conchita ran out and held a strange horse's reins while Matthew dismounted. Libby, having regained consciousness, gritted her teeth to keep from moaning as Matthew carefully carried her into the house.

"Conchita, wake Kirk and have him ride for John." Conchita sped down the hall toward Kirk's room.

Maggie was right behind her, opening Libby's door for Matthew. She went to the kitchen to heat some water, but it was already heating up. Matthew carried Libby into her bedroom, gently laying her on the bed. She looked up at him and tried to smile.

"Where's Jacques?"

"Libby, he was bitten by a rattlesnake... He's dead."

She closed her eyes, tears seeping out of her thick lashes as they lay on her cheeks. She said nothing as Matthew looked down at her. She turned her head away, not wanting him to see her tears. Matthew picked up a blanket lying on the arm of the chair and covered her with it, tucking it around her in case she was in shock.

"Kirk's going for Dr. John." He went out into the hall and tapped on Alexander's door.

"Come in." Alexander had just finished his morning ablutions and felt better for washing away the sleep. He was fully dressed. Matthew filled him in on what had transpired that morning.

"Her left arm is broken, and her chin doesn't look too good. I'm going to get some ice from the icehouse. I'll need to pick it, but there's a big block of it. It should help with the chin a bit."

Alexander clapped Matthew on the back. "I'm so thankful you rode out after her. Who knows what could have happened if you hadn't rescued her."

"That makes two of us," he said.

Alexander slipped on his sandals and quietly entered Libby's room. Her door was wide open, the way Matthew had left it. Her face was turned away, and he could see her left arm lay at an odd angle. He picked up the chair from the desk and sat it next to the bed. He sat and gently took her right hand on the coverlet, encasing it with his. Her fingers felt icy, and he wondered if she was in shock. She turned her head, looking at him with tears seeping from her green eyes.

"Jacques was so evil. I don't understand how a person can grow up from an innocent child to be such a monster and not care at all for life, or love, or any of the things that make living meaningful."

Her father replied, "Romans eight talks about the sinful mind, how it is hostile to God and does not submit to God's law, nor can it do so. Those controlled by the sinful nature cannot please God. Libby, honey, there are many people who end up just trying to please themselves and they never can because it's contrary to the law of God's Spirit. Many people fill themselves up with other things because our very being was created to worship, but they worship the wrong things."

Libby looked up at her father. She wondered that he could comfort her with so few words. Her lids felt heavy, and she closed her eyes and drifted off to sleep. Alexander continued to sit quietly holding her hand.

Kirk rode a strange horse. She was saddled and standing with her head down, munching on nasturtiums just outside the front door. He climbed easily into the saddle and backed her down the walk to the drive. He rode hard for John Meeks, catching him just as he was entering his office.

"You're needed at the Rancho, John. I don't know all the details yet, but Liberty's got a broken arm and who knows what else."

John looked at him, startled. Without saying a word, he grabbed splints and his medical bag. Kirk helped him saddle up his horse and they were off.

Diego had returned and spent some time currying the horses and feeding them. He'd take care of the other horse later. He'd seen Kirk head out on her. He washed up and went into the house for breakfast.

Maggie was in the kitchen. "You know, I think I should learn how to cook. I don't want to, but here you are slaving away, and I have no idea how to help."

"You mus learn, You can geet out the plates and cups...everyone can halp themselves."

Conchita had begun cooking the pancakes, stacking them in the oven to stay warm. Bacon was sizzling in another pan. She cooked up several pounds and decided to make scrambled eggs too.

Diego came in and was glad to sit quietly and have his first cup of coffee. Conchita didn't ask him anything until he was half-finished with it. She knew when he was troubled, and she waited until he calmed down.

Maggie didn't say anything either. The kitchen was quiet. She hoped Dr. John would hurry. She was worried about Libby but didn't want to disturb her or Alexander.

Phoebe came out to the kitchen. "Where is everyone?"

Conchita replied, "Diego, he know."

Diego was ready and related all that he knew.

When he finished his narrative, Maggie's eyes sparked. "I'm glad that hateful man is dead. Glad, glad, glad!"

"Mees Maggie...you no talk like that. Eet ees not good."

"You don't know, Conchita, how evil that man was, and he was always mean to Liberty. Before I worked for Libby, I worked for another family. That man committed suicide because of Liberty's husband and her father...I mean Jacques Corlay. Liberty thought all these years he was her real father and he was vile. Yes, I am glad he's dead."

Phoebe went over to get a cup of coffee. "Evilness is like a disease. It doesn't get better—it gets worse unless we ask Jesus to forgive us, come into our hearts and change us."

They heard the front door bang open, and Dr. John Meeks followed Kirk inside. Conversation stopped in the kitchen, and they all wondered how Liberty was.

EPILOGUE

Fear not; for thou shalt not be ashamed: neither be thou confounded;
for thou shalt not be put to shame:
for thou shalt forget the shame of thy youth, and shalt not remember
the reproach of thy widowhood any more.
ISAIAH 54:4

EVERYONE WAS IN THE COURTYARD, relaxing after dinner. It had cooled off a little, and the air felt fresh and pleasant. Birds were singing their evening song, and across the courtyard, quail could be heard calling to each other.

Liberty was sitting in the bench swing with her father. Dr. John had come back for dinner. He'd told her it would take about six weeks for her arm to heal. She was glad there'd be no permanent damage. Her heart still mourned for what Jacques could have been and chose not to be. As she thought about it, she realized that could be said about anyone. *We all have choices to make.* She was so happy she had family. They could help her build. Her own loving father and grandmother could help her start over again.

Phoebe sat looking at Alexander and Libby. How grateful she was to know she had a granddaughter. It was as if her son, Alexander, had been granted new life. He was like a new man. The hurt from Violet's marriage that had lain deep within him had turned to peace. She watched in gratitude

291

as Liberty Alexandra and Alexander Liberty sat engrossed in conversation, getting to know each other.

Maggie sat in the courtyard and glanced over at Kirk. *I don't think he's the one for me. I like him a lot, but he is always flirting with Consuelo. I wonder what the future holds for me? Will I end up working at the mission for Abigail and Elijah? Will I stay with Libby? I love her so much. She's the best friend I've ever had.* Maggie looked at Liberty sitting next to her father. *I think I'd better start thinking seriously about what I believe about God and Jesus. I wouldn't like to end up like Monsieur Corlay and die without really knowing the truth.*

Elijah sat thinking about what he would find in San Francisco. Was Cabot Jones all right? What unspeakable cruelty those women have endured, what heartache. *I hope Abigail and I will be able to begin harboring and ministering to these women very soon. Is San Rafael the right place to open a mission? Time is of the essence. I'm not going to allow Abigail to go with me to San Francisco this trip. It's too dangerous. Perhaps Matthew will accompany me.*

I thank Thee, gracious Lord. How I praise Thee for the protection Thou hast provided for Liberty. I thank Thee for bringing this family together and pray their years might be long. Oh my Father, how I give Thee praise. May it be continually in my mouth for healing Abigail. Thou art precious to me, oh Lord, may all of us be a delight to Thee. Tears of thanksgiving misted his eyes.

𝔄 Woman of Entitlement
Book II
Liberty's Land

Preview ~ Prologue

"Ah LORD God! Behold, Thou hast made
the heavens and the earth by
Thy great power and by Thine outstretched arm!
Nothing is too difficult for Thee,"

JEREMIAH 32:17

I WISH I KNEW WHERE I WAS. *I suppose it wouldn't make the situation any better, but I think I'd feel better, knowing. What city is this? New York? Boston? We got here some time after dark last night. At least those filthy rafter windows let in enough light to know day from night.*

The trip was longer than I'd anticipated. Perhaps, we're in South America. Maybe Rio de Janeiro. We stopped sailing and made port yesterday afternoon, but those men brought us to this place in the dead of night.

I've tried to be strong, but I feel I can't do this anymore. How can these girls bear it? Is this a warehouse? Some distribution center? I'm so cold. The damp feels as if it's crept into my bones. I see no way out, and those men keep staring at us. I'm so frightened.

Far *and* Mor *would be horrified if they could see me now. Me, with my big ideas of going to America. Of being independent and free. Oh, how I wish I'd never left!* Looking around her, the young woman saw such abject misery. She'd tried to be an encouragement to the ones sitting nearby, but she was running out of hope herself. Dozens upon dozens of girls sat, huddled upon blankets, on the damp, cold floor.

If they plan to sell us, they can't keep us here too long. No one wants to buy skinny, unkempt women.

I've heard of people being sold, but I thought it only happened to Africans, not Europeans. I've recognized many languages here besides Norwegian: French, Spanish, Danish. Although most of these girls don't talk at all.

God, if You're real, if You really exist as the Bible says You exist, rescue us. I learned about You growing up but, after confirmation, I forgot all about You. Mor *and* Far *never talked about You. Only* Mormor *has. She said You're a God of love and compassion. I've done a great deal of thinking since being locked in my cabin on board ship. If my grandmother believed You're real, perhaps, You are. If You have any compassion at all, please, please help us. If You're real, if You'll deliver us from captivity, I promise to serve You all the days of my life.*

CHAPTER I

"So your barns will be filled with plenty,
And your vats will overflow with new wine."

Proverbs 3:10

DUSK FADED INTO INKY NIGHT. Heavy fog blanketed the world in a cold, moist shroud. Sounds were muted, dulled by the thick damp. Lanterns cast a rainbow of light around themselves. They glowed weakly, visibility obscured by the curling mist.

"Easy does it men. Easy does it. Don't go stacking 'em on top of each other. You realize each one of these sweet things is worth a lot of money. What'd you give them anyway? Opiates? They're out cold." The man who directed the moving of some of the women looked unkempt. His hair greasy, his face needed a shave, and his coat rumpled. He'd sold this batch of girls to a man in Hong Kong and stood to make a huge bundle of greenbacks from the shipment. He had gone through and picked each girl, specially, for his Far East client. It wasn't the first time he'd filled an order for Cheng Wu. He was in the process of lining up another shipment to go out next week to a client in Chile.

Several men wore gray uniforms; others were dressed in regular clothes. They all took orders from the rumpled looking man with the educated speech. The man standing next to him looked like a dandy, but when he opened his mouth he betrayed the fact he was not a part of the educated, higher class society. The two men looked disparate, but they were business partners. Although they were not friends, they were in accord in their efforts to make money in the selling of human flesh.

"How many ya gots on this shipment, Brooks? How many goin' out?" Saul Simmons, nearly illiterate, clothed himself like the best dressed in San Francisco.

"I've got twenty-five head going out on this load." He yelled at a man on the second wagon. "Don't drop them like a sack of potatoes, Smitty. We don't want 'em bruised up."

Several of the men guffawed making lewd comments to each other.

Ethan Brooks turned toward Simmons, "This is the last time I'm going to ask you, and I want a straight answer. When is that bookkeeper, Jones, going to be finished with the books? Does he have any idea, besides putting ink on those pages, what we're about here? Has the man a clue why the books have such huge discrepancies?"

"Naw. He's jest workin' the books an' he don't know nothin' 'bout where the extra money's comin' from. He should be wrapping them up afore long."

"When he does, I want you to take care of him. No loose ends. You hear me? No loose ends."

"Yeah, I hear ya. I know 'xactly what ta do." His smile didn't reach his cold eyes.

Neither man trusted the other. They were simply partners with a common goal of making money. Once all three wagons were loaded, they headed slowly across the cobbles toward the pier where a ship awaited them.

Liberty Alexandra Bouvier sat in Matthew Bannister's great room in Napa, California. Her splinted left arm was covered by a long sleeved blouse. The ache was bone deep, but she didn't complain. Her chin had an ugly bruise where her step-father, Jacques, had hit her.

Because of her dead husband's lack of interest in her, in years past, Libby was unaware of her beauty. Her slim loveliness was breathtaking, but she seemed oblivious; it was part of her charm. Winged eyebrows arched above almond-shaped green eyes. A shining, coppery crown of cascading curls framed a perfect face. With lips full and made for smiling, her teeth were even and white. She looked utterly feminine and fragile, but seemed to have an inner strength and was quite capable of taking care of herself. Her true beauty lay within her; she loved the Lord with all her heart. It showed in her dealings with people—in every relationship.

Liberty sat with a calendar on her lap and used it as a diary. As she started to record the events of the last few days, she stared at the date in surprise, March 24, 1883. She couldn't believe how fast the time had gone since she'd packed her bags in Boston. She and Maggie had been living at Matthew's Rancho Bonito since a few days before Christmas. When she'd traveled west, in December, she'd thought a house awaited her, but it had only been a shack, nothing habitable. Maggie, who'd been her maid in Boston, was now her best friend.

Liberty enjoyed her new life and reveled in her newly found freedom. The split skirts she'd begun to wear gave her a freedom her regular skirts had not. Usually, she could be found wearing long leather boots, but today she wore the *espadrilles* Conchita had given her. She'd slipped them off and sat easily in a chair made for comfort, something she'd never enjoyed in her house in Boston. She felt as if someone had let her out of a cocoon that had bound her for thirteen, long years. With legs curled up underneath her, she sat reviewing the events of the past few days.

She looked up to see Elijah enter the great room. She'd not been able to talk to him, one on one, since he arrived at the Bannister's rancho three days earlier.

"Am I interrupting anything? he asked. At her head shake he went on to add, "Wonderful breakfast. Don't believe it would take me long to get used to tortillas and salsa. It was delicious!" He sat down in a deep leather chair facing her. The light from the window behind him cast a soft glow on her face.

"I agree. Conchita's a wonderful cook. Her eggs, bacon, and cheese wrapped up in a tortilla makes my mouth water every time I dish it up. She's been teaching me how to cook." Liberty smiled at him, "Oh, Elijah, I can't seem to stop praising God for you and all you've done for me. I'd never have left that horrible house in Boston on my own. You were right. I've found a freedom I'd never known before. I simply love it here."

Elijah Humphries, her lawyer, had arrived from Boston with his wife, Abigail. An unexpected blessing was they brought her real father and grandmother west with them. She'd not known of their existence until they arrived.

AUTHOR'S SHORT BIOGRAPHY

Born in Tacoma, Washington, I was the fifth and last child of a hearing impaired father and deaf mother. My oldest sister taught me to talk, and I could also use sign language until I was about eight. We were very poor. My father died when I was six, my mother when I was seven. I went to live with an aunt and uncle, along with three sisters and a brother. The aunt and uncle were not Christians. However, they sent us to Sunday school.

Occasionally, I would stay for church. One Sunday when I was twelve, I stayed, and it changed my life. I don't remember much about the sermon, but the song was "Softly and Tenderly Jesus is Calling." Until that time, I would steal candy from stores and tell lies. Although I had many friends, I was lonely and craved affection. My aunt and uncle were not expressive, but I knew my aunt loved me. The change in my heart and actions was evident to others, but for me—I have never felt totally alone since. My father image is God, and I feel a tangible love emanating from Him. I attribute this to His promise to care for the widows and the orphans.

At fourteen years of age, my aunt died unexpectedly. I ended up living with our minister and wife and their three daughters. I will not go into detail here, but it was not an easy time for me, coming from a non-Christian home. They made a move from Washington to California and had guardianship papers on me. I had to leave the sister and brother I was close-knit to. I drew close to God during this time and became very popular in school. Graduating from high school in the top five of my class, I was offered a scholarship to San Jose State University. I turned it down because I wanted to go to a Christian college and chose to attend Warner Pacific, a small Christian school, in Portland, Oregon, where I met my husband. Attending for over two years, I then married Philip Kerr. Philip became a career officer in the United States Air Force, and we lived in various places in the United States as well as Canada, Germany, and Denmark, which was a NATO assignment. We have four sons and have traveled extensively. My books are flavored with my travels.

Wherever I have lived, I've been involved in teaching Sunday school, teens, and youth groups. I've been a church treasurer, VBS teacher, and on the church board. I've led women's Bible studies. Currently, I'm director of my church's missions council. I have spoken at several ladies' retreats and luncheons. Having a private devotion time every morning, which includes prayer, Bible reading, and a devotional reading, I am constantly renewed.

I have a BA in education and a minor in science. I taught middle school language arts for several years, until I became ill with an autoimmune disease and cancer. God miraculously healed me of colon cancer and has spoken my name once...out loud. I cannot begin to relate to you how blessed I am or how I feel so cocooned in His love...I give Him the glory and praise! I feel God has now given me a new voice—writing. :)

I received a certificate of merit from a contest by Deep River Books, and I've written *Liberty's Inheritance, Liberty's Land, and Liberty's Heritage* in the A Woman of Entitlement series. *Caitlin's Fire* is my fourth book. I am waiting on the cover for *Tory's Father*, and currently, I am writing my eighth manuscript. I am amazed at the stories God has given me to write and can't seem to stop typing! Each book has a good storyline with godly teaching woven into them. Many people do not read their Bibles but will pick up a Christian novel. My prayer is for those people to draw closer to God from reading my stories. What has been a pleasant surprise is that men enjoy the books!

I give all the glory to God...my life and work are dedicated to Him.

God is my all in all. There is nothing too difficult for Him. He has been my Savior and friend. I wish from the bottom of my heart everyone could understand how much He loves you and that His ways are right and just. He does not want you to stumble through this life all alone with its weight and burdens on your back.

Amazing Grace

Help me, Jesus, my whole life through
To know I'm uniquely made by you.
And though the trials seem hard and tough,
I am your diamond in the rough.

Polish me, Lord, and let me know
The trials come to make me grow.
Illuminate each part of me
That with your Light I'll clearly see.

In every test that comes my way
Your Word I'll follow and obey.
May every trial that I endure
I see your love to make me pure.

Each facet cut by your loving hand
To let me shine and know I am
A glorious work in which you place
Your love, your Son, amazing grace.

Mary Ann Kerr

My books can be purchased on Amazon
My website: www.maryannkerr.com (signed copy)
Inklings Bookshop, Yakima, WA
Songs of Praise in Yakima, WA
Or by writing me at:
Mary Ann Kerr
10502 Estes Road
Yakima, WA (I charge no tax, sign the book, and the cost of shipping is
$5.65)

My public e-mail is: hello@maryannkerr.com
You may message me on Facebook on my author page:
Mary Ann Kerr—comments are welcome!
When readers take the time to write or e-mail me their experience reading
my stories, I sometimes put their comments on my blog if they don't mind.

Liberty's Inheritance (sale price. . . . .$15.00)
Liberty's Land   (sale price. . . . .$15.00)
Liberty's Heritage   (sale price. . . . .$18.00)
Caitlin's Fire   (full price. . . . . $19.99)

Books by Peter A. Kerr (my author son)

Adam Meets Eve (nonfiction)—$10.00 + 5.65 shipping and handling
The Ark of Time (science fiction)—$12.00 + $5.65 shipping and handling

Book by Andrew Kerr (my author son and cover and design guy)

Ants on Pirate Pond (children's black-and-white chapter book with darling illustrations)
—12.95 + $5.65 shipping and handling

Made in the USA
San Bernardino, CA
23 April 2018